METHODS OF
MADNESS

OTHER BOOKS AND AUDIO BOOKS
BY STEPHANIE BLACK:

The Believer

Fool Me Twice

A NOVEL

Stephanie Black

METHODS OF MADNESS

Covenant Communications, Inc.

Cover image: eye in the black © Pascal Genest. Courtesy of istockphoto.com

Cover design copyrighted 2009 by Covenant Communications, Inc.

Published by Covenant Communications, Inc.
American Fork, Utah

Printed in Canada
First Printing: August 2009

16 15 14 13 12 11 10 09   10 9 8 7 6 5 4 3 2 1

ISBN-10 1-59811-730-0
ISBN-13 978-1-59811-730-1

Acknowledgments

I'M GRATEFUL TO AMY BLACK for answering my questions regarding police procedure. Thank you to Kerry Blair, Jon Spell, Dianna Hall, Marshall and Sue McConkie, Bonnie Overly, Shauna Black, and Amy Black for taking the time to read and offer feedback on the manuscript.

Thank you to my editor, Kirk Shaw, for his skill, patience, and encouragement, and thank you to all the talented and dedicated people at Covenant Communications.

As always, thank you to my husband, Brian, for his constant support.

CHAPTER 1

FEAR STRUCK EMILY RAMSEY WITH such force that she couldn't move. Her body was stone, as cold and hard as the diamond that glittered against the velvet lining of the wooden ring box.

She was going to lose him.

Zachary Sullivan smiled at her, his cinnamon-brown hair blasted by the wind so it stood straight up from his forehead. "I know it's not exactly the Hope Diamond, but hey—you know all about schoolteachers' salaries."

Willing herself to relax, Emily dug her toes into the sand and drew a deep breath of briny air. "I wouldn't want the Hope Diamond. It's cursed. And this is gorgeous."

"You don't sound too sure." The teasing note in Zach's voice disappeared with his next words. "Or are you having second thoughts about taking me along with the ring?"

"No second thoughts." She rotated the box and studied the delicate wooden inlays forming a daisy on the lid. "The box is as beautiful as the ring. How long did it take you to make this?"

He smiled and shrugged. "I thought you could use one more thing for your daisy collection."

Emily smiled back. She'd never told him that every daisy-themed item in her apartment had been a gift from Tricia. Daisies had been Tricia's trademark.

She reached to take the diamond solitaire from the box, but her fingers trembled. She lowered her hand rather than risk dropping the ring into the sand.

"You're shaking." Zach took the ring box and set it on top of the picnic hamper. "You okay, Em?"

Emily intertwined her fingers with Zach's and squeezed hard, as though the combined strength of their hands could stanch the eruption of memories.

What was wrong with her? This was what she'd yearned for, prayed for, thought could never happen again. But now, with Zach Sullivan sitting beside her, an uncertain half smile on his face and sand speckling his rolled-up jeans, all Emily could feel was a resurgence of the pain and uncertainty she thought she'd finally banished.

Wind whipped dark strands of hair across her face. She didn't push the hair back; she wanted it to conceal the wetness in her eyes.

"Emily, what's wrong? We did talk about this, right? I wasn't hallucinating?"

Emily forced a laugh past the catch in her throat. "Nothing's wrong. I'm just happy." Knowing the unsteadiness in her voice had made it obvious she was crying, she stopped trying to conceal it and wiped her cheeks with both hands. "I can't believe myself." She tucked her hair behind her ears; the wind promptly blew it loose again. "I thought mothers were the ones who cried at weddings, and here I am bawling before I even have the ring on my finger."

Zach smiled, relief plain in eyes that were a muted gray-blue under the cloudy skies of this northern California beach. "Let's make it official, and the thought of being stuck with me for eternity will really give you something to cry about." He took the ring from the box and stretched to his feet, drawing Emily with him. In a gesture both courtly and awkward, he knelt in the sand in front of her.

"Emily Ramsey, will you marry me?"

Emily's throat constricted. Despite the bony breadth of Zach's shoulders and the athletic leanness of his tall body, he looked fragile, almost spectral, as though if she closed her eyes, he might disappear. She reached forward and trailed her fingers through his windblown hair, along his cheekbones, over his jaw, needing to feel the warmth—the reality—of him. "I love you," she whispered.

Zach drew her down onto the sand next to him. "Is that an answer, or are you trying to distract me?" He kissed her, his lips moving from her forehead to her neck, his touch making her feel as wobbly as driftwood tossed on the surf. "I love you." His lips brushed her ear. "Will you marry me?"

"Yes. Yes and *yes*."

Zach took her hand and slipped the ring onto her finger. The band of this ring was platinum. The band on the ring tucked in the back of her dresser drawer was gold, but other than that, the rings were almost identical. What would Zach think if he knew she still had Ryan's ring?

Zach wrapped his arms around her. Emily tried to feel only the strength of his embrace and the warmth of his mouth against hers, letting the sensations fill her and crowd out memories.

She was marrying Zach Sullivan. Everything would be fine.

* * *

"Oh, honey, we're so happy for you!" Carolyn Ramsey reached for Emily's left hand. Emily hastily picked up a dishtowel and started drying a china platter. Her mother had a habit of grasping Emily's hand when she was excited, and the sparkle of a new diamond apparently made her fingers an even more attractive target.

Carolyn turned back to the leftover dinner rolls she was placing into a bag for Emily to take home. "Zach's such a good man. I can tell. He's perfect for you."

"That's what Nicole kept hissing in his ear until he finally asked me out."

Carolyn laughed and brushed bobbed gray hair back from cheeks that had grown flushed from vigorous kitchen work. Whether cooking or cleaning up, Carolyn moved at double-speed the instant her feet touched kitchen tile. "I don't know what you'd do without Nicole."

Emily kept smiling, but the words burrowed so deeply into tender truth that they hurt. Without Nicole she *would* have fallen apart, and it made her cringe to remember how broken and helpless she'd been that first year. She thought of Nicole removing Ryan's ring from Emily's finger—almost forcibly—and shutting it in the ring box with a decisive click. *"If Ryan were alive, he would have come back by now. He's dead. You know it. It's time to move on. Do it for Tricia. She'd want you to be happy."*

Do it for Tricia. Nicole's mantra, the words Emily could never combat. If it weren't for Nicole, she probably never would have emerged from her protective shell enough to catch Zach Sullivan's attention. And Zach *was* perfect for her.

So far this Sunday afternoon, everything had been perfect—her parents' transparent joy at Zach and Emily's announcement, the cheerful conversation during dinner, Zach's arm brushing affectionately against hers when he reached for something on the table. And naturally the dinner had been another of Carolyn's culinary triumphs—the beef tenderloin a succulent, medium rare, the salad an intriguing combination of baby greens, goat cheese, lemon zest, and toasted pine nuts.

Perfect. And this time, everything would stay perfect.

"He looks like such an athlete," Carolyn remarked. "Does he coach basketball as well as teach math?"

"No. He always says he'd rather play a pickup game with a few friends than add all the stress that comes with organized sports." Emily slid the china platter into the cupboard.

"Tall, dark, and handsome. With such a beautiful wife, he'll have a crop of beautiful children."

"You're sweet, Mom." Emily mentally recorded the bet she'd just lost with herself. She'd predicted that her mother would mention grandkids before dinner ended, but Carolyn had lasted half an hour beyond that. *Pay up, Em. That's one more bottle of Welch's you owe yourself.* "We won't have any blond kids, that's for sure."

Carolyn wiped a smudge of flour off her sleeve. "You and Zach do have similar coloring, though your skin is more olive and your hair is a darker brown. I really like your haircut, honey. It's very—hip."

Hip? Had her mother ever used that word before? Emily ran dish-damp fingers over her hair. "Nicole gave me two choices. I could either agree to get my hair cut and highlighted, or she'd knock me out, take me to the stylist, prop me up in the chair, and I'd get my hair cut and highlighted anyway. I wasn't sure she was kidding about the second option, so I thought I'd better go voluntarily."

Carolyn laughed. "Do you like how it turned out?"

"Yes, I do." It had taken her a few days to decide that she *did* like the shorter, layered, artfully tousled look the stylist had given her, but from the number of people who had raved about the haircut, she knew it must really flatter her. Either that or people were just relieved to see she was capable of trying something new.

"It's good to try something new, isn't it?" Carolyn asked.

Suppressing a sigh, Emily nodded and turned back to the rack of dripping dishes.

"I'm proud of you." From the intensity in Carolyn's tone, she wasn't just talking about the haircut.

Emily picked up a plate and dried it vigorously, glad Zach was outside admiring the new brick patio her father had installed and couldn't overhear this conversation. "I figured if my first graders could manage to get haircuts without kicking and screaming, maybe I could too."

"You look beautiful. You're doing so well, and Dad and I couldn't be happier for you and Zach."

"Zach's great." Emily's response sounded ridiculously generic to her own ears, the type of remark she'd make about anyone from her visiting teacher to a helpful bag boy at Safeway.

"It's easy to see why you love him. And it's so good to see you *in* love."

Emily focused on the gilt-edged plate she was drying. "You never thought it would happen again, did you?"

"I was afraid you wouldn't let it happen."

"Mom, for goodness sake." Emily added the plate to the stack on the counter. "If I didn't want to meet someone, I wouldn't have been hanging out in the singles ward."

Carolyn smiled, but her eyes were serious. "I think that most of the time you were there in body but not in spirit. We worried about you, sweetie."

"You worry too much."

"We can't help it. You're everything to us now."

You're everything to us now. Emily had been waiting all day for someone to refer to Tricia, simultaneously aching to hear her name and dreading it. She thought of the way Tricia had teased her when Tricia went off to college. *"You're doomed, Em. The only kid left at home. I won't be around to take the heat off you. You won't be able to get away with anything."*

"After what you went through, didn't we have a right to worry?" Carolyn asked. "I don't blame you for keeping to yourself for a while. I know it took a lot of courage for you to let Zach into your life."

Emily dried a handful of forks, letting the clink of stainless steel take the place of a response. She hadn't paid much attention when Zach and his girlfriend had broken up last year, putting Zach back in circulation, but Nicole's matchmaking sensors had gone on high alert. For a while Emily had tried to ignore Nicole's hints and prodding, but Nicole's expert maneuvering had thrown Zach and Emily together so many times that, to Emily's amazement, sparks began to fly.

"Life is good," Emily said, realizing her mother was waiting for her to speak. "Life is wonderful. Will you make my wedding dress? Your sewing beats anything in the bridal shops."

Carolyn beamed. "Do you even need to ask? I've been waiting for this day for—" She stopped, and Emily knew she was thinking of the nearly finished bridal gown packed in tissue in a box in the attic.

Silence pulsed between them. Emily could picture every detail of the dress—the beading on the sleeves; the voluminous, gathered skirt; the panels of lace. A frothy, romantic dress. To spare her mother the awkwardness of asking if she wanted to wear that dress, she said matter-of-factly, "Something simple, I think. No train or beading or anything glittery. I'll pay for the fabric, of course."

"You don't need to do that." Carolyn removed her apron. "It's my gift to you."

"I don't expect you to pay for two wedding dresses. Maybe I should—I could wear the other dress—"

"Do you *want* to wear it?"

Emily twined the dishtowel around her hand, remembering Ryan's voice as he looked at the picture of the dress-in-progress that Carolyn had e-mailed Emily. *"Wow! You'll make Cinderella look shabby. But isn't there some kind of law about the groom not seeing the wedding dress before the big day? I hope this doesn't jinx us."*

"No," Emily said quietly. "No, I don't want to wear it."

"I planned to pay for two wedding dresses." Carolyn hung the apron on the hook. "I refuse to spend the money on anything else. That's settled."

Two dresses. One for her and one for Tricia. Instinctively, Emily knew what Tricia would say if she were here. *"Are you nuts, Em? Let her buy the new dress. She wants to do this for you. Don't take that pleasure away from her. Think of it as my dress if you can't stand having her spend the money on you. Wear it for me, okay?"*

"Would you like me to look at some patterns and bridal magazines to get ideas for you?" Carolyn asked. "I know you're busy, and I'd love to do a reconnaissance mission to see what's out there."

"I'd appreciate that." Emily hung up the dishtowel and glanced around the clean kitchen to see if they'd forgotten anything. She loved this room with its terra-cotta tile floor and honey-brown cabinets. Her parents' house was small, but every room exuded welcome and warmth.

Sometimes she wanted to hide here, crawl backward in time until she was a child, carefree and confident and sure that bad things could never come closer to her than newspaper headlines.

"Honey." Carolyn's voice was soft. "I hope you don't expect too much from yourself right now. It's a happy time for you, but I'm sure there must be a lot of anxiety too."

Emily suddenly felt naked. Were her feelings that plain on her face? "I'm fine." She removed the apron that shielded her sweater and skirt and hung it on one of the sunshine-yellow hooks on the pantry door.

"I know you're doing well, honey, but you may hit some bumps. It might not hurt to have you and Zach go together to talk to someone. Your bishop, or a professional counselor. We have a good friend in the stake—"

"Mom, please. I'm fine. We're fine." Emily straightened a couple of soup cans on the pantry shelf.

Carolyn was silent. Emily ran out of things to straighten in the tidy pantry. Reluctantly, she stepped back and closed the door.

She and Carolyn faced each other. Carolyn looked calm and steady, her Sunday dress a simple navy shirtwaist, her makeup minimal but expertly applied. "Have you talked to Zach about Ryan?"

"He knows. Everyone knows. He probably heard the whole story within a week of moving into the ward."

"I understand that. But have *you* talked to him?"

"He knows about Tricia."

"Emily, have *you* talked to him?"

Emily's dry tongue stuck to the roof of her mouth. Swallowing, she turned away and straightened the dishcloth draped over the edge of the sink. "Mom, everything's fine."

"Sweetheart, I can tell you're anxious. I don't want a cloud hanging over you. You and Zach need to start your marriage on a strong footing, and that means trusting Zach enough to trust him with your feelings. A bit of premarital counseling can go a long way toward—"

"I'm a grown woman. I think I can handle my own relationships." Emily was instantly ashamed of her curt words, but she'd gotten similar advice from her mother at least a dozen times over the past three years— that she should see a professional counselor, that no one could handle this type of stress on her own. Maybe she shouldn't have resisted. But if she suggested to Zach that they go to counseling now, what could Zach think except that she was still hung up on Ryan?

"I'm sorry." She smiled. "I know you just want to help me, but I promise, we're fine. The past is past. Let's talk about the future—like how you're going to spoil your first grandchild."

Pain still flickered in Carolyn's eyes, but she chuckled and opened the fridge. "If you'll slice this cheesecake, then I'll make the blueberry sauce."

"Deal," Emily said, grateful for her mother's willingness to change the subject. Emily *was* fine. And the last thing she wanted to do was to scare Zach into thinking she had enough emotional baggage to fill the cargo hold of a 747.

CHAPTER 2

"I'M A FOOL, I'm a fool, I'm a fool." Monica Fife sing-songed the words, her personal pop ballad of love gone bad, as she drove downtown and parked behind the small stucco shopping center that housed her candle shop, the Amber Flame.

She'd been so positive she'd done the right thing in unloading Zachary Sullivan. He was too dull, too plain, and too poor. She'd envisioned them living in a tiny fixer-upper of a house, with Zach spending all his free time in the garage hammering together new kitchen cabinets. They'd drive a used minivan and occasionally go out for a wild Friday night at Fuddruckers, where Zach's idea of a splurge was to get a piece of cherry pie with his burger.

It wasn't until she'd turned around in Sunday School today and seen the ring on Emily Ramsey's hand that the truth had swept over Monica like a wave, knocking her head over heels and leaving her drenched and dazed on the sand.

She wanted Zach Sullivan back. Boring career, small bank account—what did any of that matter stacked up against his sweetness, his steadiness, his integrity, the way he worshipped her? Even his looks—nobody would ever mistake him for a movie star, but how could she have forgotten the way his smile made his whole face glow, the way his button-down shirts draped over those bony shoulders, the way his hair curled around the tops of his ears if he waited too long between haircuts? He was adorable. She'd noticed it the moment he'd moved into the ward a year and a half ago and had stood up in Sunday School to introduce himself. She still remembered the cute way he'd fidgeted with the knot on his tie and shifted his weight from foot to foot as he spoke, reporting that he'd moved here from the Sacramento area and was teaching math at Los Coros High. She'd decided right at that moment that she'd have a date lined up with Zachary Sullivan by the following weekend. And she had. And when Zach had finally confided in her the reason he'd moved here, she'd been pleased that he trusted her, and she was sure that she was just what he needed. But four months into what had rapidly become a serious relationship, she'd decided she was bored.

What was *wrong* with her? She'd been an idiot to waste the past year going out with pretty boys who were so busy admiring themselves that they didn't even notice when she had a new dress or a new haircut. Zach had always noticed and commented in that shy way that made her feel like Miss America.

In the back of her mind, she'd assumed Zach would be there for her if she wanted him. She'd had no idea he and Emily Ramsey were so serious. It was only in the last couple of weeks that she'd even realized they were dating. They'd certainly been sneaky about it, and that infuriated Monica. If only she'd known, maybe she'd have come to her senses sooner.

"I'm a fool," she whispered, unlocking the back door. Inhaling the spicy-fruity scents of her store promptly improved her mood. She kept the shop closed on Sundays, but coming here on a Sunday afternoon always relaxed her. She loved sitting in her workshop and tinkering with new scents, and right now she needed the peace of the candle shop to soften the tension making her muscles feel like cold wax.

She'd been a fool, but it wasn't too late to fix things. Zach and Emily had barely gotten engaged.

Monica dropped her purse on the floor and sat at her worktable. She could get Zach Sullivan back, but it wouldn't be easy. She'd hurt him. He wasn't the type to clutch a grudge to his heart, but he didn't have amnesia either. He wouldn't look into her eyes and think *love*. He'd look into her eyes and think *pain*.

But he *wanted* her back. The fact that he'd gotten engaged to Emily so quickly—they couldn't have been dating for more than a couple of months, or Monica would have heard rumors—was evidence of rebound syndrome. He wanted Monica, but he thought she was out of reach, so he'd turned to Emily. If he knew that Monica had changed her mind . . .

Monica picked up an aluminum mold for a pillar candle and absently rolled it between her palms. She liked Emily Ramsey well enough. Emily was quiet and tended to keep to herself unless Nicole Gardiner was around to draw her out, but she'd always been nice to Monica. Monica had never heard her say anything catty about anyone, and Monica had gotten more than her share of catty remarks from girls who thought an attractive face was an open invitation for insults. And she *did* feel bad for Emily. Emily had had a rough time of it, losing Tricia in that horrible hit-and-run, and Ryan Tanner disappearing the same night.

Monica shuddered, thinking of that rainy January night when she'd driven up to Ryan Tanner's parents' home, a gift box of gardenia-scented candles on the seat beside her, and had seen a line of police cars and an ambulance. She'd barely known Emily then. Emily had moved to Los Coros only a month earlier, but Tricia had invited half the ward to Emily's combo birthday party/wedding shower.

How awful for Emily never to know what had happened to the guy she loved. At first Monica had thought that Ryan must have had something to do with the hit-and-run—it couldn't be coincidence that he'd disappeared that same night—but the police had found no evidence to support that. Ryan must have been involved in something else shady that finally caught up with him, and either he was dead or on the run from the law. He'd never seemed the type, but who could tell what secrets some people buried beneath their ties and white shirts?

Monica shook herself mentally. *This* kind of thinking wouldn't help at all. She needed to focus on Zach. Forget Emily. Emily would find some other guy. She was pretty enough, especially now that Nicole had talked her into losing that frumpy hairdo, and she was young. She'd fend for herself. No way could Monica abandon her hopes of marrying the best man she'd ever met just to keep from hurting another girl's feelings. That was ridiculous. No guilt allowed. She had to snare Zach again, and quickly, before his wedding plans went any further.

From listening to Emily talk to Brent Amherst in the hall after church, Monica knew that Emily and Zach had planned to drive to Emily's parents' house in Morgan Hill this afternoon. Zach would probably drop Emily off at her apartment around nine o'clock tonight—he was an early-to-bed-early-to-rise kind of guy and was particularly fanatical about getting to bed early on Sunday nights because he hated feeling draggy on Mondays. If Monica just *happened* to be at Emily's apartment complex, visiting . . . *let's see* . . . Justin. Of course. Justin Driscoll was a good sport. He'd get a kick out of her campaign to reclaim Zach. She'd chat with Justin for a while and then go for a stroll around the complex and manage to be near Emily's apartment just about the time Zach was leaving . . .

Round one, Monica thought. Time to start reminding Zach that there was someone better for him than Emily Ramsey.

* * *

"Can Welch's make up for the fact that it's past regular visiting hours?" Nicole Gardiner proffered the bottle of sparkling white grape juice and flashed Emily an impish smile.

Emily laughed and waved Nicole into her apartment. "You don't have to bribe your way in."

"Miss Manners has yet to approve midnight visits so I thought I'd better come armed with something you can't resist."

"It's not midnight yet." Emily checked her watch. Ten-thirty. Zach had dropped her off an hour ago, but despite her fatigue, she was too wired to sleep. "And if we're consulting Miss Manners, she'd say it isn't nice to throw people's addictions in their faces."

"As far as addictions go, I've heard of worse ones." Nicole strode into the kitchen, opened a cupboard, and took out two of the Waterford crystal goblets she'd given Emily for Christmas.

"What you really need, girlfriend, is to have this grape juice fermented." Nicole unscrewed the lid. "You need a glass of wine. Or two or three."

Emily rolled her eyes. "I thought we had an agreement. I wouldn't try to convert you if you wouldn't try to unconvert me."

"I made that contract with Tricia, not you. It doesn't transfer."

"Nice try."

"I'm just saying carbonated grape juice might be tasty, but it's not going to do much to relax you. Besides, I've gone to so many of your church events that I've earned the chance to unpreach at you."

"Yes, but you were just coming to keep me company and match-make."

"Guilty." Nicole poured grape juice into a goblet and brought it to Emily. "You know you need a fix, so drink up."

Emily took the goblet. "You're psychic, aren't you?"

Nicole pressed her index fingers against her temples and slid her eyelids half closed. "I'm sensing . . . tension. And half-digested turkey."

"Ha. Mom made beef tenderloin."

"Oops." Nicole plucked the beret off her blond hair and unwound a matching cashmere scarf. "Too warm for the scarf-beret ensemble, but I'm feeling French tonight."

"You look gorgeous." Emily sipped from her goblet.

Nicole filled the second goblet and sat gracefully on the couch. She was wearing high-heeled boots, jeans, and a suede jacket. Whether dressed in a T-shirt and shorts, a sequined evening gown, or a gabardine business suit, Nicole always looked like she was striding along a fashion-show catwalk. Normally, anyone that chic left Emily feeling tacky and inadequate, but every time she got the urge to be jealous of Nicole, she remembered what Tricia had told her about witnessing Nicole's mother tearing Nicole apart for a miniscule stain on the sleeve of her jacket. *You wouldn't have believed it, Em.*

It was like she'd disgraced the family name for generations." Nicole had obviously learned to look flawless the hard way.

"So talk to me," Nicole said. "How'd it go? Are your parents thrilled to pieces?"

"They're ecstatic. They adore Zach."

"What's not to adore? One twinkly-eyed smile from him and any parent would be falling all over him."

"Did you say *twinkly*-eyed?"

"Yeah, you know. When he smiles, his face lights up—bing!" Nicole spread her fingers wide to mimic rays of light.

Emily laughed. Nicole was right. She loved Zach's smile.

"So your parents adore Zach. Dinner was wonderful. And . . . ?"

Emily sighed. "And my mother is still worried about me."

"Worried in what sense?"

"The usual sense."

Nicole frowned, one finger tracing the intricate cuts on the surface of the goblet. "You know what I think? She still can't handle her own grief, so she projects it on you. She can't see that you're past all that, that your life is back on track and moving forward fast."

Emily looked down at the bubbles rising to the surface of her drink. Could she ever be "past" losing people she loved? Grief could lessen, but it wasn't as though time made the loss insignificant.

"I'm sorry," Nicole said. "That was tactless. You'll always miss Tricia. I miss her too. I know you wish she could be here helping you plan your wedding."

"I do," Emily said. "But I'm glad you're here."

"You need me, I'm here."

"I appreciate that more than you'll ever know." It was strange to think that before Tricia's death, Emily had known Nicole only casually as Tricia's close friend and coworker at Mariposa Interior Design. Abruptly she thought about how she'd answered Nicole's call to the Tanners' house on the night of Tricia's death, an action that stood out in her mind as the last normal thing she'd done before everything shattered. She remembered Nicole's tired voice: *"I tried Tricia's cell phone, but she's not answering. Can you let her know I won't be able to make your birthday party? I'm sorry, Emily. I'm sick as a dog. I think it's food poisoning."*

Tricia not answering her phone.

"You okay?" Nicole's voice was gentle.

"Yes."

"Nothing would have made Tricia happier than to see you with Zach. You know that, right?"

Emily touched the diamond on her finger. Tricia *would* be thrilled, sharing Emily's joy like it was her own. "I need to take Ryan's ring back to his mother," she said abruptly.

"Emily! I don't think that's a good idea. Besides, you tried before and she wouldn't take it."

"I know. But it's been three years now. I think she'll be ready."

"I doubt it."

"I can't keep the ring any longer. And it seems so callous to sell it."

Nicole set her glass aside, her violet-blue eyes scrutinizing Emily. "I don't think it's a good idea for you to talk to Ryan's mother right now."

"Nicole, I *have* to talk to her anyway. I need to tell her I'm engaged."

"Send her a wedding announcement."

"I can't just send her an announcement. She deserves to have me tell her personally."

"Because she still thinks of you as her daughter-in-law."

"I was never her daughter-in-law."

"Short of a couple of vows, you were. Face facts. She still sends you Christmas presents and birthday presents. She still invites you to dinners and family parties."

"She's just trying to reach out to me." Emily knew she wasn't being quite truthful. If she truly believed that Bethany Tanner didn't consider her a daughter-in-law, why had she never mentioned to Bethany that she was dating Zach?

"Em, trust me. Sell the ring."

A rapping on the door startled Emily. She walked to the door and peered through the peephole. "It's Brent." She swung the door open.

Brent Amherst grinned at her. Round glasses, straight straw-blond hair, and a boyish face always made Emily think he'd look more at home on an Idaho potato farm than in the Bay Area.

"Party going on?" he asked. "I saw Nicole walk past holding the bubbly and figured you were up to no good. Can I join in?"

"That depends," Nicole said from across the room. "How good are you at girl talk?"

"Decent. My sister and I used to have long conversations when we hid under the bed while my father screamed at my mother about her affair-of-the-week."

Emily could never figure out how to respond to Brent's offhand references to his parents' miserable marriage. "Well, if you hide under the bed in my apartment, the dust bunnies will eat you, so sit down and join us."

"Thanks." Brent sat on the couch and grinned at Nicole. "So what's the girl-talk topic tonight?"

Emily and Nicole exchanged a look.

"Emily's upcoming wedding," Nicole said.

"Ah, yes. The bomb that Emily dropped on our heads."

Nicole's eyes narrowed. "You make it sound like bad news."

"I didn't say that. I'm just saying she certainly kept this quiet until—whammo! I leave for New York thinking Emily isn't even seriously dating anyone. I come back three weeks later, and she's engaged."

"That'll teach you to go on a business trip." Emily spoke lightly, but her insides scrunched with guilt. Brent was grinning, but his eyes didn't look amused, and Emily suspected she had offended him by concealing her relationship with Zach. Not that Brent had ever had any romantic interest in her, but they were good enough friends that naturally he'd expect her to confide that she was in a new relationship.

"I should have known something was up when those pictures of Ryan disappeared from your bookshelf," Brent said.

Emily hadn't realized he'd noticed that.

"So why the clandestine routine?" Brent asked. "Or is this one of those whirlwind engagements and you've only been dating for three weeks?"

"It's not whirlwind," Nicole shot at him. "And it's none of your business if Emily and Zach didn't want to become gossip fodder."

"There's a difference between not wanting to become gossip fodder and creeping around like a couple of criminals."

Embarrassed to realize she was blushing, Emily said, "It wasn't that extreme. We just wanted to keep things low-key for a while."

"Why so shy?"

"Are you really that clueless?" Nicole leaned forward, holding her glass in such a tight grip that Emily wondered if her next move would be to fling her drink into Brent's face. "Emily's suffered through enough gossip—everyone picking her life apart, speculating about Ryan. Is it any wonder she wanted to keep a new relationship beneath the radar for a while?"

"No, it's not surprising. I just didn't know I was out of radar range."

"I wouldn't have even told Nicole, but she knew before I did," Emily said with what she hoped resembled a natural laugh. "Do you want some sparkling grape juice?"

"Sure."

Emily filled a goblet and brought it to Brent.

"Thanks." He raised the goblet. "A toast—to Emily and Zach." He clinked his goblet against Emily's. "Now, what's the problem?"

"What do you mean 'what's the problem'?" Emily returned to her seat, an ugly, pink-and-orange overstuffed armchair that Tricia had intended to reupholster.

"Well, let's analyze this," Brent said. "I didn't hear any giggling or shrieks of excitement when I approached your apartment. When I asked what you were talking about, you exchanged a 'should we change the subject?' look. If you were talking about the wedding, you were talking about a problem with it. Do your parents not like Zach?"

"My parents love Zach, and there are no problems. You have a suspicious mind."

"When do you meet his parents?"

"In about six months when they return home. They're on a mission in Denmark."

"Oh, yeah. So are you going to hurry and get married before they get home so they won't have a chance to disapprove of you?"

"They'll *love* Emily," Nicole said, her tone so harsh that Brent looked startled. Emily knew Nicole was thinking of her own brother, cut off by her parents when he married a girl they disliked. "Why are you convinced that an engagement has to spell trouble on some level?"

"You know me. I'll be a bachelor 'til I die and be happy about it. Better bachelorhood than dealing with a cheating little snake."

"You'd better not be talking about Emily."

"Don't be stupid. But there are always snakes in the grass, aren't there? In fact, tonight . . ." Brent gulped from his glass and started coughing.

"Tonight what?" Nicole said sharply.

He eyed his glass. "That carbonation is a killer."

"Sip it," Emily advised.

"What happened tonight?" Nicole repeated.

"I saw Monica Fife."

Nicole arched her eyebrows. "You went out with Monica?"

"Yeah, didn't you know? She's been obsessed with me for a while now, but we wanted to keep it *beneath the radar*. No, I mean I saw her standing in the parking lot, talking to Zach."

"So what?" Nicole said.

"So she was flirting up a storm while Zach stood drooling—"

Nicole's eyes flamed. "That is *not* true. Quit exaggerating and trying to spook Emily. We know you cringe at the idea of marriage, but that doesn't mean you have the right to foul things up for everyone else."

"I'm not trying to make trouble. I wish Emily the best, but I call 'em

like I see 'em, and Monica was flirting. If Zach were wc
would have told Monica to get lost, not stood there revelin

"What were they saying?" Emily made her voice casua
conversation was silly. Gorgeous Monica with her flowing ;   ..... anu
eyes the color of the hills that winter rains had turned emerald. *Stop it. Zach
loves you, not Monica.*

But he had loved Monica once.

"Monica was asking him how the meet-the-parents episode had gone,"
Brent said. "I didn't hear more than that."

"Then how do you know they were flirting?" Nicole snapped.

"Body language. Look, obviously you think Emily and Zach are the
couple of the year, but Emily is my friend, and I don't want her to get hurt.
And unless Zach shows more backbone than he showed tonight, Monica is
going to make trouble."

"Why would she make trouble?" Nicole said. "If she cared about Zach,
she wouldn't have dumped him."

"I'm not trying to read her mind. All I'm saying is that she was flirting."

Emily tilted her hand so the diamond caught the light and tried not to
imagine Monica edging closer to Zach, touching his hand, smiling up at
him . . .

"Emily, you're not letting this get to you, are you?" Nicole asked
urgently. "Monica Fife would flirt with anything male. It doesn't mean
anything. You can't trust Brent's take on this. Brent is a nearsighted, woman-
hating nutcase."

"I've known *that* for a long time," Emily joked.

Brent removed his round glasses, examined the lenses as though
checking for flaws, and returned them to his face. "Apparently the shoot-
the-messenger attitude is alive and well."

"There is no 'message,'" Nicole said. "Except that you're creating trouble
out of thin air. Some people *do* manage to have happy marriages, you
know."

"So what are *you* doing at Emily's late at night instead of staying home
with Mitch the millionaire?"

Nicole flushed. "He's out of town until—"

"Truce," Emily broke in. "Brent, get your lens prescription checked.
Monica may have been flirting, but Zach wasn't drooling. He's just too nice
to walk away while she's talking to him. I think I can trust my fiancé
enough not to get jealous when he chats with an ex-girlfriend in a public
parking lot."

Brent still looked unhappy, and Nicole's cheeks were scarlet.

"Sorry," Brent said after a moment. "Let's change the subject. So is Mitch still thinking of going into politics? You two would look charming in the governor's office."

CHAPTER 3

TUESDAY AFTERNOON, EMILY FELT a familiar tightness in her throat as she drove carefully along the rural back road that led to the Tanners' home. No matter how glowing the sunshine, no matter how azure the sky, she could never glimpse the white mailbox that Ryan had painted with a picture of a galloping horse without imagining black skies, lashing wind, and Tricia struggling to tie a cluster of balloons to the mailbox—balloons that would mark the site for Emily's party. Until the wind ripped the balloons out of her hands and she chased them, or so the police assumed, along the shoulder of the narrow, pitch-black road, and a car, driving too fast . . .

Emily drew a deep breath and steered into the driveway, almost ashamed that her anguish was for Tricia right now, not Ryan. She ought to be mourning Ryan at this moment, silently honoring him in a last farewell as she finally returned the engagement ring to his mother.

An unfamiliar black Corvette was parked in the Tanners' driveway. Emily's heart sank. When she'd told Bethany she wanted to stop by for a few minutes this afternoon, it hadn't occurred to her that other guests might be present. The thought of having to make her announcement in front of a stranger appalled her. She'd have to stall until the visitor left.

Her limbs felt cold and uncoordinated as she climbed the porch stairs and rang the doorbell. Fingering the ring box in the pocket of her chocolate-brown sweater coat and clutching the oversized tote bag hanging on her shoulder, she waited for Bethany to answer.

"Emily, it's so good to see you. Please, come in." Bethany's tanned face radiated welcome, but the lines around her eyes and mouth were deeper than her age warranted. In the entryway, she gave Emily a firm hug. "You look wonderful."

"Thank you."

"Come sit down. How are you doing? It's been a few months since I've seen you."

"I'm doing very well." There was no one else in the living room, to Emily's relief. Maybe the car was Bethany's—though a Corvette seemed an unlikely choice for her. "How are you? How's Princess Leia?"

"Not living up to her name." Bethany settled on the leather sofa. She looked comfortable and casual in faded jeans and a flannel shirt with the sleeves rolled up. "Why anyone ever named that grouchy mare after royalty—even make-believe royalty—is a mystery to me. But she'll come around. She's good for a challenge, anyway. How's school? Your students treating you well?"

"They're fine. It's an easygoing class. Mellow. No major problems." Emily kept her right hand curved around her left, hiding the new ring on her finger.

"Have a cookie." Bethany gestured at the plate on the coffee table.

"Thank you." Emily stretched out her right hand and took a cookie. She wished she could make this purely a social visit—enjoy Bethany's chocolate chip cookies and leave without mentioning Ryan's name.

"So what else is going on in your life?" Bethany asked. "How are your parents?"

Emily's gaze drifted to the watercolor hanging above the fireplace, a painting of the sun setting over cultivated fields. Ryan had won three different awards with that painting, but no ribbon had meant as much to him as his grandfather's pleasure in seeing his farm as the subject of Ryan's artwork. "They're doing very well. Mom keeps busy trying every new recipe in existence, and every pair of pants Dad owns is stained with dirt from yard work."

"Good for them. Nice people. I'll have to invite them over one of these days. Logan is here, by the way. He had the afternoon off work. He's out riding right now but should be back soon. He wanted a chance to say hello to you. Said he hasn't seen you in a while."

"It *has* been a while." So the Corvette was Logan's. She tried to think when she'd last talked to Ryan's cousin. At the Tanners' New Year's Day brunch the year previous? Had it really been over a year?

Emily laid her half-eaten cookie on a napkin and steeled herself. She couldn't wait any longer to deliver her news, or she'd be in the awkward position of returning the ring with Logan looking on.

"Bethany, I wanted to let you know that I'm engaged." The words seemed loud and jarring. "I don't know if you've ever met Zachary Sullivan. He teaches at the high school. He moved to Los Coros about a year and a half ago."

Silence overtook the room, the kind of silence that dried Emily's throat and made her cheeks burn. She opened her mouth to start babbling about how Zach had moved here from Sacramento, but Bethany spoke at last, her voice quiet.

"Well. Congratulations."

"Thank you," Emily said, even though "congratulations" sounded like the opposite of what Bethany was thinking. "We haven't set a date yet, but we're thinking summer. After school gets out, since we're both teachers. It's nice to have our vacations line up." She smiled. Bethany smiled back with her lips, but her eyes were cloudy.

"I thought—" Emily's throat was so parched that she had to swallow before she could go on. "I need to give this back to you." She drew the velvet box from her pocket. "I know you said to keep it, but I can't. I don't feel right about it. It should belong to you."

Bethany wasn't even trying to smile now. "Ryan gave it to you. It's yours."

"It's an engagement ring. A symbol of something that can't happen."

"Not if you marry someone else, that's for sure."

"Bethany . . ." What could she say? *You're not being rational. Ryan is dead.* Bethany couldn't accept that Ryan was dead unless she had proof. And there was no proof. There was nothing.

"It's been three years," Emily began gently. "And we both know Ryan would never have disappeared of his own free will. He—"

"We don't know what happened. He could have been kidnapped. He could be injured. He could be ill. He could have amnesia. He could be living out there somewhere, wondering who he is. But when his memory returns, he'll remember us. He'll come home."

That only happens on television, Emily thought, but she kept quiet. She and Bethany had done this together in those first agonizing months after Ryan's disappearance, frantically conjuring up any explanation for his absence that could possibly have a happy ending. None of the explanations had been very plausible at the time, and now they sounded like pure fantasy.

"Ryan loves you." Bethany's eyes glistened.

Emily placed the ring box on the coffee table and fought the responsive prickling of tears in her eyes. "I know. But he . . ." She pried the words from her throat. "He's not coming back."

"You don't know that."

"If he were alive, the police would have found some hint of that. Or those private investigators you hired after the police—"

"I see it the other way. If he were *dead,* they would have found some hint of that. If he had been attacked by some psycho or druggie, the police

would have found his body, or the killer would have left other . . . evidence
. . . behind."

Emily bit her lip. It seemed beyond callous to point out that it had been
pouring rain that night, and evidence might have been washed away. "None
of us knows what happened. But I do know I need to move on."

"You're the woman he wants to be with for eternity. You felt the same
way about him. And now you can't even wait a few years for him?"

Emily couldn't think of a response that wouldn't hurt Bethany. How
could she be so deep in denial, talking like Ryan was on a mission and
Emily wanted to Dear John him?

*But how can she not be in denial? He's her son. Until she receives concrete
evidence of his death, how can she stop hoping the phone will ring and she'll
hear his voice explaining where he's been for the past three years?*

What if Bethany was right? What if Ryan was alive? Inside Emily,
confusion, yearning, and despair swelled, then popped like a bubble. *You
can't do this to yourself. He's gone. He's not coming back.* Chilled, Emily drew
her sweater coat more tightly around her, hyperconscious of the ring on her
finger. The symbol of her betrayal.

"I'm sorry," Emily said. "You've been so kind to me, and I'm grateful for
that."

Bethany closed her eyes. For a long moment, she sat that way, her face
taut, her fingers digging into the arm of the couch. "No, don't apologize."
Tears trickled down her face, and her expression softened. "You're right, and
I'm sorry. It's not fair of me to think you could put your life on hold indefi-
nitely. You're a beautiful young woman. You want to start a family. It's just
hard for me because I know how Ryan feels about you."

Emily wondered if she should go sit next to Bethany, put her arm
around her, and try to comfort her, but she sensed that doing so would only
make things more painful between them.

A small smile curved Bethany's lips. "I remember the way he used to talk
about you in his e-mails when you started dating. He'd slip your name in so
casually—this girl in my racquetball class, we went to a movie, we were
studying together last night, we tried a new recipe for dinner—it was always
Emily, Emily, Emily. I could tell he was crazy about you, but he wasn't going
to come right out and admit it. But I knew a wedding was coming."

Emily reached into her tote bag and withdrew a large cardboard envelope. "I . . . brought you some pictures," she said. "I thought you might like
to have them."

She brought the envelope to Bethany. Bethany wiped her face with the
back of her hand and took it. Emily had hoped she wouldn't open it right

away, but she did, tipping the stack of pictures onto the couch cushion next to her.

Bethany picked up the photos of Ryan one by one and examined them. "These are the pictures that used to hang in your apartment, aren't they?"

"Yes."

"I imagine you took them down a while ago." There was no edge on Bethany's voice, but the words still stung, and Emily didn't respond. She hadn't actually taken them down. Nicole had gone systematically through her apartment and gathered up every framed photo of Ryan while Emily sat and watched, unwilling to help her, unwilling to stop her. *Girlfriend, you're dating Zach now. Sooner or later, he's going to come to your apartment. What's he going to think if he sees you've got the whole place decked out as a shrine to your former fiancé?* Nicole had been exaggerating; Emily did have a dozen framed pictures of Ryan, but only two of those were in the living room where Zach would see them. Still, she knew Nicole was right. If she was planning on moving on emotionally, surrounding herself with pictures of Ryan wasn't the way to do it.

"Did you take all these pictures?" Bethany asked.

"Yes."

"You're a talented photographer."

"It's easy to get good shots of such a handsome subject." Emily blushed at how stilted the words sounded.

"You're sure you don't want to keep at least a couple of these?" Bethany asked, her gaze on the photo in her hand.

"I still have everything on my computer." Emily felt slightly ridiculous. Here she was giving these prints to Bethany like it was a significant step forward, and yet she could easily print out new copies. Was she wrong not to delete the pictures altogether? Zach wouldn't expect her to do that. Ryan was part of her past, and it wasn't as though he was a romantic rival. He was gone. But she should probably get the pictures off her computer and consign them to backup archives.

At the sound of the front door opening, Bethany looked up. "That'll be Logan," she said, swiping her hand across her wet eyes.

Emily turned automatically and smiled, ready to greet Logan, but inside, she felt as though she'd swallowed a handful of thumbtacks. She had no idea how Logan would react to the news of her engagement. He and Ryan had been close—buddies throughout childhood, roommates at BYU. Would he too think she was betraying Ryan?

Logan Tanner strode into the room. His hair was several shades lighter than Ryan's coal-black hair, his build stockier, and his nose more prominent, but the family resemblance to Ryan was distinct. People had often assumed they were brothers, not cousins. "Emily! It's great to see you." He embraced her. "How are you?"

"I'm good." Emily suppressed the urge to hide her ringed hand in her pocket. "How are *you?*"

"I'm great." Logan's gaze flicked to the stack of photographs on the couch.

"Emily brought me these pictures of Ryan." Bethany spoke softly, but Logan obviously read the distress in her face. His smile flattened.

"You okay, Aunt Beth?"

She nodded. Logan took the photos and flipped through them. Emily watched him, her cheeks hot. Why had it ever seemed like a good idea to bring the ring and the pictures back on the same day she told the Tanners of her engagement? She shouldn't have brought the prints at all—should have copied all her pictures of Ryan onto a CD and given that to Bethany months ago. Giving her the prints now felt tacky, even heartless. *Take these old photos of your son. I don't want them anymore.*

Logan handed the pictures to Bethany. If Bethany's expression hadn't given him adequate evidence that something was amiss, the thick silence in the room had done the job by now.

"I'm engaged," Emily said. She couldn't think of any subtle way of working up to her announcement, and she knew Bethany wouldn't deliver the news for her.

Logan stared at her. "You are?"

"Yes." Emily's vision blurred. She blinked hard; she would *not* cry.

"Congratulations."

"Thank you."

Logan glanced at Bethany, who sat clutching the pile of photographs. "Listen, I've got to run. Thanks for letting me play cowboy for a few hours."

"Anytime."

"Emily, why don't you walk me to my car?" Logan suggested.

"Sure." Emily was glad for an excuse to escape. "I need to get going as well." She picked up her tote bag and looked at Bethany. "Thank you for everything."

"Come to dinner this weekend," Bethany said. "Just you. I promise I *will* be happy for you, but I'd like a little more time before I have to say good-bye. And I know Ted would like to see you."

"We're not saying good-bye," Emily said, but she knew Bethany wasn't talking about losing all contact with her. She was talking about losing Emily as her almost-daughter-in-law. Emily wanted to refuse the invitation—how could the dinner be anything but difficult for all of them?—but she couldn't bring herself to do it.

"Saturday?" Bethany asked.

"That's fine."

"Come over around five if that works for you."

"That would be fine." Emily uncomfortably pictured herself telling Zach she couldn't see him on Saturday evening because she was going to dinner at the home of her former fiancé's parents, and he was definitely not invited.

Logan led the way out the front door.

"Nice car," Emily said, feebly attempting to sound like she was interested in a hunk of metal and glass. "When did you get it?"

"Last month. Got to spend my money on something, since I can't seem to lure a girl into marrying me. Speaking of which, I'm sorry I gaped at you like an idiot. You caught me off guard. I talked to Brent Amherst just a couple of weeks back. He always gives me updates on you, and he told me you weren't seriously dating anyone, so your announcement knocked my socks off."

"Yes, Brent's already read me the riot act for not keeping him in the loop. Zach—my fiancé—and I wanted to keep things private for a while. I've had my fill of being talked about."

"I totally understand. So tell me about Zach."

Emily gave the standard thirty-second bio—raised in Tucson, served a mission in Virginia, graduated from Arizona State, taught math for three years in the Sacramento area, moved to Los Coros a year and a half ago.

"So why Los Coros?" Logan asked. "Did he come here for you?"

"No, I didn't meet him until after he moved here, and we didn't start dating until last year. He just said that he wanted a change, and Los Coros High had an opening." She wondered what Logan was thinking. He didn't seem upset, but he didn't look happy either. He wasn't meeting her gaze; he stood, tapping his fingers on the glossy black hood of his Corvette.

"Bethany took it hard, didn't she?" Logan said.

"Yes."

"I figured she would. She thinks of you as Ryan's wife. We all did."

Emily didn't know what to say.

Logan's expression was remote. "Funny," he said. "I know he's dead—it's the only explanation that makes sense—but one corner of me keeps waiting for him to come home and pick up where he left off. Seeing you marry someone else makes me realize how stupid that is. He's gone. And I'm glad you've found someone, Emily. I'm happy for you."

* * *

"This is for you, Miss Ramsey."

Emily turned from where she'd been erasing the whiteboard to see seven-year-old Annie Chen holding out a drawing of a smiling, brown-haired woman in a blue dress standing in a grassy field with flowers the size of beach balls blooming around her.

"Do you know who it is?" Annie grinned, showing off permanent front teeth halfway emerged from her gums.

"Of course I do. It's me. Thank you, Annie."

"Did you see the big smile? I made it *big*."

"It's a very happy smile."

"It's for you to take home and put on your fridge." Annie twined the end of her black ponytail around her finger. "You're happy because you're standing in flowers. You were sad today, so when you look at this picture you'll be *happy*!"

Annie's words caught Emily by surprise. "That's very thoughtful, honey. But I'm not sad. I'm just fine."

"Your eyes are sad," Annie said. "Bye!" Whipping around, she raced out the door.

Emily stood holding the picture, the warmth of discomfort in her cheeks. Annie was an unusually empathetic child, and Emily had often noticed her comforting other children, but Emily was still disconcerted that one of her first graders had sensed something was wrong.

She *wasn't* sad—at least not for herself. It was Bethany's pain that haunted her. It must have hit her like a punch in the stomach to hear Emily say bluntly that Ryan wasn't coming home. In the beginning, they'd both spoken of Ryan as though he would return. As one year then two had passed, and all efforts to figure out what had happened to him had come to naught, they'd spoken of him less and less often. Emily hadn't fully realized that Bethany still refused to face the likelihood that Ryan was dead.

Ryan hadn't run away. Emily would find it easier to believe that the earth was flat than to believe Ryan Tanner could be involved in some kind of illegal or immoral activity that would have caused him to go into hiding. His credit cards had not been used. His bank account had not been touched. None of his belongings were missing except the clothes he'd been wearing, his keys, his cell phone, and his wallet. His car—with a dead battery—had been found in the Safeway parking lot.

Emily thought of the last time she'd heard his voice, the message he'd left on her phone while she was in a conference with the parents of a challenging student.

"Hi, it's me. I'm stuck—my car's dead again. I got a jump, but it didn't work this time. Call me when you finish your meeting to see if I'm still stuck or if I found another ride home. I hope Tricia doesn't skin me alive for being late with the cake."

She'd tried to call him back several times, but when he didn't answer his cell phone, she'd assumed he'd gotten another ride, so she'd headed for the Tanners' home.

The police had located the man who'd attempted to jump-start Ryan's car, and he reported that when the jump failed, Ryan had thanked him and said he'd call his fiancée for a ride. The police investigation turned up nothing remotely suspicious about the man, a young father who'd had his toddler daughter along as he stopped at the store for milk and cereal.

The cake Ryan had picked up at Safeway was not in his car. Had he taken the cake and started walking toward the elementary school in the pouring rain to meet Emily? Cell phone company records didn't show any calls after the one to Emily, so he hadn't called a taxi or anyone else for a ride. But what could have possibly happened to him in the middle of family-friendly, low-crime, suburban Los Coros?

Was it any wonder Bethany thought soap opera–style amnesia was as likely an explanation as murder?

Emily drew a deep breath and slid Annie's picture into her tote bag. She was dreading Saturday night's dinner and felt guilty that she hadn't told Zach anything more specific than that she'd been invited to the home of some old friends. Zach hadn't asked for details or seemed bothered that he wasn't invited as well; he had plenty of work to catch up on and could use the time.

Why hadn't she confided in him? Why did she feel so unable to even speak Ryan's name in front of him, like doing so would push Zach from her life?

At least she'd gotten through the awkwardness of returning Ryan's ring to his family. She *was* moving forward, and she couldn't let this upcoming dinner upset her. She loved Bethany and Ted. Marrying Zach didn't have to change that. Maybe Emily's marriage would help the Tanners move on as well.

And at least Logan was happy for her.

Emily settled at her desk and slid a pile of writing assignments toward her. Soon she was in the rhythm of deciphering first-grade handwriting, her tension gradually unwinding like thread off a spool.

It felt good to be in love again. It felt good to have Zach Sullivan constantly jumping into her thoughts.

Her classroom door swung open. Emily looked up and smiled, enjoying a tingle of excitement. "Hey."

"Hi, Teacher. Am I interrupting you?"

"Yes, thank heavens." Emily pushed aside the stack of papers.

"I came to offer you an early dinner—if you're okay with a cheap burger at In-N-Out." Zach crossed the room in a few long-legged strides, leaned over Emily's desk, and kissed her. "Unless you've already got plans for dinner this evening."

"None at all." Emily moved from behind her desk so she could embrace Zach. She wanted to feel his arms around her.

Zach hugged her and kissed her again. When they broke apart, he grinned down at her. "Greet me like this, and I'll come back fifty times a day."

Emily smiled back, feeling warm and light, as though a weight she hadn't even realized she was carrying had lifted from her shoulders. There was nothing to be afraid of. "Do you have any idea how much I love you?"

"If it's half as much as I love you, you adore me with mind-boggling intensity." He touched his lips to her forehead. "I'm just hoping you won't figure out that you could do a lot better than Zach Sullivan."

"Oh, please. No one could ever do better than you."

He grinned. "Well, on Friday night, I'll show you I can offer something a lot more elegant than a burger and shake. How does a multi-stake Valentine's dance in a church gym grab you?"

"Hey, don't knock it. This is supposed to be quite the event."

"Yeah, they're really pulling out the heavy artillery in the romance department. I heard that if at least five couples don't end up getting engaged due to the dance, they're going to make the stake presidents pay out of pocket to reimburse the budget for money spent on red and pink glitter and ice sculptures of Cupid."

Emily laughed. "You should have waited another week to propose to me in order to help the stats."

"Tough luck for them. I couldn't wait."

"So you'll really dance with me? I thought the only time you like to move around a gym floor is when you've got a basketball in your hands."

"I'll dance, I swear." Zach swayed in time to imaginary music. "I even bought a special pair of shoes to fit my two left feet. I recommend that *you* wear steel-toed work boots—in self-defense."

"No way. I've got darling new shoes that match my dress. And a few crushed toes are a small price to pay for an evening of dancing with you."

A mischievous grin lit Zach's face. "We ought to record this romantic conversation and play it for our students. Show them another side of their teachers."

"Good idea. My students would get bored. Yours would get sick."

Zach laughed.

* * *

Emily was still smiling when she arrived at her apartment after dinner. She would have loved to spend the entire evening with Zach, but they both had work to do.

She stopped at the mailbox to retrieve her mail and headed up the stairs to her second-floor apartment. Swiftly, she flipped through the envelopes and flyers, tossed the junk mail in the trash, and plopped the electric bill into the beautifully scalloped wooden tray Zach had made for her when she mentioned needing a to-do basket for bills and letters needing attention. It was far too elegant a tray to use for such a mundane purpose, but Emily loved the sight of it on her kitchen counter.

The last item in the stack was a white cardboard envelope. Her name and address were printed on an adhesive label, but there was no return address or company logo. It was probably a credit card offer trying to make itself look mysterious. All it lacked was a "Do Not Discard" warning on the front.

Emily ripped open the envelope and found a smaller manila envelope, along with a folded piece of white paper. Puzzled, she opened the note. It was printed in the same font as the address label.

> *Sorry to stick my nose in your business, but I have to warn you. I took this picture two weeks ago at Seacliff Beach. They didn't see me. I snuck a shot—thought I'd use it to tease them later. I thought they'd gotten back together. But when I heard you and Zach were engaged, I knew I had to show you what I saw. Sorry to do this anonymously, but I don't want you to hate me.*
> *—A friend*

The blood seemed to drain from her muscles, leaving her hands cold and stiff. Clumsily, she lifted the flap on the manila envelope and shook the picture onto the table.

It was a photograph of Zach and Monica Fife, sitting side by side on the sand. Monica's auburn hair blew wildly in the wind as Zach leaned toward her, one hand on her shoulder.

He was kissing her.

Two weeks ago. That was the weekend Zach had told her he couldn't take her out; he was swamped catching up on homework for the class he was taking toward his master's degree.

Calm down, Emily told herself fiercely. *Look at this logically.* An anonymous picture? It easily could have been taken over a year ago, before Zach and Monica broke up. She had only the word of an anonymous tipster that the picture was current, and anyone too cowardly to break this news in person might easily be a liar trying to stir up trouble. It could be from someone with a grudge against Zach. A student, maybe, angry over a failing grade?

Emily picked up the picture and studied it, her heart bumping violently against her ribs. Brent Amherst's warning raced through her mind.

"She was flirting up a storm, and he stood there drooling."

At least she knew this picture hadn't come from Brent. If he were the one who'd seen Zach and Monica at the beach, he'd have thrown this picture in her face the instant she'd told him of her engagement. Brent was forever convinced that all relationships were on the verge of breaking down, and there was nothing he liked better than an I-told-you-so.

You don't know the picture is current. You can't assume it is.

She jammed the picture and note into the envelope. She'd call Zach right now and ask him for the truth.

Ask him if I should believe an anonymous tip over his word? Ask him if he minds that I'm suspicious and neurotic and that my immediate reaction to the work of a troublemaker is to assume he cheated on me?

There was no reason whatsoever to think the picture was current, any more than there was reason to believe Brent's biased report from a couple of nights ago.

Emily sank into a kitchen chair, staring at the plain white envelope in her hand.

CHAPTER 4

"THAT DRESS IS BEAUTIFUL." Zach reached across the small table decorated with crimson roses and pink electric tea lights and touched Emily's shoulder. "I don't think I've ever seen you wear red. You look gorgeous."

"Thank you." Emily hadn't been able to figure out which ached worse—her feet or her wallet—after spending six straight hours shopping with Nicole. The scarlet jersey dress with a square neckline and cap sleeves had delighted Nicole immediately—*"It's perfect, Em! It totally makes you glow."*—but the price tag had left Emily gasping. Only the fact that the odds were a million to one against finding another dress that she liked in time for the dance had induced Emily to open her purse.

Emily fingered the gold beads of the necklace she'd borrowed from Nicole and watched the couples moving around the dance floor. She was determined to forget about that anonymous letter and thoroughly enjoy tonight. No malicious rumormonger was going to ruin what she had with Zach.

"I'm glad they didn't ask me to be on the decoration committee." Zach waved his hand to indicate the walls of the cultural hall, where plywood cutouts, lit with white Christmas lights and painted to resemble a Parisian skyline, had completely transformed the room. "They must have worked on this for months."

"It's amazing," Emily said, unnerved at how quickly her mind jumped to the thought that Ryan would have loved to design and paint something like this. Why was she thinking about Ryan now?

Zach popped a last bite of a cream puff into his mouth. He looked particularly handsome tonight in his dark suit and red patterned tie, his hair newly trimmed, but Emily kept involuntarily picturing him in a sweatshirt and sandy jeans, Monica Fife's auburn hair blowing across his face as he leaned toward her—

"Would you like something more to eat?" Zach asked. "You haven't had much."

"I'm fine," Emily said cheerfully. A few tables away, Monica Fife was sitting with Justin Driscoll. It looked like she was having a good time, leaning close to Justin as they chatted. *You're crazy jealous if you think she's still interested in Zach. Or vice versa.*

Nicole had agreed that it would be a rotten idea to confront Zach about the picture. *"It drives Mitch insane when I get whiny and insecure. You know that picture is garbage. Zach Sullivan could put Honest Abe to shame. He'd never cheat on you. Know what I think? Monica sent that picture herself. Who else would be likely to have a kissy-kissy picture on hand? She probably thinks any guy she ever dated is her property, and even if she doesn't want him, no one else gets him either. Don't give her the satisfaction of showing it upset you."*

Could Nicole be right? Monica had never seemed that conniving to Emily.

Zach rested his hand on hers. "You all right? You seem quiet tonight."

"Just tired," she said. "Busy day."

"Emily." Zach rubbed a fingertip over the diamond on her hand. "You really do seem tense. Are you sure there's nothing bothering you?"

"I'm fine." She had shoved the photograph to the bottom of her to-do tray. Why hadn't she thrown it away? If she thought it was just a vindictive trick, why had she kept it?

Tears stung her eyes. Not wanting Zach to notice, she rose to her feet. "I need to run to the ladies' room. Back in a minute."

She picked up her purse and hurried away from the table. The last thing she wanted was for Zach to see her crying like some immature, insecure little head case. Why did it seem like the question she kept getting from him since their engagement was "What's wrong?"

Nothing's wrong, Emily told herself, catching the tears with a paper towel before they could drip down her cheeks. *Why are you so determined to believe that you're going to lose Zach? You act like you'll return to the cultural hall and he'll be gone. Disappeared. Out of your life forever.*

"He isn't Ryan," Emily whispered, snatching another paper towel.

* * *

Oh, sweet timing! Monica Fife, sipping casually from a glass of San Pellegrino, watched as Emily Ramsey rose from her chair and headed toward the door.

"Time to move in?" Justin Driscoll followed Monica's gaze.

Monica winked at Justin. "And it's even a slow song. Wish me luck."

"I'd rather wish you *bad* luck." Justin shook his fashionably shaggy blond hair back from his forehead. "So you'll crawl to me in defeat."

Monica dabbed her lips with a napkin and hastily applied a fresh coat of lipstick. "Surfer boy, you know we'd kill each other in a month if we ever got hitched."

Justin grinned. "I'll take the chance. Come on. How can you prefer that Sullivan nerd over me?"

"You realize if we got married, you'd have to give up all your other girlfriends."

"You serious? Deal's off, then. Go chase Sullivan. And once you've trapped him, *I'm* going on the hunt."

"The hunt?"

"Emily Ramsey will be free."

Monica wasn't sure why that comment annoyed her. "You and Emily? I don't think so."

"Jealous?"

"Get real."

"I like the Ramsey women. I had a serious crush on Tricia."

"Tricia was more your type." Monica pictured Tricia with her glossy dark hair and teasing smile. "Emily's too quiet for you."

"She's a pretty girl."

"I didn't say she wasn't. She's just not your type."

"She looks beautiful tonight, doesn't she?" Justin's smile widened. "She'd make a wonderful wife."

"Justin!"

"You *are* jealous. Truth is, Monica, I've had Emily in my sights for a while now."

"More power to you." Monica shoved her lipstick back in her purse. "I hope you and the schoolmarm have a happy life together."

Justin's expression was strangely serious, and there was a shaded look to his eyes that made her wonder what he was thinking. "Maybe we will."

Forget Justin and Emily. You're going into battle. You've got to focus. Monica slipped out of her chair, smoothed the skirt of her emerald silk dress, and glided toward where Zach sat alone at a table, watching the dancers on the polished gym floor.

Monica came up behind him and squeezed his shoulders. "Hey, Zach. How are you?"

"Monica." His shoulders gave a small twitch beneath her hands. "Hi."

He turned, and she enjoyed the way his eyes moved from her hair to her toes, taking in every detail of her appearance. She knew she looked good in this dress. The green formed a luscious contrast to her auburn hair, and the flowing silk accentuated curves where she wanted to be curvy and slimness where she wanted to be slim.

"Wow, you really—" Zach closed his mouth, and Monica hid a smile. He'd wanted to compliment her but had censored himself.

She moved so she was standing next to him. "Enjoying the dance?"

"Sure."

"I'm shocked. I could never get you to take me dancing, and now I see you out on the dance floor playing Fred Astaire." Monica brushed a fingertip along his arm. "You look great. Dance for old time's sake?"

Zach swallowed. "Thanks, but you must be here on a date, and I'm sure—"

"Justin won't care. He's just a friend." Monica took Zach's hand and pulled him to his feet.

He spoke quietly, bending toward her. "I really can't. Emily—"

"You *can't*? Or you don't want to?"

"I'm here with Emily. I can't just walk away from—"

"I'm sure Emily wouldn't begrudge me one dance." Monica slid her hand into the crook of his arm and guided him onto the dance floor. She rested her hand on his shoulder, and his hand move awkwardly to her waist in response. Clasping his other hand, Monica smiled up at him.

"What are you trying to do?" he whispered as they swayed to the music. "I'm engaged."

"Congratulations." Monica leaned a little closer and saw his gaze flick toward her lips then quickly away.

"Listen, I need to go back to the table. Emily—"

"The song's not over. And Emily's still in the ladies' room."

"I don't know what kind of game you're playing, but—"

"I'm not playing a game." She looked into his eyes—those clear, candid eyes that revealed everything Zach was feeling. "I'm admitting I made a mistake."

He drew a deep breath, and Monica knew he was appreciating—unwillingly—the perfume she wore, a scent he'd always loved. "You thought I wasn't good enough for you."

"I never said that."

"Not straight out." Even in the dim light of the gym, she could see his neck blotch red above his crisp white collar. "But you got the message across. You thought you could do better. You told me it was over. Now I'm engaged to a woman I love very much."

"You're engaged to the first runner-up. Zach, I was so stupid. I don't know what I was thinking. I acted like a selfish little girl. I've grown up now. I want to try again."

Zach's body was rigid, and he moved mechanically as they pivoted on the dance floor. "I'm not available."

"You're engaged. Not married. Big difference." With her hand on the back of his neck, Monica drew his head down so she could whisper in his ear. "You know if you don't give us a chance, you'll wonder for the rest of your life if you made the wrong decision."

Zach straightened up so forcefully that Monica could either remove her hand from his neck or end up looking like a clingy fool. He was looking toward the table where he and Emily had been sitting. Monica didn't need to look to know Emily had returned.

Monica settled her hand back on his shoulder, and after a slight stuttering motion, Zach continued moving in time to the music. No matter how embarrassed he was to have Emily see him dancing with an old flame, he was too sweet to publicly humiliate Monica by abandoning her on the dance floor. It was *such* a relief to be with a man who cared so much about her feelings. How could she ever have been crazy enough to dump him?

"What do you want with me?" He held her hand a little too tightly. "Does it bother you that I actually found someone who thinks I'm worth something?"

"I made a mistake. I was a fool. You're the best thing that ever happened to me."

Zach's mouth flapped opened and closed like he was trying to speak with jaws made of rubber.

Monica fought the urge to run her fingers through his cropped brown hair and stroke her fingertips over the sharp angles of his face. "I know I don't deserve another chance, but could you maybe . . . think about it?"

"Monica—"

"Think about it. That's all." Deliberately, she made her voice too quiet for Zach to hear over the music. As she had anticipated, he leaned his head closer to hers in an effort to catch her words. Monica looked into his eyes, her face only a couple of inches from his.

"It was over a long time ago," he whispered.

"That doesn't mean we can't start it again." With a small, soft movement, she touched her lips to his.

His body gave a little spasm. Dropping his hands, he stepped back. Monica smiled and turned away from him as the last few bars of music drifted through the room.

So exhilarated that it was almost difficult to walk a straight line, Monica headed back toward the table where Justin waited. Out of the corner of her eye, she could see Emily Ramsey watching her. Emily's expression would have made ice look toasty. *Good.* Either she'd give Zach a blast of the Arctic silent treatment or she'd swoop at him with claws out—which meant that no matter how much Zach professed his devotion to Emily, when he remembered tonight, he'd recall Monica's smile, the way she moved in her emerald silk dress, the touch of her lips, her humble plea for another chance—contrasted against either Emily's coldness or her shrewish anger.

Round one to me, Monica thought as she settled in her seat.

"You're a vicious little creature." Justin grinned, but the chill in his eyes surprised Monica.

"I know what I want," she said. "When it comes to love, you either go for what you want with all you've got, or you lose. I'm not going to lose."

"Better be careful, or Emily might decide to fight dirty," Justin said. "Sometimes the quiet ones are the dangerous ones."

Monica laughed.

CHAPTER 5

"DON'T WORRY ABOUT IT," Emily said. "It's not your fault she kissed you."

Zach clutched the steering wheel so tightly that his skin stretched taut over knobby knuckles. "Yeah, she really caught me by surprise."

If you're dancing with your faces an inch apart, you shouldn't be that surprised if she pounces. Emily buried the sarcastic words and looked out her window at the city lights whipping past. She was determined to maintain her composure, but everything inside her seemed formed of glass. A wrong word. A glance. Anything could shatter her.

"What did she say to you?" Emily asked quietly.

"Nothing important. Congratulations on your engagement, how about a dance for old times' sake—that kind of thing."

Zach wasn't a good liar. Emily would have known he was holding back even if she hadn't seen him return from the dance floor red in the face and so flustered that he'd nearly missed the chair when he sat down. Whatever Monica had said to him, it hadn't been "Congratulations on your engagement."

Emily and Zach had both tried to pretend nothing was wrong, dancing a few more dances, dropping by the refreshment table for another glass of punch, chatting with a couple of friends. But when Emily suggested they leave, Zach had leaped on the suggestion with transparent relief and all but sprinted out the door.

Brent was right. Monica was after Zach, and Zach didn't seem to know how to handle it.

"I don't blame her for falling for you again," Emily said, careful to sound good-humored. "I feel the same way."

Zach gave a fake chuckle. "Monica tossed me out of her life because I was the human equivalent of stale bread to her. We were finished a long time ago. Don't let her get to you."

She wouldn't, Emily thought, *except for the fact that she obviously gets to* you. "Sending an old picture of the two of you and saying it was new was a pretty desperate trick." The words jumped from her lips, and Emily felt both relieved and panicky to hear herself speak them. "I don't think she'd have resorted to that if she wasn't interested."

Zach shot her a confused look. "What are you talking about?"

Emily pulled her evening wrap more tightly around her, but she only felt colder. "I got a . . . strange letter in the mail on Wednesday."

"Who from?"

"I don't know. It wasn't signed."

"What did it say?"

"It was a picture. And a note."

"A picture of Monica and me?"

Without looking at him, Emily described the picture and the contents of the note.

Zach gripped her hand, holding it so tightly that the band of her ring dug into her finger. She waited for him to say something, but he didn't speak, and she finally risked a glance in his direction.

If she'd driven a knife between his ribs, she imagined he would have looked about as he did at that moment—rigid with shock, his face so pale that it looked almost inhuman in the darkness. When he spoke, his voice was low but filled with more anger than she had ever thought could come from easygoing Zach. "That letter is a ridiculous lie. The picture was not taken in the past year, and whoever sent it to you claiming it was new is either sick or evil or both. I've had nothing to do with Monica since we broke up. The only times I've seen her are at church or church activities, and we've hardly spoken to each other. Why didn't you call me and clear this up the instant you got that letter? Why did you wait?"

"I didn't want to make it seem like I didn't . . ." Her voice trailed off.

"Like you didn't trust me?"

"I do trust you," Emily said, embarrassed at the way her actions had already marked this statement as insincere. If the picture hadn't rattled her, of course she would have mentioned it to Zach.

"I'm not upset with you for wanting an explanation. If someone had sent me a picture of you kissing Brent Amherst, I would have asked *you* for an explanation."

"If someone sent me a picture of Brent kissing *anyone,* I'd sell it for a million dollars on eBay, since it'd be a rare find right up there with Loch Ness Monster sightings."

"All right, but you get my point. It kills me to know you've been worrying about this for two days. If something's bothering you, talk to me. *Immediately.* Don't let rumors come between us. Promise?"

"Promise." Emily's throat seemed to close on the word so it emerged faint and raspy.

"And Emily, I can't imagine that Monica sent the picture. She wouldn't sneak around sending anonymous letters. That's not her style at all. She's very direct."

That's one word for it, Emily thought.

"I'm sorry all this happened." Zach released her fingers and returned his hand to the steering wheel. "Rotten way to end a great evening."

"Not a big deal."

"I'll make it up to you next weekend. I'll take you up to San Francisco. We'll eat somewhere classy and see a show. And promise me you'll wear the same dress. You look stunning."

"Thank you." Emily tried to sound warm and ended up sounding flat. She wondered if Zach noticed.

Or if he was too busy remembering Monica Fife's kiss to care.

* * *

Justin Driscoll locked his front door behind him and dropped the careless, good-natured expression from his face like he was shedding a Halloween mask. The muscles ached in his jaw and temples, and his lungs throbbed like he'd been running in frigid air. Monica had chattered about Zach Sullivan all the way to the dance and all the way home, each word a red-hot sliver of steel stabbing Justin's heart.

The buddy, the brother, the brainless pretty boy with no more depth of emotion than a Ken doll—*that* was how Monica regarded him. Justin could still feel the heat of her hand on his arm and the softness of her lips on his cheek when she'd given him a careless kiss good night—all those little flirty things she did without caring how they affected him. Just the thought of Monica in that green dress, her hair rippling down her back as she looked up at that geek Sullivan . . . Sullivan's bony hand on her waist . . .

Easy. Take it easy. Justin forced deep, slow breaths into his lungs and picked up the photograph of Monica that she had given him a couple of days ago, a shot she was thinking of using in an ad brochure for her candle shop. She'd wanted his opinion of the picture. He'd told her it was too beautiful. *"You trying to sell candles or collect stalkers?"* She'd giggled.

He *should* be feeling triumphant right now. He'd seen the sparks of jealousy in Monica's eyes when he'd pretended to be interested in Emily Ramsey.

She'd taken him for granted. They'd been friends since they were nine years old, and Monica thought he'd always be there, a shoulder to cry on and a listening ear for her romantic woes. But when he'd made her think for a moment that she wasn't the star of his life, it had nettled her.

He'd avoided chasing Monica. Chasing her would only inflate her ego to the point that she'd float to another man. Playing the buddy role had kept her in his life this long. But now she had this insane idea that she wanted to marry Zach Sullivan, and if Justin didn't act, he was going to lose his chance.

How dense could Monica be? *Zach Sullivan*? A high school math teacher who liked to go to bed by ten-thirty and get up before the sun? Had Monica forgotten how she used to grouse to Justin about Zach's early-bird habits, along with everything else that put him squarely in Boring Central?

No, she hadn't forgotten. She just had that all-too-common female brain ailment that let her believe she could change a man once she married him.

It didn't take a degree in psychology to figure out why Monica was suddenly obsessed with Zach. She'd had a bad run this last year, dating every flake in the area code. Zach, by contrast, was stability personified. That was what had drawn her to Zach in the first place. The father figure, designed to fill the gap left by the father who had abandoned Monica and her mother when Monica was eight. Monica was so shrewd in some ways and such a child in others.

This charade had gone on way too long. If Monica married Zach, she'd be comatose with boredom within a year. Monica and Justin were meant for each other. Who did she turn to when things went wrong in her life? Who did she trust with her secrets? Who'd been holding her hand and supporting her through every bump and twist in her life since they were in elementary school?

Justin.

Justin looked down at the picture of Monica and was dismayed to realize he'd crumpled both sides of it. He tossed it on the table and flexed his cramping fingers. *Take it easy. You know Monica loves you.*

You just need to let her know she does.

* * *

"See you later." Zach waved as he jogged down the stairs outside Emily's apartment, his footsteps loud on the concrete and metal steps. Emily kept a smile on her face until he was out of sight. She and Zach had managed light conversation the rest of the way home—too light, neither of them daring to say what they were thinking—and Zach had kissed her good night like everything was fine between them.

Did he think she couldn't sense the phoniness in his laughter or the tension in his arms?

A folded paper with her apartment number written on it hung from an elastic band around the doorknob. Another notice from the management. What was the issue this time? Parking problems? Scheduled tests of the fire alarm system? Who cared? Emily unhooked the notice and stepped inside her apartment.

Monica wasn't going to back off. Flirting with Zach in the parking lot on Sunday night . . . flinging herself on Zach the instant Emily stepped away from the dance. And that picture.

Emily removed her gold silk shawl—another loaner from Nicole—and draped it over the back of her overstuffed chair. She believed Zach's insistence that the picture was an old one, but the fact remained that Monica wanted to make it current. If she hadn't mailed the picture personally, Emily suspected that Monica knew who had and had approved it.

What did Zach think of Monica's pursuit?

Emily needed to sleep—sleep and find strength to cope. Tomorrow morning she'd be able to see things clearly. Whether or not she'd like what she saw was a different question entirely.

Weary and with a tightness in her stomach that made the refreshments she'd eaten sit like rocks, Emily absently flipped open the notice that she'd taken from the doorknob. Even as her fingers moved, it registered in her brain that the notice was unusually heavy—the paper was cardstock.

A picture of Ryan Tanner holding a WELCOME, EMILY! sign filled the top half of the paper. Crimson trickles of blood ran down his face, and red blotches stained his shirt. Beneath the picture, written in red marker, were the words *Forget me already?*

CHAPTER 6

"THIS IS THE LOWEST TRICK I've *ever* seen." Nicole threw the picture of Ryan onto the kitchen table. After Emily's call, Nicole had rushed to her apartment, her haste evident in her lack of makeup and her hair swept into a messy pony-tail. "I knew the woman was a snake, but I didn't think even *her* skinny little tummy would drag this low in the dirt. Did you call the police?"

"Not yet. And we can't assume it was Monica."

"Who else besides Monica Fife has it in for you?" Nicole's voice was rapid and hard, like stones flung onto concrete. Emily felt somehow comforted to know how upset Nicole was in her behalf.

"I can't think of *anyone* who would do this," Emily said. "Besides, Monica was at the dance tonight, and that's half an hour away."

"So what? Did she arrive right when you did?"

"Um . . ."

"I know you were watching for her, so you might as well admit what you know."

"She was late," Emily admitted. "She arrived about an hour after the dance started." *Right when I'd started to relax, thinking she wasn't coming.*

"I rest my case." Nicole pointed to the bloodied picture of Ryan. "Do you recognize this shot? Was this taken right when you moved here?"

Pain wrenched Emily as she studied the photo of Ryan wearing a BYU sweatshirt and holding the welcome sign decorated with several sketches of Emily drawn in black marker. Ryan was grinning at the camera, a grin rendered macabre by the blood trickling down his face and splotching his shirt. "Yes, I'd just finished school. When Tricia and I arrived at my parents' house, he was there to meet us with that sign he'd drawn for me."

"I remember Tricia flying to Utah to drive home with you," Nicole murmured, studying the picture. "Who took the shot?"

"I did."

"Did you ever give it to anyone? E-mail it? Post it online?"

"Let me think," Emily said, though at the moment, thinking clearly sounded about as feasible as defying the law of gravity. "I didn't post it anywhere. That would have embarrassed Ryan. I don't think I sent it to anyone, but I don't really remember. Wait—I probably sent it to Tricia. She liked collecting family photos, so I sent her a lot of pictures."

Nicole frowned. Her lips looked flat and pale without her usual lipstick or gloss. "How about Ryan's family? You said his mother was upset about your engagement and didn't want Zach coming to dinner with you tomorrow night—"

"Forget it. I'd bet my life that Bethany Tanner would never do anything like this. She can't even face the probability that Ryan is dead, let alone create something so . . ." Why had she said *probability* instead of *fact*? *Because it's not a fact. No matter how convinced you are, you're only guessing. And who's to say your guess is right and Bethany's is wrong?* Not wanting Nicole to read her thoughts, Emily said quickly, "What *is* that on the picture anyway?"

Nicole scraped at a trickle of red. "Fingernail polish. I'm betting Monica Fife has this exact shade of red in her collection."

Shivering, Emily stood with her arms folded tightly against her body. The shimmering fabric of her dress hung cold and limp against her legs. "But why would she—or anyone—do this?"

"Why do you think? Anything to shake you up and cause trouble for you and Zach. First she sends you that old picture of them smooching on the beach, and then to make sure you're *really* rattled, she follows up with—"

"There's more. At the dance tonight she . . . kissed Zach."

"She *what*?"

"She was there with Justin Driscoll. When I went to the ladies' room, she jumped into my place. I came back to find Monica and Zach on the dance floor while she whispered in his ear. Next thing I knew, she kissed him."

Nicole's eyes smoldered. "That little—"

"Don't say it. You'll have to wash your mouth out with soap."

"Ooh, I just want to *smash* something. Or someone. How did Zach respond to Monica's hussy routine?"

"Deer in the headlights. And he wouldn't tell me what she said to him."

"No big mystery to *that*. She said, 'Oh darling, my ego can't stand seeing you in love with someone else. Dump Emily and come back to me so I can turn your heart into Kibbles 'n' Bits.'"

Emily surprised herself by smiling. With the comfort of Nicole's presence, her shock at the sight of the bloodstained picture was fading. "Somehow I don't think that's *exactly* what she said."

"It's what she meant. She's a heartless, greedy—"

"Soap."

"Grr." Nicole bared her teeth. "There are some people you can't describe with nice words."

"I still can't believe she'd—" Emily waved toward the picture. "Zach would certainly never believe she'd do this. He wouldn't even consider the possibility that she sent me the photo of them on the beach."

"That's why you called me and not the police, isn't it?" Nicole said shrewdly. "Because you think it *is* Monica, but you have no proof, and you know Zach would never believe it. And if he heard you sent the police to pester Monica, he'd think you're being jealous and irrational—"

"—or even that I staged the whole incident myself in a desperate attempt to make Monica look like a villain."

"Ouch. You're right. That's probably what Monica is hoping for. Better to leave the police out of it." Nicole tiredly pushed at a clump of blond hair that had escaped her ponytail. "I must look horrible. Mitch would die if he knew I went out in public looking like this."

"You're not in public. You're at my apartment. And you look fine."

"Well, he's in Chicago until Monday, so he'll never know anyway. Now—change out of that dress, put on some old sweats, and pack your bag. We're having a sleepover at my place tonight."

"I'll be ready in a few minutes." Emily was grateful for the invitation. She hated the idea of being alone in her apartment tonight. She knew she was going to dream about Ryan. And Tricia.

In her bedroom, she looked at herself in the mirror over her dresser. Her face was a pallid, lifeless contrast to the vivid red of the dress. *"Promise you'll wear that dress. You look stunning."*

Stunning next to Monica Fife? *Ha.*

Emily stuffed pajamas and a change of clothes into her overnight bag and headed into the bathroom for a few essentials.

Back in the living room, she picked up her purse and jacket. "Ready. I just need my keys—" She looked around. Where had she put her keys? She usually kept them in a misshapen ceramic bowl on the counter, a gift from a student whose generosity outstripped her dexterity. "Darn it—I hate it when I—"

"Your purse?" Nicole suggested.

"I don't usually—oh, right. I must have dropped them in here without thinking." Sheepishly, Emily reached into her purse. "Okay, let's—" She stopped. At the bottom of her purse, half wedged under her wallet, was something red and smooth. Emily lifted her wallet and picked up a bottle of red nail polish.

A shiver tingled along her spine. Silently, she extended the bottle to Nicole.

"I'm guessing you didn't put that in your purse." Nicole took the bottle.

"I own two colors of nail polish. Clear and pale pink."

Nicole looked at the blood-red polish with distaste in her eyes. "Did you have this purse with you tonight?"

"Yes. I don't have an evening bag."

"You should have borrowed one from me. Well, this clinches our theory that Monica was hoping to make it look like you staged this yourself. She slipped the polish into your purse at the dance."

Emily hesitated. It seemed nightmarishly unreal that Monica Fife would do something like this. Surely Monica wasn't that cruel—or that desperate. "This just seems so . . . horror movie. Chasing Zach is one thing, but planting a picture like this—"

"By hiding the polish in your purse and using a picture you took yourself, she's hoping to make it look like you're the one who's come unglued—and that you're still obsessed with Ryan. Just one more way to drive a wedge between you and Zach."

Emily picked up the photo of Ryan. Thinking back to the day when she took the picture was like remembering a fairy tale—the thrill of being reunited with Ryan after four months apart while Emily finished her degree at BYU and Ryan started his new job here, the anticipation of their wedding, scheduled six weeks later for the end of January. A fairy tale, encrusted in glitter and magic, until—

"Get rid of the picture for me." If she had to look at it for one more second, she'd start screaming. "And take the polish too."

"Not a problem." Nicole took the picture. "Let's get out of here. It's time for hot chocolate, popcorn, and revenge planning."

"Lead on." Listening to Nicole plot elaborate revenge schemes that neither of them would ever carry out would be diverting, and at this point, Emily welcomed any diversion that could keep her thoughts from cutting too deeply into fears she didn't want to explore.

* * *

Emily sat up in Nicole's guest room bed, her heart thumping crazily. In tonight's dream, she'd been screaming for Ryan to help her as she chased a cluster of white-and-yellow balloons carried on the wind, but Ryan just drove alongside her in his car, yelling at her to run faster. She'd tripped and fallen in the road, and the wheels of his car were headed straight for her, but then it was Tricia sprawled in the road, her eyes staring at nothing, blood dripping from her mouth, while Zach stood next to Emily and repeated over and over, *"Why did you kill her? We haven't had cake yet."*

At least she'd netted a few hours of sleep before the nightmares had set in. She and Nicole had talked until two in the morning, until Emily was so tired that she knew even the stress of her disastrous evening wouldn't keep her awake. But now, the familiar tension in her limbs and the knots in her chest told her she had as much chance of falling back asleep as she did of beating Monica Fife in a beauty contest.

The more she thought about the picture of Ryan, the more anger displaced her pain. Maybe it wasn't fair to assume Monica was responsible, but if she was ruthless enough to pursue a man who was engaged—and kiss him in front of his fiancée—maybe she *was* ruthless enough to seek out other ways of shaking up Emily. No one else had a reason to want to push the memory of Ryan between Emily and Zach—except for Bethany, and the thought of Bethany daubing fake blood onto a picture of her son was so ludicrous that it wasn't even worth considering. How Monica could have gotten a copy of that picture, Emily had no idea, but Emily guessed it must have come through Tricia. Tricia had probably passed the shot of Ryan along to friends, and it had eventually made its way to Monica.

Emily switched on the bedside lamp, hoping the light could lift mental darkness as well. The guest room was beautifully decorated in tones of sage and shell pink. Nicole's entire house was so perfect that it almost made Emily uneasy, as though a mismatched cushion or a chair with frayed arms would be a sin beyond forgiveness. To Nicole's mother, it probably would be. Emily wondered if Mitch was that particular. She hoped not.

She slouched down in the bed and tucked the covers under her chin. Through a tangle of fear and jealousy, only one thought was clear: she needed to confront Monica. If Monica thought she could manipulate and intimidate Emily, Emily needed to look her straight in the eyes and tell her she was wrong.

Would she listen? If she was coward enough to pull anonymous stunts, she probably wouldn't have the guts to continue with them if Emily stood up to her.

But even if the pictures stopped, that didn't solve the core problem— that Monica wanted Zach. Emily twisted the diamond ring on her finger. More than anything, she wished she could confide in Tricia, but Tricia was gone, and all Emily could see in her memory were those balloons, snagged in the branches of a tree, jerking hideously in the wind.

Emily shoved back the blankets. She needed to do something productive. Not wanting to disturb Nicole, she tiptoed through the chilly house and into the study. Using Nicole's computer, she located Monica's e-mail address from the ward Web site and sent her a message.

We need to talk, immediately and in person. I can meet you anytime tomorrow except between five and nine in the evening.

If Monica claimed to be too busy for the conversation, Emily would simply show up at her candle shop. But somehow she doubted Monica would want customers to overhear anything Emily had to say.

* * *

Monica Fife yawned as she stumbled toward the kitchen. *Too early. It ought to be illegal to get up before ten on a Saturday.* She should hire someone to work Saturday mornings so she could sleep in, but she hated the thought of leaving the store in the hands of a less competent salesperson on her busiest day.

The kitchen had a chemical smell to it that vaguely reminded her of a beauty salon. Blinking in the gray light from a cloudy dawn, she flipped the light switch.

Puddles and streaks of red covered her kitchen table. Blood.

Monica screamed, jumping back so wildly that she knocked her shoulder against the doorframe. Suppressing a whimper of pain, she stood in the hallway and goggled at the table.

In the middle of the table lay a photograph of Monica, one from her recent sitting. It was torn down the middle, and the halves were streaked with red.

Monica pressed both hands to her mouth and flung a terrified glance at the phone on the wall, afraid to so much as walk across the room to dial 911. What if the intruder was still here, waiting to attack her?

Mustering her courage, she sprinted to the front door, intending to go hammer on a neighbor's door and call the police from there, but when she pulled the door open and her apartment remained quiet, she hesitated. She really didn't want to go staggering over to a neighbor's, shrieking like a banshee and looking like one too. Obviously whoever had done this was long gone or they would have grabbed her already.

She clicked the door shut and turned back toward the blood-streaked table. Was it a threat? A warning of some kind? She inched toward the gruesome display, nausea wriggling in her empty stomach. Real blood? No. Some kind of costume blood.

With her initial panic fading, Monica started to get angry. If someone thought they could spook her, too bad for them. It was going to take more than a scene from a Halloween party to spook Monica Fife.

But who would want to scare—

Emily Ramsey. After last night, Emily was surely furious with her. But would calm, dignified Emily do something so freaky and disgusting?

Emily probably hadn't done it herself. She might have talked a friend into doing it for her, or hired a teenager—some kid eager for a few dollars to restock his supply of weed.

Monica glared at the table. Was this the best Emily could do? Some cheap fake blood and that picture—Monica hadn't given a sample picture to Emily, but she'd passed a few of them to friends, asking their opinions, and it wouldn't have been hard for Emily to get her hands on a copy. But how had Emily—or her flunky—gotten in here? Monica returned to the front door and opened it. There were no signs of damage to the door, the lock, or the doorframe. Nobody had forced the door open. She walked through the apartment and checked each window. All were locked.

Whoever had come in here had a key. That should narrow things down for the police—except that Monica couldn't remember ever giving a key to anyone, let alone Emily Ramsey. The culprit must have picked the lock. Monica shuddered at the thought that someone had crept in here while she was sleeping, splashed fake blood all over her table, and slipped out again with Monica never hearing a sound. Maybe she should be grateful she *was* a heavy sleeper. If she'd awakened and confronted the intruder, who knew what would have happened to her?

But if Emily was responsible, she'd never actually *hurt* Monica.

Would she?

She seemed so sane. But serial killers were always the quiet ones, weren't they? Isn't that what shocked neighbors always said? *"He was so quiet. We never would have guessed he had a duffel bag full of heads in his basement."* And Emily Ramsey had been through enough to drive anyone around the bend. It would be a shocker if she *wasn't* warped.

Monica's lips curved in a little smile. Didn't Emily realize that in her effort to scare Monica, she had handed Monica the tool for plucking Emily out of Zach's life? Once Zach learned what Emily had done, he'd be both sickened at her cruelty and shaken by this evidence that she was mentally unbalanced. Monica doubted that Emily and Zach's wedding plans would go forward if Emily was in prison, charged with making death threats—or whatever the legal term was for leaving a blood-soaked picture on someone's kitchen table.

Monica hurried into her bedroom. She drew a green fleece pullover and a pair of jeans out of her closet and dressed quickly. In the bathroom, she ran a brush through her hair and swished a hasty coating of mascara on her eyelashes. Now it was time to call the police.

After she called the police, she'd call Zach.

CHAPTER 7

"DIDN'T EXPECT TO SEE YOU out so early after last night. It was the big lovey-dovey dance, wasn't it?"

Emily turned from where she'd been about to unlock her front door and saw Brent Amherst at the bottom of the stairs with several bags of groceries slung over his arm.

"Oh . . . yes . . . I just . . ." Self-conscious at Brent's seeing her with an overnight bag in her hand, Emily tried to think what to say. She didn't want to give him the wrong impression. But telling him she'd spent the night at Nicole's would require a lot of painful explanation.

Brent must have sensed how flustered she was, because he started climbing the stairs, his teasing expression darkening to concern. "Is everything all right? You look stressed."

Emily tried to smile, wishing she'd stayed at Nicole's long enough to miss running into Brent. She probably should have waited for Nicole to wake up, but at seven-thirty Nicole was sound asleep, and Emily had been up and restless for over two hours. She'd called a cab and left Nicole a note, figuring it would be more therapeutic to return home and plunge into cleaning and laundry than to sit in Nicole's guest room and brood.

"Time to talk." Brent took the key out of her hand, unlocked the front door, and pushed it open. "You sit down, I'll make breakfast, and you can talk."

Emily sighed, but she allowed Brent to follow her into the apartment. "I'm not sure I want to talk. And don't you need to get those groceries into the fridge?"

"The groceries can wait. What did Sullivan do?"

"Who says Zach did anything?"

Brent plopped the bags on Emily's counter and surveyed her owlishly through his round glasses. "I'm not dumb, kiddo. Last night was the big date. Then you sleep over at Nicole's and come home at the crack of dawn looking like death. Sullivan did something. Confess."

"How do you know I was at Nicole's?" Emily asked, annoyed at Brent's clairvoyance or her transparency or both.

"Because you needed a best friend's shoulder to cry on, and Mitch the millionaire is probably still out of town, so I figure Nicole's house was a good place for a venting session. It's about Monica Fife, isn't it?"

Emily sank onto the couch and said nothing.

"I know," Brent said. "None of my business. The perpetual bachelor should keep his know-it-all opinions about relationships to himself." He drew a carton of eggs out of one of the bags. "Omelet?"

"No, thanks."

He opened her fridge. "One salsa and cheese omelet coming up."

"Brent, don't bother—"

"I'll cook it, and if you don't want it, you don't have to eat it. Okay?"

Emily smiled tiredly, realizing she *was* hungry. "How did you remember what I like on my omelets?"

Brent cracked eggs into a bowl. "That New Year's Eve party. Make your own omelets. Remember?"

"That was two years ago! You've got a great memory."

"I'm a formidable opponent at trivia games. Go on, ask me Attila the Hun's favorite color."

"Um . . . I'll guess a bold cranberry."

"I said his favorite color, not his favorite snack. You women and your need to turn the color wheel into a salad. What's wrong with plain old red?"

Emily giggled.

"Hmm," Brent said, "I see you're a lot more cheerful when I talk about something unrelated to the dance. How about rock climbing? Logan Tanner and I are meeting at a new gym in Sunnyvale tonight. Want to join us? Might take your mind off everything."

"Sure it will, because I'll be preoccupied with my imminent death."

"It's perfectly safe."

"For Spiderman, maybe. Besides, I have other plans. But have fun."

"Thanks." He gave Emily a small smile. "It always feels like we're short a climber."

If Brent's intention had been to change to a lighthearted subject, he wasn't doing a very good job of it. "I'm just glad Ryan had you two as part-ners in crime, or he would have tried harder to drag *me* up one of those crazy walls. I'm okay with hiking, but rock climbing—in a gym or else-where—no thank you."

"I appreciated him inviting me along. New kid on the block and all that."

"Are you kidding? He was always thrilled to find new recruits. I remember when he met you while he was home from BYU for Christmas break—he must have talked for ten minutes about how there was a new guy in the ward who loved hiking and rock climbing but had never been to Yosemite. He and Logan couldn't wait to initiate you."

"He was a good guy. One of the best people I ever knew." The humor left Brent's face. "He deserved a lot better than—" He cut his own words off with a shrug. "Well, who knows what happened."

Emily couldn't prevent the image of the bloodstained picture of Ryan from settling at the front of her thoughts. "I'm going to talk to Monica," she said abruptly. She hadn't intended to share her plans, but it was suddenly easier to speak than to sit silent with miserable thoughts trapped inside her. "She was at the dance last night."

"So were a lot of people. But I'm guessing she didn't stay with her date and give Zach a sisterly wave."

"She kissed him." Emily described the scene.

Brent grimaced, his gaze focused on the eggs he was mixing with a fork. "So you think confronting her will help? Get a clue, Emily. She knows she's hurting you. She doesn't care. Monica's a scorpion, but at least she doesn't camouflage her poison. It's the women who hide behind a façade of sweetness and devotion who cause the most pain."

Emily suspected Brent was referring to a failed past relationship, but she knew if she asked about it, he wouldn't elaborate. "It's more than what happened at the dance. And no, I don't want to explain."

Brent rummaged through the drawer under the stove and brought out a frying pan. "When are you going to talk to her?"

"As soon as possible. I hope today—"

The doorbell rang. Surprised, Emily started to stand up, but Brent waved her down. "Allow me."

"No, that's—" But Brent was already approaching the door. He swung it open.

"Brent. Uh . . . good morning." It was Zach's voice.

Emily jumped to her feet and hurried to the door. "Zach, hi. Come in. Brent's . . . making omelets."

"Put me down for a ham and mushroom." Despite the lightness of his tone, Emily blushed at the oddness of the situation. Explaining why Brent was here at eight in the morning would involve explaining that she'd been at Nicole's last night and had returned home looking so stressed that Brent had followed her into her apartment to try to coax her worries out of her. And the last thing she wanted to discuss right now was that horrible picture of Ryan and her suspicions about Monica.

What was Zach doing here so early? He was almost always up by six-thirty but had never stopped by her apartment before nine without making prior arrangements.

Brent tossed a pat of butter into the hot frying pan. Emily wished there were a tactful way to ask him to leave, but she couldn't think of a non-offensive way of tossing the cook out the door mid-omelet.

"I tried to call you last night." Zach sounded as awkward as Emily felt.

Emily glanced at the phone on the wall to see the voice mail light blinking. "I . . . was out for a while."

Zach's gaze flicked toward Brent. Emily's cheeks went hotter. "With Nicole," she said.

Brent tipped beaten eggs into the pan with a buttery sizzle. "Girls' night out," he said. "I ran into Emily coming back from her sleepover and volunteered to make her breakfast, since she looked too tired to remember how to do it."

"You stayed at Nicole's?" Zach's expression took on the strained-polite look he got when he was annoyed and trying to hide it. Emily could guess what he was thinking—that after she'd arrived home last night, she'd called Nicole to vent about Monica. Zach hated gossip.

Emily wanted to take the spatula out of Brent's hand and whack him across the seat of his jeans. He was trying to jockey her into a position where she had no choice but to confront Zach about how upset she was.

"It's a long story," she said lamely. "Mitch is out of town," she added, as though that were relevant.

"A long story." Brent drizzled salsa on the quivering mass of egg, added grated cheese, and deftly flipped the omelet in half. "Once upon a time," he said, "the princess was bugged when the serf was lurking in her kitchen making omelets when she wanted to talk to her prince alone. 'Forsooth, fool, get thee hence,' she said.'"

Emily forced a laugh.

"Listen, I can't stay anyway," Zach said before Emily could take the spatula Brent held out to her. "I'm meeting Jonathan at the gym. I just wanted to drop by, and you weren't answering either of your phones."

"Oh—I must have forgotten to turn my cell phone back on after the dance last night. I'm sorry."

"No problem," Zach said. "Have a good day, and enjoy your dinner party tonight. I'll see you at church tomorrow."

"I'll walk you to your car."

"That's okay," Zach said as Brent flipped the omelet onto a plate. "Your breakfast is ready."

"You eat it, Brent," Emily said. She couldn't let Zach leave like this. "I'll have the next one."

She and Zach were both quiet on the way to the parking lot. It was a chilly, gray morning, and Emily shivered, wishing she'd grabbed her jacket.

When they reached his car, Zach turned to face her.

"I was trying to call you to apologize about last night," he said. "I was so caught off guard by Monica acting like she did that I didn't handle it very well. She was completely out of line, and I stood there like an idiot. I'm sorry."

The pain level inside Emily instantly dropped by half. "It's all right."

Zach shook his head. "Especially considering that picture some anonymous jerk sent to you, I don't blame you for being upset enough to need Nicole's support. I'm glad she was there for you. I'm sorry I wasn't."

She should tell him what had really driven her to call Nicole but couldn't seem to force the words from her mouth.

"I had an idea of who might have sent the picture, but it didn't pan out," Zach said.

Emily's pulse rate jumped. "You think you might know who sent it?"

"When I was living in Sacramento, I had a student who was both vicious and unstable, and she made some trouble for me. I wondered if somehow she had followed me here, but I checked with the police in my old area, and they told me she died of a drug overdose last year. So clearly it wasn't her."

"Oh. I'm sorry," Emily said. Zach had never told her about this student. "It sounds like you had a rough time with her."

"It's over. Not something I like to talk about."

Emily wanted to ask if Zach was willing to consider that Monica herself might be the culprit, now that his trouble-causing former student was eliminated as a suspect, but she didn't dare.

"Zach, I hope you didn't get the wrong idea." She tilted her head in the direction of the apartment building. "Brent saw me arriving home and kind of elbowed his way in the door."

"It would never occur to me to think you were sneaking around with Brent Amherst. I know you better than that." He wrapped his arms around her. Emily rested her cheek against his shoulder, comforted in his embrace, wishing she didn't have to let go.

Finally, they drew back from each other. "You look tired." Zach touched her cheek. "You must have had a bad night, and it's my fault. I'm sorry. But you can quit worrying. No one is going to come between us—not some anonymous creep, and not Monica Fife."

He kissed her and climbed into his car. Emily walked back to her apartment. The damp coldness of the air made her want to hurry, but the thought of Brent waiting for her slowed her pace. She didn't want to talk to anyone right now.

She should have told Zach about the picture of Ryan. But if she had, would he still believe she could quit worrying?

* * *

Emily absently paired two socks together and rolled them, her gaze flicking for the tenth time to the bookshelf. Finally, she pushed the basket of laundry aside, rose from where she'd been sitting cross-legged on the living room floor, and slid the daisy-covered photo album from its spot between two daisy-painted bookends. The bookends had been a Christmas present from Tricia and the album a birthday present—the present that had been sitting, wrapped, on the Tanners' coffee table while Emily found Tricia's broken body by the side of the road.

Emily curled up in her overstuffed chair and opened the album. On the inside cover, Tricia had written, *Happy birthday, Em! Here's to the next twenty-three years!*

She turned the pages, examining each picture that Tricia had chosen for her. Tricia and Emily dressed as witches, ready for trick-or-treating. Tricia and Emily on Christmas morning, chocolate smeared all over their chins. Tricia and Emily grinning next to a huge sandcastle. Tricia with her arm around Emily the day Emily graduated from high school.

As Emily studied each photo, her tension level lowered a fraction until by the last page, she felt almost at peace. If Tricia were here, Emily knew what she'd say.

"No worries, Em. This whole Monica thing will blow over. Keep your cool."

Emily slid the daisy album back on the shelf and checked her e-mail to see if Monica had responded to the message Emily had sent early that morning.

No answer yet. If Emily didn't hear back by this afternoon, she'd go to Monica's candle shop. She wasn't going to let this drag on.

The doorbell rang. Hoping Zach had decided to stop by on his way home from the gym, Emily opened the door to see two strangers: a woman with a lean face and gray-streaked hair cut short, and a younger man with dark hair. His brown eyes, though pleasant behind his glasses, nonetheless seemed to assess Emily in one glance. Both visitors exuded an air of authority that made Emily sure of their identity even before they spoke.

Police. Ice shot through her veins, a million prickles of pain poised to coalesce into one razor-edged mass of agony slicing her heart in two. Zach was dead. These officers were here to tell her Zach was dead.

"Emily Ramsey?" the woman asked.

Emily nodded. She wanted to clamp her hands over her ears to keep whatever this woman was about to say from entering her consciousness and becoming reality, but she couldn't do anything but stand and wait.

The woman showed her a badge and an ID that Emily didn't even try to read. "I'm Detective Helen Lund with the Los Coros Police Department. This is Detective Nimish Kapoor. We'd like to ask you a few questions. May we come in?"

A few questions. Emily's frozen mind moved sluggishly, trying to catch up with the words emerging from the detective's lips. They wanted to ask her questions. *Ask* her, not tell her. Not deliver bad news.

Blood flowed back into her limbs and swept into her cheeks in waves of heat. "Yes—of course, come in," she said, too relieved to bother feeling foolish for her unwarranted panic. Had Nicole called the police and told them about the bloodied picture of Ryan? That didn't seem like something Nicole would do without Emily's permission.

Lund and Kapoor stepped into the living room. "Have a seat," Emily invited, embarrassed by the assorted piles of laundry littering the living room floor. Hastily, she gathered the piles, tossed them in the basket, and shoved it into the corner. Detective Lund watched her with an unreadable expression on her face.

"What can I do for you?" Emily sat in her armchair and tried to look politely interested, but Lund's gaze was so sharp that her relief rapidly buckled to apprehension.

"This morning, Monica Fife found a threatening picture someone had left in her apartment," Lund said.

The words jarred Emily. "A picture! What kind of picture?"

"I understand you're having a disagreement with Miss Fife. Could you tell me the nature of the disagreement?"

Emily fumbled for words, feeling like her brain had turned upside down. Someone had left *Monica* a threatening picture? Of whom?

"We haven't had any kind of confrontation. But Monica used to date Zachary Sullivan. Zach and I got engaged last week, and since then—" Her thoughts sped to the obvious conclusion: the police thought Emily had threatened Monica, which meant Monica had accused Emily. Had Monica planted the picture of Ryan and then planted a similar picture in her own apartment so she could blame Emily? Was she that devious?

"Miss Ramsey?"

"I'm—I'm sorry. I'm just trying to make sense of this. I've received a couple of pictures too."

"What kind of pictures?"

"The first was a picture of Monica Fife and Zach Sullivan kissing. It came in the mail with an anonymous note claiming it was taken a couple of weeks ago."

"When exactly did you receive the picture?"

Emily gave the details while Lund jotted something on the notebook in her hand. Detective Kapoor was taking notes as well. His dark eyes were friendlier than Lund's gray ones. Emily wished he were the one asking questions.

"You have no idea who sent the picture?" Lund asked.

"Not really."

"Not really?"

Emily shifted in her chair. "I suspected Monica," she admitted. "I had no proof, of course, but she was the only person I could think of who would be interested in causing trouble between Zach and me, since she's made it obvious she wants him back. But the picture was an old one, taken over a year ago, before Monica and Zach broke up."

"Mr. Sullivan told you that?"

"Yes, and I believe him. Zach wouldn't cheat on me." Did she sound confident or just entrenched in denial?

"You said you'd received a couple of pictures," Lund said. "What was the second one?"

Emily's tongue turned leathery. Why hadn't she called the police last night? Any reasonable citizen would have called the police after finding that gruesome calling card. "It was a picture of my former fiancé, Ryan Tanner. Ryan disappeared three years ago. Are you familiar—"

Lund and Kapoor both nodded.

Relieved that she wouldn't have to explain the whole history, Emily said, "Last night, I found a picture of Ryan fastened to my front doorknob. It—" The prospect of describing the picture for Lund and Kapoor made Emily feel as though her stomach had contracted to the size and hardness of a piece of gravel, but she kept the words coming. "Red nail polish had been painted on his face and shirt to simulate dripping blood. Beneath the picture was written 'Forget me already?'"

"Why didn't you call us?" Lund asked.

"I should have. But I—again, I suspected Monica Fife." Could Lund possibly believe that Emily was telling the truth, or would she assume Emily was pointing a finger in Monica's direction in response to Monica's accusing her? It was like some twisted version of junior high school. *She did this to me." "No, SHE did this first."*

"Why would the fact that you suspected Miss Fife keep you from reporting it?"

"I didn't have any proof it was Monica. I just couldn't think of anyone else who'd want to shake me up. It obviously wasn't the work of a stranger, because the picture was one I took myself."

"You took the picture?"

"Yes, I recognized it. I don't know how the culprit got a copy of it. After three years, I can't remember exactly who I sent it to. My sister, probably, and she might have passed it on . . . I just don't know."

"We don't require people to know the perpetrator or all the details of a crime before they report it," Lund said.

"I know. I was just afraid that accusing Monica without proof would look petty."

"You were afraid Mr. Sullivan would think you accused her out of jealousy?"

Heat spread over Emily's cheeks. "I had no proof that it was Monica," she repeated, embarrassed at how easily Lund had read her insecurity.

"Do you still have the picture of Mr. Tanner?"

Emily's heart sank. "No. I called a friend last night, Nicole Gardiner. I asked her to get rid of the picture. And the bottle of red nail polish. I found a bottle of red nail polish in my purse last night, the same shade used to paint 'blood' on the picture."

"You found the polish in your purse?"

"Yes. I don't own any polish that color, and I didn't put it there."

"Do you have any idea when the polish could have been inserted in your purse?" Lund's voice remained bland, and Emily couldn't tell if she believed anything Emily had told her.

Emily thought back. Was she sure the polish hadn't been in her purse before the dance? No. Had she even opened her purse yesterday before she'd discovered the polish late that evening? She hadn't opened her purse to insert or retrieve her keys. At work, she was in the habit of leaving her personal keys in her jacket pocket, and her school keys were on a lanyard with her staff ID. She hadn't done any shopping yesterday. What about the day before? She'd gone to the grocery store. If the polish had been there, she would have noticed it when she lifted her wallet. Her purse was small, and she kept it tidy, so she wouldn't have missed seeing the polish.

"I know it wasn't there on Thursday evening, so it got put there some-time between Thursday and Friday night." In response to Lund's questions, she detailed the times when the purse had been out of her possession: at school, she kept it in a desk drawer; yes, she locked the drawer sometimes but wasn't scrupulous about it; they'd never had any trouble with theft; no, the door to her classroom wasn't always locked when she was away; she'd had the purse with her at a church dance on Friday evening; yes, there were times when she'd left it unattended. By the time Lund finished exploring this angle, Emily was both relieved that she was taking this seriously enough to follow up on Emily's story and humiliated by the certainty that Lund must think she was the most careless woman on the planet, and it was a wonder someone hadn't stolen her identity, emptied her bank account, and fled to Argentina.

"Does your friend Nicole Gardiner still have the picture or the polish?"

"I don't know. She probably got rid of them, but you can ask her." She recited Nicole's number, and Lund wrote it down. "You probably won't be able to get in touch with her right away," Emily added. "She told me she was going sailing with her dad this afernoon, and he doesn't like her to bring—I mean, she doesn't usually have her cell phone on board. But I can show you the picture of Monica and Zach that came in the mail. I still have that one." Emily hurried to retrieve the envelope from the bottom of her to-do basket. Could the police lift fingerprints from cardboard and paper?

She brought the envelope to Lund. Lund opened it, studied the picture for a moment, then returned it to the envelope. "Do you mind if we take this?"

"Please do." Emily resisted a somewhat hysterical urge to add, *"I'll cancel the appointment I made to have it matted and framed."*

Emily resumed her seat and spoke as firmly and calmly as she could. "I did not threaten Monica Fife. I didn't leave her any picture. I haven't even spoken to her since Zach and I got engaged. I did send her an e-mail this morning, asking if we could meet today to discuss this issue. But I didn't threaten her in any way. I can show you the e-mail if you like."

"Why did you want to meet with her?"

"Like I said, I thought maybe she'd left me the picture of Ryan. I wanted to tell her she couldn't intimidate me like that, and if she kept trying, I'd see her in prison. I thought if I confronted her directly, I had a better chance of getting things to stop before they escalated."

"Did she respond to your message?"

"Not yet."

"Where were you from one this morning until eight?"

"I was at Nicole Gardiner's until about seven-thirty. I was upset over the picture of Ryan and didn't want to be alone, so I slept at Nicole's last night. This morning, I woke early but didn't want to wake Nicole—we'd been up late—so I took a taxi back here. I have—" Emily reached into her pocket and pulled out the card the taxi driver had given her. She handed it to Lund. She wanted to ask more questions about the picture someone had left Monica—who was in the picture? What threats had been made?—but she didn't dare. This whole thing was absurd, a tacky soap opera.

Lund and Kapoor exchanged a glance and rose to their feet in unison. Emily stood as well, not sure if she should be relieved that they were leaving or bracing herself because she was about to be arrested.

"Thank you for your time." Lund opened a small leather case and pulled out a business card, which she handed to Emily. "If you think of anything that might be helpful, call me."

"I will."

Emily closed the door behind Lund and Kapoor, not sure whether to feel shaken, furious, or completely ridiculous.

CHAPTER 8

ZACH'S BLUE EYES WERE STORMY with shock and fury, and Monica had to work hard not to smile at how much her report had affected him. He looked ready to don his armor, grab his sword, and go slay dragons for her. "Monica, that's horrible. What did the police say?"

"They asked questions, took notes, dusted for fingerprints and all that. They said they'd talk to the neighbors, check if anyone saw anything."

Zach looked so endearing standing there in the middle of her workroom, his curly dark hair still damp from the shower at the gym. She'd invited him to sit down, but he'd refused, clearly making the point that he didn't want to stay any longer than necessary.

He'd been curt on the phone when she'd called this morning, and only her insistence that something awful had happened and that she needed his advice had prodded him into coming over. She was almost pleased that she'd had to push him a little—he'd hardly be worth having if she didn't have to work for him.

"The thing that creeps me out the worst is knowing that this intruder came in while I was home, while I was asleep." Monica shuddered.

"I don't blame you for being shaken up. You'll change your locks, right?"

"The locksmith is coming this afternoon." Monica slid off her stool and took a few steps toward him, careful to stop before she got close enough to make him feel crowded. "I'm sorry I dragged you over here. I was scared out of my wits and needed a shoulder to lean on. Seeing my picture all covered in blood—realizing some psycho had been in the house with me . . ."

Zach touched her arm then yanked his hand back like he'd burned himself. "I'm sorry you had to go through this. But if you need a friend to support you, you'd better call Rochelle. I can't—"

Monica gave an impish grin. "I need a strong male friend. Rochelle is all of five-foot-two and a hundred pounds."

Zach didn't smile. "Then call Justin Driscoll. I don't mean to sound callous, but this isn't a role I can play for you."

"We're not friends?"

"From what you . . . uh . . . said last night, you're not looking for me to be just a friend."

Monica retreated to her stool and sat, lowering her eyelashes so they shadowed her eyes. "I'm sorry." She picked up a spool of wicking and played with the loose end of the thread. "You're right. It wasn't fair of me to call you. I guess I'm not thinking very clearly."

"That's all right. I understand why you're upset. Anyone would be. Do you have any idea who did this to you?"

It was the question Monica had been awaiting. She frowned at the wicking and said, "It's hard to believe that anyone I know could do something like this. But obviously *someone's* furious at me and wants to scare me, so I keep thinking . . . wondering . . ." Monica looked up. She held Zach's gaze until she saw a flicker of comprehension—and horror.

"You can't possibly believe Emily did this! That is the most ludicrous—"

"I *know.* I like Emily. She's such a doll. But Zach . . . I can't stop thinking about the way she looked at me last night. You probably didn't see it—you were too far away—but—"

"Emily wouldn't do this."

"I didn't say she would, but when my safety is on the line, I need to consider every possibility. And Emily is the only person I can think of who's angry enough with me to want to—"

"I can't believe *that's* true." Blood darkened Zach's neck and ears. "Unless you've had a personality transplant. How many broken hearts have you added to your tally in the past year? There was that Johansen kid who was so dizzy-crazy for you that he was walking into walls . . . then Paul Huntington . . . You give men just long enough to lose their minds over you, and then you—"

"I can't help it if someone has a crush on me," Monica snapped. "And those guys all forgot me a day after we quit dating. Whoever left that picture is someone who's deep-down furious with me . . . and disturbed. And considering what Emily's been through, it would almost be a miracle if she weren't fighting some demons. The kind of pain she's experienced might break out in unpredictable ways—"

"What are you trying to do here?"

Monica jumped to her feet with an angry clack of heels. "What do you mean what am I trying to do? I'm trying to stay safe. Someone threatened me today. I'm not saying Emily did it. I'm only saying she's got a reason to hate me, and—"

"Did you give Emily's name to the police?"

"I had to! They asked if I could think of anyone with a grudge against me, and—"

"Emily does not have a grudge against you. The fact that you made a fool of yourself last night at the dance doesn't constitute a grudge on her part."

Blood rushed into Monica's face. "Caring about you makes me a fool?"

Monica had never heard Zach raise his voice, but now he was almost shouting. "So now you care about me? I have a two-year-old niece just like you. She doesn't want a toy until some other kid takes it, and then all of a sudden it's the best toy in the world, and if she can't have it, she's going to die."

"I've always loved you. It just took me a little while to grow up and realize it."

"And if I break up with Emily for you, within a couple of months Prince Charming will be a toad again and you'll toss me aside. Thanks, but I'm not interested. I'm marrying Emily."

Scalding tears filled Monica's eyes. "I know I hurt you. I can't tell you how much I regret that. But I'm not that way anymore. Just give me a chance. You used to love me."

"I used to love taking an entire bag of Oreos, eating the filling, and throwing the cookies away. I grew out of that, too."

Even as she recoiled from Zach's harshness, one reassuring fact blazed brightly, and she smiled at him through the tears. "If you didn't still care, you wouldn't get angry like this. You'd shrug and walk away."

For a long moment, Zach stared at her. She couldn't read his face—too many emotions battled in his eyes—but she knew she'd scored the point.

The jingle of a bell signaled a customer entering the shop. It was normally a sound she loved, but this time, Monica repressed a scowl. Of all the moments to be interrupted! "Just let me take care of whoever that is, and I'll be right back to—"

"No, we're finished talking." Zach's voice was cool. "I'm sorry to hear about the frightening picture. I'm sure the police will figure out who is responsible." He turned toward the back door.

"Zach, wait—"

Zach turned around and looked directly into her eyes. "I'm marrying Emily Ramsey. I swear I will not let you ruin this for me." He pivoted and strode out of her workroom. The door banged shut.

* * *

The bell over the door jingled, and Monica nearly lost the thread of the sales pitch she was giving an elderly gentleman. All day, she'd been waiting for Zach to return and apologize. He *would* come back. As soon as he calmed down, he'd feel awful about how rude he'd been, especially with Monica already traumatized by that picture. He wouldn't be able to rest until he apologized to her.

It wasn't Zach opening the door of the Amber Flame. It was Justin Driscoll. The sight of a young male who wasn't Zach rubbed like steel wool on Monica's raw feelings. With effort, she kept her smile in place and turned her attention back to her customer.

"The honeysuckle has a touch of jasmine as well." Monica popped the lid off the jar and held it out to him. "It's a fresh, springlike scent."

The white-haired man took the candle and sniffed. "Nice and light. She loves lilac, but she might like something different for a change." He picked up the lilac candle from the row of four other floral candles he was contemplating and sniffed for what must have been the tenth time. "We had lilac bushes near the porch of our first home. Massive things. Nearly took over the yard. I wanted to get rid of half of them, but she wouldn't let me. Every time I smell lilac, it takes me back forty years."

"In that case, no senior discount for you," Monica said with a wink.

He laughed. "Do you offer one?"

"No. But if I did, I wouldn't offer one to you regardless. They're for old people." Usually the flirty banter was easier to pull off, but today Monica felt she was straining to read lines from a blurry script. Why couldn't Gramps make up his mind and buy something?

Her gaze drifted to Justin. He was standing near the Valentine's display at the front of the store, feigning fascination with a chocolate-cherry scented candle. In one hand, he held a dozen red roses. Roses?

Their eyes met. Monica quirked an eyebrow in question. Justin grinned.

"This one," her customer decided, pointing to the honeysuckle candle. "I've got too much sense to want to be forty years younger."

"Sense definitely isn't part of the standard package in younger men." Monica pulled out several sheets of tissue paper and rolled them around the chosen candle.

When her customer was out the door with his purchase, and the shop was empty except for Justin and her, Justin said, "Lucky for you women that sense *isn't* part of the standard package, or none of us would ever be dumb enough to marry you."

Monica scowled at Justin. Her faux good humor had departed along with the customer. "Those roses had better be for me. After the day I've had, I need *something* to cheer me up."

Justin bowed and handed her the bouquet.

"They *are* for me? What's the occasion? Is it my birthday?"

"Do I need the calendar's permission to give roses to a beautiful woman?"

"That's a little cheesy, but I'll take it." Balm began to spread over Monica's sore emotions. It was good to talk to a friend. "I don't think you've ever given me flowers before."

"That's because I don't have much sense. Or so I've been told."

"It's part of your charm."

Justin smiled, but he was looking at her in an intense way he'd never looked at her before. "Go to dinner with me tonight."

"Tonight?" Monica stroked one of the rosebuds with her fingertip, uneasiness stirring inside her. Red roses were a very romantic choice. Did he mean something by them? No. They were the best of friends—had been forever. "I'm pretty booked. I've got a batch of candles I'm going to do after the store closes, and then I've got—drumroll, please—an appointment with Emily Ramsey."

"An appointment with Emily!"

"She e-mailed me, saying we need to talk." Monica had intended to ignore Emily's e-mail, but the thought that Emily might think she was too scared or too ashamed to face her had impelled Monica to consent to the meeting. "I'm guessing she has some threats she wants to make face-to-face, since breaking and entering is old hat."

"What do you mean 'breaking and entering'?"

Monica told him about the picture she'd found on her kitchen table. By the time she finished, rage had so transformed Justin's handsome face that Monica felt a flicker of concern. She'd wanted Justin's sympathy and anger in her behalf, but she didn't want him losing his temper and doing something irrational that would get him in trouble.

"The police will take care of things," Monica emphasized. "Don't freak out and go break Emily's neck."

"The police can only work with evidence." Justin picked up one of her promo magnets from the bowl on the counter and started bending and twisting it like he couldn't rest until he'd torn it apart. "Emily's a smart cookie, and she probably covered her tracks. How did she get into your apartment?"

"No idea. There were no signs that she broke in. Maybe she got a key somehow. Like you said, she's smart."

"She threatens your life, and then you agree to *meet* with her? Have you lost your mind?"

"I'm not scared of her. She ought to be scared of me."

"Monica, she's dangerous!"

"Come into the back." Monica picked up the roses and led the way. "I don't want a customer seeing you when you're foaming at the mouth like a rabid dog."

Justin followed her into her workroom. "Tell me you aren't going to meet with her."

"I'm not going to hide from her. I told her to meet me at the Starbucks across the street."

"So you can make nice over hot chocolate? This is nuts."

"We'll keep the meeting in a public setting, so I'm sure she won't try anything weird. But I'm hoping she'll *say* something weird. I have a digital voice recorder."

"Good luck with *that*." Justin picked up a wick bar and rotated it in his hands. "Even if you get her to admit something, will the police be able to use your recording as evidence?"

Monica rescued the wick bar from Justin before it could go the way of the mangled magnet. "I'm not a lawyer. But legal or not, I can play the recording for Zach." She expected to see a flash of admiration or even humor break through the anger in Justin's eyes, but instead he caught her shoulders in a grip so hard that it startled her.

"What is *wrong* with you? Your life gets threatened, and all you can do is plot ways to use the situation to get your claws into Zach Sullivan?"

"You think I shouldn't tell Zach what Emily is?"

"I think you need to wake up. Sullivan's not right for you, and you know it. You dumped him once. The only reason you're chasing him now is because you're tired of the flakes you've been dating and you think a dull, steady clod is safe. The daddy you never had."

Monica wanted to shout at him, but she kept her voice low. "I am *so* not in the mood for this. This has honestly been the worst day of my life."

"If you'd quit chasing some nerd who's already engaged to another girl— a psycho girl who'll probably burn your store down if you steal her fiancé— maybe your day would be a lot better. Maybe your *life* would be a lot better."

She twisted her shoulders, pulling free of his grip. Why was Justin acting like this? "It's none of your business who I marry."

"Maybe it is my business."

She could no longer pretend she couldn't read the message in his face. Monica looked down at the roses she was holding, her mind limping through a clutter of stock phrases that usually served her well in dealing with this kind of situation. She couldn't stand to recite any of them, not for Justin. How did this happen?

She looked up. For a silent moment, they stared at each other.

"You know I'm right," Justin said. "You'd never be happy with Sullivan."

She had to stop this immediately. She couldn't hurt Justin by letting it go any further. "Justin, we're *friends.*" Monica laid her hand on his arm. "We've always been friends. It's never been more than that. Please, let's not ruin things now."

"*Ruin* things?"

"I've been honest with you. You know I love Zach."

"A brainless obsession with a guy completely wrong for you is not love."

Monica's temper flamed, and she dropped her hand from his arm. "I thought you were the one man in the world I could count on not to go gaga on me. Go home and get some sleep, and you'll be back to normal in the morning."

The jingle of the bell signaled the arrival of a customer. "I have to go," Monica said, relieved to have an excuse to end the conversation. "Thank you for the roses."

Justin reached forward, planted his hands on either side of the clustered rosebuds and gave several quick, savage rubs. Bruised petals scattered over Monica's shoes.

"You're welcome," he said.

* * *

So tired that she ached all over, Emily slid behind the wheel of her car. The dinner with Bethany and Ted had gone better than she'd expected, but she still felt as though she'd just staggered across the finish line of an emotional marathon.

The Tanners had asked her politely about Zach and their wedding plans. They'd discussed a number of pleasant, neutral subjects. But, inevitably, midway through the evening, the topic had turned to Ryan. Ted's words kept echoing in Emily's thoughts: *The thing that hurts the most is wondering if I could have prevented this. I knew he'd been having car trouble. If I'd loaned him a car—bought him a car—anything to keep him from getting stranded that night . . ."*

Hadn't she gone through similar if-onlies thousands upon thousands of times? If only she hadn't scheduled the parent meeting for that night, then she would have been with Ryan when his car broke down. If only she hadn't agreed to the combined wedding shower/birthday party idea of Tricia's, then Ryan would have been somewhere completely different that night. Or if only they had decided to hold the party somewhere other than at the Tanners' spacious home, then Tricia wouldn't have been struggling to tie balloons to the mailbox in a rainstorm.

If only, if only, if only.

"Enough," Emily said aloud as she turned off the Tanners' rural street onto the frontage road. She'd known the dinner tonight was going to stir up painful memories, but that didn't mean she had to wallow in them. She needed to keep herself focused if she was going to derive any benefit from her meeting with Monica Fife tonight.

Monica's e-mail answer had come late that afternoon, angry words that reaffirmed the fact that Monica blamed her for the threatening picture—or at least wanted Emily and everyone else to *think* she blamed Emily.

"I'm surprised you're bothering to ask if we can meet. Why not just break in and stand over me wearing a Halloween mask? Meet me at the Main Street Starbucks tonight at nine. Don't mess with me, Emily. You're no match."

Emily's exhaustion made it tempting to postpone the meeting, but putting it off would only make things worse. She needed to talk this out with Monica and get a feel for what was really happening. She didn't expect Monica to admit it if she was responsible for all the pictures—including the one left in her own apartment—but Emily hoped she might inadvertently give something away, if not in her words then in her attitude.

And if Monica *was* innocent and truly thought Emily was behind the pictures?

Then somewhere there was a third party with a grudge against both of them. Monica could help her figure out who that was—*if* Monica was willing to think about this rationally rather than simply blaming Emily.

Emily arrived at Starbucks at ten minutes before nine. She didn't see Monica anywhere in the café, so she bought a bottle of water—the only thing she could possibly fit into her overfull stomach after Bethany's pasta extravaganza—and sat down to wait.

Half an hour later, with no sign of Monica, Emily's edginess had turned to anger. How childish could Monica be—agreeing to the meeting and then standing Emily up? Did she think this was a clever way to put Emily in her place?

Emily tossed her empty water bottle into the trash and exited Starbucks. Monica's candle shop was on a side street not more than a block away. It was a long shot, but maybe Monica was still there. Although it was well past closing time, maybe Monica had stayed at her shop to get some work done. *And maybe she lost track of time and didn't mean to stand you up. Sure.*

Emily crossed the street and headed toward the small, stucco plaza that contained the Amber Flame. Four stores formed the plaza—Monica's shop, a bakery, a vacant shop, and on the end, Rochelle's Shoes and Boots.

The lights glowed inside Monica's store. Emily paused outside the window, looking at the colorful candle displays and trying not to feel inadequate at this evidence of Monica's talent. A gifted entrepreneur as well as a skilled candlemaker, Monica had turned a home-based candlemaking hobby into a thriving small business before she hit her thirtieth birthday, and it was hard for Emily to feel either glamorous or competent as she reached for the doorknob.

She didn't expect the door to be unlocked, but it was. Why hadn't Monica locked up? According to the sign on the door, the shop closed at seven on Saturday evenings, and it was now nine-thirty.

Emily swung the door open, causing a bell overhead to jingle. She stood in the empty showroom, waiting for Monica to respond to the bell, but no one appeared.

"Monica?" Emily called.

No answer. Emily raised her voice. "Monica?"

Nothing. Emily exited the shop and walked around the side of the plaza to check the parking lot. It was empty except for one car—Monica's old black Honda Civic. The sight of Monica's modest car always made Emily feel a little guilty for being judgmental. She would have expected Monica to go into debt to drive something flashy and pricey, and this evidence that she was careful with her money evoked a respect Emily didn't want to feel.

But if Monica's car was here, so was Monica. Emily strode back into the store. This was getting ridiculous. "Monica? It's Emily Ramsey. If you don't have the guts to talk to me—" Emily stopped. She sounded like an idiot.

The silence of the shop began to trigger shivers along her nerves. If Monica were here, surely she'd answer. It was absurd to think she'd sit in the back, smirking, waiting for Emily to give up and go home. Had she stepped out for a moment to grab some dinner at a nearby restaurant?

Without locking up or turning out the lights?

"Stop it," Emily whispered. Was she really paranoid enough to make Monica's absence into something ominous? Should she call the police? *"Detective Lund, I'm trying to meet with the woman who's attempting to steal my fiancé, and I can't find her. I think you should issue a missing persons alert."*

Monica was probably in her workroom, engrossed in her work, unable to hear Emily over the music playing on her iPod. Emily knew where the workroom was; they'd toured Monica's shop once for an enrichment activity.

Emily marched to the back of the showroom and pulled open the door marked STAFF ONLY. A short corridor led to Monica's workroom in one direction and her stockroom in the other. The door to the workroom was ajar, and the lights were on. Too irritated to feel self-conscious at her intrusion, Emily walked into the workroom.

Monica was nowhere in sight. Emily walked farther into the room, moving past Monica's cupboard and worktable. "Monica? Are you—"

For a long moment, it was as though everything inside Emily turned to stone—her heart motionless, her blood solid in her veins, her lungs incapable of expanding. She stared at the lithe figure sprawled behind the worktable, at the droplets of red spattered on the tile, at Monica's auburn hair, a jumbled mass of curls concealing her face.

She wasn't moving.

"Please." Emily choked out the word—a cry, a plea, a prayer that the scene in front of her would disappear in a puff of theatrical smoke and Monica would stride toward her, smiling widely.

Was that movement in Monica's ribcage? Was she breathing? Maybe there was time to help her—to save her—not like Tricia . . .

"Monica." Emily dropped to her knees next to the prone figure. With shaking fingers, she lifted the hair that had fallen forward to cover Monica's face. "Monica, can you—"

Monica's face was purple, her mouth gaping, her eyes blank and bulging. A gash marred her forehead, and blood streaked her face and stained her white sweater. Her neck—something was digging into her throat. A scarf?— twisted fabric, sinking into bruised skin—

With a cry, Emily jerked backward, trying to stand and retreat at the same moment. She wanted to scream, but she couldn't even breathe. Dizziness buzzed through her skull, and her stomach convulsed with nausea. She couldn't get sick—she had to call the police, had to call for help. The blood on Tricia's lifeless face mingling with streaming rainwater—

* * *

Her cheek was resting against something hard and icy. Disoriented, Emily tried to push herself up. Pain battered her skull. She sank back to the floor, too dizzy to stand. Where was she?

Heat trickled across her forehead and dripped into her hair. She touched her head and felt wetness beneath her fingertips. What had—

A tumble of auburn hair caught her eye, and reality shone through the fog in her head. Monica. Monica Fife had been murdered.

She grabbed the edge of Monica's worktable and dragged herself to her feet. Another wave of dizziness hit, and she stumbled, slamming her shoulder against the storage cupboards. *Steady. Breathe.* She lurched toward the back door and fumbled blindly for the doorknob.

Please don't let this be real. Let it be a dream, just a bad dream. She twisted the doorknob and tottered out into the darkened parking lot. Call the police—a phone—her cell phone—where was her purse? She must have dropped it in Monica's workroom. Next to her body.

She couldn't go back in there. She'd stop someone and ask to use a phone, or go to a store or restaurant. The ice cream shop across the street, with lights blazing and couples lined up at the door—

Emily staggered into the street, distantly aware of the screech of brakes, and headed toward the ice cream shop. The ground swayed beneath her feet as she pushed through the line of people waiting to be served.

"Hey, lady—whoa, are you okay?"

She grabbed for the glass-topped counter to keep herself upright. The boy behind the counter gaped at her, an ice cream scooper in his hand.

"Call the police," Emily said hoarsely. "Monica's dead."

CHAPTER 9

EMILY PRESSED HER PALMS TO the countertop as the tubs of ice cream underneath the glass swirled into a sickening blur of colors. She blinked hard, struggling against the dizziness. "She's dead. She's dead."

The boy with the ice cream scooper stared at her, his jaw slack. As though they'd choreographed it, the entire staff behind the counter stepped backward.

"Monica Fife," Emily said. "In her shop."

It wasn't just the staff shrinking from her. The customers were drawing back as well, and she heard a sharp voice. "Let's get out of here."

"The—the candle shop—across the street . . ." Warmth slid down the side of her face, crawled along her neck, dripped onto her jacket. Emily brushed her hand across her cheek and saw blood smeared on her fingers.

"What's the name of the shop?" A man with gray hair and a San Francisco Giants sweatshirt was at her side. Emily looked at him, grateful someone had finally responded.

"It's the—the . . ." Why couldn't she remember the name of Monica's shop? Those pale green scarves with the little flame motif that Monica sold at her shop and occasionally gave away as promotional freebies . . . flames . . . gold . . . "The—the Amber Flame—Monica is in the back . . . in her workroom . . ." Sickness rose again. It was hot in here, stifling. She took a wavering step toward the door. Fresh air . . .

"Hang on, miss." The man caught her arm. "You're hurt."

Emily tried to tell him to let her go, that she had to get fresh air or she would faint again, but her lips tingled, and her tongue flopped wordlessly.

"She needs to sit down. Get her a chair." A woman's voice. "And grab some napkins; we need to stop that bleeding."

"I'll call the police." Another voice. Chair legs scraped on tile, and Emily felt herself being pushed into a cold metal seat. Someone pressed a pad made of folded napkins against the stinging pain near her hairline. How had she cut her head? She must have struck the sharp metal corner of Monica's worktable when she fainted.

"Emily. *Emily.*"

A tall man with shaggy blond hair pushed his way into the ice cream shop. Justin Driscoll. Emily's relief at seeing a familiar face mingled with horror. She'd have to tell him Monica was dead.

Justin grabbed her shoulders in a crushing grip. His face was gray. "Someone said—Monica—tell me it's not—"

"I'm—I'm so sorry. She's—I found her—Justin, I'm sorry."

"What happened?" His voice slammed into her; his fingers bruised her shoulders.

"I don't . . . I don't know. She—there was blood . . . her head—but I think she was strangled . . ."

Justin's face contorted in agony. His fingers gouged deeper into her shoulders, loosened, then tightened again in a spasmodic rhythm.

"I'm sorry," Emily whispered.

"What did you do to her?"

"What did *I*—What do you mean?"

Justin jerked her to her feet. "You killed her. Because of Sullivan. I *told* her not to meet with you—"

"No—*no*—"

He shook her viciously, and her head snapped backward. She tried to pull free of his grasp, but the floor heaved, her vision blurred, and nausea rose so strongly that she was sure she would vomit.

Abruptly, the pressure of Justin's grip was gone, and gentle hands lowered her to the floor. Her head rested on something soft. The man in the Giants shirt knelt on one side of her; a plump woman in a tan coat knelt on the other, holding the folded napkins against Emily's forehead.

"Take it easy, honey," the woman said.

" . . . *murderer*—she's a murderer—let *go* of me—" Justin's voice hammered her eardrums. She caught a glimpse of him struggling to break free of three men who'd pinned him against the wall.

Sirens lashed the night. Emily closed her eyes and tried to slow her breathing. She had to get control of herself. She had to be able to tell the police what had happened, but her head hurt so badly she couldn't think. Justin's shouted accusations—Monica's blank, bulging eyes—the blood on the floor—Emily's blood would be there as well—

"—hear me, ma'am?" A hand on her arm. Emily opened her eyes. A police officer was leaning over her, a young woman with a brown ponytail.

"I—I didn't hurt her—" Why had she said that first, like she assumed they would blame her? Sounds splashed against her like an incoming tide, mingling with the throb of her pulse. Had the officer asked her another question? She couldn't remember what it was, but the officer was watching her expectantly.

"My name is . . . is Emily Ramsey. I—found Monica Fife in her workroom. I had an appointment to meet her at—at—" Reconstructing simple facts was like groping for scattered puzzle pieces. "At nine," she said finally. "At Starbucks. She didn't come."

"What did you do when she didn't show up?"

"I walked to her shop. The Amber Flame. Her car was there—she had to be there . . ." Emily tried to remember the exact sequence of events, but everything jumbled in her head. How badly was she hurt? She moved her hand toward the wound on her forehead, but someone caught her wrist and drew her hand away before she could touch it.

"An ambulance is coming," the officer said.

"I don't need—I'm all right—"

"Do you have some ID, ma'am?"

"I—left my purse—dropped it—in Monica's workroom. My name is Emily Ramsey." Words and images crowded into Emily's mind. The picture of Monica and Zach kissing on the beach—Monica, sinuous in green silk as she danced with Zach—the bloodied picture of Ryan hanging on Emily's doorknob—

"You've got the murderer right there." Justin's voice was fainter; they'd taken him out of the room, but Emily could still hear his shrill accusations. "She hated Monica, she was jealous—"

Emily struggled to push herself onto her elbows. "I didn't—*please*, I didn't—"

"Just lie back, ma'am. For your safety and mine, I'm going to do a quick pat-down."

Emily slumped against the sweatshirt someone had formed into a makeshift pillow. The officer's hands moved over her body, checking for weapons.

Weapons.

"I didn't kill her," Emily whispered. "I didn't kill her."

* * *

"Zach." Emily started to sit up on the hospital gurney, but Zach took two quick strides to her side and nudged her back onto the pillow.

"Lie quietly," he said. "You look like you're going to pass out if you get up."

"No—I'm—"

Zach gripped her hand. His fingers were clammy and trembling—or was she the one shaking? He bent and touched his lips to her forehead. "Emily," he whispered, his lips moving against her skin. "Oh, Emily."

His touch infused a small ripple of comfort. Zach was here. She'd be all right.

He straightened up. "Nicole's in the waiting room; they wouldn't let us both come in. What happened? I heard that Monica . . ."

Emily stumbled through the story, watching as the blood drained from Zach's face.

"Why had you arranged to meet her?" he asked.

"Because I thought—because she—" Emily's voice trailed off. It was too much to explain. The picture of Ryan, her suspicions of Monica, the visit from the police, Monica's claim that Emily had threatened her—

Justin screaming that she was a murderer.

"Emily." Zach rested his palm against her cheek. "Can you talk to me?"

She rallied her strength. "I—there was—last night when I got home I found a picture hanging on my doorknob."

"Another picture!"

"Yes." Emily described it. "I thought maybe Monica . . . I couldn't think who else . . ."

"Emily." Zach slipped his arm beneath her shoulders and drew her into a tight embrace. "Why didn't you tell me?"

Emily drew a deep breath. Zach smelled soothingly of laundry soap and leather jacket. "Because I—I thought maybe it was better to just take care of things, talk to Monica myself."

To take care of things?

To intimidate Monica? Threaten her?

Kill her?

Zach eased her back to the bed, his face still and blank. Emily wondered if his thoughts were following the same line as hers. "Monica received a threatening picture as well," he said.

"I know . . . I know. She told the police . . . they asked me about it. She told you about the picture?" It was a stupid question, Emily realized. Of course Monica had told Zach. She would have rushed to make sure Zach knew that Emily had supposedly threatened her.

Had Zach believed Monica?

"What was the picture?" Emily asked. "Did she describe it?"

"It was a picture of her, torn in half and spattered with fake blood. Fake blood was also splattered over her kitchen table."

"Fake blood?" Emily asked, thinking of the fingernail polish on the picture of Ryan.

"Some kind of costume blood, she thought. She said it didn't seem like paint, exactly. More like something you'd buy at a party store. What did the police say to you about it?"

"They wanted to know about my 'disagreement' with Monica." Emily sat up and swung her legs over the side of the gurney, ignoring the pounding in her head. She couldn't lie here any longer, helpless to dispel the suspicion darkening around her. "I didn't threaten Monica, and I didn't hurt her. I—"

"Lie down." Zach caught her by the shoulders before she could stand up.

"I don't need a doctor. I need to talk to the police. I—"

And what made her think the police would believe her? Someone had threatened Monica; Monica told the police it was Emily. Emily had a reason to hate Monica. She had been on the scene where Monica died. She'd even touched the body. She might have Monica's blood on her hands or clothes. Emily's blood and fingerprints were all over Monica's shop.

"Lie down." Zach pressed her back onto her pillow. "The doctor should be in soon."

Emily looked up at Zach, frantically searching his face. "I'd never hurt Monica. You know that."

"Of course I know that. Don't be a fool."

But he didn't meet her eyes as he spoke.

* * *

Nicole sprang to her feet as Zach entered the waiting room. His face was chalky, his expression brooding.

Nicole rushed to Zach. "Is she all right?"

Zach rested his hand on her shoulder. It was a tired gesture, and Nicole had the feeling it took all his energy to lift his arm. "She seems to be. The doctor just came in to examine her, so they asked me to leave. She's got a gash on her forehead, right here," he touched his fingers to the right side of his forehead near the hairline, "and a lump on the side of her head. From how she describes things, it seems she fainted in Monica's workroom. She must have struck her head, once on the corner of the worktable as she was falling, and again on the floor."

Nicole winced. "But does she seem—you know—aware? Does she know who she is and everything?"

"Yes. She's just very pale. Weak."

"What was she *doing* at Monica's anyway?" Nicole balled her hands, wanting to slam a fist through the wall. A mother holding a whimpering toddler shot her a frightened look.

"Don't yell," Zach said roughly. "Do you want to get us thrown out?"

Nicole gritted her teeth, but the sight of a couple of police officers standing near the reception desk was enough to get her to lower her voice. "What was she doing there?" Nicole repeated in a whisper. "Monica was the last person she'd want to see. And I thought she was at the Tanners' tonight."

"At the Tanners'? Ryan's parents?"

Mentally, Nicole cursed herself. Her fear for Emily must have short-circuited her brain; she knew Emily hadn't told Zach she was going to the Tanners', and here Nicole was blabbing about it.

Not wanting to reveal that she'd blundered, Nicole gave an impatient shrug. "She was going over there for dinner, to tell them about your engagement. I can't imagine what would have made her go to Monica's instead."

Zach stole a glance at the police officers. "She said she had an appointment with Monica at nine. She wanted to confront her about that picture, the one of Ryan Tanner. She just told me about it—I had no idea . . ."

Nicole growled and ran clawed fingers through her hair, trying to restrain herself from crashing around the waiting room in blind frustration. "This is *your* fault."

"*My* fault?"

Nicole leaned close to Zach so she could speak in a whisper impossible for the officers across the room to overhear. "She was afraid to tell you about the picture because she was afraid you'd take Monica's side of things."

"What do you mean?"

"It's a no-brainer that Monica gave her the picture of Ryan, but Emily was afraid that if she told you, you'd think she planted it herself to make Monica look bad. She thought she had to cope with this on her own and *now* look what's happened—she's ended up at the site of a murder. They'll suspect her. *They'll suspect her.*"

"Take it easy." The gentleness in Zach's voice contrasted with the alarm in his eyes, and Nicole realized she must look like a lunatic. "No one could ever believe Emily is a murderer."

"You idiot." Nicole trapped her hands under her arms to keep herself from punching Zach in the jaw. "Sure, the police are Emily's best friends. They know what a sweetie she is and that she'd never hurt a fly."

Zach opened his mouth, clamped it shut on the angry response he was obviously about to make, then said, "I don't think Monica gave Emily that picture. She got a threatening picture as well—one of her promo pictures, covered in fake blood."

Nicole was taken aback. "When?"

"Yesterday morning. She thought Emily did it. She called the police. Emily said the police came and talked to her."

Nicole launched a barrage of profanity that made Zach grimace.

"Take it easy," he snapped. "Losing your temper won't help Emily."

"It's a lot more helpful than anything *you've* done."

"What was I supposed to do? *You're* apparently the one she trusts enough to confide in. Why didn't *you* do something?"

They glared at each other. Zach drew a deep breath, his bony shoulders rising and falling.

"We should call her parents," he said.

"Emily wouldn't want that."

"What do you mean she wouldn't want it? They're her parents."

"She hates worrying them. Don't you get that? They've had enough grief, after Tricia—" Nicole turned and stalked to the other side of the waiting room. She had to get away from Zach, or she *would* hit him. This *was* his fault. Didn't he understand how much Emily feared losing him like she'd lost Ryan? Didn't he understand what it had done to her to see him with Monica Fife? How could he ever have let Monica drag him onto that dance floor?

Nicole punched every button on the vending machine with savage jabs of her thumb, desperate for some way to release the anger building inside her.

Emily had already suffered more than anyone should have to suffer in a lifetime. She was supposed to be happy now. Emily and Zach—the perfect pair.

She glanced at Zach. He was talking into his cell phone. Calling Emily's parents. Nicole thought how her own parents would react to such a phone call and felt another spasm of rage. They'd rather see her dead than involved in a sordid situation like this. Better the victim than an accused murderer. Sympathy and flowers from their friends instead of ostracism and raised eyebrows at the country club.

Calm down, she told herself, pressing her forehead against the cold plastic of the vending machine. *Calm down or you'll never be able to help Emily.*

Calmer, Nicole sat in a padded chair and stared fixedly at the door through which Zach had emerged. She wanted to rush through that door and clamp her hand over Emily's mouth before excruciatingly honest Emily started babbling about how angry she'd been with Monica, how jealous, how afraid that Zach would fall for Monica again.

Shut up, Emily, Nicole thought. *Just shut up.*

Why did Emily have to be at Monica's tonight?

CHAPTER 10

"YOU SIT THERE IN YOUR armchair, hon, and I'll bring you some soup."

"Mom, for crying out loud, I'm not sick." Emily regretted the edge on her voice. She didn't want to snap at her mother. Carolyn was just trying to help.

"You have a concussion." Carolyn ladled soup into a bowl.

"A minor concussion."

"And a laceration."

"Three stitches. I've done worse rollerblading."

"I'm here to keep an eye on you for twenty-four hours, like the doctor ordered." Carolyn sprinkled chopped cilantro on the soup and picked up the pepper grinder.

Humor flickered beneath Emily's exhaustion as she watched her mother work. Making chicken soup for a convalescent was a classic thing to do, but curried chicken soup with lemongrass wasn't the usual chicken soup on the menu.

"Smells delicious," Emily said, but despite the prospect of enjoying her mother's cooking, she didn't like being waited on. Having Carolyn bustling around her apartment, making soup and fussing at her to lie down heightened the fear and humiliation she felt whenever she thought of how she'd fallen apart last night. Fainting in Monica's shop—and even after that, there were some blurry and blank spots. She couldn't remember exactly what she'd said when she'd raced into the ice cream shop to seek help. She couldn't remember everything she'd said to the police, and in some cases she wasn't sure if she'd said something or only thought it.

Emily moved to the cupboard near the sink and removed a bottle of ibuprofen. "The police are coming at three o'clock."

Carolyn frowned. "Why? You said they talked to you last night."

"They did for a few minutes, but I wasn't really up to answering questions. But I'm fine now." It was a lie; slight background dizziness still made her feel she needed to step carefully when she walked, and her headache alternated between hammer blows and sledgehammer blows. But the less Carolyn knew, the less she'd worry. Emily wished she could avoid telling her mother that the police were coming at all, but there was no hiding it.

Last night, Emily had wanted to talk to the police immediately, face their questions head-on and prove she'd had nothing to do with Monica's death. But now that Detectives Lund and Kapoor would soon be ringing her doorbell, Emily kept having fantasies of fleeing the country.

How *could* she prove she hadn't killed Monica?

She couldn't. And after Lund and Kapoor's visit yesterday, she'd have been number one on the list of suspects even if she hadn't been at the murder scene last night.

"I don't think you're up to questioning today either." Carolyn arranged some crackers on a plate. "After what you went through, you need time to rest and heal."

Emily moistened her dry mouth. "Mom, I have to do everything I can to help the police."

"I know, hon, but you already told them you didn't see anything, right? Are there any clues you can give them? Do you know anyone who was threatening Monica or angry with her?"

Queasiness lurched through Emily. She hadn't told her mother *why* she'd gone to talk to Monica last night, and Carolyn had assumed Emily was meeting a friend. Carolyn had met Monica once or twice when she'd visited Emily's ward, and she didn't know that Monica and Zach used to date, let alone anything about Monica's recent campaign to reclaim Zach. Or about the threatening picture Monica had blamed on Emily.

"A lot of people may have been upset with her," Emily said. "Monica didn't spend much time worrying about other people's feelings." Guilt swelled inside her. It sounded like she was suggesting Monica had brought her death on herself. Monica wasn't a monster, and people didn't resort to murder over hurt feelings.

Usually.

Should Emily come clean with her mother? The thought made fear clog her chest like waterlogged sand. *Mom, I just wanted to let you know that the police are probably going to arrest me for murder. Thanks for the soup. You're the best.*

Justin Driscoll thought she was a killer, and everyone in earshot last night probably believed the same thing. Even Zach—she couldn't forget the way he'd averted his eyes when she'd said she could never hurt Monica. Was he doubting her?

"Sweetheart, you need to sit down." Carolyn took her by the elbow and led her to the couch. "You're so pale, I'm afraid you're going to pass out. I'll call the police station and tell them you're in no shape for an interview. They'll have to come tomorrow."

"No—no, don't do that." Emily settled onto the couch and burrowed her bare feet under the mohair blanket Ryan had brought her when he returned from a six-week art study program in Ireland. She couldn't delay the interview. She couldn't risk doing anything that might appear suspicious. What if the police thought she was stalling because she needed time to cover her tracks? She wanted to talk with them while they were still *asking* to come interview her, not hauling her off to jail.

Carolyn brought the tray of soup and crackers and set it on the lamp table next to Emily. "What would you like to drink?"

"Water, please." Emily wondered how she could get her mother out of here before the police arrived. The thought of Carolyn's overhearing that conversation made her shrivel inside.

"Thank you." Emily took the ice water that Carolyn set on the tray and sipped. Water was all she could handle at the moment; the soup that had smelled so delicious a few minutes ago now had a too-tangy, too-spicy aroma that nauseated her.

Carolyn was back in the kitchen area, busily wiping countertops. If Emily wanted her to leave, subtlety wasn't going to work.

"Mom . . ." Emily dunked her spoon into the soup and swirled it through bits of spinach and cubes of chicken. "I don't want you to be here when the police come. You shouldn't have to go through this."

"Neither should you. And you certainly shouldn't have to go through it alone. You've already had more than your fill of answering questions."

Emily knew she was thinking of the police investigation that had followed Ryan's disappearance. As Ryan's fiancée and the last person he'd called before he disappeared, Emily had fielded a lot of questions. Though the police had never said so directly, she knew they'd been scrutinizing her life for any reason she might have had to want Ryan gone.

"I'll be fine," Emily said, amazed that such short, simple words could shape so big a lie.

"The doctor said to keep an eye on you. I'm keeping an eye on you. Now eat your soup." Carolyn turned back to the sink full of soapy water. "You need the energy."

Emily picked up the tray that held the bowl of soup and set it on her lap. Her mother was right. She needed to eat if she wanted the energy and focus necessary to get her through police questioning. If she was light-headed with hunger, she'd be a lot more likely to stumble over her words and incriminate herself.

The doorbell rang. Emily jumped, slopping soup over the edge of her bowl. It was only two-thirty, too early for the police to be here. It must be Zach, stopping by after church.

"I'll get it." Carolyn dried her hands on a towel.

It was Brent Amherst. "Hi, Sister Ramsey."

"Brent, it's good to see you again." Carolyn gave Emily a questioning look, silently asking if she wanted Brent admitted into the apartment. Emily gave a slight nod.

"Come in," Carolyn said. "Emily's having some lunch. Would you like a bowl of soup?"

"Didn't mean to drop hints, but if you're offering . . ." Brent grinned. "Smells tasty." He walked over to Emily and squeezed her shoulder. "How are you holding up?"

"Not bad. How was church?"

"It was pretty much an endless session of gossip and questions about Monica Fife."

"I'm sure everyone is very shaken." Carolyn set a full bowl on the table. "Here's your soup."

"Thanks." Brent lingered near Emily. "Yeah, everyone's in shock. Even the people who hated Monica are acting like they lost their best friend."

"My goodness, I can't imagine Monica had enemies at church," Carolyn said.

Brent lifted one eyebrow and said nothing. Carolyn turned curious eyes toward Emily. Emily shot daggers at Brent before saying neutrally, "Everyone has disagreements sometimes."

"Good grief, Saint Emily, you don't have to be so nice," Brent said.

Emily was tempted to kick him in the shins. Did he *want* Carolyn to know that Emily had a reason to hate Monica?

Did *Brent* suspect her of killing Monica? He couldn't possibly believe she was capable of murder. But what were other people saying about her? By now, the entire ward knew everything about the Zach–Monica issue, and Justin Driscoll was probably taking every opportunity to proclaim that Emily Ramsey had murdered Monica. Emily bit her lip, wanting to ask Brent what gossip was flying around but feeling she'd sooner die than ask that question in front of her mother.

Carolyn looked troubled, but she occupied herself with filling a water glass for Brent. Emily was relieved at her silence. Carolyn no doubt didn't want to ask questions for fear of appearing to gossip about Monica.

"You sure you're okay?" Brent studied Emily's face. "You look like death. What did the doctor say about your head?"

Emily touched the bandage on her forehead. "Just a few stitches and a mild concussion. I'm fine."

"Anything with the word *concussion* in it doesn't sound fine. You'd better take it easy."

"What does it look like I'm doing? Hiking Mount Kilimanjaro?"

"Don't worry, Brent. I'm taking care of her," Carolyn said. "Come eat your soup."

Brent patted Emily's shoulder and went to the table. "Thanks. Looks a lot better than the ramen noodles I was going to have for lunch."

Emily sneaked a glance at the clock on the wall. The police would be here soon, and now she had her mother *and* Brent Amherst to get rid of.

"I keep telling Emily she should wait until she's feeling better to talk to the police." Carolyn handed Brent a napkin.

Brent gave Emily a look so penetrating that she felt he could count her accelerating heartbeats. "The police are coming to talk to you today?"

"It's just routine. They didn't get much chance to talk to me last night."

"They don't suspect you, do they?"

"Brent!" Carolyn exclaimed. "Don't be ridiculous!" But despite her words, Emily saw surprise—and fear—flash in Carolyn's eyes. "Why in the world would Emily want to hurt her friend?"

For an instant, Emily had an absurd image of herself grabbing Brent by the collar and throwing him out the door before he could answer that question.

"I wouldn't want to hurt Monica," Emily said flatly, her gaze locked with Brent's. "And the police didn't say anything about my being a suspect. They just have to talk to everyone who knows anything, and obviously I was there last night."

Brent spooned soup into his mouth and said nothing, clearly getting the message. Emily glanced at her mother and was relieved to see some of the tension leave Carolyn's face.

But the relief was transient, as fragile as a single snowflake. She could soothe Carolyn all she wanted, but none of her comforting words would be worth anything once Carolyn learned the truth, and she was about to hear it from the police—if Brent Amherst didn't beat them to it.

* * *

Emily got what she thought she wanted—neither Carolyn nor Brent stayed for the police interview. The first thing Detective Lund did upon arriving with Detective Kapoor at Emily's apartment was to ask to speak to Emily alone. Carolyn, a mother-bear glint in her eye, opened her mouth to protest, but to Emily's surprise, it was Brent who gracefully ushered Carolyn out of the apartment, saying he needed her opinion on a new recipe he wanted to try, and would Carolyn give him some advice?

Emily's relief lasted almost until the door closed behind them. She'd wanted to be alone for the interview, but she didn't want her mother and Brent alone together. The two of them would discuss her—that was inevitable—and Brent might well say something about Monica's man-stealing ways, generating a host of frightening thoughts in Carolyn's mind. Brent wouldn't deliberately upset Carolyn, but sometimes he was tactless, and he might not understand how much Carolyn worried about Emily. Emily thought of Tricia's caveat before she'd introduced Emily to Brent: *"Great guy, but he's kind of an acquired taste, and he racks up a lot of frequent-flyer miles on the foot-to-mouth route."*

"How are you feeling, Miss Ramsey?" Detective Lund's words were polite but not friendly. Her austere face reminded Emily of a woman who worked yard duty at the school and could scare errant children into paralysis with a glare.

"I'm fine," Emily said. "Just a headache."

"We'll get right to the point, then," Lund said, "so you can rest."

"I'm fine," Emily repeated, afraid she'd sounded whiny by mentioning the headache. "I'm willing to do whatever I can to help you find whoever—" The words *killed Monica* stuck in her throat. Part of her still wanted to believe last night had been nothing more than a nightmare.

Lund opened her notebook. "You had arranged to meet Monica Fife last night at nine."

"Yes."

"When did you set up that meeting?"

"Saturday afternoon. Via e-mail. I mean—I e-mailed her Friday night, or rather Saturday morning—" *Terrific.* Five seconds into the interview, and already she sounded like a blithering fool. Emily sat up straighter and started over.

"I e-mailed Monica Fife very early Saturday morning and asked to meet with her. She responded Saturday afternoon and told me to meet her at the Main Street Starbucks at nine last night." Lund already knew this, Emily realized. She'd told Lund yesterday morning that she'd asked Monica to meet with her, and by now Lund and Kapoor would have checked out Monica's recent e-mails and seen Monica's response.

"Why did you want to meet with Miss Fife?"

Emily resisted the urge to say she'd already told this to the detectives yesterday. Was Lund checking to see if she could maintain a consistent story? "I thought Monica might be responsible for the picture of Ryan Tanner left on my door. When I asked her to meet with me, I didn't know she'd received an upsetting picture as well, but after you told me about that incident, it seemed even more vital to talk with her and try to figure out what really happened."

"What time did you arrive for your appointment last night?"

"I arrived at Starbucks at about ten minutes to nine. I waited until about twenty past nine then walked over to the Amber Flame to see if Monica was there."

"What were you doing yesterday evening between five and nine?"

"I was at the home of Bethany and Ted Tanner, Ryan Tanner's parents. They'd invited me to dinner."

"Their address and phone number?"

"It's—" Her brain stalled, unable to retrieve anything but the street name. Emily felt oddly glad about the lapse. The details of her time with Ryan were fading. "Hang on. I've got it written down." She rose, careful not to stand up too fast. In the kitchen, she opened the drawer where she kept her address book—another daisy-covered gift from Tricia.

The address book wasn't there. Where had she put it? Embarrassed, Emily closed the drawer and tried to remember when she'd last used it. At work. She'd taken it to school when they'd been discussing letter writing, and she'd wanted to use her grandparents' address when she wrote a sample letter. It would be in the oversized canvas bag she used to transport materials to and from school.

"Sorry—just a minute." Emily went to the coat closet where she kept the bag, drew it out, and set it on the counter. As she rummaged through the bag, a plastic sack wrapped around something cylindrical caught her eye. Not recognizing it, she opened the sack and saw a plastic tube containing some kind of red liquid. It was three-quarters empty.

Puzzled, Emily reached for it, then froze. Zach's voice, describing the picture someone had left in Monica's apartment, echoed in her memory. *It was a picture of her, torn in half and spattered with fake blood.*

Fake blood? Emily smoothed out the sack and saw the Party City logo. She'd never purchased anything like this. The only paint she owned was in big plastic screw-top jars or watercolor trays, and she'd certainly never purchased fake blood. Her Halloween costumes ran more toward Little Bo Peep than zombies and grim reapers.

Her back was to Lund and Kapoor, and with her hands deep in the tote bag, they couldn't see what she was doing, but she could sense them both staring at her, wondering why she was standing motionless.

She should take the tube of costume blood and show it to Lund. She should explain that she had no idea how it got in her bag, that it wasn't hers.

And would Lund believe her? It would sound like a roundabout confession—that the guilt was devouring her but she couldn't bring herself to confess directly.

Her hands trembled as she reached past the Party City sack, grabbed her address book, then shoved the canvas bag back into the coat closet. She set the book on the counter and fumbled to find the Ts, so flustered that she had to chant the alphabet in her head to remember the order of the letters.

"Did you find what you needed, Miss Ramsey?"

"Yes—it's in here, just a sec . . ." When and where had someone slipped the fake blood into her bag? She used this bag constantly—at school, at church on the weeks she was teaching Relief Society; she frequently left it in her car; she even took it to the beach and the gym. Had Monica slipped the incriminating tube of blood in there before she called the police to accuse Emily of leaving the picture? Or was someone else responsible for the pictures both Monica and Emily had received? A killer who had murdered Monica and was now targeting Emily?

She should show Lund and Kapoor the tube of fake blood. Confide in them. Trust them to figure out the truth. *You have the right to remain silent. Anything you say can and will be used against you in a court of law—*

The tread of footsteps behind her made her jump. She turned to see Detective Kapoor walking toward her.

"Come sit down. You're not well." He held out his hand. "I'll find the address."

Emily passed him the book. With a light touch on her elbow, he guided her back to the armchair. Emily's hands and feet were ice, but her cheeks blazed with heat. She must look as guilty as anyone Lund and Kapoor had ever arrested.

"What time did you arrive at the Tanners'?" Lund asked as Kapoor flipped through the address book.

"About quarter past five. I stayed until eight-thirty. It takes about twenty minutes to get downtown from the Tanners' house, and I had the appointment with Monica at nine." What time had Monica died? Emily didn't dare ask if the police had figured that out yet.

Lund watched her with incurious eyes, but despite the blandness of her expression, Emily had the sense that Lund was reading her mind. "When you went to the Amber Flame, what did you do?"

Emily described her actions, step by step. Why hadn't she given up and gone home when Monica didn't come to Starbucks? If she'd walked away, she wouldn't have found—wouldn't have had to see Monica's beautiful face, swollen and dark purple and streaked with blood, her eyes staring, the spatters of red surrounding her . . . Tricia's eyes had been open too, sightless eyes, blood trickling over . . .

Distracted, Emily stopped in her narrative and swallowed hard. *Calm down. You've got to calm down. You can't think of Tricia right now. Stay focused.*

"Why did you think she might still be alive?" Lund prompted when Emily didn't resume the story.

"I—she—I thought maybe I saw her ribcage move, like she was breathing. It must have been the light—or wishful thinking."

"You hoped she was alive?"

The question made Emily's stomach cramp. She knew what Lund was implying. *"Monica Fife was trying to steal your fiancé. Her death would erase what was potentially a huge problem for you."*

"Of course I hoped she was alive," Emily said coolly. "The fact that Monica and I were at odds doesn't mean I wanted her dead."

"When you thought you saw her breathing, what did you do?"

"I knelt next to her and lifted the hair covering her face. When I saw her face . . . it was obvious she was dead. I think I jumped backward—maybe I screamed, I can't remember . . . I must have fainted, because the next thing I knew, I was lying on the floor." She described going to the ice cream shop to get help. Her heart pounded so loudly that she wondered if Lund and Kapoor could hear it. What if they asked to search her house and found the fake blood?

Tell them. Don't hide it. You need to tell them. Why couldn't she force the necessary words out of her mouth?

"Witnesses report that Mr. Justin Driscoll tried to attack you in the ice cream shop and accused you of killing Miss Fife. Why would he make that accusation?"

"Monica and Justin were friends. Justin is the one who was with Monica at the dance Friday night when she was . . . pursuing Zachary Sullivan. Justin knew I had a reason to be upset with Monica, and when he heard she was dead, he made an unfounded assumption." Emily was amazed that she could sound so clinical when the memory of Justin's shouted accusations was enough to drench her in cold sweat. "He was out of his mind."

"Witnesses report that when you first came into the store, you told them Tricia was dead."

An electrical shock shot from Emily's scalp to her toes. "I did?"

"Yes. You don't remember?"

"Some memories of last night are a little blurry." She'd said Tricia? Had she been *that* out of it?

Lund waited for Emily to elaborate.

Swallowing to moisten her dry tongue, Emily said, "Tricia is—was—is—my sister. She was killed in a hit-and-run accident three years ago." Emily was positive Lund already knew all this, but she continued anyway. "She was hit by a car when she was walking by the side of the road near the Tanner home. I'm the one who found her. Finding Monica must have reminded me . . . after hitting my head, I wasn't thinking clearly . . ." Sweat trickled down Emily's back.

What else had she said that she didn't remember?

Lund glanced at the bookshelf where an 8 x 10 photograph of Emily and Tricia held a prominent place on the middle shelf. Her gaze returned to Emily. "Did you feel responsible for Tricia's death, Miss Ramsey?"

CHAPTER 11

EMILY GAVE UP TRYING TO nap and lay in bed staring at the ceiling. The apartment smelled of baking bread, simmering beef, and something involving cinnamon and nutmeg. Though Emily felt too shaken to eat much, she knew that cooking helped relieve her mother's stress. Let Carolyn whip up a banquet if it would make her feel better. Heaven knew Emily wasn't doing anything to ease her worries.

When she'd retreated to her bedroom, she hadn't really expected to sleep, but she'd wanted to get out from under her mother's eye. The last thing she wanted to do was report on Lund and Kapoor's visit. To Carolyn's question of how the interview had gone, Emily had answered with a one-word lie: "Fine."

Sickness rose every time she thought of Lund's question: *"Did you feel responsible for Tricia's death?"* She'd told Lund no, but it was a lie and a futile lie at that. Lund had assuredly already read the reports regarding the accident—had probably even talked to the officers who had interviewed Emily that night, officers who had listened to her sobbing about how Tricia's death was her fault: she had told Tricia to tie those stupid balloons to the mailbox so guests wouldn't miss seeing the driveway in the dark. The balloons Tricia had almost certainly been chasing when a car driving too fast had struck her.

Emily closed her eyes. She knew what Lund had been aiming at. Emily had mixed up Monica's and Tricia's names in reporting the murder. Why? Because the shock of finding Monica dead had evoked memories of finding Tricia by the side of the road? Or because she'd again been wracked with remorse for causing a death—Tricia's inadvertently by sending her out on that windy, rainy night and Monica's deliberately with a blow to the head and a scarf knotted around her neck?

Lund thought she'd killed Monica Fife. Why hadn't they arrested her? They must not have adequate evidence yet, but how much more evidence did they need?

Emily eyed the drawer of her dresser where she'd hidden the tube of fake blood. Holding it by the very tip so as not to smear any fingerprints, she'd taken it out of her tote bag and concealed it in her room before her mother returned from Brent's apartment.

Why had she been worried about marring fingerprints when she was already certain there weren't any prints on the tube? If someone was trying to frame her, he or she wouldn't be careless enough to leave fingerprints.

Had Monica done this? With Monica dead, it seemed ludicrous to imagine that she might have faked the threat against herself in order to implicate Emily.

Emily rolled over and tugged her quilt up to her shoulders. Why did the room feel so cold? Sun glowed through the window; it was a gorgeous day outside. That seemed wrong, to have the sun shining on millions of people who neither knew nor cared that a formerly vibrant, beautiful young woman was in the morgue. Emily remembered having the same sensation after Tricia's death and Ryan's disappearance—a confused sense of envy and disbelief that, for almost everyone else, life was chugging along like normal.

As much as she'd disliked Monica, she'd never wanted Monica to get hurt, let alone killed. How could anyone have done that to her? Hit her, strangled her—

Was it possible Monica's death wasn't related to anything else that had taken place that week? That the threats were red herrings, and Monica was the random victim of a robber or a kid high on drugs?

You're stretching credibility ten feet past the breaking point. You just want to believe there's no threat to you—that Monica was the one harassing you and that now that she's dead, you're in no danger.

It *was* absurd to think that, but it was also absurd to imagine that someone would murder Monica and try to frame Emily. Emily could fathom some unbalanced former boyfriend killing Monica in a jealous rage, but she couldn't imagine someone cold-bloodedly preparing for the crime by planting those gruesome photographs and making it appear as though Emily were responsible.

Responsible for the pictures . . . the picture of Ryan . . .

Emily glanced at the laptop sitting on her dresser. She shouldn't assume that it was impossible to track the picture to the culprit. If she'd sent the photo to Tricia, whom might Tricia have sent it to? Someone she thought would enjoy it—a friend of both Tricia's and Ryan's. If Emily made a list of everyone who . . .

Or had the killer taken the photo directly from Emily's computer?

Emily flung back the covers and went to fetch her laptop. She clicked on the application where she kept all her photos. It would open on the last photos she had viewed—which *should* be pictures of Zach and her at Golden Gate Park when they'd gone to that new art exhibit a few weeks ago.

The application seemed to take forever to load. Her head pounded as she stared at the screen, waiting for images to appear. Maybe this was ridiculous. The killer wouldn't have—

Rows of pictures appeared on the screen. Ryan holding the welcome sign and grinning widely. Ryan and Emily side-by-side on the couch in her parents' living room, Ryan's arm around her shoulders—Tricia had taken that picture. Another shot by Tricia—Emily opening a gift wrapped in silver paper, an early Christmas present from Ryan. Emily holding up the gift, a double-strand freshwater pearl bracelet.

Her hand so shaky she could hardly control the mouse, Emily shut down the program. Whoever had left the picture *had* used her computer to retrieve the photo. They could have slipped into her classroom and used her computer there. She had a laptop lock, but she didn't bother to log out every time she walked away. Someone could even have crept into her apartment and used it here. Los Coros was a low-crime area, and she was sometimes careless about locking her door when going to the laundry room or to collect her mail. If she'd gotten delayed—stopped to talk to a friend or gone to the office to pay her rent—she could have been gone long enough for someone to mess with her computer.

She imagined herself reporting everything to Lund. *"The picture of Ryan Tanner came from my computer. The costume blood used on Monica's picture was in my tote bag. I had a reason to hate Monica and to want her out of the way, and I was at her store the night she was killed. But I didn't do any of this. I'm innocent."*

Sure she was. Even her mother would have trouble believing that.

Suffocating fear crept over Emily. *"Did you feel responsible for Tricia's death, Miss Ramsey?"* She didn't remember mixing up Tricia's and Monica's names, but multiple witnesses had heard her. Was it possible she had done other things she didn't remember? Like printing a picture of Ryan and telling herself Monica had done it?

Stop this. You were confused at the ice cream shop because you'd had a horrible shock and you'd cracked your head. It was a wonder you could talk at all. You're perfectly sane.

Perfectly sane. Until last night's concussion, she'd never experienced any kind of blackouts or memory loss—well, not really. After Tricia's death and Ryan's disappearance, when she'd been at her lowest, there were days when everything blurred together, and she'd had difficulty remembering how she'd passed the time. But forgetting unimportant details in a fog of gray emotion was far different than blocking out a sharply repugnant or illegal act.

Wasn't it?

How could she imagine even for an instant that she could or would plant that bloodied picture of Ryan?

Subconscious guilt, stirred by the conversation with Bethany when you returned Ryan's ring? A sense that you're betraying him by marrying Zach? Emotions you can't deal with on the surface so they push their way out in—

"What are you, some kind of Freud wannabe?" Emily whispered, slapping the computer shut. Stress couldn't cause a sane person to snap overnight, commit acts that were wildly out of character, and then forget about them. Like planting threatening, bloodied pictures.

Or committing murder.

* * *

"If all the good food is in there, then why are we out here?" Lloyd Ramsey's eyes twinkled with humor, but the twinkle was a brief flicker of light glancing off the darkness of anxiety.

Carolyn shut the door of the car and gestured for Lloyd to drive out of the parking lot of Emily's apartment complex. "It's not finished simmering anyway."

"What is it?"

"Swiss steak. With a few modifications. Emily was missing a few staples."

Lloyd chuckled. "When the cook considers gray Norman sea salt, saffron threads, and semolina flour to be staples, *everyone's* kitchen is missing staples. Except yours and Julia Child's."

Carolyn smiled good-naturedly, but she felt the same strain in her smile that she heard in Lloyd's laughter. They were both hiding, thinking if they didn't mention what had happened that maybe it wouldn't hurt them.

"How's Emily?" Lloyd loosened his tie with one hand as he drove. He'd come to Emily's straight from this afternoon's high council assignment.

"She's . . ." Carolyn held a quick internal debate. She didn't want to burden Lloyd with the fears weighing on her. But how could she hide what she'd learned? If their roles were reversed and Lloyd concealed anything from her, she'd be livid.

"She's not doing very well," Carolyn said.

Lloyd frowned at the windshield. "Then what are we doing out here driving around? You should be with her."

"I told you, dear, Zach is there. He's been anxious to see her all day, but she's been sleeping. When he came by this evening, I could tell he wanted to see her alone. Obviously he's been worried sick about her."

"That doctor should have kept her in the hospital last night. Fainting like that—gashing her head, then hitting it against the floor—"

"The doctors checked her out thoroughly." Carolyn bypassed the fact that she'd thought along similar lines every time she looked at Emily's bloodless cheeks and dazed eyes. "I'm sure she's fine."

"You just told me she wasn't doing well."

"She—" Carolyn looked down and brushed a spot of flour off her slacks. She wanted to confide in Lloyd, but every time she started to speak, panic swelled inside her.

Lloyd pulled into the parking lot of the library and parked at the far end, away from other vehicles.

"Why are we here?" Carolyn asked.

"For a place to talk." He intertwined his fingers with hers. "How are *you* coping?"

"I'm just worried about Emily. The police came to talk to her today."

"Had a few questions they couldn't ask her last night, I imagine."

"Yes. I kept telling her she should wait to talk to them until she was feeling better, but she insisted she was fine."

"Sounds like Emily. And it's better she talks to them promptly. If she saw anything that might help them figure out who killed that poor girl, they need to know it."

"Lloyd . . ." Carolyn's heart gave a few heavy, jerky beats. "While Emily was talking to the police, I was at Brent Amherst's apartment. Do you remember Brent?"

Lloyd scratched his scalp through his thinning gray hair. "Sounds familiar, but I don't—"

"He was a friend of Tricia's. They dated a few times, but it never went anywhere. Blond boy. You met him the night Tricia died. He'd come for Emily's party."

"Oh, the blond kid. Looks like he spends all his time on a surfboard."

"No, you're thinking of Justin Driscoll."

"Hard to keep track of Tricia's boyfriends."

"Brent's the one who—" Carolyn paused. It still cut right through her to think about that night, but she could speak calmly through the pain. "He was the one helping Emily that night."

"Helping Emily," Lloyd murmured, and Carolyn knew he was picturing the scene that had greeted them when they'd walked through the door of the Tanners' home, forewarned by a phone call from a stricken Bethany Tanner, who didn't want them to arrive at the house expecting a joyous celebration only to be greeted by the sight of police cars and an ambulance. Emily had been on the couch, rain-soaked hair clinging to her ashen face. Bethany was attempting to wrap a blanket around her while Emily struggled against Brent Amherst's grip. *"Let me go, let me go, I have to stay with her, I can't leave her."* Carolyn had later learned that Emily had refused to leave Tricia's side until two police officers had taken her forcibly into the house. It was Brent who had kept her there, holding her while she sobbed, comforting her while she waited for Ryan.

Ryan had never arrived.

"Brent," Lloyd repeated. "The one Tricia called the 'Eternal Bachelor.'"

"Yes. For a while I thought something would develop between Emily and him. He's been a great help to her, and he obviously cares about her. He's the one who helped her find this apartment, and he lives just downstairs from her. But I think he's like an older brother to her."

"What did he say to you today?"

"Well, he seemed very concerned about what the police might ask Emily. When we were alone in his apartment—he had a question about a pie crust recipe—he said he was worried they'd try to blame Monica Fife's death on Emily."

Lloyd stared at her. In the dimming light of early evening, his face looked pale and bluish. "Why would they suspect Emily? Just because she had the bad luck to find her friend dead?"

"From what Brent said, Monica and Emily weren't friends."

Lloyd absently tightened the knot of his tie that he had loosened a moment ago. "What do you mean they weren't friends? I thought Monica was in Emily's ward. The red-haired girl, right?"

Carolyn repeated what Brent had told her about Monica and Zach's former relationship and Monica's recent efforts to reclaim Zach, culminating with the kiss at Friday's Valentine's dance.

Lloyd's lined face went slack. "Oh, no."

"Brent said Emily spent the night at Nicole Gardiner's on Friday—it sounds like she didn't want to be alone—and was visibly upset on Saturday morning."

"Sounds like Zach didn't handle things very well."

"Well, this is all secondhand," Carolyn admitted. "But Brent was sure the reason Emily was at Monica Fife's candle shop last night was because she went there to confront Monica about Zach."

Lloyd removed his glasses, took a tissue from his pocket, and began to polish the lenses. His voice was unnaturally calm. "Did Emily confirm all this?"

"I haven't dared ask her. When I came back to the apartment after the police left, Emily looked awful. Very white and kind of glazed. I was about to call the doctor, but she told me not to, and she was perfectly coherent, so I didn't push it. She said she was just tired. She stayed in her bedroom the rest of the afternoon. She never said anything about what happened with the police."

Lloyd kept polishing his glasses. "Maybe this Amherst kid is full of baloney."

"Why would he lie? He's a good friend of Emily's, and he's worried about her."

Lloyd slid his glasses back on his face. "You think the police will say Emily killed Monica out of jealousy."

"They'd hardly be worth their pay if they didn't suspect her." Fear made Carolyn's voice curt. "She had a motive, and she was there. And she—there's the background. They investigated her when Ryan disappeared. They dug into the possibility that Ryan might have taken up with another woman while Emily and Ryan were apart during those last few months while she was finishing school."

"They never came up with anything."

"I know that. But it still might affect their judgment now."

Lloyd removed his glasses again and reached in his pocket for another tissue. "Honey, you're assuming too much. Emily may have had a reason to dislike Monica, but that's not proof of anything. We don't know what kind of evidence the police have found, or what witnesses there were to the incident last night. Emily may already be in the clear."

Carolyn thought of Emily's chalky face and the blank fear in her eyes. If she was in the clear, the police hadn't told her so. "Tricia's friend Justin Driscoll was there last night after Emily found Monica's body. He thought Emily had killed her and yelled to everyone in earshot that Emily was a murderer."

Anger tightened Lloyd's face. "I'm sure the police will look hard at this Driscoll boy. He may have rushed to blame Emily to turn suspicion away from himself. Was he involved with Monica?"

"Brent said they were close friends, but he wasn't sure if it was more than that. But even if—when—Emily is cleared, what will this experience do to her? Finding Monica's body, being under suspicion . . . She can't cope with this on her own. I want her to talk to Peter Kincaid."

Having run out of imaginary spots on his lenses, Lloyd started polishing the earpieces of his glasses. "You know Emily will refuse."

"Maybe it's time we insist. We should have insisted three years ago."

"She's an adult. We can't force her to do something she doesn't want to do."

"So we just turn our backs and let her crumble? Emily's got to get over this . . . this perfectionism, this feeling that she has to handle everything on her own."

"Dear, I *want* her to talk to Peter. I'm just saying we can't force her to do it."

"She's been so lonely. To lose Tricia and Ryan so soon after moving to a new city—she must have felt so dislocated. I've always wished she hadn't gone ahead and filled that long-term sub position that winter. She should have come home and taken a few months to heal."

"She'd committed to the job before she moved here."

"They would have understood if she'd needed to back out."

"Would she have been better off sitting at home with nothing to do?"

Carolyn sighed. "Maybe not. I can't ever thank Nicole Gardiner enough for taking Emily under her wing like she did. I don't know what would have happened to Emily without her. And ever since she started dating Zach, she's seemed so much happier. I could see she was finally letting Ryan go. She'd realized she could fall in love again. Is it any wonder that when Monica Fife tried to steal Zach she'd want to confront Monica? Emily's a fighter; she wouldn't—" Carolyn saw the horror in Lloyd's face and stopped. "What?"

"Are you saying you think Emily might have hurt—that she was the one who—?"

"Lloyd! I'm only saying it's reasonable that she would have gone to talk to Monica last night. Stop looking at me like that! Do you think I'd believe our daughter could kill someone?"

"No. But if the police heard what you just said to me—"

"I get the point. I wasn't thinking. But the idea that Emily could kill someone is so absurd—anyone who knows her . . ." Her voice trailed off.

Anyone who knows her. The police didn't know her. And if it came to the question of whether or not she was capable of murder, somehow Carolyn doubted they would take the word of her mother.

* * *

"This place smells wonderful." Zach smiled at Emily, but his lips were nearly colorless, and the shadows under his eyes made it apparent he'd gotten very little sleep last night. "How can I finagle an invitation to dinner?"

"Consider yourself invited," Emily said. "I'm sure my mother has cooked enough food for the entire complex." She settled more firmly against

Zach's side, trying to absorb strength from the weight of his arm around her shoulders.

She had to tell him everything and hear him reassure her that she wasn't crazy. She desperately needed to tell someone, and she couldn't tell her mother. Carolyn would be terrified. She'd be on the phone with a psychiatrist before Emily even finished explaining about the tube of fake blood and the picture of Ryan that had come from her computer.

I'm not crazy. I don't have blackouts.

But that meant someone was framing her. Someone who had committed murder and wanted Emily blamed for it.

But it didn't make sense. How could the killer have known she'd be at the scene the night Monica died?

Their appointment. Who had Monica told about the appointment?

One fact was excruciatingly clear. The killer wasn't a stranger, at least not to Monica.

But Emily had never resolved the question of whether Monica herself was responsible for the pictures.

Zach leaned his cheek against her hair. "How are you holding up? You look tired."

"Is that a diplomatic way of saying I look horrible?"

"I just think they were too quick to discharge you from the hospital. A head injury—you'd think they'd have kept you under observation for longer."

"You sound like my mother." Emily aimed to sound wry. "Fussing about a little cut."

Zach's smile looked as phony as Emily's smile felt. They'd been like this for the past fifteen minutes, polite, joking, inquiring after each other's welfare. Pretty soon they'd be talking about the weather.

Just tell him everything. You've got to tell him. This is the man you're planning to marry. You've got to trust him.

But what if he didn't believe her?

"The police came to talk to me today." Zach's words barged in on the silence.

Emily's heart lurched. "What did they say?"

Zach's arm tightened around her shoulders. "They wanted to know about my relationship with Monica. About what happened this weekend."

Emily gripped Zach's hand where it rested against her shoulder. "What did you tell them?"

"The blunt truth. Monica and I used to date, she dumped me over a year ago, and we were completely finished with each other. Then as soon as

I got engaged to you, she started after me, wanting another chance, and I told her to forget it. The awkward thing is, I wish I hadn't spent last night alone in my house studying."

Emily sat up straight. Zach was saying he had no alibi for the time of Monica's death. "They don't think you—I mean, you aren't a suspect, are you?"

"They didn't say. They just asked where I was between the hours of five and nine."

"I'm sure they're checking out everyone who had any recent contact with Monica." That was the same thing she'd told Bethany Tanner when Bethany had called earlier in the afternoon. Bethany, stunned by the news of Monica's death—she'd known Monica's mother—had been worried and puzzled when the police had come to her, wanting to know if she could verify that Emily had been at their house yesterday evening. *"Are you all right, Emily? What happened?"*

"Em . . ." Zach pressed his lips to her hair. "Why didn't you tell me you were going to talk to Monica last night? I would have come with you. You didn't have to do that alone."

"I know," Emily said tiredly. "I'm sorry."

Silence settled between them. The drumbeat in Emily's head grew more urgent. *Tell him. Tell him.*

"How could anyone do that to Monica?" Zach's voice tightened with pain. "I know she wasn't always the nicest person on the planet, but how could anyone—" He swallowed. "I feel horrible that I didn't take that whole picture threat seriously when she told me about it. It seemed so over-the-top. I even thought maybe she was making it up so she could blame it on you, make you look spiteful."

I'm not crazy. I don't have blackouts. Emily felt she could almost see through the wall of the living room into her bedroom, where the tube of fake blood was hidden.

"Emily, you need to be careful," Zach said. "You received pictures too. The same lunatic—"

"I know. But my pictures seemed designed to upset me, not threaten me. Not like Monica's."

"That's not much comfort."

"I know." Emily decided not to mention the unfortunate fact that she'd been unable to show he picture of Ryan to the police. Nicole had torn it to shreds and tossed it into San Francisco Bay along with the nail polish while she was out sailing on Saturday. Having the evidence gone didn't do a lot to raise Emily's credibility.

"What did the police ask you today?" Zach asked.

"Just more questions about what happened last night." Why couldn't she let the rest of the truth flood out? If she couldn't get the reassurance that Zach believed in her innocence, she was going to start bawling and wouldn't be able to stop. "I . . . Zach . . . I'm afraid the police are going to . . . I don't think they believe me."

The words hung in the air for a long, miserable moment. Coldness crept over Emily's skin. Zach didn't believe her either. Did he think—

"They don't believe you about what?" Zach asked.

"About . . . that I didn't put that picture in Monica's apartment. That I just went to talk to her last night and she was dead when I got there."

"Emily." Zach linked his fingers together, encircling Emily in his arms. "Have they accused you of anything?"

"No. Not yet."

"Then you're jumping to conclusions. They're questioning everyone who was involved. They talked to me. I know they talked to Justin. It's all routine."

"But I don't have an alibi for all of last night. Or for yesterday morning when someone put that picture in Monica's apartment."

"Em, they'd need evidence that you committed a crime. They don't *have* any evidence. That Detective Lund strikes me as a person who tries to rattle people into saying stupid things and condemning themselves. Don't let her get to you. Relax."

Relax. Ha. Emily sighed and rested her cheek against Zach's chest. Protected in his arms, she did feel a little better.

"You all right?" Zach asked.

"Better." Emily made her decision. She'd tell him everything. "I'm just rattled because . . ." Her voice caught as she stared at Zach's left wrist. With his hands linked together, his wrist was directly in front of her. His *watch*— a steel and black-enameled watch with a distinctive woven band. He'd been wearing it in the picture of Monica and him kissing on the beach.

But Emily had given him that watch three months ago, for his birthday.

Three months ago. How could he be wearing it in a picture he'd sworn had been taken over a year ago?

"What rattled you?" Zach prompted at Emily's prolonged silence.

Emily's throat was frozen, her gaze welded to the watch.

"Em?" Zach released her and turned so he was facing her. "Are you okay?"

"I'm—I'm all right." Emily couldn't make herself look him in the eyes. "Like I said, I'm just . . . a little rattled that I don't have an alibi for the whole evening. But you're right. It's ridiculous to worry."

CHAPTER 12

EMILY ARGUED THAT SHE WAS fine to go to work on Monday, but Carolyn objected so adamantly that Emily ran out of strength to protest. Carolyn was determined to keep Emily home and recuperating under her watchful eye for at least another day. Desperate to avoid that watchful eye as much as possible, Emily retreated to her bedroom.

But she couldn't rest. It was all she could do not to pace frenetically around her room. The watch Zach was wearing in the picture had haunted her all night, and she'd spent the hours twisting so restlessly that she'd untucked every sheet and blanket. She tried to tell herself that whoever was malicious enough to send the picture might be clever enough to have digitally added the watch to Zach's arm, knowing Emily would recognize it as a new gift. But that explanation sounded so strained. So willfully blind.

Weary of the fear and unanswered questions whirling in her head, Emily finally sat down with her laptop, opened her journal file, and typed out everything that had happened since she received that first picture of Monica and Zach. As morning became afternoon, the words on the page finally formed into a plan.

She needed to talk to Monica's friend Rochelle Elton. Rochelle was the person most likely to know the answer to two questions tormenting Emily: Had Zach been seeing Monica behind Emily's back? And had Monica planted the bloodied pictures and tried to make Emily look responsible?

It still seemed far-fetched that the pictures could be unrelated to Monica's murder, but no more far-fetched than the idea that someone would have plotted beforehand to frame Emily for Monica's death. To murder Monica in her shop, in the middle of downtown, with potential witnesses around—to Emily, that seemed to be a crime committed in the heat of passion, not a killing cold-bloodedly planned in advance.

And believing that Monica had sent the pictures was far less outlandish than believing that Emily had planted the pictures and fake blood herself in the midst of a psychotic blackout. She was embarrassed that she'd ever considered this possibility, even for an instant. She *really* must have clonked her head if she was dazed enough to start thinking that way.

She needed to move forward. Strange as it seemed, Monica was still the most likely culprit behind the pictures. And if she *had* been responsible, she might have let something slip to Rochelle.

The silence from the front of the apartment gave Emily the courage to open her bedroom door. Her mother loved to lie down with a book after lunch, and when she did, she invariably fell asleep. She'd looked haggard this morning and had probably been up most of the night agonizing over Emily. The odds were good that she was asleep now.

Emily peeked into the living room and saw Carolyn lying on the couch, a book and her reading glasses on the floor next to her. She was snoring softly.

As noiselessly as she could, Emily retrieved her keys from the ceramic dish and picked up her purse. Holding her breath, she eased the front door open. Fortunately, Carolyn was a heavy sleeper, and Emily knew she must be horrendously sleep-deprived after this weekend. She didn't stir.

Emily eased the door shut and hurried to her car. She'd left her bedroom door closed in the hope that if Carolyn awakened soon, she'd assume Emily was still napping in her room. She didn't want to worry her mother any more than she already had. The day of judgment would come when Emily walked back into the apartment and Carolyn sliced, diced, and sautéed her alive for leaving, but if Emily couldn't take some action toward figuring out what was going on, she *would* go insane.

Her car was in the parking lot; her father had retrieved it from where Emily had parked it near Starbucks on the night of the murder. Rochelle would be at work right now, in her shoe shop near the Amber Flame. Emily hoped business would be slow enough in the middle of a Monday afternoon that Rochelle could slip to the back for a few minutes to talk with Emily.

What if Rochelle had taken the day off? That was a strong possibility. To have her friend murdered in the shop nearby would have been a horrific shock. But from what Emily knew of Rochelle, she was a driven, perpetually busy personality, and Emily guessed she'd be more likely to cope with loss by working twice as hard than by holing up in her house. If Rochelle wasn't at her shop, Emily would track her down. She had to talk with her.

Emily parked on the street in front of the row of shops, trying futilely not to look at the yellow police tape still blocking the door to the Amber

Flame. She was relieved to see the OPEN sign on the door of Rochelle's Shoes and Boots. Rochelle might not be there, but Emily might be able to coax her phone number out of whoever was working.

Behind the counter, Rochelle sat flipping through a stack of papers, her small shoulders hunched, her straight black hair pulled back in a ponytail. At the ding of the bell over the door, she looked up, an automatic smile on her face, but when she saw Emily, her expression stiffened.

There were no customers in the shop. Emily stood for a moment in silence, realizing she had no idea how to greet Rochelle. *How are you? Good to see you again? I'm sorry about Monica?* She didn't know Rochelle very well. She'd met her several times—Monica and Rochelle were both members of a book club sponsored by the local bookstore, and Emily, under Nicole's prodding to get involved with community events, had attended a few meetings. She'd also seen Rochelle at an occasional church activity as Monica's guest, and she'd chatted with her there but didn't know her well enough to call her a friend.

The awkwardness between them made Emily feel she was wading through waist-deep slush as she moved toward the counter. Closer to Rochelle, Emily could see the thick makeup around her eyes, an unsuccessful effort to conceal the redness and swelling left by tears.

Sudden knife-edged guilt made Emily regret coming here. How could she confront Monica's grieving friend and ask her if Monica had been running around with Zach behind Emily's back—and if she'd been cruel enough to use the picture of Ryan Tanner to torment Emily?

"I—I'm so sorry about Monica," Emily stammered. "I know you were close to her."

Rochelle stared at Emily for a long moment, her expression immobile. Then words like shards of ice burst from her lips. "*Are* you sorry?"

A mixed sensation of heat and cold rose in Emily's face. "I'm sorry for what happened to her. I'm sorry for your loss."

"My loss is your gain. Don't be such a phony. You know if Monica had lived, you wouldn't have been able to hold Zach Sullivan for another day. But Monica's dead now. Lucky you. What do you want, anyway?"

Rochelle's hostility made it easier for Emily to ask questions she knew would be offensive. "I want to know the truth about what Monica was up to. Was she seeing Zach behind my back?"

Rochelle gave an angry bark of laughter. "What does *that* matter? He's yours now. You win. It's the only way you *could* have won. But you know that."

Was that an accusation? Emily's cheeks burned, and she felt she was broiling in her wool sweater. "Was she seeing him?"

"Is this your way of gloating?"

"I'm just asking—"

Eyes ablaze with fury, Rochelle sprang to her feet. A petite woman a good four or five inches shorter than Emily, she still looked so dangerous that Emily wanted to turn and run. In her hand she clutched a black cylinder.

"Pepper spray," she said. "I keep it behind the counter just in case. Get out of my shop before I call the police and tell them you showed up today to rub Monica's death in my face."

"I never said anything—"

Rochelle came out from behind the counter, advancing on Emily. With an effort, Emily stood her ground.

"I know they almost arrested you on Saturday," Rochelle said. "Why they're still letting you run around free is a mystery to me, but I suppose they have to get all their ducks in a row so you can't wriggle out on some technicality. I'm not scared of you, Emily. Did you think I'd be scared of you?"

"I didn't kill her! Someone was targeting me as well. She—he—*someone*— left a bloodstained picture of Ryan Tanner on my door. Was it Monica? I have to know. If it wasn't her, then—"

"You're insane. I'm calling the cops. Why don't you sit down on one of those chairs while you wait? We'll find you a pair of shoes. Something in a nice white canvas to coordinate with your straitjacket."

Sweat soaked Emily's palms as she clutched her purse. "Why don't you answer two simple questions and I'll leave? Was Monica seeing Zach? And did she plant the picture of Ryan Tanner?"

The bell over the door startled Emily. She swung around and saw Nicole and Brent enter the store, both looking irritable and worried.

"*There* you are," Brent exclaimed. "Good call, Nicole."

Normally, Emily would have been relieved to see allies, but at the moment, she felt only humiliation to have them find her like this—flushed, trembling, with Rochelle Elton brandishing a canister of pepper spray in her face like she was warding off a maniac.

"Get your crazy friend out of here," Rochelle said shrilly. "You'll get yours, Emily—I swear I'll see you punished for—" Her voice choked.

"Em, come on." Nicole touched Emily's arm. "Rochelle's out of her mind. Let's get out of here."

"*I did not kill Monica.* I came last night to talk to her. When I got there, I found her dead. I would never hurt anyone."

Rochelle looked as though she couldn't decide whether to blast Emily with the pepper spray or drop the spray and attack with her bare hands.

"Emily." Brent laid his hand on her shoulder. "It's time to go."

Emily swatted Brent's hand aside and kept her gaze locked with Rochelle's. "I don't know who killed her. But someone left me a couple of pictures trying to scare me. The first was of Monica and Zach. The second was of Ryan Tanner. I thought it was Monica who sent the pictures, but if it wasn't, it might have been whoever murdered her. I have to know what was going on. *Were* Monica and Zach seeing each other—"

Rochelle's lunge startled Emily, and the slap came so quickly that before Emily could process what was happening, she was staggering backward, her hand pressed to the scorching pain in her cheek.

Rochelle retreated, clutching her fingers. "A picture of Ryan Tanner? Death just follows you, doesn't it? What really happened to Ryan? Was he messing around with your sister, so you ran her down and strangled him?"

Brent grabbed Emily's arm; Nicole caught her other arm, and Emily found herself being dragged out the door before she could even catch her breath enough to protest.

Tears blurred her view of the street in front of her, and she wasn't sure where Brent and Nicole were taking her until she caught a glimpse of Nicole's car parked at the curb.

"I'll take you home," Nicole said. "We'll go back and get your car later."

"I'm not going home."

"Yes, you are." Brent swung the back door open.

Making a scene on the street was the last thing she wanted, so Emily didn't resist as Nicole prodded her into the car. Instead, she shot a hand out and grabbed Nicole's purse.

"Em!"

Clutching Nicole's purse along with her own, Emily slid over to the opposite door.

"Emily, give me my purse. I need my keys."

Emily shook her head and wrapped her arms tightly around the purse, her teeth gritted and her eyes squeezed shut in an effort to keep tears from becoming hysterical sobs. They couldn't leave yet. She had to go back and talk to Rochelle Elton. She had to make her see how wrong she was.

Nicole slid into the backseat next to Emily. "Em, come on." Her arms went around Emily, and Emily leaned against her, sobbing on her shoulder, the same shoulder Emily had drenched in tears multiple times after Tricia died and Ryan disappeared. "I need to . . . I have to talk . . . Rochelle doesn't understand . . . I need to go back and . . ."

Nicole rubbed Emily's neck in a gentle, circular motion. "Forget everything she said. She's so upset over Monica that she's crazy."

"She—she thinks I—"

"No, she doesn't," Nicole said. "She doesn't know what she's saying."

Brent settled in the driver's seat and closed the door. "Your mother was scared cross-eyed when she woke up and you weren't there. Give us the keys. You don't want her to worry."

"I can't . . . go back like this. I can't let my mother—Brent, no!" Brent's hand reached between the front seats, grabbing for the purse. It slipped partway out of Emily's grip, and before she could tighten her fingers, Nicole caught both her wrists. With strength that surprised Emily, Nicole held her hands while Brent slid the purse out of her grasp.

Realizing the ridiculousness of what she was doing, Emily crumpled back onto Nicole's shoulder and didn't try to interfere as Brent removed the keys from Nicole's purse and started the engine.

No one spoke until Brent steered into the parking lot of Emily's apartment complex. "I can't talk to my mother yet," Emily murmured, trying to mop tears from her face with the sleeve of her sweater. The wool scratched her skin, smearing the tears rather than absorbing them. Her cheek throbbed where Rochelle had struck her, and she was afraid to look in the mirror to see what kind of bruise was forming. "She already worries about me 24/7. If she sees me like this—"

"You don't have to go home," Nicole said. "I'll take you wherever you want to go."

Where *did* she want to go? Nowhere. Anywhere. *Back in time.*

"How about your sacred yoga cabin, to which only the select few are admitted?" Brent suggested to Nicole. "Tricia always said it was the ultimate de-stresser, and Emily needs to get away from everything for a couple of days."

"I don't really use the cabin anymore. Too many memories of Tricia. It must have an inch of dust everywhere."

"Shame. You ought to sell it if you aren't going to use it. A mountain getaway would be worth a lot of dough."

"Thanks for the real estate advice, but can we concentrate on Emily right now?" Nicole smoothed a clump of wet hair off of Emily's cheek. "She can come to my house and rest there for a while. Mitch won't be home until late tonight."

"And I'll go up and explain to her mother," Brent offered.

Emily sat up straight. "No! Just—no, I'll call her. As soon as I . . ." As soon as she could speak without her voice trembling and cracking. "I'll call her from Nicole's."

Brent passed Nicole's keys and purse back to her. "Nice car," he said, patting the dashboard of the BMW. "Thanks for letting me take it for a spin."

"Don't count on ever doing it again." Nicole matched Brent's smile, and Emily knew her friends were doing their best to lighten the mood. Nicole opened her purse, took out a tissue, and handed it to Emily.

"Thanks." Emily wiped her face and tried to offer a reassuring smile of her own. But all she could think about was the hatred and accusation in Rochelle's face.

What really happened to Ryan Tanner? Was he messing around with your sister so you ran her down and strangled him?"

* * *

The ringing of Emily's doorbell drew a moan from Carolyn's throat. When she'd heard footsteps coming up the stairs outside, she'd thought Emily was home, and now . . .

Had the police come to tell her something had happened to Emily? Had Monica Fife's killer struck again?

I should have kept her here. I shouldn't have let her out of my sight. Why did I take that wretched nap?

A rap on the door followed the doorbell, and Carolyn steeled herself. She had to answer it. Her joints moved like rusted iron as she pushed herself toward the door.

It was Brent Amherst. "We found her," he said. "She's with Nicole now. She's fine."

Relief flooded Carolyn, and without thinking, she stepped forward and hugged Brent. "Thank you."

Brent patted her shoulder. "Not a problem. Just glad I was home when Nicole came knocking. Telecommuting has its advantages."

"Come in," Carolyn said, stepping back so Brent could enter. "Where was she?"

"She . . ." Brent's voice faded. "Now, Sister R., I don't want you to worry."

Carolyn's relief started a new descent into fear. "Where *was* she?"

Brent sat gingerly on the couch and looked at the faded knees of his jeans. "She . . . listen, Emily didn't want me to tell you any of this, but I can't stand making a mother worry. You won't rat on me, will you? I don't want Emily to feel like I betrayed her trust."

"I won't say anything to Emily."

"She'll probably tell you herself anyway, once she calms down." Despite his words, Brent wore a guilty, uneasy look.

Afraid he'd change his mind about confiding in her, Carolyn said quickly, "I know you only want to do what's best for her. You've been a great support to Emily all along."

"Yeah, I try, but sometimes doing what's best for someone isn't much appreciated, you know?"

"Tell me about it."

Brent chuckled. "Anyway, it was like I guessed. She went back to Monica's store."

"The place where the murder—"

"Yeah, there. Well, a couple of stores down, actually. I'm not sure what all she was doing, but when Nicole and I got there, she'd—hey, it's probably good if you sit down. You look kind of wobbly."

"No, no, I'm fine." Carolyn realized she was twisting the hem of her apron, winding the fabric around her hands. She shook her hands loose and folded her arms. "Tell me what Emily was doing. And why didn't she come home with you?"

"Like I said, she's with Nicole. She was pretty upset—*really* upset—and said she didn't want you to see her like that."

Carolyn dropped into Emily's armchair. Why would Emily cut her out? "What do you mean she didn't want me to see her?"

Brent shifted his feet and eyeballed his shoes. "I think she's trying to keep up a good front. Doesn't want to worry you. But I felt like you ought to know. I mean, if you were my mom—well, anyway. Emily was in the shoe shop near Monica Fife's candle shop. That shop is owned by Rochelle Elton, who is—was—Monica's best friend."

"Why was Emily there?"

"Not sure. But when Nicole and I got in there, Emily and Rochelle were having some kind of argument. They were both so upset that it was hard to tell exactly what it was about, but Rochelle seemed to think Emily had something to do with Monica's death, and Emily . . . she was demanding to know if Zach had been cheating on her with Monica. Then she . . . well, it got physical."

Carolyn gasped, and Brent said hastily, "It's all right. Rochelle slapped Emily, but we hauled Emily out of there before anything else could happen. Emily's fine."

Carolyn's heart thumped frantically, but she kept her voice steady. "Did Emily say anything? Explain why she went to Rochelle's store?"

Brent squirmed. "No. She was pretty hysterical. She didn't want to come home—we got her in Nicole's car, but then she grabbed Nicole's keys, and we had to wrestle them away from her. She kept saying she wanted to go back and talk to Rochelle."

Carolyn sat very still, her back straight, her hands folded in her lap. In one corner of her mind, she wondered why she needed to feign composure in front of Brent Amherst when what she wanted was to race out the door, screaming for Emily to come home.

"I'm sorry to shake you up like this." Brent gave a small, wry smile. "But it shook *me* pretty bad, and I thought you should know Emily's fine. I'm just glad Nicole and I got there when we did."

CHAPTER 13

"PEPPERMINT-CHAMOMILE. WITH A TOUCH of sugar." Nicole extended the china cup. "Guaranteed to soothe."

Emily dragged the corners of her mouth upward. It was only a distant cousin to a smile, but at least it was an improvement over bawling. "Thanks." She took the cup of herbal tea. "Are you sure my mother is all right? How did she sound?"

"Anxious. But I did a good job of calming her down. Trust me."

Emily inhaled the steam from her cup and said nothing. She shouldn't have accepted Nicole's offer to call her mother for her, but at the time it had seemed a welcome compromise between letting Carolyn worry and speaking to her personally.

"Stop feeling guilty," Nicole reproached, obviously reading her thoughts. "You're supposed to be relaxing, not winding yourself up."

"I am relaxing." It was almost true. With each minute that separated her from Rochelle's vicious accusations, she felt a little more able to view her words as absurd—and to reassure herself that other reasonable people would too.

But what now?

She struggled to focus her thoughts. Going to Rochelle had been a colossal mistake. How could she ever have thought Monica's friend would help her while the grapevine blossomed with rumors that Emily had killed Monica? Chances were Rochelle had now called the police to tell them about the visit, and Emily would soon face another visit from Lund and Kapoor. *You told me you trusted Zachary Sullivan, Miss Ramsey. Why did you go to ask Rochelle Elton if he was cheating on you?*

The faint sound of the front door opening made Nicole sit up straight and set her cup aside. "Oh, Mitch is early! He didn't think he'd finish up in time to catch the early flight."

"I'd better head out," Emily said. "I'm sure you two would like time alone."

"Relax." Nicole stood. "You haven't even tried your tea yet. He'll head straight for the shower anyway. Stay put."

Nicole strode from the room, her skirt swishing around her designer boots.

Emily sighed and took a tentative sip from her cup. She was less worried about intruding on Mitch's homecoming than about having him see her like this. Mitchell Gardiner—and everything around him—always seemed so put-together, so polished, so flawless. She hadn't looked in a mirror, but she could imagine how she looked—makeup smeared, eyes red and puffy from crying. A bandage concealed the stitches on her forehead but didn't conceal all the bruising surrounding them. And her cheek—she touched her cheekbone where Rochelle had struck her. What an idiot she'd been to go to Rochelle.

Alone in Nicole's expertly decorated living room, Emily made it halfway through her cup before deciding she didn't like peppermint-chamomile tea, soothing properties notwithstanding. She set the cup on the table next to her.

The longer Nicole was gone, the more uncomfortable Emily felt—a tangled mess of fear and emotion intruding on Nicole's peaceful household. She wished Nicole *could* take her to the yoga cabin and leave her there alone for a couple of weeks until everything in Los Coros calmed down. She'd never been there—Nicole took only a small number of her closest friends to her retreat, and before Tricia's death, Emily had only recently met Nicole. But in e-mails, Tricia had rhapsodized to Emily about the serene simplicity of Nicole's cabin, the isolation, the beauty of the mountain setting, the way Nicole refused to allow anything electronic through the door. A place cut off from the outside world sounded like bliss to Emily right now.

Of course, it would look acutely suspicious to Lund and Kapoor if she left town. And alone in a cabin, she'd have nothing to do but sit and think.

On second thought, staying at the cabin sounded like torture.

It was time to stop leaning on Nicole and go face her mother. She should tell Nicole she was leaving, but she didn't have her car here, and Nicole would never agree to let her call a cab.

Lacking anything better to do, Emily reached for the teacup but fumbled the delicate china and tipped it. She snatched at the cup and managed to set it upright before more than a single splash of tea hit the tabletop.

Emily hunted through her purse for a tissue or something else she could use to mop up the spill but found only a crumpled receipt. Taking the cup with her, she hurried to fetch a paper towel, her shoes noiseless on the thick carpeting of the hallway.

To her dismay, as she neared the kitchen she heard Nicole's and Mitch's voices. Mitch must have wanted a snack after returning home, instead of following Nicole's prediction that he'd want an immediate shower. There was no way around it—she'd have to face him. *Don't be so vain,* she chided herself. *Don't you have better things to worry about than facing Mitch Gardiner with your makeup smeared?*

She'd wipe up the spill in the living room, tell Nicole she was leaving, and call her mother to come pick her up. Carolyn would be more than happy to make the trip.

". . . know you care about Emily, but do you really think this is wise?" Mitch's words, spoken in a low, stern voice, penetrated her ears. She stopped in her tracks, still out of sight of the kitchen.

"What's that supposed to mean?" Nicole's voice was quiet but edged with broken glass. "She's my friend. She needed a place to decompress, so I brought her here."

"I admire your compassion." A dish clinked against the counter. "But I imagine that soon you won't want your name associated with hers. I'd guess it's only a matter of time until they arrest her."

Emily's heartbeat turned to hammer blows inside her chest. She shouldn't stand here and eavesdrop. She should march into the kitchen, face Mitch, and tell him he was wrong.

And he'll believe you. Just like Rochelle believed you.

"She didn't kill Monica Fife." Nicole came to Emily's defense with a fierceness that sent a surge of gratitude through Emily.

"I've heard the buzz. I have friends, contacts. She had a motive, she was there—"

"That doesn't mean she's guilty."

"Unlike on TV, most of the time the obvious candidate *is* the guilty one."

There was a brittle clunk, like someone had set a bottle down too hard. "She's innocent. She could never hurt anyone."

"Your friend Emily is one messed-up lady, and no wonder. Losing her sister in that terrible accident, and her fiancé disappearing—how could she not be damaged by that?"

"People heal."

"Healed wounds leave scars. And sometimes, scars conceal deeper damage. I'd say Emily made a mistake jumping back into the ring so soon. She wasn't ready for marriage and the emotional strain—"

"It's been three years since Ryan disappeared."

"Has it been that long?"

"We'd just gotten engaged, remember?"

"Oh, that's right. But my point—"

"You're not being fair."

"Your life may be in danger, and you're talking about fair? You're running around with an unstable woman who could crack at any moment."

Emily couldn't take it anymore. She filled her lungs and blew the air out slowly, concentrating on relaxing her expression. Then she walked into the kitchen.

"Welcome home, Mitch," she said. "Sorry to barge in, but I spilled a little of my drink on the table. I need a paper towel. Just a tiny spill—didn't hit the carpet." She strolled to the paper towel holder and ripped off a couple of squares, watching Nicole and Mitch out of the corner of her eye. Mitch, who usually moved with athletic grace, was standing as stiffly as the Tin Man in need of oil. Emily fought a perverse temptation to jump at him and yell *"Boo!"* He'd spill his wine down the front of that Armani suit.

"Don't worry about the mishap, Em. I'll take care of it." Nicole sounded casual, but she looked worried, plainly wondering if Emily had overheard any of Mitch's words.

"I'll just wipe it up quickly," Emily said. The anxiety in Nicole's eyes quelled any desire she had to confront Mitch with what he'd said about her. If she argued with him, it wouldn't convince him of anything, and it would be agony for Nicole to get caught in the middle. "I need to get going. My mother will go crazy twiddling her thumbs without me around to baby. I'll give her a call. She'll come get me."

"Don't be silly," Nicole said. "I'll take you home."

Emily risked a glance at Mitch and saw dismay in his eyes. "Don't abandon me when I just got home, Nicole," he said smoothly. "I'll pay for a taxi for Emily."

Emily mentally finished Mitch's statement: *So the taxi driver, not you, will be in danger of getting strangled at the first stoplight.*

Nicole's face was taut with unhappiness, and her mouth opened like she wanted to speak but didn't dare. Emily could sense how torn she was, hating to clash with Mitch but wanting to support Emily.

"My mother is a regular taxi service, so that's settled." Emily smiled, trying to relieve Nicole's inner conflict. "Let me go clean up my mess, and I'll give my mom a quick call—"

She started for the door. Nicole followed her. "I'll drive you home." Nicole's voice was firm. "Mitch, I'll be back in half an hour or so."

* * *

"Hey, Shel." Justin Driscoll flashed a bleak version of his normally charming grin at Rochelle Elton. "I stopped by the store, and Kim told me you'd gone home. I came to see how you're doing."

Rochelle tried to smile back, but she was so tired that it was hard even to fake it. "Thanks for the thought. Come on in if you want. Seth's at my mother's."

"How is he?"

"Fine, I think." Rochelle led the way to her small, wood-floored living room. It was where she always brought guests, but this afternoon she wished too late that she'd taken him into the TV room, never mind Seth's Hot Wheels cars and the goldfish crackers scattered across the carpet. The living room contained too many reminders of Monica. Her candles were everywhere—pillar candles on black wrought-iron stands, votives in mosaic glass bowls, a round candle she'd designed especially for Rochelle laced with lemons, cloves, and cinnamon sticks. The room even smelled like Monica, a faint mingling of candle fragrances.

"Did you tell Seth what happened?" Justin slumped onto the couch.

Rochelle rubbed her eyes with both hands, knowing but not caring that she was destroying the last remnants of the makeup she'd used to camouflage the signs of tears. "I didn't tell him any details." She sat across from Justin. "I told him Monica died and I'm sad about it. He's only five. He shouldn't have to deal with something like this."

"Did you go to work today?"

"Yeah, but it was a mistake. I thought it would be better to keep busy, but . . ." Rochelle pressed her fingertip against the curved surface of the lemon candle. "It didn't work out very well. I called Kim this afternoon and had her take over."

"You're a trooper to go in at all." Justin propped his elbows on his knees, his shaggy hair falling around his face. *He looks awful,* Rochelle thought, *like he hasn't slept since he heard the news of Monica's murder.*

"I still have trouble believing this is real," she said. "How can Monica be alive one minute and then . . ." Tears stung Rochelle's eyes, but she didn't bother blinking them away. After struggling for hours to maintain her composure at work, she lacked the energy to fight her emotions.

At least she *had* done a good job of containing her feelings in public—until Emily Ramsey had walked through the door.

"When did you last see her?" Justin lifted the candle nearest him, brought it close to his face, and inhaled.

Rochelle wished again that she had chosen another room in which to talk to Justin. "I stopped by the Amber Flame Saturday morning before our stores opened. Monica had called me all upset about that horrible picture."

"Yeah, the police asked me about that." The muscles in Justin's jaw tightened. "Even after getting that picture, she couldn't believe that Emily Ramsey was dangerous. If Monica hadn't been such a fool, chasing Sullivan like that—"

The bitterness in his voice made Rochelle sure of what she'd suspected for a long time. "You were in love with her, weren't you?"

Justin set the candle on the table, his face flooded with an emotion Rochelle couldn't identify. Was he startled? Furious? Embarrassed? "She told you."

"Told me what?"

He shrugged curtly.

"She didn't know how you felt, or she *would* have told me," Rochelle said. "But it's not like I needed subtitles to figure out the play. Not all of us are as dense about men as Monica was."

"*Monica* dense about men? She could wrap any guy around her finger."

"Yeah, but she never completely figured out that men were real people with real feelings."

"I can't blame her. She didn't exactly have a great male role model growing up. But I never thought *you'd* criticize her like this. You two were buddies."

Rochelle wiped her eyes. "Monica was my closest friend, but that doesn't mean I was clueless. You played the whole guy-friend, flirty role like you didn't care, and she played it right back, but I could tell every time you looked at her that it was killing you the way she played with you."

"You're full of it."

"I wish you'd told her, Justin. Because maybe if you had, you could have woken her up to what a fool she was being about Zach Sullivan. She and Zach were *so* wrong for each other, but the instant he got engaged to Emily Ramsey, Monica got obsessed with him, thinking he'd be the perfect husband. If she hadn't—if she'd only left Zach alone . . ."

Justin looked haunted, but he said nothing.

Rochelle drew her knees up to her chest and picked at the fraying hem of her jeans. "The stupid thing is, she never would have married Zach. She'd have gotten cold feet before the wedding and called it off."

"I wish the police would arrest Emily and get it over with," Justin said gruffly.

"They probably have to establish the time of death first and all that. The thing that gets me is that I—" Absently, she dug her fingernail into the lemon candle then regretted marring it. "I might have been in Monica's store after she was killed. She might have been lying there, dead, and I had no idea."

Justin's hand closed jerkily around the fringe of one of the beaded throw pillows Rochelle had arranged on her couch. She bit her tongue against an urge to tell him to be careful not to tear the beads off, that the cushion was expensive. *He's not your child, and who cares about a few dumb beads?*

"What do you mean you were there after she was killed?" Justin asked.

"Well, I don't *know.* I don't know what time she died. But she called me maybe an hour before closing time. She said it had been a horrible day and I wouldn't *believe* what had happened—as if the picture wasn't enough—and if I had a chance, could I pop over after closing time? I said sure. I had a last-minute customer who couldn't make up her mind, so I was late closing and didn't get over there until almost seven-thirty. She hadn't locked the front door yet, which was weird, so I went in, but she wasn't anywhere in sight. I called to her, but she didn't answer, which was also weird, but right then my cell phone rang, and it was my mother. Seth had cut his finger on a piece of glass, and she thought he might need stitches . . ." Was she babbling? Justin didn't seem to mind. He was scrutinizing her so intently that she felt he was devouring every word.

"I hollered to Monica that I had to run, but I'd call her, and I raced out. She didn't answer, but I thought maybe she was in the bathroom. After I finished taking care of Seth, I tried to call her, but she didn't answer her phone. Later that night, she still wasn't answering her phone—any of her phones—and I got worried. I headed back downtown to see if she was still at work, and . . ." She swallowed. "I saw the police swarming all over the place."

"Did the police talk to you?" Justin's eyes reminded her of coals in a campfire—gray with red heat showing through. A new sense of uneasiness tickled Rochelle's nerves.

"I ran up and asked them what happened," she said.

"Did you go into her store? Did they have you look around?"

"Yes, to see if I could identify anything that didn't belong or anything missing. Her body was . . . covered. I didn't see her." Realization pierced Rochelle. Among the things the police had asked her was if she knew who might have given Monica roses that day. They'd found a dozen red roses, with petals bruised and missing, stuffed in her trash can. Rochelle hadn't known anything about it and hadn't thought much about it after the fact— it was far from unusual for Monica to get flowers from admirers, and if she were in as bad a mood as she'd seemed to be in on the phone, she might have destroyed the roses in a fit of annoyance that they weren't from Zach.

But who *had* sent the roses?

Justin?

She thought of the expression on his face when she'd brought up his feelings for Monica. *"She told you."* Told Rochelle what? That Justin had sent—or brought—her roses along with a declaration of his feelings for her, and she'd rejected him and destroyed his gift?

Rochelle's tongue went dry. She'd been so busy blaming Emily Ramsey that she hadn't stopped to examine all the possibilities.

"What else did they ask you?" Justin said.

"Just if I had any idea who had it in for Monica," Rochelle said carefully. "I told them about Emily."

"Did they say anything about a digital voice recorder?"

"Yes, they found one in her workroom. It was mine. She'd borrowed it to record her conversation with Emily. It had one of my address stickers on it—I always slap a sticker on things when I lend them out—so they asked me about it."

"Was there anything recorded on it?"

"No, it was empty. She'd never turned it on."

"Emily must have shown up before Monica expected her."

"Maybe."

"I saw Emily that night. She was completely wacko. White as a ghost and rambling like a nutcase."

"Justin, I'm so sorry. This must be awful for you. I know Monica cared about you."

Justin gave a couple of beads a hard twist. "Yeah, sure she did. I could tell by the way she invited me along to watch her kiss Sullivan."

"She would have come to her senses. If only she'd had a little more time, she would have realized you were much better for her than Zach."

He stood up. "I'd better go."

Rochelle tried not to look too relieved. "Thanks for stopping by."

"No problem." Justin hugged her, and she was suddenly conscious of the strength in his arms. He was a lot stronger than Emily Ramsey. It would have been a breeze for him to . . .

What was the matter with her? Justin loved Monica. He wouldn't have hurt her. Emily was the one who had a reason for wanting Monica dead.

But Justin *did* have a temper, and Monica could be callous when she got overly focused on a goal—like pursuing Zach—and got tunnel vision. What if Justin told Monica he loved her, and she had refused to take him seriously? What if she had laughed in his face and invited him to help her the next time she went out stalking Zach?

The memory of mangled rose petals flickered in Rochelle's mind as she escorted Justin to the door. Was it really Emily Ramsey's voice that Justin had thought might be on that voice recorder?

* * *

"Hello, Zach." Carolyn stood with her hand on the doorknob and looked hard at Zachary Sullivan. He appeared drained, like misery had sapped him of energy.

Had he been cheating on Emily? Or if not outright cheating, had he still harbored feelings for Monica Fife? Or was the fear and jealousy Brent Amherst had witnessed in Emily just evidence of her insecurity? How could she not be insecure after losing Ryan?

Zach gave a half smile. "How are you holding up, Carolyn?"

It was a sweet smile, Carolyn thought, and it was sweet of him to inquire after her welfare before asking about Emily. But what if the courteous façade hid a man who was unfaithful at best, and at worst a murderer?

The latter thought startled Carolyn. How could she ever imagine that Zach would harm Monica?

If he had feelings for her—if he was seeing her behind Emily's back and Monica threatened to tell Emily, and Zach panicked—

Carolyn tried to shake off these ridiculous thoughts. She'd seen too many movies if she could believe that a nice boy like Zach Sullivan was a murderer.

A nice boy? Or a two-faced, two-timing . . .

Zach shifted his weight from foot to foot and ran his fingers through his hair. His fidgeting made Carolyn realize she must appear very strange, standing here and staring at Zach like she was trying to read his mind. She wished she *could* read it. She'd give almost anything for a peek into Zachary Sullivan's soul.

"I'm fine." She answered his question at last. "But I'm afraid Emily's not home. She's at Nicole's."

"I'm glad she's feeling well enough to go out." His positive words clashed with his grim expression. "Do you know when she'll be home?"

"I'm afraid I don't. I'll tell her you stopped by."

Transparently unhappy, Zach shoved his hands in the pockets of his jacket. "I tried to reach her on her cell, but she must have it turned off. Would you ask her to call—"

Footsteps clacked on the concrete stairs, and Zach turned. At the sight of Emily approaching, Carolyn's heart plunged. She'd been frantic to see

Emily all afternoon, but why did she have to arrive right this minute while Zach was here? If she'd been upset enough to yell accusations about Zach at Monica's friend, there was no telling how the sight of Zach himself would affect her.

"Hey." Emily offered Zach a smile Carolyn instantly pegged as phony. As Emily reached the top of the stairs, Carolyn gripped the hem of her apron in an effort to stop herself from shoving Zach aside, snatching her daughter, and whisking her into the apartment.

"How are you?" Zach drew Emily into a hug.

"I'm all right." Emily quickly broke the embrace. "How about you?"

"Been better. Been worse. Listen, I don't mean to crash the party. I know your mother's here taking care of you. I just wanted to check to see how you're doing."

Carolyn wondered if she was the only one who thought the phrase "here taking care of you" sounded ludicrous in light of the fact that Emily had been running around all afternoon in a state of nervous breakdown. At least Emily seemed calm now, in contrast to Brent's report.

"Thanks for coming by," Emily said. "I'm exhausted, so I think I'll go lie down. I'll call you later."

Discouragement in his eyes, Zach nodded and stepped back as Emily walked into the apartment and closed the door.

* * *

"It's only an hour away." Carolyn's voice was almost strident, a rarity for her, and her harsh tone caught Emily off guard.

"I need to be back at work tomorrow, Mom. If I hang around being lazy any longer, I might start liking it too much." Keeping her response pleasant strained Emily's self-control, but she'd fed Carolyn enough fear today. She didn't want to make things worse.

"Emily, you need to take it easy. Right now, home is the best place for you. You can take a few more days off work. Your principal will be more than happy to accommodate you."

Was her mother staring at her bruised cheek? She'd tried to conceal the developing bruise with makeup borrowed from Nicole, but Nicole's complexion was lighter than hers, and Emily wondered if in trying to hide the bruise, she'd only highlighted it. "I appreciate your concern, but I'm not sick, and I have a job to do. First graders are very young. They don't like subs. They don't like disruptions. Besides, the police might have more questions for me." Had anyone ever worked so hard to make terrifying words sound so casual?

Mitch Gardiner's voice still echoed in her thoughts. *"Usually the obvious candidate is the guilty one."*

At least Nicole believed in her innocence. Emily knew how much Nicole hated arguing with Mitch or disappointing him, so she was deeply grateful for Nicole's standing up for her. They hadn't talked much on the drive back to Rochelle's shop to pick up Emily's car. Emily had been tempted to mention that she'd overheard Mitch's words but couldn't bring herself to make Nicole feel even more torn between her friend and her husband.

"I'll tell Detective What's-Her-Name where we'll be," Carolyn said. "If they have other questions for you, they'll know where to find you, but I can't imagine they will. You've already told them everything you know, probably five times over."

Emily looked down at the glistening, buttery surface of the turkey, basil, and sun-dried tomato sandwich Carolyn had grilled for her. The sandwich was delicious, but it was hard to eat when her stomach was in knots. She half expected Lund and Kapoor to ring the doorbell at any moment to question her about the incident at Rochelle's store.

Maybe she *would* be better off going home with her mother. At least that might slow Lund down. But it wouldn't do anything to clear the storm of confusion inside her. She still didn't know if Monica had sent her the pictures or if someone else was targeting her. She still didn't know if Monica and Zach had been seeing each other.

The memory of the watch Zach had been wearing in the picture of him kissing Monica kept shoving against her emotions in a way she couldn't ignore. If only she *had* the picture, she could examine it for signs that it had been doctored. But Lund had taken it. And how could she call and ask to see it without exposing the extent of her mistrust and jealousy? She might as well invite Lund to arrest her.

Why couldn't she trust Zach enough to talk to him directly? Less than two weeks ago, she'd trusted him enough to want to marry him. Why couldn't she now trust him enough to ask him about a watch in a photograph? She'd taken the coward's way out by brushing him off with a fake claim of exhaustion, not even inviting him inside for a few minutes.

Carolyn set a plate bearing a fudgy brownie topped with toasted pecans next to Emily's water glass.

"No wonder it smells so good in here," Emily said. "You've been baking all day. You're spoiling me."

"That's my goal." Carolyn ruffled Emily's hair. "Let me do it for a couple more days. Come home and rest."

Relieved that good humor had returned to Carolyn's voice, Emily looked up at her. Carolyn was smiling, but she had lines of anxiety and exhaustion around her eyes that Emily hadn't seen since Tricia's death. *And it's my fault,* Emily thought. *She's terrified for me, and everything I do makes things worse.*

"One more day," Emily conceded. "I'll take one more day off work, and you can baby me. But then I've got to start acting like a grown-up."

Carolyn chuckled. "You'll always be my baby."

"The curse of the youngest child. But I'm taking my own car to your house so you don't have to drive me all the way home tomorrow night."

Carolyn frowned, and Emily could tell she was debating whether or not to endanger her victory by fighting Emily on this point. "If you're feeling up to it," she said at last.

"I am." Emily picked up her fork, deciding to sneak a bite of brownie before finishing her sandwich. Carolyn headed into the kitchen and started running hot water into the sink.

"These are wonderful knives, by the way." Carolyn held up a chef's knife. "A pleasure to work with."

"They ought to be, seeing as how you bought them for me."

"I'm going to have to sharpen my knives." Carolyn put the knife under the running water. "Or buy new ones. I'm spoiled now."

Emily watched her mother, wondering what she was really thinking. Carolyn had never asked her where she'd gone today when she'd sneaked out, and Emily knew Nicole hadn't told her.

Had Brent? Probably, and it was hard to blame him for wanting to keep Carolyn in the loop. He'd known Carolyn longer than he'd known Emily, since Brent and Tricia had dated for a little while before Emily moved to Los Coros.

Had he repeated anything Rochelle said? Emily felt she'd rather die right now than imagine that Carolyn could, even for the tiniest instant, wonder if her daughter had murdered Monica Fife.

And Ryan Tanner as well.

CHAPTER 14

IT PROVED HARDER THAN EMILY had anticipated to hide her restlessness during dinner at her parents' house, but she was determined to maintain a calm demeanor. She wanted to reassure her mother that she no longer needed either a babysitter or a watchdog, so Carolyn would willingly send her home tomorrow with a hug and a smile.

Granted, it was a long shot.

"This chicken is superb. How do you make it so flavorful?" The plump, balding man seated across the table from Emily reached for the serving fork and helped himself to another slice of chicken.

Carolyn launched into an explanation of marinating techniques. Whenever she began to slow down, Emily inserted a question to keep her rolling, wanting to keep the subject light and harmless.

Emily had been surprised when her mother told her a friend was coming to dinner, but she figured it was a good thing—the presence of grandfatherly widower Peter Kincaid would take some of the pressure off Emily and keep her mother from bringing up topics Emily didn't want to discuss.

"Are you a kitchen diva like your mother, Emily?" Brother Kincaid asked.

"Oh, no. I'm a decent cook, but I don't have her talent."

"Time, not talent," Carolyn corrected. "All it takes is time."

"And I have just enough time to punch START on the microwave so it heats my chicken nuggets," Emily said.

Brother Kincaid laughed. It was a pleasant, rumbling sound.

"Emily is a busy young woman," Carolyn said with a smile. "She's a teacher."

"What do you teach, Emily?"

"First grade."

Carolyn was silent a few beats before adding, "She's taking a few days off, of course, to get some rest after that heartbreaking situation with Monica Fife."

The forkful of garlic mashed potatoes Emily had placed in her mouth now felt like a mouthful of glue.

"Yes, I'm sorry." Brother Kincaid's eyes were gentle as he surveyed Emily, but she felt she would choke. What was Carolyn trying to do to her? At the head of the table, her father studiously buttered a roll, not looking at anyone.

"It's been difficult convincing Emily that she ought to rest," Carolyn said. "She's ready to go charging back to work, but for heaven's sake, the girl has a head injury."

"Mom, I'm fine." Emily spoke too sharply. Under the table, she wadded her napkin in her fist, willing herself to keep calm. Infusing a touch of humor into her voice, she said, "You worry too much, Mother Hen."

"And you push yourself too hard to be perfect. It's not a failing to admit you need help."

"I've rested, and I'm fine." Emily tried to sound confident. Instead, she sounded flat and fake.

"What do you enjoy most about teaching school, Emily?" Brother Kincaid asked kindly. Emily couldn't decide whether to be relieved that he'd redirected the subject or humiliated that he'd clearly done so because he'd sensed her agitation.

"I love the enthusiasm of young children." With each word, the tension in her throat eased a little. "Enthusiasm, excitement—everything is so new to them. So fascinating."

"True," Brother Kincaid said. "After my grandchildren come to visit, I find myself noticing every fire engine or cow or motorcycle—and pointing it out to imaginary children in the backseat."

Emily laughed, but she didn't dare look at her mother. Carolyn yearned for grandchildren. Emily had thought she'd finally be able to give her that gift, but now . . . did Zach still love her? Had he ever loved her, or had he only wanted her because he thought he couldn't have Monica?

Emily lifted her fork to her mouth, methodically chewing bite after bite. If she showed a lack of appetite or left the table early, Carolyn would pounce on that as more evidence that she wasn't well, and clearly Brother Kincaid's presence wasn't enough to keep Carolyn from hassling Emily about her health.

To her relief, Brother Kincaid deftly kept the conversation going, relaxing Emily by sharing anecdotes from his own long-ago school days, engaging silent Lloyd in the conversation by asking about his planned summer garden, and quizzing Carolyn about the virtues of homemade pasta versus dried. By the time the meal had progressed to where Emily could rise and offer to heat the fudge sauce Carolyn would pour over the mint chocolate cake, Emily felt she might actually make it through the evening without a meltdown.

"I'll heat the sauce, honey. You relax," Carolyn said, but Emily waved her off and hastened into the kitchen before Carolyn could rise from her chair.

As soon as she was alone, she heaved a deep sigh and brushed her fingers across the bandage on her aching head. Thank heaven for Brother Kincaid's tact; if not for him, she would have been weeping on her grilled asparagus before dinner ended. He seemed to understand, far better than Carolyn, that she emphatically didn't want to discuss anything related to Monica Fife.

No, that wasn't true. Carolyn *knew* she didn't want to talk about the events of the weekend. She just thought Emily needed to get her feelings out in the open in order to deal with them. But the only kind of talking that would help her was talking to someone who could tell her the truth about Monica, Zach, and everything else.

Who was that person?

Emily ignited the flame beneath the pan of fudge sauce and stirred the sauce slowly, her mind sorting through her options.

Justin Driscoll? Emily grimaced. He probably knew the truth about what Monica had been up to, but approaching him would be even stupider than approaching Rochelle Elton.

The familiar rhythm of her mother's footsteps on the terra-cotta tile brought Emily on alert. She should have known Carolyn wouldn't stay in the dining room.

Carolyn set a stack of soiled dinner plates on the counter. "I'll do the sauce, sweetie."

"You could cut the cake." It was useless to try to banish Carolyn.

"You really don't know how to relax, do you?" Carolyn took dessert plates from the cupboard. Emily smiled blandly and kept stirring. She wished she could take some Tylenol from the cupboard and down a couple of pills for her burgeoning headache, but she didn't want her mother to see her reaching for painkillers.

"I sent the men off to the living room," Carolyn said. "I thought it would be nice to eat dessert there in front of the fire. It's a cold evening, isn't it?"

"Yes."

Carolyn drew the powdered sugar–dusted cake toward her. "Brother Kincaid is easy to talk with, isn't he?"

"He's very nice. He's in your ward?"

"In the stake. He moved in after you left for school."

"How long has his wife been gone?"

"Five years. It's been hard on him, but he's coping very well."

Unlike me? Emily bit back the question. What was wrong with her that she read criticism into such an innocent remark?

"He's comforting to talk to." Carolyn selected a knife from the cupboard. "He understands how crushing it is to lose someone you love. He was a great comfort to me after Tricia died."

"That's wonderful." Discomfort seeped through Emily. *Comforting to talk to . . . wait a minute.* "Is Brother Kincaid your psychiatrist friend?"

"He's a psychiatrist, yes." Carolyn cut a slice of cake. "And a friend who cares deeply for our family."

Blood rushed into Emily's cheeks as her mother's full agenda became clear. Carolyn had invited Peter Kincaid here because she wanted Emily to meet him. She'd tried multiple times to get Emily into counseling after Tricia's death and Ryan's disappearance, but Emily had always refused. Tonight, Carolyn had apparently decided to set things up on her own.

Emily lowered her voice to ensure that it wouldn't penetrate beyond the kitchen. "It wasn't fair of you to do this to me."

"For heaven's sake." Carolyn slid the slice of cake onto a dessert plate. "What's wrong with inviting a friend of the family to dinner?"

"This wasn't a social invitation."

"He's a friend. One who might be able to help you through a difficult time."

Emily kept stirring the sauce, but inside, humiliation ate at her like acid. What had Carolyn told Dr. Kincaid about her?

"I don't need that kind of help," Emily whispered. "And I don't appreciate being put under the microscope during dinner. If you planned for me to meet him, you at least could have been honest about it."

"If I'd told you, you would have refused to come. You wouldn't have had the chance to learn that he's a delightful, compassionate man."

What had Peter Kincaid thought of her? His trained eyes would easily have discerned the turmoil beneath her feeble efforts to appear calm. She must have looked like an idiot, pretending nothing was wrong, chatting about chicken marinade and first graders with all the finesse of a child who thinks that if she covers her eyes, no one can see her.

"You're going to burn that." Carolyn took the saucepan off the heat and switched off the flame. "Sweetheart, please don't get upset. No one will force you to do anything you don't want to do."

The thought of facing Dr. Kincaid again made Emily cringe. "I can't go sit by the fire and eat cake and pretend this is a social visit."

Carolyn's lips pressed together. She spooned fudge sauce over four pieces of cake, her movements jerky. "If you're so worried about getting analyzed, feel free to sit and glower like a sulky teenager and not say a word."

Anger scalded Emily. Because she didn't like getting invited under false pretenses for some after-hours psychiatry, she was a sulky teenager? "Maybe I should go home."

"Maybe you should calm down," Carolyn snapped, sounding as though she were struggling to take her own advice. "Just eat the cake, then go to bed early."

Emily pictured it: strolling into the living room, cake plate in hand, talking and laughing, a bad actress in a travesty of a play. She couldn't do it. Not tonight, not on top of everything else that had happened. She walked to the wooden coat tree near the back door and took down her purse and coat.

"Emily!" Alarm overtook the anger in Carolyn's face. "Don't go. You're blowing this completely out of proportion. If you want to skip dessert, skip dessert. Go to bed. I'll tell Dad and Peter that you have a headache. But don't drive all the way back to Los Coros."

"I know, I know. I'm not up to it. I'm not up to much of anything." Emily twisted the doorknob.

Tears glittered in Carolyn's eyes. "Has it ever occurred to you that the reason you fight this so hard is because in your heart you know you can't go it alone—and you're panicked that someone else might figure out that you're human?"

Emily walked out and closed the door behind her.

* * *

With his body clock skewed by jet lag, Mitch fell asleep by nine o'clock. Nicole knew she didn't stand a chance of falling asleep that early, so she sat in the entertainment room, flipping channels and staring mindlessly at the TV.

When she'd returned from driving Emily home, she'd walked into the house braced to launch a defense of her behavior, but to her surprise, Mitch had said nothing about Emily for the rest of the evening, nor had he seemed angry at Nicole. They'd eaten a companionable dinner, watched TV for a while, and Mitch had gone to bed.

Why had he changed his attitude? Had he discovered something in her absence? Mitch had friends in the police department, including the chief of police. Could he have called one of his contacts and elicited an update on the investigation? Nicole wasn't sure if they could give out any information, but she hoped they could—and that Mitch's contact had told him the police were far from convinced of Emily's guilt, or even that Emily was in the clear altogether. After all, she *did* have an alibi for most of the evening, so if they'd concluded by now that Monica died during the hours while Emily was at the Tanners', Emily couldn't have done it.

Nicole imagined the wheels turning in Mitch's mind as he analyzed the situation in light of his burgeoning political aspirations. *"Not convinced of her guilt . . . good chance she's innocent . . . If Nicole turns her back on Emily, that will make Nicole look heartless, abandoning her innocent-until-proven-guilty friend after Emily went through such a traumatic experience. I can't afford to have my wife look heartless. An opponent would love to trot that story out for the press. Better to let Nicole keep treating Emily like her pet project. It'll look noble."*

Nicole sighed and reached for the remote to switch off the TV. At least Mitch wasn't going to be a problem. *One less thing to worry about.* Why did life have to be so messy? Just when everything was going smoothly—*crash.* But she *was* picking up the pieces, and soon she'd have everything back in order.

Nicole wandered into the music room. She opened the piano bench and selected a book of Beethoven's piano sonatas. She'd play the piano for a while then go to bed early.

The first few passages flowed easily from her fingers, but on the second page, she stumbled—once, twice. Lifting her fingers from the keyboard, she closed her eyes, fighting the reflexive tightening in her back muscles. Her mother wasn't here. No one could hear her mistakes; no one was going to materialize at her shoulder to criticize her. It was all right.

She started over, playing more slowly. Everything would work out.

But what about Emily and Zach's relationship? She'd thought Emily believed that Zach wasn't sneaking around with Monica. But if Emily believed what Zach told her, she wouldn't have been at Rochelle Elton's store this afternoon.

Nicole had tried to coax Emily into confiding why she'd changed her mind about Zach's fidelity, but Emily had shrugged off every question with glib statements of "Of course I trust him," which Nicole translated to mean, "I don't want to talk about it."

She couldn't let this tear Zach and Emily apart. Even if Zach *had* been cheating, it didn't have to be an issue anymore. Monica was dead. If Zach handled things correctly, everything would be fine.

If he handled things correctly. Zach wasn't exactly a slick talker.

Nicole played a few more passages, trying to concentrate on the music, but the anxiety inside her intensified, and the mental picture she tried to maintain of Emily and Zach happily surrounded by a bunch of dark-haired kids seemed out of focus and unrealistic.

When she couldn't endure it any longer, she rose from the piano bench. She'd call Zach. If he was with Emily, she'd make a quick excuse and hang up. If he wasn't with Emily, she'd find out what the problem was—and fix it. Nothing was going to mess up Emily's happiness, and if Zach was too much of a dork to repair things on his own, Nicole would walk him through it.

"Hey, Nicole." Zach's tone was unusually curt. *Not a good sign,* Nicole thought.

"Hi." Nicole plunged in. "You with Emily?"

"Not at the moment." His tone headed from curt to cold. "If you need to talk to her, call her. She might be home, or she might be at her parents', but I'm sure she'll have plenty of time for *you.*" The slight emphasis he put on the last word of the sentence both annoyed Nicole and confirmed her fears.

"Don't go all petty on me," Nicole said. "You know I'd never get in the way of your time with Emily."

Zach was silent for a moment. "All right. Sorry. What do you need?"

"To know what you're talking about. Did you see Emily today?"

"For about ten seconds, until she told me she was tired and shut the door in my face. After spending the afternoon running around with you, apparently."

Nicole swore under her breath. "Are you at home?"

"Yeah. Why?"

"I'm coming over. We need to talk."

"This is none of your business, Nicole."

"Really? Too bad. I'll be there in twenty minutes." Nicole banged the phone into the base and went to get her purse and shoes.

CHAPTER 15

CURLED UP IN THE MOHAIR blanket Ryan had given her, Emily huddled on her couch, refusing herself permission to cry. If Carolyn was desperate enough to sneak a psychiatrist in to dinner, did that mean she *did* have doubts about Emily's innocence? Had she convinced herself that Emily's grief over the dual loss of Tricia and Ryan had rendered her so unstable that the possibility of losing Zach had pushed her into violence?

Could her own mother think that of her?

You can bet the police do. Why don't you call Detective Lund and tell her you just happened to find some fake blood in your tote bag? See how sane you look then.

What now? Should she ask Lund if the police had any evidence implicating Monica in sending the threatening pictures? Emily grimaced as she imagined how Lund would react.

Justin Driscoll? His name kept popping into her head, despite her conviction that talking to him would be inviting trouble.

She tugged the soft blanket more tightly around her. Was she putting too much stock in Justin's knee-jerk accusations? He'd been in shock the night of the murder, venting his anguish on Emily because she'd had the bad luck to be on the scene. Maybe now that he'd had a few days to calm down, he'd realize he'd been premature in blaming her.

Maybe. The only way to find out was to ask him.

Knowing she was a fool, but unable to sit still when there existed even a tiny possibility that Justin could help unsnarl her confusion, Emily pushed the blanket aside. She found Justin's number on the ward list taped to the inside of her cupboard and dialed rapidly. What was the worst that could happen? Justin would yell accusations at her and tell Lund she'd called. She'd have to face Lund sooner or later anyway.

Justin answered on the first ring, his voice guarded. "Hello?"

Emily swallowed to moisten her mouth. "This is Emily Ramsey. I need to talk to you." Her tongue stuck to the roof of her mouth, and she swallowed again, waiting for Justin to speak.

Justin said nothing.

Emily's pulse thudded in her ears. She should hang up now and cut her losses, but she couldn't make herself push the button to end the call. Let Justin hang up first. At least he hadn't started screaming at her.

"Emily," he said at last. "What do you need?" He didn't sound angry—just cautious.

"I need to ask you some questions. I know you don't want to hear from me, but—"

"It's okay." Justin cut across her explanation with the last words she'd expected to hear. "I owe you an apology. I was cruel the other night. Crazy."

Relief draped itself around Emily, so warm and heavy that she felt her knees would buckle. "It's all right. You were upset. I understand."

"Are you doing all right? How's your head?"

"It's fine. Just headaches here and there. I'll be back at work tomorrow." Emily let her knees give way, and she sat cross-legged on the carpet, hope bubbling inside her. "Justin . . . I have some things I need to ask you. They aren't easy questions, but I really need some answers."

"If they're not easy questions, let's not do this over the phone. I'll come over. You're upstairs from Brent, right?"

"Yes. Apartment 210."

"I'll be there in five minutes. Are you sure you're all right? You sound shaky."

"I'm just relieved. I wasn't sure how you'd react to hearing from me."

"My fault. Sorry. See you soon." He hung up.

Emily headed into the bathroom to comb her hair and refresh her makeup. She wanted to appear calm and composed, a total contrast to how she'd been the last time Justin had seen her.

Despite the fact that she expected it, the doorbell still made her jump. Steadying herself, she went to answer the door. She'd have to be careful in how she questioned Justin. If her questions about Monica sounded too accusatory, Justin might feel compelled to get defensive in Monica's behalf.

"Thanks for coming." Emily waved Justin into the apartment and closed the door. "Have a seat."

Justin shed his jacket and sat on one end of the couch; Emily sat at the opposite end. "Thanks for coming," she said again. "This must be a rough time for you."

"Yeah, it's rotten." He slumped against the back of the couch and stretched his legs out. "But Monica . . . don't repeat this, but I'm not *that* surprised at what happened. She had a way of getting under people's skin."

Startled, Emily searched for an appropriate response. "No matter how many people she offended, it's hard to believe someone would kill her."

"Life as an Agatha Christie novel." Justin's opaque expression gave Emily no hint of what he was thinking. "What's on your mind, Emily?"

"For a few days before Monica died, someone was working hard to shake me up." She told him about the picture of Monica and Zach and the picture of Ryan.

"I'm not making any accusations," she added, watching Justin's expression for any signs of anger. "But the only person I could think of who had a reason to be upset with me and drive a wedge between Zach and me was Monica."

"Are you asking me if she sent you those pictures?"

"You were close friends with her. You were with her last Friday at the dance, so I'm assuming you knew what she was up to."

The calm veneer covering his expression cracked for an instant then resealed itself before Emily could see what lay behind it. "Yeah, I knew what she was up to. I knew everything she was up to. She didn't keep secrets from me."

"Did she send the pictures?"

"No. She never would have done that. Tacky tell-all tabloid pictures . . . horror movie threats—no way. That wasn't her style at all. Besides, someone sent *her* a threatening picture."

The hope inside Emily flattened to cold discouragement. "I know. I thought maybe she did it herself. To make it look like I was responsible. Are you sure she never even *hinted* that she was trying to spook me with—"

"That kind of stunt isn't how Monica operates. Operated. With her face, her body, her brains, her charm—" Justin's hands twitched in his lap. "She didn't need any other tools to get the men she wanted."

"Maybe she just didn't tell you . . ." Emily began, but Justin shook his head.

"Uh-uh. She would have told me if she was doing something like that. Would have wanted my help. She trusted me. But she didn't do it. Monica's style is what she pulled at the dance when she was bewitching your fiancé. She wouldn't skulk around pasting horror pictures on people's doors."

Justin scooted along the couch so he sat next to Emily and reached for her hand. His fingers were warm, and Emily wanted to pull away; the iciness of her own fingers would belie her controlled demeanor.

"Emily, look. I understand. I really do, better than anyone. I know how charming Monica could be. And you'd been through so much, losing Ryan Tanner like you did. To see Monica moving in on Zach . . . who *wouldn't* crack under those circumstances?"

Paralysis seized Emily as she stared into Justin's eyes.

"I understand," he said. "I know I was upset with you the other night, but I've had some time to put it in perspective. How can I blame you? Monica was my friend, but I'm not blind to how cruel she could be. She used people. She hurt people. And she was going to steal Zach from you. Once she switched on that charm, there was no escaping it. Zach had been in love with her before. It would have been a snap for her to stir up those feelings again."

Emily's voice emerged as a nearly inaudible rasp. "Justin—"

"I don't blame you. In your position, I think I'd have done the same thing."

"I didn't *do* anything." Emily tried to pull her hand out of Justin's grasp, but he took her other hand and held them both in a tight grip.

"I understand why you need to blame Monica for those stalkerish things that happened. If you want me to say she was responsible, I'll tell people she was. It's not like it will hurt her reputation. She's not here to care. You can trust me. You need to trust someone. The need to talk about this must be eating you alive."

Emily couldn't do anything but stare at him.

"I wouldn't ever betray you. I wouldn't go to the police. What's the point in ruining your life? Monica's dead, and nothing's going to bring her back. She brought her fate on herself. We both know it."

"I didn't—" Emily's lips formed the words, but no sound came.

"Let me help you. You've got to lean on someone or you're going to collapse. I know you didn't mean to hurt Monica. You probably don't even remember doing it. You woke up on the floor of her workroom, and you were injured and she was dead. You never meant for it to happen. You just wanted to get her to leave Zach alone." Justin stroked his thumbs along the backs of her hands. "But you can't reason with Monica."

"I—I never even talked to her. I was at the Tanners' house all evening— they told the police I was there—"

"The guilt must be destroying you. I understand, better than anyone, because I knew Monica better than anyone. Let yourself talk. Let the pain spill out so together we can wipe it away."

Emily closed her eyes. Justin's kindness was a poisonous sham. He thought she was a murderer and that he could wheedle a confession out of her.

For a bleak, pitch-black moment, Emily searched her memory, rooting for any blank spots, any evidence of time lost, any loose fragments broken from memories she'd buried under piles of guilt.

No.

Emily opened her eyes. With an abrupt twist of her hands, she yanked them from Justin's grasp. "I didn't kill Monica."

"Em, don't get panicky. Take a little while to calm down. You need a friend. I'm here for you. We don't have to talk yet. Just sit and relax."

"You're recording this conversation, aren't you? You're hoping I'll say something you can take to the police. Here's something for you: I didn't kill Monica. I didn't send her that picture, and I certainly didn't send the pictures to myself."

"Okay. All right."

"I want you to leave."

"Hey, take it easy. I didn't mean to upset you."

"I'm not upset." Emily spoke coldly, glad her voice wasn't shaking. "I want you to leave."

"I don't think you ought to be alone—"

"Get out, Justin."

"All right, fine. I'm just trying to help." Justin stood. "But if you change your mind, call me." He picked up Emily's cell phone where it sat on the counter and rapidly punched buttons. "There. I put my cell number in your phone so you can call me anytime you need to talk."

Emily sat stonily silent as Justin picked up his jacket and walked out the door.

* * *

"So how come you're here and Emily is at her parents' house?" Nicole faced Zach, her hands on her hips. "You should be together right now."

Zach's hand closed around the doorknob as though he was contemplating shutting the door in her face. Nicole stuck her foot across the threshold, just in case. Zach wouldn't slam the door on her foot, or even push her backward to get her out of the way. He was too much of a gentleman.

"I don't know where she is, Nicole. She's not answering her home or cell phone, and since her mother was there this afternoon, I assume she went back to Morgan Hill with her."

"Have you checked?" Nicole pushed her way into the house. "Have you driven over to her apartment to see if she's there?"

"To check if she's home and avoiding my calls, you mean?"

"That's exactly what I mean."

"No, I haven't been stalking her." Zach closed the door and turned to face her. The circles under his eyes and the pallor of his skin made him look like he had a bad case of the flu. "If she doesn't want to talk to me, I'm not going to force—"

"I'm not talking about stalking. I'm talking about showing Emily that you care enough to come after her."

Zach glared at her. "There's a fine line between helpful and pushy. You've passed it. Why don't you go home?"

"So you can resume being alone and miserable, pacing around your house and wishing Emily would call?"

Zach looked taken aback. Nicole waited for him to deny it and say he'd been busy with lesson plans, but instead he said flatly, "Yeah, if you don't mind, I'd like to get back to that."

Nicole almost laughed. She'd always liked Zach's sense of humor. "How about if we call a truce: you tell me what you know, I tell you what I know, and we figure out the best way to reach out to Emily."

Zach sighed and ran both hands through his hair, leaving it a mess. "Fine. Since I'm clearly not getting rid of you unless I call the police, we might as well talk. Come sit down."

They sat in Zach's tiny, nearly empty living room, a room that always gave Nicole the urge both to offer emergency decorating advice and propose a ballot initiative banning futons.

Zach told her about his visit to Emily's that afternoon, finishing with, "It was obvious she didn't want to talk with me. I understand her being tired, but that wasn't the real reason. She wouldn't even look me in the eye. Her mother said she'd been out with you this afternoon. What's going on?"

Nicole decided candor was the best strategy. "I stopped by Emily's at lunchtime to see how she was doing. When I rang the doorbell, I woke her mother up from a nap. She thought Emily was in her room, but when she checked, Emily was gone. She was very worried—couldn't figure out why Emily would sneak out without at least leaving a note. I said I'd go check to see if Brent had seen her."

"Why Brent?"

"He works from home a lot, so I thought he might be there, and maybe Emily had been going stir-crazy and decided to pop over and say hi." Seeing the sudden tightness in Zach's jaw, Nicole shook her head. "Oh, come *on*, Zach. Tell me you're not jealous of Brent Amherst! He and Emily have never been anything more than friends. And he'd rather climb Mount Everest barefoot than get married anyway."

Zach shrugged irritably. "So he says. But go on."

"Brent was home but didn't know anything. I figured Emily had gone somewhere she didn't want her mom to know about, hoping she could get back before her mom woke up. I talked to Emily last night, and she mentioned how she still didn't know if Monica was responsible for those freaky pictures. It was really bothering her, for obvious reasons. If Monica didn't do it, Emily still has an enemy out there."

Zach's big hands gripped the arms of the chair. "An enemy who killed Monica."

"Yes. Anyway, I tried to think of who Emily might approach for answers and came up with Rochelle Elton, Monica's friend. Brent and I drove over to Rochelle's shoe shop." Speaking steadily, her eyes fixed on Zach's, Nicole reported what she'd witnessed at the shop. The shock and hurt in Zach's expression were painful to see.

"I never would have cheated on Emily. How can she . . . I thought she believed me. That picture—"

"I don't know. But she didn't get any answers from Rochelle. Rochelle was too busy screaming that she was a murderer, then she slapped Emily. Brent and I ended up dragging Emily out of there before things could get worse. It was ugly."

"Rochelle slapped her! Is she all right?"

"Physically."

Zach lowered his face into his hands. His fingertips massaged his forehead.

"You need to talk to her," Nicole said. "You've got to work this out."

Zach lifted his head. "I've been trying," he said tiredly.

"Is that the best you can do? Walk meekly away when she tells you to go, and then make a few phone calls?"

"What do *you* recommend, since you obviously think I'm too much of a loser to handle this on my own?"

"I didn't say you were a loser. I figured you didn't know how upset Emily was this afternoon, so you didn't know how urgent this is. You can't let this fester. If she won't answer her phone, go to her house. If she isn't there, drive to her parents' house. Do whatever it takes to talk to her. You two were made for each other. Don't let the stress of this business with Monica tear you apart. I don't care if you were still drooling over Monica, but you'd better make it look like you weren't."

Zach's neck blotched pink and crimson. "I wasn't drooling over her."

"Good. But what matters now is what Emily thinks. Talk to her and say whatever it takes to convince her you never even looked at Monica after you met her. If it isn't true, lie through your teeth. But make her believe it."

"Lie through my teeth?"

She was on the wrong track, Nicole realized, offending Zach instead of convincing him. "I'm not saying I think you cheated on Emily. I'm trying to make you understand that you've got to get out there and fix this, no matter what it takes."

"And a mouthful of clever words will fix it, huh?"

Zach's sarcasm gave another turn of the crank to the tension inside Nicole. She fought the pressure, fought the urge to leap from her chair, sink her fingernails into Zach's reddened face and vent her pain by inflicting it on him.

"I'm sorry," Zach said curtly. "I know you're trying to help. I'm frustrated because my side of the story doesn't seem to matter to anyone. Monica starts chasing me, and everyone—including Emily and the police—assumes I must have fallen for her."

"The police don't suspect *you,* do they?"

"I don't exactly have an alibi, Nicole."

"Most of the world doesn't have an alibi. Just because you can't prove you were somewhere else isn't any kind of evidence against you."

"Maybe not. But that doesn't stop something like this from trashing reputations and ruining lives."

The anger in his voice unnerved Nicole, and the remote look in his eyes gave her the impression he was talking about more than the situation with Monica. "Zach, you don't have something nasty in your past, do you? Something the police *are* going to jump on?"

"My record is clean, Nicole." Zach rose to his feet. "Thanks for coming over. I know you care about Emily, and I promise you, I would never do anything to hurt her."

Reluctantly accepting her dismissal, Nicole stood. "Go find her and talk to her. She wants to believe in you. She's just very rattled right now."

"I wonder why." Zach opened the front door. "If you hear from Emily before I—" He stopped, his gaze on the porch mailbox.

A piece of white paper was folded over and taped to the mailbox. Not a piece of paper, Nicole realized, as Zach unfolded it. A paper sack, sporting the In-N-Out hamburger logo.

"What the heck—" In the porch light, Zach's face looked as still and gray as concrete.

"What is it?" Nicole plucked it out of his hands. A message was written on the bag in black felt-tip pen, the neat, curvy handwriting a contrast to the harshness of the words.

I belong to Ryan. Stay away from me.

The wind caught the edge of the bag, flapping it in Nicole's hand as she and Zach stood in silence, neither of them willing to say what Nicole knew they were both thinking.

That was Emily's handwriting.

CHAPTER 16

EMILY CLOSED HER EYES, JUSTIN'S deceptively gentle voice still slithering through her mind. To have her hopes rise and then slam so viciously to the ground left her feeling too stunned to move.

She could no longer even pretend to hope that Monica had been the one targeting her. Beneath the surface, hadn't she known all along what Zach and Justin had both told her—that the gruesome pictures weren't Monica's style?

Someone else was targeting her, someone who was alive and unlikely to stop until they'd achieved whatever sick goal they sought.

Her death?

But Monica had received a bloodstained photo of herself—a threat directed at her. Emily had received items meant to upset her, frighten her, and cause trouble in her relationship with Zach, but nothing that seemed to be an immediate threat.

Who would do this to her?

There was always Justin's solution. He thought she'd done these things to herself in a lunatic effort to make herself—a murderer—look like a victim.

At the thud of footsteps ascending the stairs outside her apartment, she stifled a groan. She couldn't think of a single person she wanted to see right now.

The doorbell rang. Maybe she'd ignore it.

Ignore it and stir up even more of a frenzy in the people who are worried about you? She'd already ignored a couple of calls from Zach, one from her mother, and one from Logan Tanner, who had no doubt gotten a report from either Bethany or Brent.

Emily shuffled to the door and pulled it open.

"Hey, kiddo." Brent Amherst's boyish face wore a crooked grin as he extended a bottle of Welch's sparkling grape juice. "Want to spend a few minutes with a listening ear and a friend who doesn't think you're a murderer?"

Emily stepped back, tacitly giving Brent permission to enter. "I take it you saw Justin leaving."

"Yep. Couldn't figure out why you let him through the door."

"I asked him to come," she admitted.

"Why in blazes would you do that?" Brent walked to the cupboard and removed Emily's crystal goblets. "Rochelle wasn't enough for you?"

"Do you think I'm crazy?" The instant she spoke the words, she regretted them, but there was no retracting the question.

Brent turned from where he'd been opening the bottle of Welch's. "Crazy in the sense of making some bad judgment calls because you're under an avalanche of stress? Or crazy in the psychotic lock-you-up sense?"

"The latter."

"Are you worried about what I think of you after that dustup at Rochelle's? Gee, Em, if that's the best crazy you can do, work on it for a while and check with me again later."

Emily smiled, abruptly glad Brent was there. She resumed her place on the couch and wrapped the mohair blanket around her shoulders.

"So why *did* you call Justin?" Brent stood with his back to her while he poured the grape juice. "Boredom?"

Should she tell him? She hadn't told him anything about the pictures, especially the picture of Zach and Monica. Brent wouldn't be able to restrain a smug *"I told you so."*

"Hmm. Long, weighty silence." He screwed the lid back on to the bottle. "In that case, I'll have to guess. You're afraid the police think you killed Monica and are waiting for some last piece of evidence so they can arrest you. You know Justin—like Rochelle—was a good friend of Monica's, and you thought he might have an inkling of what really happened to her, something that might turn police attention away from you. So even though Justin blamed you originally, you thought he might have come to his senses and could help you solve the crime. Am I close?"

Emily sighed. "Yes and no. But that's all you're getting."

"That was some serious bad luck, you being at Monica's shop the night she died." He tossed her a wry, sympathetic smile. "Bet you wish you'd decided to go rock climbing with us that night after all."

"I do, actually." She would have been able to tell Detective Lund that Brent Amherst, Logan Tanner, and a gym full of rock climbers could testify she'd been forty minutes away from Los Coros the night Monica died. *Little decisions. Big regrets.* "Can we talk about something else?"

"We could. But it won't be what either of us is thinking about." He brought her the goblet of sparkling grape juice.

"Thanks." Emily took it. "It's a little embarrassing to have everyone know I'm addicted to this."

Brent rolled his eyes. "Wow, what a vice. So who *do* you think killed Monica?"

"I honestly have no idea. Who do you think killed her?"

"Don't know. Someone who hated her guts, I guess, which leaves it wide open. She was good at grinding hearts into hamburger. Ask Sullivan."

Emily's hand tightened on her goblet. "Unless someone's paying you by the insensitive remark, maybe you could come up with a better example."

"Sorry." Brent settled into Emily's armchair, glass in hand. "But I've been doing a lot of thinking, and it creeps me out to realize it's probably somebody I know who killed her."

"I've been thinking the same thing."

"Chilling, isn't it? We all put on our Sunday best and our Sunday faces, but what are we hiding beneath those sunny masks?" He grinned at her. "What are *you* hiding?"

"Right now, I'm just hiding a headache."

"Just a headache? I doubt it, Emily."

Emily averted her eyes. Brent was right. She was hiding such a pile of fears that trying to conceal them was probably about as effective as hiding a mountain under a Kleenex.

"What are you hiding?" she asked.

"Don't change the subject. Don't you want to vent a little? Might help."

"You sound like my mother."

"Your mother is a smart lady."

"Most of the time." The thought of Dr. Kincaid brought heat to Emily's cheeks.

"Penny for your thoughts?" Brent asked.

"You're way behind the times. I only take Visa or PayPal."

"Seriously, Em." Brent took a large swallow from his goblet. "Unload. You know it'd make you feel better to talk about it."

"I just want everything resolved." Emily kicked off her shoes and tucked her feet underneath her. "I want the police to solve the case, I want the murderer locked away, I want to go on with my life."

Brent looked at her keenly. "Never got to do that last time, did you? That must dice you up, deep down."

Emily sipped from her glass, fighting the tightening in her throat.

"Not that you show it," Brent said. "You keep up a good front. But it goes back to what I said. The Sunday faces. Take Sullivan—you're engaged to marry him, but do you really know what's behind *his* Sunday face?"

"Don't you *dare*."

"Don't get defensive. I'm not accusing Sullivan of anything, but you can't dispute my point. You think you know him, but do you? Be honest. I heard what you said to Rochelle. You're afraid he was cheating on you with Monica."

"Change the subject or leave, Brent. I'm not kidding."

"Interesting. You can't even discuss this without getting panicky."

"He didn't cheat on me." The image of that cursed birthday watch stenciled itself on her brain.

"Nice try. I wouldn't bug you about this, except for one thing. You're my friend. When it comes down to it, you don't know what's going on inside Zach Sullivan. What you *do* know is that he used to be wildly in love with Monica Fife. She dumped him. Then a year later, she comes back, playing with his affections, upsetting his life. Maybe he falls for her again. Maybe he sees her behind your back, but he knows it won't last. He tries to tell her it's over. She threatens to tell you the truth about what he's been doing. He's afraid of losing you. After that stunt she pulled at the dance, he cracks and does the only thing he can think of to shut her mouth and get her out of his life permanently."

The words brought stunning pain, far worse than Rochelle's slap. "I don't know what you're trying to do to me, but that's enough. Go home and keep your crackpot theories to yourself."

"Emily." Brent leaned forward in his chair. "I'm trying to make you open your eyes and look at all the possibilities. I'm not accusing Zach or anyone else. I'm being objective—pointing out it could be *anyone,* and you need to be careful. You've got a murderer somewhere close to you."

"It's *not Zach*."

"Take it easy." His blue eyes were soft behind round glasses. "I'm sorry I upset you."

Emily was too drained to stay angry at him. So Brent thought Zach might have killed Monica. Half the city thought Emily had killed Monica, but that didn't make it true.

Since her engagement, she'd sensed that Brent harbored some animosity toward Zach, though she couldn't think why. It was absurd to think he might be jealous. Brent had never asked her out or shown even a flicker of romantic interest in her. She was just a friend to him, Tricia's little sister.

"Em, I'm really sorry." Brent stood up and went to refill his glass. "I'm just shooting my mouth off. I don't really think Sullivan is guilty."

"I can't believe this is happening. I thought that at last things were . . ." Emily looked away from Brent. What was wrong with her? She didn't want to confide in Brent, expose the guilt-ridden thoughts twining around her heart like barbed wire.

"I'll bet you wish you could rewind time." Brent sat next to her on the couch.

"I used to pray for that," Emily confessed.

"After Tricia?" Brent's tone was matter-of-fact, like he didn't find anything kooky in her praying for supernatural abilities.

"I couldn't see any other way to cope with . . . everything."

"The loss?" Brent asked. "Or the guilt?"

Emily didn't answer.

"Tricia's death wasn't your fault, Emily."

"Yes, it was." The words burst from her throat without her permission.

"You weren't driving the car that killed her."

"I told her to hang those stupid balloons. I was afraid people would miss the driveway in the dark. She was out there because of me." The crack of crystal striking wood made her jump. She'd tried to set her empty glass aside and had knocked it on the edge of the lamp table. Brent took it out of her hand and examined it.

"Not damaged," he said, carefully setting it aside. "Emily, it's normal to wish you could rewind. Who wouldn't wish that? One minute you're madly in love with the man you want to be with forever, sharing your wedding plans with the sister so close to you that you practically share a brain. You'd tried so hard to do everything right, even staying in school to finish your degree when Ryan moved here to start his new job. You thought a brief separation would be well worth it—what's a semester apart balanced against the rest of eternity? You finish school, you come home, everything is bliss—until a month later your sister is dead, your husband-to-be is gone, and your life collapses. I saw you go through all of it, remember? I know how bad it was for you. And now, when you thought you'd started over with Sullivan, everything falls apart again. *Any* sane person would want to rewind, rewind all the way back to when you were planning a future with Ryan Tanner. That's what you really pray for, and I'll bet your hyperactive conscience hates it—hates acknowledging that you're still yearning for Ryan."

"I love Zach," Emily murmured, so emotionally weary that she hardly cared what Brent was saying.

"Okay. Maybe I'd better go. You look exhausted, and I suspect I've worn out my welcome." He brushed his finger along the double-strand pearl bracelet she was wearing. "Nice bracelet. I haven't seen you wear that in a while. Gift from Ryan, wasn't it?"

Emily said nothing.

* * *

"She's not here, Zach. She was here for dinner, but then she . . . left." Carolyn Ramsey sounded tense, and Zach's hopes nose-dived. He'd called the Ramseys hoping to hear that Emily was there, that she'd been there all evening, and hence there was no way she could have been at his door sometime in the last half hour to tape a note to his mailbox.

"She went home?" he asked.

"I assume so. Maybe she went to Nicole's. She—" There was a pause and what sounded like a stuttering intake of breath.

Zach pressed the phone more firmly against his ear. "Carolyn?"

"If you get in touch with her, can you tell her I'm sorry that I . . . no, never mind." Carolyn's voice went wry, but it was edged with pain. "She'd probably be angry at me for confiding in you."

A chilling prickle of adrenaline spread through Zach's bloodstream. "What's wrong?" he asked. "What happened?" Behind him, he heard Nicole rise to her feet and come to stand next to him in an undisguised effort to eavesdrop on both halves of the conversation.

"She was going to stay with us tonight, but we had a . . . disagreement," Carolyn said.

"A disagreement?" Zach tried to imagine Emily arguing with her mother and leaving in a rage. He couldn't picture it any more than he could picture Emily creeping onto his porch and—

"She's not herself, Zach. She's under so much stress, and I made a tactless attempt to—" With a sniffle, Carolyn composed herself. "I tried calling her, but she isn't answering her phone. If you can get in touch with her, will you make sure she's all right? Without mentioning that I asked you to?"

"Absolutely." Zach's gaze drifted to the folded fast-food sack on the counter. "Try not to worry. I'll talk to you soon." He hung up.

Nicole smoothed a strand of blond hair back from her face. Zach had never seen Nicole Gardiner look so worn out, and he felt a flash of guilt at how rude he'd been to her that night.

"She has no idea where Emily is?" Nicole asked.

"No," Zach said. "Emily left Morgan Hill a few hours ago."

"It can't have been Emily who wrote that note." Nicole poked the hamburger sack with a French-tipped nail. "That's the work of the same sicko who left her the picture of Ryan. He copied her handwriting."

"I agree." Zach feigned confidence. "Let's go see if she's at her apartment."

* * *

Emily's car was parked in its reserved slot next to her building, but her apartment was dark, and there was no response to Zach's rap on the door.

"I'll ring the bell." Nicole reached for it, but Zach caught her wrist.

"Don't. It's ten-thirty, the lights are off—she's asleep."

"I doubt it. And if she is, she'll be awake soon if I ring the bell enough times."

"Don't," Zach repeated, though the urge to kick the door down was making his leg muscles cramp. "If we want her to trust us and talk to us, we're not going to make that happen by battering down her door and dragging her out of bed."

Nicole scowled. "Maybe not. But *swear* you'll stop by tomorrow."

"You really don't think much of me, do you?"

Nicole sighed and tucked her hands under her hooded wool cape. "Sorry. I'm worried about her."

"Yeah," Zach said, looking at Emily's closed door. "So am I."

CHAPTER 17

IT WAS REMARKABLE HOW a good night's sleep could shrink things into perspective, and Emily was amazed at how well she'd slept, when nightmares and broken sleep had long since become the norm. With a solid night of rest behind her, she could see far more clearly, and what she saw made her want to crawl under a rock.

What had possessed her yesterday when she'd stomped out of her mother's kitchen like a petulant thirteen-year-old? Just because she didn't want Dr. Kincaid's professional services didn't mean she couldn't have sat in her parents' living room with him, eating cake and talking about inconsequential topics. He wouldn't have pushed her to confide in him or embarrassed her in any way.

What had her mother said to Dr. Kincaid to explain her abrupt departure? The truth as she saw it—that Emily had fled because she was too terrified to even remain in the house with a psychiatrist? If he hadn't thought she was mentally ill before she left, he certainly thought so now, and she couldn't blame him. If he didn't think she was ill, he probably thought she was the most selfish, thoughtless, immature woman he'd ever met.

She'd almost rather have him think she was insane.

Steeling herself, Emily lifted the phone off the hook. It was only six-thirty in the morning, but her parents would be up. She hit speed dial.

"Emily, hello." Carolyn's voice was odd—as though she was dulling her tone, afraid to show too much relief, anger, or emotion of any kind.

Emily jumped in with both feet. "Mom, I am so sorry. I don't know what came over me last night. I shouldn't have gotten angry and stormed out like that."

"Oh, honey." Relief was now naked in her voice. "It's all right."

"The way I acted was *not* all right. You can ground me if you want. I deserve it."

Carolyn gave a tremulous laugh. "I'm sorry for getting angry and snapping at you. It *wasn't* fair of me to invite Brother Kincaid without telling you."

"You should be free to invite whoever you want to your own home. And you ought to be able to count on your adult daughter to show a little maturity."

There was a long pause, and Emily suspected Carolyn was hunting for the right words, fearing the wrong ones might set Emily off again. "I know this is a difficult time for you."

"That doesn't excuse my behavior. I'm sorry for acting childish, and I'm sorry for causing you so much stress."

"Honey, don't worry about it. We're just concerned about you."

"I know that, and I appreciate it." For a moment, Emily teetered on the verge of asking for Dr. Kincaid's number and saying she would apologize to him personally—but she couldn't make herself do it. "I'd better go. I've got to get over to the school and do some catch-up before the day begins. I love you."

"I love you too, honey. And I'm sorry I made you feel like I was setting you up."

"It's fine, Mom. I'm fine. Talk to you soon." Emily disconnected and dialed Zach's number. She wasn't going to talk to him about the watch in the picture—that wasn't a conversation she wanted to have over the phone—but she could arrange a time to meet.

"Emily! How are you?"

"I'm good. I'll be back at work today."

"That's great. So you're feeling okay?" The relief in Zach's voice added another boulder to the weight of guilt on her shoulders.

"I'm fine," she said. "I'm sorry about acting like I didn't have time for you yesterday. It was a lousy day, times ten. And I'm sorry I didn't call you back."

"No problem. I know you were tired." Now Zach sounded like her mother had—cautious, afraid of saying the wrong thing. "Let's get together after work, all right? Five o'clock? We'll do takeout."

"It's a date. Are you coming to my place?"

"Sounds good. I love you."

Do you? "I love you, too." Emily fought down the image that sprang into her head—a bloodstained picture of Ryan Tanner and the caption: *Forget me already?*

* * *

Emily almost expected the principal to stop her at the gates and order her away, but he greeted her with warmth and sympathy. Emily was deeply grateful that the news reports had identified her only as the person who'd found Monica's body, and had said nothing of the animosity between them. Apparently the press hadn't interviewed Justin—or hadn't dared print his accusations, lest Emily call in the lawyers.

It soothed Emily to spend the day dealing with six- and seven-year-olds, all of whom were oblivious to the upheaval in her life and none of whom thought she might do anything crazier than don her striped Cat-in-the-Hat hat during story time. But shadowing her comfortable routine was the knowledge that tonight she would ask Zach about the watch—and his answer might destroy everything she'd thought they had.

The instant her students swarmed out of the classroom, heading for home, Emily opened her laptop and clicked on her journal file where she'd started making notes yesterday. Recording her thoughts would help her prepare mentally for tonight and let her rehearse a calm, nonaccusatory way of telling Zach her concerns.

A few minutes later, a soft knock at the door made her look up. "Come in," she called.

The door opened, and Bethany Tanner stepped into the room.

"Bethany." Surprised, Emily closed her laptop. "How are you?" A look at Bethany's face answered that question. Bethany appeared pale and sleep-deprived, and she moved tentatively toward Emily as though not sure how Emily would react to her presence.

"Here, sit down." Emily lifted her desk chair and brought it to Bethany. "Let me just grab another chair . . ." Emily took one of the chairs she used for parent conferences and sat next to Bethany. "I'd use one of the kids' chairs, but the older I get, the harder it is to sit with my knees in my face."

Bethany gave a feeble chuckle. "You're still a child in my book."

"What can I do for you?"

Bethany fiddled with the strap of her purse. "I'm surprised you're back at work already. I thought you'd be with your parents, but when I called, your mother told me you were determined to get back in your classroom."

"It was only a little conk on the head. If I were an action hero, I'd have jumped to my feet and saved the president, the world, and a convent full of nuns before the closing credits."

"Those shows aren't exactly true to life." Bethany studied the tissue-paper Valentines taped to the wall. "A concussion is a serious thing."

"I'm fine. But are *you* all right? You look tired."

Bethany shifted in her seat, tightened her grip on her purse, and looked squarely at Emily. "Hon, why didn't you tell me the police are treating you as a suspect in Monica Fife's murder? You said that their checking with us about where you were that evening was routine, that they were doing it to everyone."

"I—well, they never said that—who told you I was a suspect?"

"One of Monica's friends came over last night. He said he'd heard we were 'covering for you' the night of the murder, claiming you were at our house all evening." Bethany's tanned face stiffened, but her expression appeared on the verge of cracking like dried mud. "He said it would be on our hands if you killed someone else."

For a sickening moment, Emily feared that Bethany was going to tell her she *hadn't* been there all evening—she'd disappeared from their house without explanation after dinner and had returned later, looking dazed, and now Bethany needed to go tell the police the truth.

"He told us we were insane to protect you," Bethany said, "especially since it couldn't be coincidence that someone connected to you had died again. He kept hinting that you'd had something to do with Tricia's death—and Ryan's disappearance."

"Justin Driscoll," Emily murmured. "It was Justin Driscoll, wasn't it?"

"Yes."

"What did you tell him?" Her voice was small, shrinking in her throat.

"What do you think we told him? We told him you'd been there until eight-thirty, just like we told the police detectives. But Emily, I thought you should know what he's saying, because if he's saying it to us, he's saying it to the police and anyone else who'll listen. Do you have a lawyer, honey?"

Emily shook her head.

"We could recommend someone. Ted's brother was a lawyer and knows—"

"I'll think about it."

Bethany smoothed her denim skirt over her knees. "You have a very appealing classroom," she said, looking around. "You have a knack for using color to create a cheerful atmosphere."

"Thank you," Emily said mechanically, knowing that at the moment, Bethany couldn't care less if the walls were an artistic triumph or bare wallboard.

"Emily . . . Justin said you claimed someone left you a picture of Ryan. A picture covered with blood."

This was the last thing Emily wanted to discuss with Bethany, but there was no denying it. "Yes. Red fingernail polish was used to simulate blood."

"Why didn't you tell me about it?"

"I . . . didn't want to upset you."

"It came with a message accusing you of forgetting him."

"Yes. And I'm sure Justin told you I left the picture for myself or lied about finding it. I didn't."

Bethany hesitated. "Was there anything else to the message or picture? Any clue as to . . . what happened?"

Tingling spread over Emily's skin. She'd been so focused on connecting the picture with Monica Fife and her killer that she hadn't stopped to think that it might be a message from whoever was responsible for Ryan's disappearance. "No. I'm sorry."

"Do you have any idea when or where the picture was taken? That might help us figure out who gave it to you."

"I took the picture," Emily said quietly. "At my parents' house, the day I arrived home from BYU. It was a picture of Ryan holding the welcome sign he'd drawn for me."

Bethany looked intently at Emily, as though she were straining to see in the dark. "Does anyone else have a copy of that picture?"

"I don't know. I never posted it online. If I sent it to anyone, it would have been to Tricia or my grandmother. Or maybe my roommate in Utah. No one who could have had anything to do with this." She didn't want to tell Bethany that the picture had come from her computer.

"Can you check to see if you did send it to someone else and forgot?"

"No. I clean out my e-mail folders every few months. I wouldn't still have a message that old."

"Honey . . . you called me last night, very late."

"Last night?" Puzzled, Emily reviewed what she'd done the previous evening. "We talked on Sunday. Is that what you're thinking of?"

"No. No, it was last night. In the middle of the night, actually."

"The middle of the night?" Emily's confusion thickened. "I went to bed early last night. I was very tired—I was asleep before ten."

"Two o'clock in the morning." Bethany spoke gently. "You don't remember?"

Chills crawled along Emily's nerves. "Why would I call at two in the morning?"

"You—sounded very strange."

"What did I say?"

"You asked to speak to Ryan. When I told you that you knew he wasn't there, you kept repeating that you needed him. I tried to break through to you, but it was like you were . . . I don't know . . . completely out of it. Finally, you hung up."

Emily's heart thudded so violently that it seemed to shake her whole body. "Are you *sure* it was me?"

"Well, you . . . the caller . . . spoke very softly, almost a whisper, so I suppose I couldn't swear it was your voice. But the call came from your home phone number. Was anyone else staying at your apartment last night?"

"No." Emily racked her memory. She didn't even recall waking in the night, let alone getting up and making a call. *I didn't do it. I couldn't possibly have called her and then forgotten it. And why would I ask about Ryan, when—*

Emily touched the pearl bracelet she wore under her sleeve. She'd gone to bed thinking about Ryan. She'd been worried that she'd dream about him. Had she been sleepwalking? She'd never sleepwalked in her life. And to pick up the phone, dial a number, and make incoherent requests to speak to a man who'd been gone for three years was far more bizarre than going for a nighttime stroll.

"Emily." Bethany squeezed her hand. "I think everything that's happened to you lately—getting engaged, finding poor Monica's body, having the police ask you a bunch of questions, not to mention hitting your head—it's been too much for you. You need to take some time off and recover."

Emily pulled her hand away, not wanting Bethany to feel either her trembling or the cold sweat breaking out on her skin. "When you talked to my mother, did you tell her about the call?"

"Sweetheart, we're both worried about you."

She could imagine the conversation between Bethany and Carolyn as they discussed this evidence of her disintegrating sanity. Carolyn must be in a panic right now. Had she already called Dr. Kincaid to apprise him of this new development?

But I didn't make the call. I'd remember—I'm sure I'd remember . . .

But if she hadn't made the call, someone else had made it from *her* phone. Did she really think someone had broken into her apartment and used her phone to torment Bethany Tanner and make her think Emily was losing her mind?

And how would an intruder have gotten in? The deadbolt had been locked when Emily rose in the morning, and the anti-theft bar had been nestled in the track of the sliding door. Her windows were locked. She'd checked everything before she went to bed and again before leaving for work that morning.

"But you're not sure it was my voice," Emily said. "You're not sure."

"Hon . . . did you and Ryan have some kind of inside joke about 'Ryanair'?"

Emily jerked like someone had splashed boiling water down her neck. "Why do you ask?" It was an idiotic question, and she knew the answer before Bethany gave it.

"The . . . caller . . . last night used it a couple of times as a nickname for Ryan. I'd never heard you call him that, but I wondered . . ."

Emily could barely breathe. She'd never—how could anyone have known—

"You don't have to tell me if you don't want to," Bethany said.

"It's all right." What was the point in hiding it? Obviously the expression on her face had already told Bethany that the name meant something. "Ryanair is an Irish airline. When Ryan got home from that art study program in Ireland, I used to tease him that I was so glad to have him home that I wasn't just walking on air, I was walking on Ryanair . . . stupid little joke. I called him that sometimes, but never . . ."

"Never in public?" Bethany finished.

Emily nodded. Never where anyone else could have overheard her and, several years later, used this name in a 2:00 AM phone call. And Ryan wouldn't have told anyone. He was too private a person to joke with friends about an affectionate nickname his then-girlfriend had given him.

Emily wanted to slide off her chair, curl up on the floor, and sink into numbing sleep.

"Will you take some time off?" Bethany asked. "If you don't want to be an hour away from Zachary at your parents' house, you're welcome to stay with us. I've got a very comfortable guest room."

"Thank you. I just . . . need a little time to think about what to do."

"I understand." Bethany rose to her feet. "Take care, honey. I'll call you tomorrow."

Emily nodded without looking at Bethany.

* * *

At home, Emily examined every lock and checked both doors for any scratches or scrapes that might indicate tampering. There was nothing to indicate that anyone had broken into her apartment last night.

Which meant she'd probably made the call herself. No one else would have used that nickname.

Emily dreaded the call she knew was coming—her mother wanting to discuss Bethany's report. But the phone remained silent, which perversely made her feel worse. If Carolyn hadn't called, it was because she feared Emily's reaction. Emily knew she should place the call herself but couldn't bring herself to do it.

Coward.

At five o'clock, the doorbell rang. Zach. What would she say to him? Her thoughts were an incoherent mess. She twisted the deadbolt and pulled the door open.

"Hey." Zach smiled at her, but it was a brief smile that didn't reduce the concern in his eyes. "How was work?"

Emily started to say it was all right, but to her horror, tears came instead of words—tears that flooded her eyes so rapidly that there was no hope of either hiding or stanching them.

"Emily." Zach shut the door behind him and took her into his arms. She wanted to say something humorous, dismissing the tears even as they fell, but all she could do was cry.

"Emily." His lips touched her hair, her cheeks, her eyelids. "Let me help you."

How could she tell him what had happened—that she was still so obsessed with Ryan that she'd called his mother in the middle of the night and begged to talk to a dead man? Under her sleeve, the pearl bracelet seemed to sear her wrist.

Zach led her to the couch. He took the folded mohair blanket, draped it around Emily, and drew her close to him. "Let me help you. Tell me what's wrong."

She told him. It came in a flood, as unstoppable as the tears—her fears that Detective Lund was on the verge of arresting her, her frantic quest to find out if Monica was responsible for the pictures, the disastrous meetings with Rochelle and Justin, her mother's efforts to push her into meeting with Dr. Kincaid, Bethany Tanner's visit and the nightmarish phone call Emily had allegedly made. And the picture, the picture of Zach and Monica with Zach wearing the watch Emily had given him only three months earlier.

Through the rush of tears and anguished confession, Zach remained calm, his hands gentle, smoothing her hair back from her face, wiping away her tears.

"First, let's deal with the issue of that cursed picture," he said. "Why didn't you ask me about the watch? Why did you go to Rochelle instead?"

"I'm sorry." She felt weak, limp in Zach's arms. "I thought if I could verify . . . if I didn't have to confront you, to let you know I doubted . . . if Rochelle could have just confirmed that . . ."

"Why are you so afraid to talk to me? Am I a monster?"

"No. I just . . . I'm just . . . so afraid of losing you." The tears started again, dripping steadily down her cheeks.

Zach traced his fingers over her face, wiping away the tears. "You couldn't lose me if you tried. And tomorrow, we're going to the police station. I don't care what it takes, but we'll get a look at that picture, examine it pixel by pixel if we have to. An examination will show that someone doctored the photo, because, Emily, that picture was *not* taken after I started dating you. I would never have cheated on you."

"I'm sorry . . . sorry for doubting . . ."

"Don't apologize. Someone is going to a lot of effort to try to tear us apart, but they won't win. Tomorrow we'll get a look at that picture if we have to stay there all day and stage a hunger strike in the police department lobby."

Emily giggled, then wondered if she sounded punch drunk.

"About the phone call to Ryan's mother." Zach played with her hair, running his fingers the length of the strands. "There's something I need to show you. Please understand that I'm not making any judgments on it yet. I want you to look at it and tell me what you think."

Zach slid his hand into his jacket pocket and withdrew what looked like a folded white paper sack. "This was taped to my mailbox. I found it at about ten o'clock last night." He handed it to Emily.

She unfolded it and read the words written in her handwriting on an In-N-Out sack.

I belong to Ryan. Stay away from me.

Fear penetrated Emily's chest like a knife. She sat clutching the sack until Zach loosened her fingers and took it back.

"Did you leave me that note?" he asked simply.

"I . . . I don't think I did. I don't remember doing it." It was all she could do to force her lips to shape words. "It looks like my handwriting, but my handwriting would probably be easy to copy . . . first-grade teacher . . . you have to write neatly or the kids can't read it . . ."

"Any idea why it would be written on a hamburger sack? That's a strange way to leave a note."

Her head buzzed and her limbs felt heavy and numb. She knew exactly why it was written on an In-N-Out sack, and, like the nickname, it was something only she or Ryan would have known. She'd never told anyone else about the drawing on the sack, and she was sure Ryan hadn't either; he'd been so embarrassed.

But—

"I couldn't have left it. It's not possible. I couldn't do something like that and forget it." She could *almost* believe she'd made the phone call while half asleep, propelled by dreams. But to leave the note for Zach, she would have needed to go get the sack, write the note, drive to his house, and tape it to the mailbox—all before ten o'clock at night. Sleepwalking might explain the call, but not the note.

"If I had done it, there would have had to be *time* for it," Emily said. "Blank spots in my memories of yesterday. There aren't any." She wondered if Zach would notice that she'd bypassed the question about why the note was written on an In-N-Out sack. "I'm not crazy. And I'm not obsessed with Ryan." Never had words sounded so hollow. Why should she expect Zach to believe her?

She didn't even believe herself.

If she could blot out her memories of making the phone call to Bethany and the entire process of leaving the note taped to Zach's mailbox, what else was she capable of forgetting? Dripping red fingernail polish on a picture of Ryan and hanging it on her doorknob? Leaving a blood-spattered picture for Monica?

Murdering Monica?

CHAPTER 18

"Okay." Zach slid the folded sack back into his pocket. "Why don't I order us something to eat? A blood-sugar boost might help us sort this out."

Emily fought to rally her concentration. She needed to be alone for a few minutes to regain control of herself. With Zach's concerned gaze on her, her panic bubbled up until overflow was imminent. She didn't want to break down again. She needed to think. "Would you mind running to Jamba Juice? I need a smoothie. Get me anything—you can't go wrong there. Pick up some sandwiches too."

From the frown that creased Zach's forehead, it was obvious he wasn't fooled by her casual tone. "Are you sure you don't want me to call out for something?"

"I'm sure." Fake smile. "Besides, I need a few minutes to wash my face and comb my hair so I can feel human again."

"Okay." Zach kissed her on the cheek and stood up. "Back in a few minutes."

As soon as Zach was gone, Emily splashed water on her face and yanked a brush through her messy hair. Without bothering to look in the mirror to see if her efforts had helped, she returned to the living room and took her laptop out of her bag. Right now everything was scrambled in her mind, but if she could organize the facts, she'd be able to see answers beyond the knee-jerk assumptions—either she was losing her mind or Ryan had lost his mind three years ago.

She wrote rapidly, but this time, writing her thoughts down didn't seem to help, and finally she slapped the laptop shut. Zach would be back soon. He would hurry, not wanting to leave her alone for too long.

She *hadn't* sent herself the picture of Zach and Monica. Beyond that, she wasn't sure of anything.

Was she crazy? If everyone else thought she was, was it likely they were all wrong and she was right? How could you judge your own sanity? Didn't insanity imply the inability to rationally evaluate behavior?

"Calm down," she whispered. "Get control of yourself. You're not crazy. You don't forget things. You don't have blackouts or spells of amnesia."

She needed to unwind, needed the comfort of someone generous, good-humored, and practical—someone who knew her better than anyone and whose laughter and reassurance would shrink her anxiety until she could handle it. She needed Tricia.

Emily walked to the bookshelf and reached for the daisy photo album. As she slid it off the shelf, a piece of fabric followed, trailing along behind the book, its corner snagged between the album pages.

Bewildered, Emily tugged the fabric loose. It was a scarf, a piece of filmy green fabric stamped with a pattern of golden flames springing from small white candles. This was one of Monica's Amber Flame scarves.

Emily dropped the photo album and seized both ends of the scarf, spreading it out in front of her eyes. The fabric had been rolled, twisted, and stretched—it was torn in one spot and bunched and wrinkled in others. Splotches of reddish-brown stained the green.

Blood. Blood from the gash on Monica's head, dripping down—

Monica's scarf—Monica's blank, bulging eyes, a scarf digging into her throat—had Emily taken the scarf after . . .

Her own hands, grabbing Monica's scarf, twisting it, a rope of silk sinking into Monica's milky skin . . .

Emily dropped the scarf and leapt back from it. It lay on the carpet, a streak of green and brown. Evidence. The last evidence Detective Lund needed to arrest her, the evidence a jury needed to convict her.

Hide it. Destroy it.

She couldn't. She couldn't even touch it. She scrubbed her hands on her thighs. Her palms must be speckled with flecks of Monica's blood. Tricia's photo album lay on the floor, wildly cheerful, dotted with daisies.

Screams clawed at her throat, fighting to escape. In the back of her mind she could hear Carolyn urging her to talk to a psychiatrist and her own protests that she was fine, strong, perfectly able to cope . . .

A light knock at the door made her whirl around as Zach swung the door open.

"Hi. I got you a roast beef and—" He stopped. "Em—"

A welter of emotions surged in Emily's brain. She tried again to make herself move toward the scarf, pick it up, hide it. But what good would it do? If she'd killed Monica, she needed to pay.

Zach set the smoothies and bag of sandwiches on the counter and came to her. "What is it?"

Emily stared at the scarf, amazed that Zach hadn't noticed it. To her, it seemed to emit a deadly brightness that made everything else in the room dim by comparison.

"Emily." Zach took her face in his hands and tilted it upward so she was looking him in the eyes. "Listen to me. You're going to lie down, and I'm going to call your doctor. You're sick. You've been pushing yourself too hard—"

"No." To Emily's surprise, the word came with a brittle snippet of laughter. "No, don't call the doctor. Call Detective Lund."

* * *

"You didn't kill Monica." Zach's voice was rock steady as he dropped the scarf into a paper lunch sack. "You're not crazy, but someone would like you to think you are. Someone who'd like you to get blamed for Monica's murder."

"I have to turn that scarf over to the police. And Detective Lund is never going to believe I'm not the one who hid it. Or the one who used it." She felt strangely calm now, like she'd expended her quota of hysteria for the evening, and the only emotion left to her was bleak determination.

"She'll believe you, because she's going to find the person who's really responsible," Zach said. "Let's work through this. How many people know about that photo album?"

"Quite a few people. We had it displayed at Tricia's funeral."

"How many people know that you use it to help you cope when you're under stress?"

The question brought Emily up short. "I'm not sure. Why?"

"Whoever hid that scarf meant for you to find it when you were already at the end of your rope. Why else would they hide it behind the album instead of somewhere more obvious?"

Maybe I hid it there. Emily couldn't help groping through her mind for any memory of unwinding the scarf from Monica's lifeless body, carrying it home, and stuffing it behind the album. "I don't know exactly who I've told. My mother knows, of course, and Bethany Tanner . . . oh, no. This is no good at all. Lots of people know. I mentioned it in a Relief Society lesson once. The topic was on keeping family histories, and I talked about what a comfort the album was to me. But Zach, I can't imagine that—"

"Okay, word could have spread to anyone." Zach started to roll the bag shut, but Emily held up her hand.

"Hold on. I have something else." She retrieved the tube of fake blood from her bedroom and added it to the sack. "Give me the note you showed me."

Zach slowly reached into his pocket. "Are you sure you want to—"

"Put it in the sack, please. I'm going to call Lund right now. If I wait, I'll lose my nerve."

Zach dropped the note into the bag. "Everything's going to be fine," he said. "She'll figure out what really happened."

Emily appreciated his confident words, but they didn't match the fear in his eyes. He had no idea what would happen when Emily handed this evidence to Lund, but she suspected that, like her, he was picturing an ending that included the bang of a gavel and a sentence for murder.

* * *

Detective Lund didn't answer her office phone, but apparently she did check her messages frequently, because within half an hour, she returned Emily's call and asked her to come to the police department.

Zach and Emily had barely sat down in the lobby when Detective Lund emerged from the back and told Emily to come with her. She left Zach flipping aimlessly through the local paper he'd picked up from the table next to him.

"How are you feeling, Miss Ramsey?" Lund was cool and formal, as always.

"Fine," Emily said, which was not nearly as complete a lie as it would have been an hour ago. Taking the decisive step of going to the police had cleared much of the panic from her brain and left her ashamed of her self-doubt.

She didn't remember making the call to Bethany, leaving the note for Zach, or hiding the scarf because she hadn't done any of it. Someone was playing stalker games with her, and it was Lund's job to figure out who.

Lund led her to a room with a small round table and a couple of chairs. She offered Emily coffee, which Emily refused, and water, which she accepted.

A recorder lay on the table, and as Lund sat down, she pressed the button to switch it on. Emily had the fleeting, irrelevant thought that she'd always hated the way her voice sounded on tape.

Emily tipped the contents of the bag onto the table. As calmly as she could, she told Lund everything that had happened over the past couple of days, starting with finding the fake blood and culminating with finding the scarf. "Calm" in this instance meant that her voice was tight, her hands shook, and her cheeks burned, but at least she could speak coherently.

Lund prodded the bloodstained scarf with the end of her pen. "You say this scarf is one Miss Fife owned?"

"She had a lot of scarves with the Amber Flame's logo on them. She sold them in her shop and sometimes used them as giveaways. I couldn't swear that this scarf is one Monica wore personally, but it is an Amber Flame scarf."

Lund studied her. "Why the hamburger sack, Miss Ramsey?"

Emily tried not to show her discomfiture at how quickly Lund had zeroed in on this.

"I didn't write the note," she said.

"I didn't say you did. But a fast-food bag is not the usual paper for a note. I doubt the writer used it because he or she couldn't find a piece of writing paper. The sack has some significance. What is it?"

Emily swallowed. "When Ryan Tanner and I first started dating, we picked up lunch at In-N-Out after a matinee and took our burgers to a park. I spilled a little chocolate shake on my shirt and went to the restroom to wash it off. On the way back to our picnic table, I ran into an old friend, and it took me a few minutes to get back to Ryan. While I was gone, he occupied himself by doodling on the sack."

"Doodling?"

"Ryan was an artist and a chronic doodler—he always had a pen handy. He folded up the sack, and I didn't see what he'd been drawing, but when we went to throw our trash away, the sack fell to the ground. I picked it up and was curious to see what he'd been drawing, so I unfolded it. It turned out to be a cartoon sketch of the two of us, with him on one knee, offering me a diamond ring." She attempted a smile, hoping Lund's expression would soften. It didn't.

"He was very embarrassed," Emily continued. "This was maybe our second date, and he'd never meant for me to see the picture."

"Who did you tell about this incident?"

Emily dropped her gaze to the recorder; it was easier than looking Lund in the eyes. "Nobody."

"Do you know if he told anyone?"

"I don't know." Technically, it was true—she didn't *know*—but she was almost positive Ryan would have kept it to himself. "I didn't leave Zach that note. Yes, it looks like my handwriting, but let me give you a handwriting sample. I'm sure if an expert compares the two, they won't match."

Lund tore a page out of her notebook and passed it to Emily along with a pen. Emily copied the message written on the hamburger sack and passed the paper and pen back to Lund, not sure how good of a sample she'd given with her hand trembling.

"So to the best of your knowledge, both the phone call to Mrs. Tanner and the note left for Zachary Sullivan contained information shared only between you and Ryan Tanner."

"I . . . thought so, but . . . someone must have found out . . ." It sounded so feeble that Emily let her voice trail off. With Ryan gone, there was only one likely culprit, and that was Emily. Lund couldn't possibly think that Ryan was back. Emily couldn't even begin to believe that Ryan had somehow reappeared—a psychotically cruel Ryan bent on tormenting her. *And killing Monica?* Why would he kill Monica?

Not even Bethany—as determined as she was to believe Ryan was still alive—had suggested he might be involved in any of this.

"Do you have any idea who would want to cause trouble for you?" Lund asked.

"No. I don't have any enemies—not that I know of. But if Monica Fife was the real target, the culprit wouldn't necessarily need to have a grudge against me. Maybe he or she just wants a convenient person to get blamed for Monica's death."

"If someone simply wanted to frame you for the murder of Monica Fife, why would they plant evidence for *you* to find, rather than dropping an anonymous tip to the police? The fake blood, the scarf—the perpetrator couldn't know you'd bring these things to me."

"I . . . guess none of this makes much sense. I have no idea who would do this to me, or what they want."

"Miss Ramsey, would you be willing to provide a blood sample?"

Did Lund think she was drunk or on drugs? She was probably wondering why anyone in her right mind would walk into the police department to surrender evidence that might mark her as a murderer. "Of course I'd be willing."

Lund scrutinized her. Under the table, Emily clenched her hands together and tried to look composed. She doubted she was achieving it. There was too much speculation—condemnation?—in Lund's gaze. "According to the coroner's report, Monica Fife died between six-thirty and seven-thirty last Saturday night," Lund said.

These matter-of-fact words sent a burst of adrenaline through Emily's bloodstream. She'd been at the Tanners from five o'clock until eight-thirty.

"Thank you." It was the wrong thing to say, but relief and gratitude swept the words out of her mouth before she could censor them. She *couldn't* have killed Monica, and Detective Lund knew it. Did Justin know

about the time of death, and that's why he'd gone to Bethany, hounding her to retract her story about where Emily had been during the critical time?

I didn't kill her. Fears she hadn't even wanted to admit harboring broke free and floated away. *I didn't kill her.*

Lund said nothing, but knowledge glinted in her eyes. Emily had the feeling Lund knew very well that Emily's relief wasn't exclusively inspired by the fact that she wasn't going to be arrested. Had Lund sensed her fears? If she had, she must think Emily was insane, but Emily was too relieved to care.

Slightly giddy, she told Lund about the new watch Zach was wearing in the picture of Zach and Monica and her opinion that the picture had been doctored to make it appear current.

"I'll have an expert look at it," Lund said. "I'll notify you if we find anything."

"Thank you." Emily knew Lund was too shrewd not to see through Emily's pretense that she'd never doubted Zach, but at least she didn't say so.

"Call me immediately if you think of anything—or find anything—that might be relevant," Lund added.

"I will." It would be easy to do that now. Why had she ever hesitated?

Lund watched Emily in silence, her gaze thoughtful. The interview seemed to be over, yet Lund did not turn off the recorder or rise to her feet. Emily shifted in her seat. Was she supposed to say something to indicate that she had no more information to give?

"Miss Ramsey." Lund's tone was kinder. Almost gentle. "Have you ever experienced a period of time—even very brief—where you lost awareness or couldn't account for your activities?"

Jolted, Emily looked down at her hands, her gaze drawn, as always, to the diamond ring on her finger. "Never. Not really."

"Not really?"

"I . . . right after Ryan disappeared and my sister died, there were days when everything blurred together, and I couldn't quite remember everything I was doing or where I was supposed to be, but that was nothing like . . . it wasn't blackouts, it was . . . more exhaustion, I guess. Fogginess."

"Did you ever see a doctor?"

"No," Emily admitted. "No, I didn't."

CHAPTER 19

"TOLD YOU THEY'D SORT IT out." Zach's tangible relief seemed to warm the chilly evening as Emily and he drove away from the police department. "You're in the clear. And once Lund's people take a good look at that picture, they'll nail that watch as an added element."

"I don't need photographic proof in order to believe you."

"I appreciate that. But all the same, I want the proof."

Emily leaned against the headrest. She wished she could feel as wholly relieved as she'd felt in the instant she realized she was no longer a suspect in Monica's murder, but already her anxiety was rising.

In reporting to Zach on her conversation with Lund, she'd skipped mentioning that Lund likely thought she was responsible for the Ryan-related incidents. Zach didn't ask about that angle, and at first Emily was glad, but as the minutes passed and Zach still didn't mention it, she began to feel worse. If he didn't ask Lund's opinion on the phone call and the note, was it because he harbored the same suspicion Lund did—that Emily was the one responsible?

It was painfully likely.

"Where are we going?" Emily asked, realizing Zach wasn't heading to either his house or her apartment.

"Home Depot," he said. "We're buying a new lock for your front door. There are no signs of forced entry on any of your doors or windows. Whoever hid that scarf might have had a key."

Emily shuddered at the thought. "I ought to check with the rental office before changing any locks."

"No. I don't want this lock installed by anyone but me. I don't want any copies of keys hanging in your manager's office. I don't want any handyman having access to your place. When all this is settled and Monica's killer is in prison, then we can deal with the rental office."

He was right, Emily conceded. She'd feel a lot better knowing that no one else could possibly have the key to her apartment.

Zach selected the strongest, highest quality deadbolt on the shelf. They stopped briefly at Zach's house so he could collect his tools then headed to Emily's apartment.

Emily opened the lid on one of the smoothies they'd abandoned on the counter. "While you do the handyman thing, I'm going to go replace these melted smoothies."

"Don't bother." Zach flipped open his toolbox. "I don't mind drinking it warm. Still tastes good."

"It's not the same," Emily said lightly. "It's a texture thing."

"Let me do it, then."

"No, get going on the lock. I'll be back soon."

"Em, you really ought to take it easy. You've had a rough night."

"All the more reason I need a fresh smoothie. See you in a few minutes." Emily picked up her purse, gave Zach a quick kiss, and headed out the door.

In truth, she couldn't have cared less about the state of the smoothies, but the simple act of going to Jamba Juice would help reinforce the notion that she was all right, she was functional, she was sane. Intellectually, she knew it was ridiculous, but she still wanted to do it.

Damping down the memory of Lund's probing gaze, she hit the button to unlock her car.

"Emily."

Emily turned. Rochelle Elton was standing on the sidewalk a few feet away.

"Obviously, you're going somewhere, but do you have a minute to talk?" Rochelle's voice was pitched higher than usual, and she was gripping a large leather handbag like she anticipated using it as a weapon.

"I have a minute," Emily said. "But are you planning to listen to me or just lob accusations?"

Rochelle licked her lips and edged closer to Emily. "I owe you an apology. I said some things yesterday that were unfair."

"Unfair?"

"I had no right to accuse you like I did." In an ankle-length trench coat, petite Rochelle looked tiny and almost childlike. "I was feeling so awful about Monica, and I wanted someone to blame. But I had no evidence that you . . . what I'm trying to say is I'm sorry. I lost my mind for a minute. I can't believe I said that about you and your sister and Ryan Tanner. I never really thought that you . . . And I'm sorry about—" Rochelle swished her hand through the air, miming a slap. "I don't know what came over me. I've never struck anyone in my life."

"Did you really change your mind about me, or did you come to apologize because you're afraid I'll file charges?"

"I'm trying to say I never made *up* my mind. Look . . . can we go up to your apartment? I don't want to have this conversation standing out here where anyone could walk past."

"Let's sit in my car." Emily preferred not to talk with Rochelle in front of Zach. There was no telling what Rochelle would say.

When they were settled in the car, Emily turned the key in the ignition and switched on the heat.

"For a couple of days after Monica's murder, I couldn't even think straight," Rochelle began. "And I knew you'd been there that night and that you had a reason to hate her. But when Justin Driscoll came to talk with me last night, it finally hit me that you weren't the only one who had a motive. And it takes a lot more than a motive to turn someone into a killer. I don't think you're that kind of person."

"I'm not. And the police have determined that Monica died long before I set foot on the scene. I have an alibi for the time of death."

"I'm glad." The rigidity of Rochelle's posture relaxed somewhat. "Emily, Zach wasn't seeing Monica behind your back. I'm sure of that. Monica wasn't good at keeping secrets. She liked to share her triumphs. She didn't start chasing Zach until you two got engaged. And as far as I know, Zach never did anything to encourage her."

"Thank you," Emily said, more relieved than she wanted to admit to herself.

"And about the picture you told me about—the picture of Ryan Tanner. Monica *never* would have done that to you—the whole idea would have given her the creeps. She was totally squeamish about gruesome stuff. Didn't even like Halloween decorations."

"You . . . mentioned Justin Driscoll. Do you think there's any chance—"

"I don't know. I'm trying not to jump to conclusions like I did with you. But I think he was in love with Monica. You should have seen his face—we were miniature golfing one night, the three of us, when Monica first started talking about how she'd been an idiot to give Zach up and wanted him back, and he was the guy she was going to marry. Justin was laughing and teasing her, but every now and then when he thought no one was looking at him—his *eyes* . . ." Rochelle shuddered.

"He thinks I killed Monica. I talked to him the other day and—" Absently, Emily played with the *World's Best Teacher* key ring dangling from the ignition. "He was talking to me like I was a lunatic, trying to coax me into confessing. And he talked to the Tanners—I was with them the evening

Monica died—and tried to get them to retract their statement of how long I'd been there."

"He's probably hoping the police will keep looking everywhere but at him. I think—well, there were some mangled roses in the trash at Monica's shop on the evening that she died. She called me that afternoon, kind of hyper-upset—talking really fast, saying I wouldn't believe what had happened, and would I come see her when I had a chance. I came over after closing time, but she wasn't in the front of her shop, and when I called her name, she didn't answer. I'm afraid she was . . . already dead."

"Did you . . . look around at all?"

"No. I got distracted by a phone call and left . . . I wasn't even paying attention . . . Maybe her killer had just left. Maybe if I'd been alert, I would have noticed something . . ."

"Did you mention Justin to the police?"

"Of course, but they must not have anything on him yet. I wish I'd noticed something—something they could use. I feel completely useless."

"It helps me to write things down," Emily said. "Maybe you could make a list of everything that happened that night—everything you saw—even the normal things. Seeing it in black and white might help you pinpoint something you didn't think was significant at first."

"I didn't think of that. I'm not much of a writer or list-maker. But you're right. That might make it easier. I'll try it. I'll go over everything minute by minute. Maybe I'll notice something I didn't before."

Emily hesitated, debating with herself, then plunged in. Why not confide in Rochelle? At worst she'd have one more person who thought she was a kook, and how much difference could that make?

"Someone's still targeting me." Emily told her about the phone call, the note, and the bloodied scarf.

Rochelle's eyes widened. "How awful! At least the scarf's a fake. Monica was strangled with a scarf, but it was that emerald-green one she—" Her voice caught. "The one she always wore with her white wool jacket. The police asked me if I could identify it as hers."

Mingled relief and anger filled Emily—relief that the scarf in her apartment had been nothing more than a prop meant to rattle her and anger that Detective Lund hadn't told her that when she brought the scarf in. Why was Lund so cagey? *Because she thinks you're a nutcase, that's why.*

"Do you have any idea who might have a grudge against me?" Emily asked. "I can't make sense of this. If the person who killed Monica is the person targeting me, what does Ryan Tanner have to do with anything?"

Rochelle frowned, tugging at a strand of dark hair that had escaped from her ponytail. "What exactly did the picture of Ryan look like? Was there a message with it or anything?"

"It was a print of a photo I took the day I moved back here after finishing school. Ryan was holding a sign that said, 'Welcome, Emily.'"

"Oh, yeah," Rochelle said. "I remember Monica saying something about how you guys spent a few months apart so he could start his new job and you could finish school. She was amazed you could stand being separated."

"Did Monica know Ryan well?"

"Yeah, from church, I think. Aren't you all members of the same church?"

"Yes." She knew from Bethany Tanner that Monica's mother and Monica had moved into another ward in the stake when Monica was a child. Monica's mother had now moved back east to be near her elderly parents. "Did Monica and Ryan ever date?"

"I think they went to a couple of high school dances together—prom, homecoming, that kind of thing. Monica told me he was too quiet, not her type. Emily, you don't think he—while you were off at college—I promise you, they never—"

"I'm sorry." Emily didn't bother to deny Rochelle's accurate reading of her expression. "You must think I'm incredibly paranoid."

"No. I think you're having a tough time, and between the creepy stuff with Ryan and what happened to Monica, of course you're wondering if there's a link. But as far as I know, there was none. You . . . don't think Ryan's back, do you? That he's the one doing these things?"

Emily remained silent for a moment, waiting for solidly rational thoughts to settle and baseless speculation to scatter on the wind. "No. Everything that's happened is so completely opposite of what he was. Ryan is dead. Anyway, you were asking about the picture. Whoever left it used drips of red fingernail polish on the photo to mimic blood on Ryan's face and shirt then stuck the bottle of polish in my purse to make it look like I'd done it myself. The message written on the bottom of the picture was 'Forget me already?'"

"Ouch. I assume you gave the picture to the police?"

"I was so rattled that night, I wasn't thinking straight. I gave it to Nicole Gardiner and told her to get rid of it for me. Nicole and I both thought Monica was the one responsible for it."

"She wasn't."

"I know that now. But at the time, I wanted to talk to Monica myself, not involve the police. Stupid on all counts, I know. I asked Nicole later if she still had the picture so I could give it to Detective Lund, but unfortunately, she'd already destroyed it and tossed the bottle of nail polish."

"Too bad. I can't think of anyone who would . . . Were you dating anyone before Zach? I mean, after Ryan."

"No. Well, I went out a couple of times with a couple of different guys. Nicole was hounding me to get on with my life, so she kept trying to set me up. But I never got involved enough with anyone that they'd want to stalk me."

"You never know. Sometimes the nuts look completely normal. Just ask Zach."

"What do you mean?"

Rochelle shrugged. "That girl in Sacramento, the student."

"I don't know much about that situation." Emily didn't like admitting her ignorance, but she didn't want to miss the chance to learn what Rochelle knew. "He mentioned that a student gave him trouble but didn't give me any details."

"Oh." Rochelle seemed disconcerted. "Well—I'm sure it's not his favorite thing to talk about."

"What happened?"

"You probably ought to—"

"Don't tell me to go ask Zach. I will, but first I want to hear what you know." Realizing how curt she sounded, Emily summoned a brief smile. "Sorry. I'm low on patience these days."

"Go figure. Well, I can't vouch for accuracy, because this is all second-hand. I heard it from Monica. One of Zach's students showed up at home all bruised up. She told her parents that Zach had tried to seduce her, and when she refused him, he got furious and said no scrawny little student was going to make a fool of him. He slapped her around and laughed when she said she'd tell the police. He said no one would believe her."

Emily must have looked even more horror-stricken than she realized, because Rochelle paused and said, "Are you sure you want to hear this?"

"Go on."

"Well, her parents went to the police and the school administration. Next thing you know, Zach's got police officers on his doorstep. He came within a hairsbreadth of getting arrested, but in the end, the girl's story didn't hold water. Zach's reputation was above reproach—he was always super careful to follow policy guidelines—not meeting with a student alone without his classroom door open, that kind of thing. This girl couldn't produce any witnesses, and she started getting her story mixed up. Plus, it turns out that she was flunking Zach's class, and she'd begged him to raise her grade, saying an F would ruin her chance at a scholarship. Zach had refused. Eventually a witness came forward to tell the police they'd overheard her saying she'd get revenge on him. Zach was cleared. But you know how things work in the real world—even though he was officially cleared, that didn't kill all the rumors. There were still people at the high school who thought he was guilty and parents who wanted to transfer kids out of his class. That's why he left Sacramento. He wanted to make a new start, and when a position came open in Los Coros, he jumped at it."

Emily was speechless. To endure those accusations must have been agony for Zach. No wonder he'd wanted to get away. But why hadn't he ever confided in her? *Sounds familiar, doesn't it? You don't exactly rush to tell Zach when things are bothering you.*

"I hope you don't feel bad that he didn't tell you," Rochelle said. "I think he told Monica because the events were still so raw, and he needed support. By the time he started dating you, he was probably putting it behind him and just wanted to forget about it."

Emily nodded, trying to tell herself that Rochelle's interpretation made good sense.

"If you ask me, I think that situation was one of the reasons Monica stuck with Zach for as long as she did—which wasn't long," Rochelle added. "It's not as though their personalities meshed. But she enjoyed feeling like she was the healer, mending his wounded soul, or something like that. And Zach was lonely and shaken up, so it's not hard to see why he'd have been drawn to Monica. She was all about charm and beauty and fun. A great distraction."

At least until she dumped him, Emily thought, regretting that she hadn't been more in tune with Zach's feelings. She'd been so focused on her own fears that she hadn't stopped to think that Zach might be as afraid of losing her as she was of losing him. "When someone sent me that picture of Zach and Monica, Zach wondered if this ex-student might have had something to do with it. But he checked with the police in Sacramento, and apparently she died last year—drug overdose."

"Sad story. Sounds like she was pretty messed up." Rochelle sat in silence for a moment. "I'd better go. But I'll keep my ear to the ground for any gossip about who might have it in for you."

"Thanks. I appreciate it."

Rochelle opened the car door. "Thanks for talking to me. I wasn't sure you would."

Emily smiled faintly. "Thanks for coming. And Rochelle . . . if you do think of anything about that night or about who might be targeting me, could you let me know immediately? Detective Lund doesn't seem inclined to confide in me, and it's maddening not knowing what's going on."

"Sure, I'll call you. And take care of yourself, all right? You look tired."

"I'll bet you haven't had a very restful week either. And I truly am sorry about Monica. She was an incredibly talented woman with a lot to live for."

"I'll get to work on that list of everything I remember," Rochelle said. "Even though it can't help her now, I'd feel a lot better if I could come up with something that might help the police nail the monster who killed her."

* * *

With her door secured by new locks, her assurance that she was not a suspect in Monica's murder, and new optimism engendered by Rochelle's offer of help, Emily managed a decent night's sleep, her second in a row. New locks notwithstanding, Zach had strongly urged her to spend the night at Nicole's, but Emily had refused. She didn't want to create strain between Nicole and Mitch, and she doubted Mitch would want Emily Ramsey under his roof until she was certified both innocent and sane.

We'll get there, Emily thought. In the freshness of morning, she'd finally realized how the culprit could have learned information she thought had been private between Ryan and her. The answer was so obvious that she was annoyed it hadn't occurred to her yesterday when she'd been hit with the news of the 2:00 AM phone call and the note left for Zach.

She hadn't told anyone about the Ryanair nickname or the sketch on the In-N-Out sack, but she *had* written about them in her journal, the journal she kept on her computer. If the stalker had used her computer to get the picture of Ryan, it made sense that he would have accessed Emily's journal and poked around for any useful tidbits that might help him terrorize her. *He or she.* It could be a woman. She couldn't rule anyone out yet, but she did know it was absurd to imagine that a stranger would target her in such a personal way. Whoever was slashing at her mind and heart was someone she knew. With enough digging, she'd figure out who it was.

The phone rang before she left for school, and Emily knew before she picked it up that it would be her mother. Making a point to sound cheerful, Emily reported that she'd spoken to Detective Lund last night and not only was Lund making excellent progress in solving Monica's murder, but she was also working to figure out who had used Emily's phone to call Bethany Tanner. Carolyn, plainly choosing her words with care, urged Emily not to stay on her own but to spend a few days with Nicole or Bethany until this was resolved. Emily made a big deal about the new locks and the competence of the police and ended the conversation with at least a small amount of hope that she'd eased her mother's fears.

Emily called Detective Lund and reported on what she'd figured out about her journal being a source of information on Ryan Tanner. She couldn't discern if Lund was at all impressed by her explanation, but at least Emily had given the police a possible alternative to thinking she was crazy.

Both Wednesday and Thursday passed as comfortingly normal days filled with math papers, first-grade misspellings, and an eruption of construction paper that eventually resolved into silhouette pictures of Lincoln and Washington. Thursday afternoon, Emily returned home to find Nicole and Zach standing on the sidewalk near the parking lot, chatting.

"I stopped by to see how you were doing and ran into Zach doing the same thing," Nicole greeted her.

Emily smiled. Day by day, it was getting easier to smile. "Don't you people have jobs?"

"I got my hair done." Nicole flipped her fingers through her blond hair so the highlights caught the sun. "Does that count?"

"From anyone else, that would sound flaky," Emily said. "But since you got your PhD in gorgeous, for you, trips to the salon *are* your job."

"If I wasn't worried about breaking a nail, I'd punch you for that snotty remark."

"Take your best shot." It felt good to joke around.

Zach kissed Emily. "How was your day?"

"It was great."

"I still think you should have taken a few more days off," Nicole lectured as they started toward Emily's apartment. "You ought to be taking it easy."

"Sorry, did you say something? My skull fracture with intracranial bleeding seems to have affected my hearing."

Nicole frowned. Zach laughed.

Brent Amherst emerged from his apartment as they approached, a laundry bag in his hand. "Hey, kids. Is there a party going on?"

"Not for you," Emily said with a smile. "Doesn't 'work from home' mean you're at work right now?"

"'Work from home' means flexible hours, silly girl. At least let me come up and admire your new lock. I saw Sullivan messing around up there the other night with his big boy, Fisher-Price toolkit."

"I didn't know a new lock was a tourist attraction, but come on up," Emily said. "I'll make popcorn." Out of the corner of her eye, she saw Zach's expression harden, and she instantly regretted the invitation. Zach had wanted to see her alone, and now she had an entourage. Nicole would no doubt find an excuse to keep the visit short—she was always careful to give Zach and Emily time together—but Emily might have to drop a hint to get rid of Brent.

When they reached the apartment, Brent scrutinized the new lock. "So why the new do-it-yourself hardware?" He gave the deadbolt a couple of experimental twists.

"I want to make sure I'm the only one with a key for now," Emily said.

"I can see how you'd be jumpy after what happened to Monica." Brent's gaze flicked briefly toward Zach, a glance Emily hoped Zach didn't notice. Surely Brent couldn't be tactless enough to repeat any of the "Sunday faces" speech he'd given Emily the other day. Brent couldn't really think Zach was guilty.

"Why don't you sit down and relax, Emily?" Zach said, a slight edge to his voice. "I'll make the popcorn."

"If you treat me like I'm sick, I'll ask you to leave," Emily said, but she winked at Zach.

"Wow, you must make a great patient. I feel sorry for your doctor." Nicole kicked off her shoes and curled up in Emily's armchair. "Don't bother with the popcorn. I promise we'll only stay a minute." Nicole tapped a fingernail on the arm of the chair. "And Emily, forgive me, but this is the ugliest chair in existence."

"Why are you sitting in it, then?" Brent asked.

"If I sit in it, I can see less of it. Don't you think it's time to reupholster it—or burn it?"

Emily grinned. "Don't blame me for Tricia's taste. She's the one who bought it at Goodwill."

"I know for a fact she was planning to reupholster it."

"Did you get that in writing?"

"If I send someone who'll do it for free, will you let them fix this thing?"

"I kind of like pink-and-orange splotches." Emily wanted to continue the banter, but the blinking message light on her phone diverted her attention.

She checked the caller ID, and her interest flared. Rochelle Elton had called.

"Excuse me for a minute. I need to check my voice mail." She swiftly punched buttons on the phone.

"Emily, it's Rochelle Elton." Rochelle had a nervous, almost hesitant tone to her voice. *"There's something I wanted to ask you about, something I remembered. It's—well, I didn't think it meant anything, but then you mentioned that red nail polish was used on that picture of Ryan. I thought it was kind of a coincidence, and the car—well, I just wanted to run something past you. Call me."*

"Who was it?" Zach asked as Emily lowered the phone.

"Rochelle Elton."

"Rochelle!" Fire ignited in Nicole's eyes. "Is that little brat bothering you? So help me—"

"No, not at all. She stopped by Tuesday evening to apologize for the way she reacted when I tried to talk to her on Monday. She admitted her accusations weren't fair."

"Did she admit the slap in the face wasn't fair?" Nicole asked.

Zach's expression turned stony. "She'd better have—"

"She apologized." Emily lifted her hand to her cheek where makeup camouflaged a faint bruise. "Neither of us was in fine form that day. Let it go."

Zach still looked angry.

Emily walked over to him and slipped her hand into his. "Rochelle and I are on the same page now, trying to figure out the truth. She was there the night Monica died, and she's hoping she might be able to remember some detail that will provide a clue."

"It's about time she came to her senses," Nicole said grumpily. She was the only woman Emily had ever met who could scowl in a way that made her even more attractive. "But what are you two doing playing Nancy Drew? Let the police figure things out."

"You didn't tell me you were playing detective," Zach reproached.

"We're *not* playing Nancy Drew. If we figure anything out, we'll take it to the police."

"It's dangerous for you to get involved in this," Nicole said. "If you have any sense, you'll move in with your parents until everything settles down." She gave Zach a beseeching look. "Back me up, Zach."

"Absolutely." Zach squeezed Emily's hand. "Nicole's right. Leave this to the police."

Emily thought of Lund's steel-plated eyes and repressed a sigh.

"So what did Rochelle say in the message?" Nicole asked. "Did she find a secret note hidden in a hollow tree?"

"No. She . . ." Suddenly Emily didn't want to announce details to the three people scrutinizing her. She'd never even told Brent about the picture of Ryan, and she certainly didn't feel like doing it now. "She just remembered something she thinks might be significant."

"I thought you said you'd take anything you figured out straight to the police," Nicole said pointedly. "Why is she calling you?"

"Well, she sounded uncertain. She wasn't sure it meant anything—she wanted to run it by me first." Emily bit the inside of her cheek. It would be rude to call Rochelle while her friends were here, but the thought of waiting was intolerable.

"I should call her back right now." Emily disengaged her hand from Zach's. "Excuse me for a moment."

"I don't like this," Nicole said. "If you poke a stick into a murderer's den, the murderer might wake up and eat you."

"Who's poking sticks? It's not like we're going to chase anyone down." Emily hit the buttons on her phone to retrieve Rochelle's number.

Rochelle's voice mail picked up. Disappointed, Emily left a message asking her to call as soon as she got the message. She recited her home and cell phone numbers and hung up.

"You're getting your hopes too high," Zach said. "Anything significant she's already told to the police, and they've probably already investigated it."

"Probably," Emily conceded. "But I can't stand just waiting and worrying."

"If you'd go to your parents' house like I suggested, you wouldn't have to worry about anyone bothering you." Nicole poked a pedicured toe at one of her shoes lying on the carpet. "I don't think changing the locks is enough."

"I'll call the Boy Scouts. Someone can guard me for an Eagle project."

"Cute. But you really need to get away and hole up at your parents'," Nicole reiterated.

Emily glanced at Zach. He looked as troubled as Nicole did. Brent stood with his mouth pursed and his eyebrows crinkled, looking as though he were analyzing a computer program for bugs and finding plenty.

"How about I make that popcorn?" Emily said.

CHAPTER 20

EMILY ATE DINNER AT ZACH'S, and they spent the evening together, both occupied with their own work as they sat side-by-side at Zach's kitchen table. Emily tried not to show her restlessness, but she was anxious to hear from Rochelle, and several times she checked her phone to make sure she hadn't missed a call. The only call that came was from Nicole, bored at a cocktail party where Mitch was preoccupied discussing a business deal. She planned to bail out early, and could she stop by Emily's for a few minutes later that night if she promised to bring Godiva chocolates? Emily knew Nicole was still worried about her and probably planned to hassle her about playing detective, but she agreed to the visit anyway. Even when Nicole was pushing her to do something, Emily enjoyed her company, and Nicole was unquestionably the most dedicated friend Emily had ever had. No wonder Tricia had liked her so much.

When early-bird Zach started yawning at nine, Emily took that as an opportunity to ask him to take her home. As soon as she was inside with the door securely locked behind her, she dialed Rochelle's number.

Voice mail again. Maybe Rochelle was out for the evening. Frustrated, Emily hung up, wishing she had Rochelle's cell phone number.

Don't wind yourself up. You can talk to her tomorrow. And Zach's probably right—anything Rochelle didn't notice until this late in the game isn't going to be very helpful.

The phone rang. Emily snatched it up, but the name on the caller ID punctured her hopes. Logan Tanner. Well, she owed Logan a call anyway, and she might as well talk to him now.

"Hi, Logan."

"Emily. How are you?"

"I'm okay."

"Heck, I'm sorry about everything. I heard what happened. I tried to call you a couple of times but couldn't catch you."

"I'm sorry," Emily said. "It's been a rough week."

"Yeah, I'll bet. Listen . . . uh . . . are you sure you're okay? Aunt Beth said you had a concussion."

The hesitancy in his voice nudged her with an all-too-familiar discomfort. Had Bethany told him about the 2:00 AM phone call? Probably. And now Logan thought she was losing her mind. *Calm down. You know how the caller got the information. You didn't make the call.* "I hit my head, but it wasn't serious. I'm sure she made it sound worse than it is. I'm fine. Back at work."

"I—uh—hey, I heard the police are giving you a hard time."

"They questioned me, of course, since I was on the scene. But I'm in the clear. I was with your aunt and uncle at the time Monica died."

"You're not a suspect?" He sounded relieved.

"No."

"You might want to tell Aunt Beth that. And Brent Amherst. He called me earlier tonight and went on and on about how they're trying to blame Monica Fife's murder on you and how he was worried sick but didn't know how to help you."

"He did?" *I should* have updated him, Emily thought guiltily. Why hadn't she? Was it because openly declaring that the police no longer considered her a suspect would be to confirm that she *had* been a suspect—and but for the timing of the murder, she might have been arrested?

So you let Brent and Bethany worry needlessly? Are you trying *to make a career out of tormenting the people who care about you?*

"I'll talk to them," Emily said. "I didn't realize Brent was that worried about me. I saw him for a few minutes this afternoon, and he seemed so upbeat."

Logan chuckled. "Oh, yeah, he worries. He kind of worships you, to tell the truth."

"Logan!"

"It's true. The perfect woman, high up on a pedestal. I always thought that someday he'd . . . but I think he felt it would be disloyal to Ryan."

Grateful Logan couldn't see her blushing, Emily said, "You're talking nonsense."

"Just trying to give you a heads-up. He didn't seem very happy about your engagement, and I thought you might want to know why he's bothered."

"*Your* interpretation of why he's bothered," Emily corrected. Logan had to be wrong. Brent had had countless chances to hint that he was interested in more than friendship, but he never had. Or was she inept at reading his signals?

He *hadn't* seemed happy about her engagement. And he didn't seem to like Zach.

Brent Amherst in love with her? She couldn't even begin to cope with that thought right now. She didn't want to hurt Brent, but she was in love with Zach. She was marrying Zach.

Logan had to be misinterpreting things. If Brent cared about her in that way, she would have sensed it. "I think he's upset about my engagement just because I sprung it on him out of nowhere," Emily said. "He didn't like feeling shut out."

"Yeah, okay, fair enough. Don't tell him I said anything. I don't want him pushing me off Half Dome this summer."

"I won't say anything."

"Emily . . . listen." From the new tension in Logan's voice, Emily knew he had finished teasing her about Brent and was broaching a more difficult subject. "Aunt Beth told me about that . . . phone call about Ryan. I just . . . wanted to make sure that . . ."

"I didn't make that call," Emily said. She explained about her computer being the source for both the picture of Ryan and private information about Emily and him. "Whoever dug up that information must have used my phone to make the call."

"While you were asleep? That's awful." Logan sounded almost too horrified, and Emily wondered if he was overdoing his reaction because he was faking it, thinking she'd invented the intruder. "Have you told the police?"

"Yes."

"What did they say?"

"They—don't really know anything yet."

"Did you hear anything that night?" Logan asked. "Do you have any idea how someone got in?"

"No, I didn't hear anything. I was exhausted—it probably would have taken someone screaming in my ear to wake me up. The door wasn't damaged. We switched the locks in case someone has a key."

"Good idea. But you probably ought to stay somewhere else until this is resolved. Aunt Beth would be glad to—"

"I know. She told me. Thank you. But I'll be fine."

"Call me anytime, okay? If you need anything, or just need to talk, call me."

"I will."

"Hey, uh . . ." Logan's voice shook a little, and Emily closed her eyes, bracing herself for whatever was coming.

"I hope you know you can talk with me about Ryan," he said. "I know it's awkward sometimes. I bring him up and people get all nervous and don't know what to say. And now that you're engaged, I'm sure it's twice as bad for you, because you don't want people to get the wrong idea. So if you ever need . . . anyway, call me."

"Thank you," Emily said quietly. "But, Logan—I'm fine."

"I'll talk to you soon, okay? Take care of yourself." He hung up.

Emily hung up the phone, feeling strangely cold and sore, like her muscles had cramped from prolonged shivering. *"I hope you know you can talk with me about Ryan."* Talk with him, before her stress over Ryan erupted again in a haunting middle-of-the-night phone call to Bethany? Or a note to Zach?

Somehow, she'd expected Logan to instantly accept that someone else had made the call. In her relief at figuring out how someone could have learned private information about Ryan, she'd ignored the fact that, in everyone else's eyes, the use of her computer still made her the most likely culprit.

That was sure to be what Detective Lund was thinking.

Emily double-checked the gleaming new deadbolt. No matter what Logan or Lund or anyone else thought, she was completely sane. If only she could get in touch with Rochelle Elton, maybe she wouldn't feel so worried and frustrated right now. Even the tiniest piece of information might be enough to allow Emily to start assembling this puzzle.

A hot shower would help wash away some of the mounting tension and render her sleepy as well. She took a set of long-sleeved knit pajamas out of her drawer and headed into the bathroom. Nicole wasn't stopping by until between ten and ten-thirty, so she still had time.

The steaming water soothed her tight muscles, and Emily's thoughts dulled into a blur punctuated by disconnected thoughts of Monica. Vibrant, vigorous. Young and healthy. Had Monica ever imagined she might die young? Why would she? She'd gone to work last Saturday assuming it would be like any Saturday. She would have had plans for that evening, for the next day, for the next sixty or seventy years. And then, in an instant, she was dead.

What had Monica felt when she realized she was dying? Or had she realized anything? Maybe the head injury had rendered her senseless before she had time to feel fear.

Emily shook herself mentally. *You're supposed to be relaxing. Not thinking about Monica.*

Or Tricia. Not far behind the image of Monica lying dead on her workroom floor came the image of Tricia. Two lives cut off. And somewhere, two people walking free, carrying the secret of death in their hearts.

Dressed in her pajamas, Emily blow-dried her hair, glad to feel the tug of exhaustion beginning to weigh her down. She'd keep the visit with Nicole brief and then go to bed and read for a while until she was so sleepy she couldn't keep her eyes open. She wanted sleep to come easily.

In her bedroom, she switched on the light, and the sight of her pillow evoked a yawn. She should have told Nicole to come over on a different night. She was more tired than—

A rustle from behind her triggered a burst of adrenaline. She barely had time to turn her head before something encircled her neck, digging into her windpipe, cutting off her air. Emily thrashed, grabbing at the twisted fabric that was strangling her, kicking at an assailant she could see only as a dark blur. She threw her head back in hopes of smashing a nose or a jaw and felt her head strike harmlessly against a shoulder.

The need for oxygen burned like molten steel filling her lungs. Emily groped behind her, grabbing at powerful fingers, yanking uselessly at wrists, gouging at hands sheathed in protective leather.

Help me. Emily clawed at her throat, trying to grip the slippery rope of fabric, to loosen it a fraction so she could—

She was on her hands and knees, gasping for air, her head swimming. Vaguely she heard her front door bang shut.

Emily staggered to her feet and careened into the living room, knocking alternately against the hallway walls like a bouncing ball. Her hand smacked wildly at the wall until she found the living room light switch. The assailant was gone. Why—

Someone pounded on the door, and before Emily could react, the door swung open. "Emily?"

Nicole. Emily stumbled toward her.

"Emily, are you all right—*Em.*" Nicole sprang into the living room and closed and locked the door behind her. "What happened? What is it? You—"

Emily couldn't spare the breath to answer. She stood with both hands curved around her throat and stared dumbly at Nicole.

Holding a gold-wrapped box of chocolates, Nicole stared back at Emily, her eyes wide, her lips working as though she kept starting and abandoning sentences.

"Someone—attacked me," Emily croaked at last. "Tried to—tried to strangle me . . ."

Nicole dropped the chocolates and snatched Emily's hands away from her throat. "Oh, Em—baby—you need to lie down, quickly."

"The man who attacked me—you saw—he ran out of here, just a few seconds ago . . ."

"Lie down. You're going to collapse." Nicole propelled her toward the couch.

"The police—"

"Lie down." Nicole swiped a couch pillow, placed it flat on the end cushion, and swept the other decorative cushions to the floor to clear space for Emily. "Right here. Come on."

Still light-headed, Emily complied. Nicole grabbed the mohair blanket and draped it over her. "Are you all right? Can you breathe okay?"

"Yes."

"Stay where you are. I'm going to get some ice for your throat."

Emily swallowed. Her throat felt swollen inside and out. "Call the police," she whispered.

"I will. Just stay calm. Don't get up." Nicole raced into the kitchen and opened the freezer. A moment later, she returned with a bag of ice cubes wrapped in a kitchen towel.

Emily took the cold pack and held it against her throat.

"Stay calm," Nicole ordered again. She returned to the kitchen, took the phone from the hook, and headed down the hallway. Emily wondered why she was leaving the room to phone the police, but she couldn't focus her thoughts enough to care.

Monica's killer had tried to kill her. She'd wanted to believe that he meant her only psychological harm, but the feel of the scarf around her throat had erased that delusion.

Why had he killed Monica? Was there even a reason? Maybe he was a psychopath who had become fixated on Monica and Emily for an insane reason that made sense only to him.

Details . . . the police would want to know details. Emily tried to think through mists of fear. Her attacker was tall, over six feet . . . wearing some kind of a dark mask . . . That was all she'd been able to catch in her split-second view of him before the scarf pulled tight around her throat and she'd forgotten everything except a frantic need to breathe.

Scarf . . . another Amber Flame scarf? But Monica had been strangled with her emerald scarf, Rochelle had said.

Nicole entered the room. She stepped close to the sliding door and nudged the blinds aside for a moment before turning to Emily. "Doing all right?"

"Yes."

"How did it happen?"

"I got home from Zach's around nine-thirty. Took a shower . . . dried my hair—how did he get in?"

"Everything's locked," Nicole said. "I checked. Windows, the sliding door. All locked. Except the front door—"

With the new lock. How stupid she'd been to think a new lock was enough to protect her. "He went out the front door," Emily said. "I heard it slam. But I *know* I locked it before I got in the shower. Check the lock. Is it damaged? Does it look like the door was forced?"

Nicole moved to the door and opened it. She switched the bolt back and forth and examined the plate on the doorjamb. "No damage at all. It looks perfect."

"He was waiting in my bedroom. When I walked in—" Emily touched her throat.

"Did you . . . get a look at him?"

"Not really. He wore a mask. He was tall. That's all I know."

"Back in a minute." Nicole disappeared toward the back of the apartment. Emily wanted to call out to warn her not to tamper with anything before the police saw it, but the thought of gathering enough breath to raise her voice was laughable. She shouldn't have let Nicole touch the door lock, but what did it matter? The intruder hadn't left fingerprints. He'd been wearing gloves.

The doorbell rang. Emily sat up, but before she could rise to her feet, Nicole galloped into the room and swung the door open.

"How is she?" Zach's hair was tousled, and he wore a mismatched sweat suit and no socks with his running shoes. Obviously, he'd leapt out of bed to rush over here.

"I'm fine," Emily answered for Nicole, standing up—a motion that made both Zach and Nicole swoop toward her.

"Lie down," Nicole said. "You've got to take it easy."

"I'm fine—" But two sets of hands were already pushing her back onto the couch. Giving up her protests, Emily let Zach and Nicole get her settled. The temporary weakness and dizziness that had followed the attack were long gone, and raging adrenaline made Emily want to leap up and do something, but if it made her friends feel better, she'd endure a few more minutes on the couch. She was glad Nicole had called Zach; it was comforting to have him here.

"Stay still. We'll be right back." To Emily's surprise, Nicole grabbed Zach's elbow and dragged him down the hallway.

Did Nicole think she was such an emotional wreck that she couldn't stand hearing the story of the attack repeated? It was both supremely sweet and unbearably irritating of Nicole. And where were the police? In a case of attempted murder, wouldn't they hurry to the scene?

Maybe not. The assailant was gone, and Emily was in no imminent danger.

And *was* it attempted murder? Emily relived the sequence of events in her mind: entering her bedroom, the sound of movement behind her, a dark figure, the scarf cutting off her air.

Why had her attacker fled without finishing the job? Nicole's knock at the door hadn't come until *after* he ran, so he couldn't have fled because he'd heard her coming. It didn't make sense.

Maybe the intruder hadn't meant to kill her, but to scare her. Like with the picture, the scarf, the note, the phone call . . .

Unable to lie still any longer, Emily shoved the blanket aside, set the ice pack on the table, and stood up. Time to tell Nicole to quit this coddling and come talk in the living room.

Emily expected to find Zach and Nicole standing at the end of the hall, talking in whispers, but to her surprise, they weren't there, and the door to Emily's bedroom was closed. She hadn't heard the door close, which meant Nicole had eased it shut with deliberate stealth.

Emily nearly marched down the hall to rap on the door and chastise Nicole for out-of-control mother-hen tendencies, but the strangeness of the scene with the door closed and the nearly inaudible murmur of voices coming from behind it sent a crawling sensation up her spine.

What was wrong with Nicole? What was she so intent that Emily not overhear?

The stress of the past week combined with Nicole's strange behavior was enough to quash any guilt Emily normally would have felt over eavesdropping. Her bare feet were silent against the carpet as she tiptoed to the bedroom door.

She pressed her ear to the door, planning to listen for only a moment before she knocked—*on my bedroom door, thank you, Nicole*—but Nicole's voice sent a paralyzing shock along her nerves.

". . . would have *seen* him, Zach. Emily said he left just seconds before I arrived, and I *saw* the door slam shut. But no one came out."

Zach's voice. "Then somehow he must have—"

"Gone out another way? I checked. Every window is locked. The sliding door even has a wooden bar in the track. And Emily said he went out the front door. Don't suggest he might still be hiding in the apartment, because I checked the whole place, and no one is here."

A pause. Emily pressed her ear harder against the wood, not caring how absurd she'd look if Zach or Nicole opened the door.

"What about Brent?" Zach asked.

"What about him?"

"His apartment is right downstairs from Emily's. If he was the one who attacked her, he could have run into his apartment before you—"

"Brent Amherst? You're not serious."

"I don't trust him."

"Why would he want to hurt Emily? Besides, it still doesn't work. I'm telling you, *no one* came out of her apartment or went into Brent's or anywhere else. When I was at the bottom of the stairs, I saw Emily's door fly open, then slam shut, but no one came out. I went and hammered on her door, and she told me her attacker had just fled. Zach, he *couldn't have gotten out without my seeing him.* He would have had to run right past me."

"You're saying you think Emily is lying?"

"I'm not saying I think she's *conscious* of lying. But I don't see how her story could be true."

"But her neck—the marks . . ."

"Look at this."

Emily squeezed her eyes shut, concentrating every particle of her attention on listening to the whispers from the other side of the door.

"Where did you find that?" Zach sounded shaken.

"In her dresser. Her top drawer, sitting right on top. Explain to me why an attacker would stop, stow the scarf, and *then* run away."

"This wouldn't be the first time someone planted something like this in Emily's apartment. I told you what she found last night."

"You changed the locks. You *know* no one else has a key, and there's no sign that anyone broke in."

"Why were you looking in her drawer anyway?"

"She said she was attacked in her bedroom. The weapon had to be somewhere."

"Physically, there's no way Emily could have done this to herself."

"Isn't there? Watch. If she held it like this—"

"*Stop* it."

"I'm just showing you it's possible. Emily wants me to call the police, but I don't know what to do. If the police come and she tells them this story expecting me to corroborate it and I *can't*—Zach, after all the weird stuff that's happened around Emily, they already must think she's falling apart. We both saw the note about Ryan, written in her handwriting. And if they think she's capable of staging something like this, hurting herself—"

"I refuse to believe that."

"Then what's your explanation? That she was attacked by the ghost of Ryan Tanner? Or the Invisible Man?"

No response from Zach. Emily's nails gouged her palms, and she pressed her ear against the door so hard that the side of her face ached.

"I don't know," Zach said at last. "I'm going to go talk to Emily."

"But what do we do about the police? If they see her like this, they'll lock her in a psych ward. But then again, maybe that's best. At least then we'll know she's safe, and they can—"

Emily didn't hear the rest of Nicole's sentence. She stepped back from the door, one hand clutching her bruised throat, her thoughts a hurricane of confusion.

I didn't make this up. I didn't do this to myself.

But why would Nicole lie? She *must* have seen the assailant.

Emily retreated to the living room, her heart racing, her knees shaking so much she feared they would collapse beneath her. There was no reason at all for Nicole to lie. There must be a logical explanation. Split-second timing—*could* Nicole have missed seeing the attacker? It was dark, and he was dressed in black.

But Nicole had pounded on the door almost immediately after Emily had heard it slam.

Would Nicole lie? Nicole was her closest friend. Nicole lying in order to hurt Emily was about as believable as the thought of Tricia suddenly appearing, casual and mortal, and saying sympathetically, *"Rotten evening, huh, Em?"*

There had to be some evidence that would confirm Emily's story.

Brent. He might have seen something or at least heard the thudding of someone running down the stairs.

Not caring that she was barefoot and in her pajamas, Emily sped out the front door and down the steps to Brent's apartment. She banged on the door, frantic to get a response before Nicole and Zach realized she'd left the apartment and came after her.

The door flew open. "What in blazes—"

Emily pushed past Brent and shut the door behind her. "Don't ask questions. Just answer this—did you see or hear anyone coming out of my apartment about twenty minutes ago?"

"What—oops, no questions allowed. No, I didn't see or hear anything. I was in my bedroom, watching TV. Kind of dozing. What—uh . . . can I ask questions yet?"

Despair made Emily want to grab Brent by the shoulders and shake him into remembering something he hadn't noticed in the first place. "Did you notice anyone going into my apartment tonight, anyone at my door, anyone going up the stairs? Come *on,* you must have heard or seen something—"

Brent ran both hands through his straw-blond hair. "Em, I'm sorry. I didn't notice anything. Like I said, I was in my bedroom, watching TV. Now it's *my* turn. What *happened?*" He stretched a finger toward her throat. "Did someone—"

Feet pounded on the stairs outside. *Zach and Nicole.* For a wild instant, Emily pictured herself racing through Brent's living room, escaping out his sliding door onto his first-floor patio, and fleeing into the darkness. But where would she go? And why would she run from her fiancé and her friend? Even if Nicole was mistaken about—

Mistaken? Or lying?

Or right? The last thought hit Emily like a fist in the stomach.

The doorbell rang. Brent looked at Emily. "Who's chasing you? What's going on?"

"It's Zach and Nicole. But they're not . . . they're just trying to help . . ."

"Who hurt you?"

Emily lifted her hands to her throat. "I don't know. Not them." *It was a tall man. Zach is tall—but so is Justin Driscoll—*

So was Ryan.

Help me, please help me. I'm going insane. I don't know who to trust.

"Can I let them in?" Brent asked as the bell pealed again and a fist pounded on the door.

"Yes."

Brent opened the door.

"Emily." Nicole brushed past Brent without acknowledging him. "You scared us to death. Why did you run out—"

Brent held up a hand. "Someone needs to explain what's going on here."

"Hang on a second." Nicole pulled out her cell phone and dialed. "Zach, she's at Brent's. She's okay." She returned the phone to her purse. "He went to check the parking lot for your car. We were afraid you'd driven off somewhere. Why did—"

"Give her a little space." Brent put a protective hand on Emily's shoulder. "She needs to sit down. She looks like she's going to faint."

"I don't need to sit down." Emily pulled away from Brent's hand. "Someone attacked me in my apartment tonight and tried to strangle me. He ran just before Nicole arrived."

Nicole bit her lip, and Emily knew exactly what she wanted to say: *There was no assailant. Emily did this to herself.*

Pounding footsteps approached. Panting, Zach skidded to a stop at Brent's still-open door. "Emily, thank heavens."

"Come in," Brent said. "Apparently, it's a party." He closed the door behind Zach. "Who's going to explain?"

"Why did you run out on us?" Zach asked Emily.

There was no point in feigning ignorance of Zach and Nicole's conversation. "I wanted to know if Brent heard or saw anything—seeing as how Nicole is apparently deaf and blind now."

Nicole looked aghast. "You heard what I said?"

"Since you were holed up in my bedroom, I figured eavesdropping was fair play. I'm not insane, Nicole. Someone was there."

Zach looked at Brent. "Did *you* see or hear anyone coming from Emily's apartment?"

Brent shot an apologetic look at Emily. "No. I didn't. I was in the back, watching TV and half asleep. But even if I didn't hear anything, there'll be other evidence. Fingerprints? Or did you manage to scratch his hands or arms? If you have his blood or skin cells under your fingernails—"

"He was wearing gloves and long sleeves—a leather jacket, I think," Emily said bleakly. "I couldn't scratch him. But he *was there*. Nicole—"

"Em . . ." Nicole apparently couldn't think of anything conciliatory to say, because she abandoned the anxious, guilty look and looked directly into Emily's eyes. "You can hate me all you want, but I'm not going to lie and say I saw something I didn't. That would only hurt you. You need help. I know you told me to call the police, but I didn't, because I don't want them giving you a hard time. But you can't hang around here any longer pretending you're fine, playing detective. I saw that freaky note you left Zach. I heard about the phone call to Ryan's mother. You need to go stay with your parents and talk to their friend the psychiatrist. If you won't agree to go tonight, I *will* call the police. I'll tell them everything, and they'll *make* you get help."

Everyone was suddenly, starkly silent, the faint chatter of the television from Brent's bedroom the only sound. Brent opened his mouth as though to ask for an explanation, then closed it like he didn't dare speak.

Zach moved next to Emily. "I need to speak to Emily alone. We'll go upstairs to her apartment. Nicole, would you stay here with Brent for a few minutes?"

Nicole nodded. Zach's hand closed on Emily's elbow.

"Hold it, Sullivan," Brent said. "If she doesn't want to go with you, she's not going."

For an instant, Emily again felt the panicked need to escape, to get away from all of them, maybe just get in her car and drive until hundreds of miles separated her from mistrust, uncertainty, and terror. She forced the feeling down; she wasn't going to give her friends more reason to doubt her sanity.

"It's all right, Brent. I'll talk to him."

As soon as Zach closed her apartment door behind them, Emily said, "Listen to me. I don't know how Nicole could have missed . . ."

"Emily." Zach rested both hands on her shoulders.

"You think I would—" Emily gestured at her throat, where scratches burned and each breath made her muscles ache. "You think I'd do this? Why? Some kind of desperate, attention-seeking . . ."

"Emily—"

"Whether or not Nicole saw him, someone was—"

Zach put his hand over her mouth. "You don't have to convince me of anything."

She didn't have to convince him because he already believed her? Or because no matter what she said, he wouldn't take her word over Nicole's?

Why *would* he believe her? Who was more credible? The composed, efficient friend or the ranting woman who'd clawed herself half to death trying to fight off an invisible intruder, then went racing outside in bare feet and pajamas to try to drum up witnesses to her delusions?

Zach lowered his hand from her mouth. "Okay. Can you listen to me for a moment?"

Emily nodded and regretted it; the motion hurt.

"I don't know what happened here tonight. I'm not going to pretend I do. But I know two things. The first is that I love you and will do anything I can to help you. The second is that you're in danger here."

"In danger from—"

"You're in danger. That's all I need to know. If our roles were reversed, what would you do?"

"The point is—"

"*Emily.* If our roles were reversed—if I were the one in danger—what would you do?"

"Zach, please . . ."

If Zach were the one in danger.

Ryan gone . . . if she thought there was even a chance she might lose Zach too . . .

"I'd do anything I could to protect you," she said.

"To get me out of a dangerous situation?"

"Yes." Tears ran down her face and slid along her throat, stinging the scratches.

"Would you want to stand here arguing with me about what happened? Or would you make sure I was safe first and ask questions later?"

She said nothing. Zach already knew her answer.

"All right," Zach said. "Do you trust me enough to let me do the same for you?"

For all Emily's protests that she was fine, she now felt that if she didn't sit down, she was going to crumple. "What are you proposing? Call the police and have them lock me up?"

"No. Let's go to your parents. After you've gotten some rest, we can work on sorting this out."

Emily walked over to the microwave and picked up her key ring from the ceramic dish. Her new house key was still on the ring.

Four keys had come with the new lock. She opened the utility drawer where she kept extra keys.

Three keys still lay there, undisturbed.

Zach was looking over her shoulder.

"Do you want me to talk to Dr. Kincaid?" Emily tried to make her voice dry. It came out riddled with cracks.

With his hands on her shoulders, Zach turned her to face him. His eyes were gentle, his face pale with anxiety. "Emily . . . no matter what happened tonight, you need to talk to him."

CHAPTER 21

WHEN EMILY AWOKE, SWATHED IN the faded, familiar quilt that covered her bed in her parents' home, she didn't hurry to get up. She felt warm and sleepy, her emotions still fogged by whatever pill Dr. Kincaid had given her last night. He'd told her what it was, but she couldn't remember; she couldn't remember much of anything he'd said to her. She'd been too distracted by the sight of her parents—her father's face, gray and somehow sunken, like fear had sapped years from his life; the terror in her mother's reddened eyes and the tentative way she spoke to Emily, as though expecting a furious, irrational response.

How could she have hurt them like this? Hadn't they suffered enough from losing Tricia?

She closed her eyes, letting every muscle in her body go limp. The house was quiet, but she doubted that anyone besides her was in bed. Zach and her mother were probably taking shifts outside her bedroom door to ensure that she didn't escape. Her father would take window duty. He could weed the flowerbeds in his downtime.

Zach. He'd been so kind last night, so tender, so protective—calling her parents, explaining the situation, bringing her here, sitting up with her until she fell asleep. But was it the kindness of a future husband or a friend? How could he want to marry her now, when he thought she was an emotional train wreck? If he had any sense, he'd have headed home last night and started the process of extricating himself from Emily's nightmarish life.

Emily touched a fingertip to one of the scratches on her throat. She'd have to talk to Dr. Kincaid. There was no avoiding that now. She'd have to start the process of finding out if she was capable of . . .

Not of murder, anyway. At least she knew she hadn't killed Monica.

Emily pushed back the covers and swung her legs to the floor. She was too alert now, and lying in bed allowed too much time for thinking.

She opened her suitcase to see what clothes she had with her. At Zach's request, Nicole had packed for her. Emily hadn't protested; she'd felt so overwhelmed last night that just the thought of gathering clothes and throwing them into a suitcase had been too much.

True to form, it looked like Nicole had forgotten nothing. She'd even included the daisy photo album, no doubt realizing Emily would want comfort from Tricia.

Dear Nicole, the friend who was always there for her. Emily tried again to make herself think of a logical explanation for how Nicole could have missed seeing the intruder last night, but the effort brought a dull pulse of despair.

Emily took her bathrobe out of the suitcase. The shower she'd taken last night seemed days ago. Cautiously, she stepped out of her bedroom and checked the hallway. If anyone was supposed to be on guard duty, they'd abandoned their post.

She was opening the door of the linen closet when Carolyn came around the corner, looking as though she was forcing herself not to rush. Emily was certain her mother had been waiting for hours for the sound of her door opening. It was already eleven o'clock in the morning.

"How are you feeling, sweetie?"

Shame surged anew in Emily at the sight of her mother's face. She was wearing more makeup than she usually did, but her mascara was already smudged, and dark circles showed through the concealer under her eyes. Emily wondered if she'd slept at all.

"I'm okay," Emily said. "I thought I'd take a shower."

Carolyn fiddled with the pocket of her apron. The house smelled like cinnamon and baked apples. "I'll have some brunch on the table for you whenever you want it."

"Thank you." Emily fought the urge to lift her hands to hide the marks on her throat. She reached into the closet and took a towel.

"I'll . . . be in the kitchen if you need me." From the groping tone of Carolyn's voice, Emily knew this wasn't what she wanted to say. Emily tried to think of how she could make this easier on her mother, but all that rose to the surface of her mind was a desperate plea for Carolyn to believe that she hadn't imagined last night's events.

Emily held the words back, gave her mother a weak smile, and walked into the bathroom. If she started babbling about last night, she'd only scare Carolyn more and earn herself a refrain of *Of course, honey; I understand, honey; take it easy, honey.* Soothing words, but no belief. In a way, she was glad Zach hadn't been willing to instantly accept either her story or Nicole's.

At least she knew he was being honest with her—not just saying what he knew she wanted to hear.

She showered and dressed—Nicole had thoughtfully packed a turtleneck sweater that covered her throat—and headed into the kitchen.

Zach rose from his seat at the table, relief in his eyes. Emily figured he was grateful to see her calm and dressed instead of clad in pajamas and hysterical.

"Good morning." He gave her a hug. "How are you feeling?"

"Good," Emily lied. She lingered in his embrace, resting her cheek against his shoulder, trying unsuccessfully to ward off the certainty that this was the last time he would hold her like this. Why had she ever thought this could work out? From the moment she'd started falling in love with him, she'd been afraid she would lose him. She just hadn't thought that loss would come along with her getting locked in a mental hospital.

She wanted to apologize for causing him so much pain.

Emily broke the embrace, afraid if she held on any longer, she'd be both clinging and crying. "You should have gone to work today," she said. "You didn't need to stay here."

"Family crisis trumps quadratic equations anytime," he said with a small smile. "Your principal sends his best wishes, by the way, and hopes you're feeling better soon."

"I hope you told him I have the flu."

"Apple sour-cream coffee cake," Carolyn announced, putting a plate on the table for Emily. "What would you like to drink? Milk, orange juice, grape juice?"

"Milk would be great. Thanks, Mom." Emily sat down. Zach returned to his seat and picked up his fork. She didn't have to ask where her father was. When Lloyd Ramsey needed time to think or vent stress, he worked outside. With all the stress she was giving him, Emily suspected the Ramseys' yard would shortly be worthy of a write-up in *Better Homes and Gardens*.

No one spoke as Emily ate her coffee cake and the slice of honeydew melon Carolyn put on her plate. The silence was awkward, but Emily was at a loss for how to break it. *"So, what do you think really happened last night?" "On a scale of one to ten—with one being a flesh-eating maniac and ten being as solid as Dad, who only vents stress by digging dandelions—how would you rate my sanity?" "Read any good horror novels lately? Lived any good horror novels lately?"*

"What's so funny?" Zach asked, and Emily realized that grinning at her own macabre thoughts definitely wouldn't earn her any extra points on the sanity scale.

"Nothing's funny, except for the fact that here we are, three adults too terrified to start a conversation. You can say whatever you want or ask me whatever you want. I promise I won't freak out."

"We're not worried about that, honey," Carolyn said.

"If you aren't, then you've been dealing with a different Emily. I'm sorry I've given you such a hard time."

"No need to apologize. Um . . . sweetie, Brother Kincaid said he could come by this afternoon around four. Would you be willing to talk to him?"

Emily's mouth went so dry that she couldn't finish chewing her cake until she took a swallow of milk. Apparently, Carolyn had decided to test her promise to remain calm by throwing out the statement she thought would upset Emily the most.

Fear rose in a reflex reaction, and Emily wanted to protest that she was fine—why couldn't they believe her? She didn't need to talk to Dr. Kincaid or anyone else.

Instead, she said, "Of course I'll talk to him. Four o'clock is good."

Neither Zach nor Carolyn said anything to this, but Emily could feel their relief.

Zach's phone rang. "Sorry for the bad manners," he said, taking it from his pocket. "I'm expecting—ah, excuse me." He rose and walked away from the table.

"Anyone who pulls that stunt at my table gets to do the dishes," Carolyn joked when Zach was out of earshot.

"He'd be happy to help," Emily said lightly, though she felt anything but light at the knowledge that whatever this conversation was about, Zach obviously didn't want her to hear it.

"So do you have your cruise booked yet?" Emily asked, and the topic turned to a somewhat stilted discussion of the cruise Carolyn and Lloyd were planning to take in April for their thirty-fifth wedding anniversary. Emily kept up a pretense of interest in the conversation, but her thoughts were on Rochelle Elton.

Neither Zach nor her mother would be enthusiastic if she told them about her intention to call Rochelle, but if there was even the smallest chance Rochelle could tell her something that would lead to the attacker, she had to call Rochelle immediately.

If there *was* an attacker. Hating the self-doubt that dug deeper by the moment, Emily rose and took her empty plate to the dishwasher. At this time of day, Rochelle would be at her store. Emily would have to look up the number.

Zach returned to the kitchen. "Sorry about that. Hey, it's a beautiful morning. Would you like to go for a walk?"

"Oh—yes, that would be great," Emily said, glad Zach didn't assume she was too fragile for a stroll.

Carolyn turned from where she was wiping the stovetop. "Are you sure you're up to it, sweetie?"

"I'm doing fine, Mom. Let me go get ready." There wasn't much she needed to do except grab her jacket, but she wanted an excuse to leave the room and call Rochelle. If Zach could sneak away for a phone call, so could she.

Zach took the broom from the pantry. "I'll help your mom finish up. No hurry. We'll leave whenever you're ready."

Emily slipped into her father's study and used his computer to look up the number for Rochelle's store. Rochelle might not want to talk about this while she was at work, but if she didn't, she could tell Emily when to call back.

An unfamiliar female voice answered the phone. "Rochelle's Shoes and Boots, this is Kim."

"Is Rochelle available?"

"She's not in this morning. Can I help you or take a message for her?"

"This is Emily Ramsey. I'm returning her call. I'll call her at home. Thanks."

Emily hung up and dialed Rochelle's home number. From the kitchen, she could hear the faint sounds of congenial conversation and running water.

Rochelle's voice mail picked up. Emily hung up without leaving a message. She should feel frustration, but instead, the emotion beginning to congeal in her stomach was fear.

Stop it. How can you be so paranoid? She's probably running errands before going in to work. Or she could be in the shower, or out jogging.

Feeling foolish, but knowing she wouldn't be able to relax until she checked, Emily picked up the phone and dialed the number for Rochelle's store.

"Hi, Kim. This is Emily Ramsey again. I'm sorry to bother you, but I was wondering when you expect Rochelle in to work?"

There was a moment of silence. "I'm not sure. I thought she was coming in at eleven, but she didn't show up. No big deal, though. We're not busy—" Kim stopped, seeming to realize she was sharing too much information. "Anyway, when she does come in, I'll give her the message that you called."

"It's very important that I get in touch with her. Could you possibly give me her cell phone number?"

"Uh . . . sorry, but I can't do that without her permission."

"I understand. Thanks." Emily hung up.

Who would have Rochelle's cell phone number? Justin Driscoll, for sure. Emily went to her bedroom to retrieve her cell phone. She found the number Justin had entered and called him.

"Hello?"

"Justin, it's Emily Ramsey."

"Emily." His voice went faux-gentle. "How are you doing?"

"I need Rochelle Elton's cell phone number."

"Why?"

"I need to talk to her, and she's not at home."

"She'll be at her store right now."

"She's not there. Just give me the number, please."

Justin added another layer of gentleness to his soothing tone. "Why do you need to talk to her? If you need to talk about Monica, I'm ready to listen."

Deciding it would be a good idea to delude Justin into thinking he was making progress with her, Emily put a quiver in her voice as she said, "Maybe later . . . I'm just not quite ready . . . but if I could talk to Rochelle, it would really help. Please . . . ?"

"Well . . . okay, hang on." A moment later his voice came back on the line, reciting a number. Emily wrote it down.

"Thanks, Justin."

"So what do you need to talk to her about?"

"I need some new shoes for the prom." Emily hung up. She dialed Rochelle's cell phone number, but the ringing ended with Rochelle's voice mail. Dismayed, Emily left a message.

Where was Rochelle?

A knock at her bedroom door made her jump.

"Emily? Ready to go?"

"Come in."

Zach opened the door. The smile on his face disappeared as he looked at her. "You okay? We don't have to go on a walk if you're not up to it." He gestured at the cell phone in her hand. "Who were you talking to?"

Emily debated. The only way she'd be able to pursue this was if she answered Zach candidly. "I was trying to return Rochelle's call. She left me a message last night, if you remember. She thought she might have some information. But she's not answering her phones—any of them."

Zach's fingers clenched and relaxed. "Did you leave her a message?"

"Yes."

"Do you want to go on a walk while you wait for her to call back?" A cottony-soft border framed his words. The soothing tone. Apparently, Justin Driscoll was giving lessons.

Rochelle's not at the store. She's not answering her phones. And she thought she might know something.

"Emily. What's wrong?"

"She's supposed to be at work. She's not. And she's not answering her cell phone or landline."

Zach's forehead creased. "You think she might be in trouble? You think she really did know something about Monica's murder?"

Emily wanted to give a deprecating smile and a shrug, acknowledging her concerns as paranoia, but she couldn't do it.

"It's probably nothing," Zach said slowly. "Just coincidence. She got a flat tire on her way to work. Her cell phone is dead. Come on it's ridiculous to think she knew something dangerous enough to make Monica's killer feel threatened. She's already told the police everything she knows."

Red nail polish and a car. What did that mean?

Zach was probably right. Car trouble and a dead cell phone battery were likely explanations for Rochelle's lack of response. Emily was starting to see danger everywhere, even where none existed. Besides, the timing was too perfect. Even if Rochelle had figured something out, how would the killer know about it in time to intercept her before she could speak to Emily?

But Nicole knew about Rochelle's message. So did Brent.

And so did Zach.

Shivery coldness spread through Emily. She couldn't do this to herself. She couldn't doubt everyone. Especially not Zach.

Zach's mouth was a tight line, and his eyes looked through her. Emily expected him to tell her to stop worrying, that Rochelle was fine, but instead he said, "We've got time before your appointment with Dr. Kincaid. Let's drive home and see if we can find Rochelle. Chances are that by the time we get there, she'll have resolved whatever problem is making her late to work, and you can talk to her."

Surprised and relieved, Emily said, "I'll go tell my mother we're leaving for a while. But I'll make sure she knows you'll be with me. I wouldn't want her to think the inmate is fleeing the asylum."

Zach grimaced. "Em—"

"No, it's all right. Really. If I can joke about it, that's a good sign, right?"

"No one thinks you're crazy."

Emily wondered if she should tell Zach he was a lousy liar.

CHAPTER 22

BY THE TIME THEY DROVE into Los Coros, Emily's apprehension had hardened into dread. Images kept flashing through her mind: Monica sprawled on the floor of her workroom, her auburn hair covering her face, the tile flecked with blood; Tricia by the side of the road, her body contorted, blood trickling from her mouth.

Rochelle Elton was dead. Emily would find her as she'd found Monica and Tricia. Still and lifeless, her body marked by violence.

Emily's hands strayed to her throat. If that scarf had remained twisted tight for a little longer, *she* would be dead.

Life was so fragile.

"You okay?" Zach touched her shoulder.

Emily dropped her hands into her lap. "Yes." *No.* Her stomach was cramping, and the pain in her throat seemed magnified tenfold. *Rochelle's dead, and it's my fault for asking her to write down all her memories of what happened that night.* "We should call Detective Lund," she said. "We should tell her about Rochelle."

"Tell her what?"

"That Rochelle is . . . missing." She'd nearly said "dead" but edited the word in time.

Zach flicked her a glance and returned his gaze to the road. "We don't know she *is* missing. Not answering the phone for a couple of hours doesn't make you a missing person. Look, it's no wonder you'd assume the worst after the things that have happened lately, but I'm telling you, Rochelle's fine."

Zach drove to Rochelle's neighborhood. He hadn't looked up directions; Emily suspected he'd been here many times while he was dating Monica. As he pulled up in front of a small ranch-style house, the suffocating tightness in her chest made her feel she was going to pass out.

"Her car's here." Zach sounded triumphant as he pointed at the car in the driveway. "She probably just got delayed."

But Monica's car had been there when Emily had come to the Amber Flame the night Monica died. It had been parked casually in the lot, giving no hint that its owner would never return. Ryan's car had been there in the grocery store parking lot the night he disappeared.

"We need to call Detective Lund," she said again as Zach pulled over to the curb across from Rochelle's house.

Zach drew the key from the ignition. "Stay here, okay? I'll go knock on her door."

She won't answer, Emily thought, but even through her fear, she found herself reaching for the door handle.

"Emily, I'll take care of it. If she's here, I'll come get you."

"I'll come." New fear for Zach impelled her to step out of the car. What if the murderer was at Rochelle's and he attacked Zach while Emily cowered in the car?

Zach gripped her hand as they walked to the front door. When he reached for the doorbell, Emily stifled the urge to tell him not to touch it, that he might mar fingerprints left by a killer.

Stop it. You have no reason to assume Rochelle is dead.

Except that Rochelle thought she might have evidence against a murderer. Except that Rochelle wasn't answering her phones and hadn't shown up at work.

The click of the door being unlocked startled Emily so badly that she jerked, nearly stumbling backward down the porch steps. Zach put his arm around her.

The door opened halfway, and Rochelle Elton looked out at them.

Relief drenched Emily, so overwhelming that if it hadn't been for Zach's arm supporting her, she would have collapsed onto Rochelle's porch.

"Hi, Rochelle." The relief in Zach's voice told Emily he hadn't been nearly as confident of finding Rochelle safe as he had pretended. "Sorry to bother you. When you didn't answer your phone, we got a little worried. Emily's been trying to get in touch with you. Are you . . . okay?"

Rochelle's face was blotched red, Emily realized, and her eyelids were swollen from tears. No wonder Rochelle hadn't wanted to take calls or go to work. She must have had a bad night, mourning Monica. Emily remembered well how a temporary spell of feeling back on keel could be followed rapidly by an emotional storm that left her completely unable to function.

"I'm sorry," Emily said. "We shouldn't have bothered you. I just wanted to follow up on your call from yesterday."

"I told you to leave me alone."

Emily recoiled inwardly from a glare that pierced like spikes of iron. "I—you called—you said you had something to tell me. You asked me to—"

"What's the matter with you? First you come to my store yelling crazy accusations. Then when I come to warn you to leave me alone, you start hassling me for information. I already told you—I don't *know* anything. I didn't see anything that night. I called you yesterday to say if you bother me one more time, I'll take out a restraining order."

Emily's heart was a lump of ice. "You *asked* me to call. You said you'd remembered something—something you wanted to run by me. You mentioned red nail polish and a car."

"*What?* What does nail polish have to do with anything? I never said anything like that. Get out of here." She started to shut the door. Without thinking, Emily sprang forward and caught the edge of the door.

"Emily." Zach put his hand on her shoulder. "Let's go."

"Rochelle, *please*. You left me a message saying you'd thought of something, that my mentioning red nail polish had reminded you—"

Rochelle's five-year-old son came up behind her, clutching a stuffed shark and peering nervously at Emily and Zach.

"Seth, go watch TV," Rochelle said. *"Now."*

He raced away.

"I don't know what you're raving about." Rochelle kept her voice low, obviously not wanting Seth to overhear. "I left you a message telling you to leave me alone, but maybe you're too crazy to understand plain English."

"I have the message, Rochelle. I saved it."

"You're insane." Rochelle's face was so pale and wild that she looked like something out of a ghost story. "Zach, get her out of here, or I'll call the police." Rochelle tried to push the door shut.

"Wait." Emily pushed back, but Zach's arms went around her from behind. He caught her wrists and pulled her against him while Rochelle slammed the door.

"Let go of me! She's lying. I don't know why she—"

"We can't stay here. We can't argue with her in front of her son. Come on." Zach forced her down the porch steps.

"She's *lying*."

"Okay. But we'll talk about it somewhere else." Zach unlocked the car door. Emily let him nudge her onto the seat, though her muscles remained rigid with the need to rush back to Rochelle and force her to speak the truth.

Why would Rochelle lie?

Rochelle and Nicole too?

So now everyone is lying to you. They're all crazy or evil—except you.

Every time she thought she'd regained her balance, the earth heaved beneath her. But this time was different. This time she had proof that she wasn't losing her mind.

She fumbled in her purse for her cell phone.

"What are you doing?" Zach reached toward her like he feared she was digging for a weapon.

"I want you to hear the message. I want you to hear what she said."

"I never said I didn't believe you. But go ahead and play the message for me if it'll make you feel better."

Clumsy with adrenaline and eagerness, Emily could hardly dial the number to retrieve her landline voice mail. After all the terrifying episodes to which she was the only witness, after all the accusations of broken sanity, after *everything*, she finally had a sliver of proof in her favor.

"You have no saved messages," the recorded voice said in Emily's ear. "To change your voice mail options, press two. To—"

"*No.*" She must have dialed wrong. She disconnected and tried her voice mail again, acutely conscious of Zach watching her.

The result was the same. No new messages. No saved messages. Nothing. The message was gone.

"I saved it," Emily whispered, so chilled it was hard to keep her teeth from chattering. "I *know* I saved it. I distinctly remember—"

"It's gone?"

Emily squeezed the phone as though she could wring the erased message from plastic and circuitry. "How could it have gotten erased? I saved it."

"Some glitch with the voice mail program, maybe. Don't worry about it. I didn't need to hear the message anyway. I was there when you first listened to it, remember?"

"But did you *hear* it? Could you overhear anything she said?"

Zach shifted the car into drive and sped down Rochelle's street.

"Did you hear anything? Zach, I need to know if—"

"No," he said. "No, I didn't hear anything."

Emily wanted to hurl her phone through the windshield. He had no idea what Rochelle had said to her, either on the message or when she'd talked to Emily in the parking lot. He had only Emily's word for what had passed between them.

A glitch with the voice mail program? How convenient. Did Zach really believe that was the explanation for the lost message?

What *was* the explanation? Did she think someone had gotten her voice mail password and deleted her message?

The most likely explanation—at least to Zach—would be that she had deleted the message herself or never bothered to save it, because it contained nothing more than Rochelle's threat to take out a restraining order.

"Rochelle is lying." Emily shoved her cell phone into her purse. "I have to talk to her. *Now.* Someone got to her, someone who thought she knew something dangerous. Maybe they threatened her son. Why else would he be home today? He should be at school. Turn the car around."

"You can't talk to her right now. If you go back there, she'll call the police."

"Who cares? Let her call the police. Maybe she'll tell them what she won't tell me."

"Let's think this through, okay? Let's head back to your parents' house."

"Not yet. Something's horribly wrong. She's terrified. Didn't you see how she looked?"

"She just lost her best friend. Of course she's been crying. That doesn't mean—"

"Turn the car around. Turn around, or I'm getting out. I'll walk back to Rochelle's if I have to, but I'm talking to her *now.*"

"You won't get anything rational out of Rochelle right now. If you don't want to go to your parents' house yet, let's go to my place. We can talk this out."

"Talk *what* out? Rochelle is lying. We need to talk to her. Turn the car around, or I'm getting out at the next stoplight."

Zach's hand closed around her wrist in a firm grip. "No, you're not. Don't be ridiculous."

"Let go of me."

"When you're threatening to bail out into traffic? I don't think so."

"So now you think I'm nutty enough to throw myself in front of a truck?"

"You threatened twice to jump out of the car. And if you're irrational enough to think you could get any information out of Rochelle in her current state of mind, maybe you're irrational enough to do it. I'm not taking chances."

Anger collapsed into a rubble heap of despair. Zach was right. In her desperation to make Rochelle retract her false story, she was talking like a lunatic.

Emily's free hand moved to the bruises concealed by her turtleneck sweater. For an exhausted instant, she wanted to quit fighting. It would be so much easier to sink into the madness everyone already thought had possessed her, to stop scrounging for answers, stop meeting defeat every time she thought she'd made progress. A hospital bed behind a locked door sounded like a refuge. At least she knew she'd be safe there.

You'd be safe there. And a killer would roam free out here. Someone got to Rochelle. Someone threatened her. Monica's killer. My attacker. Someone who knew Rochelle called me and wanted to give me information. Someone who can break into my apartment, dig up my voice mail password—

Zach's fingers were tight around her wrist, iron fingers like those that had knotted the scarf around her throat.

Zach had installed the new locks. Could he have slipped a key into his pocket, made a copy, and returned the key before Emily noticed it was gone?

Zach knew she kept all her passwords written on a paper in her filing cabinet. She'd told him that a long time ago; they'd laughed at how bad she was at remembering which password went with which account unless she wrote them down.

No. Zach would never hurt her.

The story Rochelle had told her about the girl in Sacramento. *". . . covered in bruises . . . he laughed at her, saying no one would ever believe her . . ."* She'd caused trouble for Zach, and she was dead. Monica had caused trouble for Zach, and Monica was dead.

Stop this. You trust Zach. He would never hurt anyone.

Sunday faces.

"You can let go of me." Emily made her voice calm. "You're right. I can't talk to Rochelle right now. I'm not going to try."

Zach returned his hand to the steering wheel, but slowly, like he anticipated having to grab her again.

"Take me to the police department," Emily said. "I want to talk to Detective Lund. If she isn't there, I'll leave a message for her."

"Are you sure you want to do that?"

"Yes. I'm the one who got Rochelle into this by asking her for information. Now she's in trouble. I need to talk to Lund."

"Are you sure you don't want to think about it for a little while? Maybe head back to your parents' house, get a little rest—"

"Because rest will somehow change the facts? Even if Lund thinks I'm a kook, she'll go talk to Rochelle. And Rochelle might tell her the truth. Are you one hundred percent positive that I imagined all this? Because if you're not, then there's a chance that I'm right and someone's threatening Rochelle. Do you want it on your conscience if something happens to her or her son?"

"Okay." Zach's voice was grim. "I'll take you to Lund."

* * *

"She knew something, but instead of taking it to us, she was taking it to you." Detective Lund's tone was as featureless as ever, giving Emily plenty of room to interpret contempt and doubt in her words.

"From what she said in her message, she wasn't sure it was significant. She wanted to run it by me."

"Red nail polish. And a car."

"That's what she said. I don't know what she meant. But red nail polish was used on that picture of Ryan Tanner that someone left on my door."

"Did you tell anyone that Rochelle Elton claimed to have information for you?"

Emily didn't want to hear herself speak the words. The instant she acknowledged them to Lund, she'd have to fully acknowledge them to herself, cope head-on with the possibility that someone she cared about—loved—

"Miss Ramsey?"

Emily's heart beat in her ears, loud and hollow. "When I listened to the message, Nicole Gardiner, Brent Amherst, and Zachary Sullivan were in the room."

"Did they hear the message?"

"No. I told them only that Rochelle and I were trying to figure out what happened, and Rochelle had come up with something she wanted to run by me." Pain burned like a ring of fire encircling her neck. She needed to tell Lund about last night's attack. How could she expect Lund to carry out an accurate investigation if Emily withheld information?

"We got the lab report back on the scarf you turned in," Lund said.

A whiplash of surprise made Emily sit up straight. "What did it say?"

Lund's eyes focused directly on hers, a gaze that made Emily feel like her mind and soul were being inventoried. "The blood on the scarf was yours, Miss Ramsey."

A rock slammed into her chest. "That's impossible. They must have made a mistake."

"They didn't make a mistake."

But it was impossible. How could it be her blood? She would have known if someone had hurt her—if she'd hurt herself—

"Is there something you need to tell me, Emily?"

Emily's vision blurred, and Lund's face became murky. *I didn't put the blood on the scarf. Someone else must have. Someone came in my apartment and—*

And what? Took her blood without her noticing? Emily realized she was twisting her hands back and forth, staring at palms, then the backs of her hands as if searching for injuries she hadn't noticed previously.

Think. You've got to think. How could this have happened? There's a logical answer if you'll just look for it.

"Emily," Lund said. "Did you put your blood on the scarf?"

"No."

"How did the blood get there?"

"I don't know."

"Have you been injured recently, besides the head injury sustained at Miss Fife's shop?"

"No."

"Any cuts or marks you can't explain?"

"I haven't noticed anything."

"How often do you drink alcohol?"

"I don't. I don't drink at all. I don't take drugs." She was so cold, so tired, losing the battle against the icy riptide dragging her out to sea. *Think. You've got to think.*

Tell Lund about last night's attack now, her mind gibed. *Tell her about the attacker that Nicole couldn't see and Brent couldn't hear. Tell her about the knotted scarf Nicole found in your drawer.*

Without thinking, Emily pulled her sweater up higher on her throat to ensure no scratches or bruises were exposed. Zach was out in the lobby, waiting his turn with Detective Lund. She'd indicated that she wanted to speak to them separately. What would Lund ask him? Would she tell him that the blood on the scarf was Emily's? Would he tell her about last night's "attack"? That would be the final proof Lund needed that Emily was a danger to herself and possibly to others. She'd be locked up by the end of the day, as soon as Lund jumped through whatever legal hoops were required for an involuntary commitment.

She couldn't stay here. She had to be alone, she had to think, and she couldn't do it with Lund's gaze on her. "Am I free to go?"

Lund raised one eyebrow. "Yes, you're free to leave. But you're holding something back. What haven't you told me?"

Emily rose to her feet, bumping the table as she tried to push her chair back.

Lund rose as well. "If you think of anything you'd like to say—and you will—call me."

Emily nodded. When they reached the door to the lobby, Lund stopped and faced Emily. "Call me," she said again. "I'm not your enemy. I'd like to help you."

"I know."

In the lobby, Zach sprang to his feet as Lund and Emily entered. Zach gave Emily a penetrating look, and fear sharpened his expression. "Are you all right?"

"I'm fine," Emily said flatly.

"Mr. Sullivan." Holding the door open, Lund gestured Zach into the hallway.

Emily sank into one of the lobby chairs, but within seconds she was on her feet again. She couldn't sit here, waiting for Zach. She didn't even want to imagine what was about to pass between Lund and him. And she couldn't face Zach until she'd had some time to figure this out.

She walked to the glass partition that separated the lobby from the clerk's area. The clerk looked up and offered a wary smile.

"I need to leave," Emily said. "If I give you a message for Zachary Sullivan, will you give it to him when he comes out?"

"What would you like me to tell him?"

"Do you have something I could write on?"

The clerk took a pad of paper and a pen and slid them through the opening to Emily.

Emily wrote quickly.

> *Zach,*
> *I'm sorry to run out on you, but I need to be alone for a while.*
> *I'll be back at my parents' house by four.*
> *—Emily*

She folded the note, wrote Zach's name on the outside, and handed it to the clerk.

* * *

When she'd walked a couple of blocks away from the police department, Emily paused long enough to call a taxi to take her the rest of the way home. She had a frantic, look-over-your-shoulder feeling that she was a fugitive, despite the fact that Lund had told her she could leave. Zach was going to be worried and angry when he came out and found her gone, but Emily's relief at being alone outweighed her guilt at sneaking out.

With some reluctance, she gave the taxi driver her address. She was afraid to go home after what had happened last night, but she needed somewhere she could close the door and shut everything out.

Her heart started to race the instant she stepped over the threshold into her living room. Everything looked peaceful, but never before had the place felt so ominous. Maybe this was a mistake. Maybe she should go to the library or a bookstore—anywhere she could sit and think. But she wouldn't be able to concentrate in public, struggling to keep her expression neutral and her eyes free of tears, wondering who was watching her. She needed to hammer this out in her mind, and she could only do it in private.

Emily opened her coat closet and fished out the bat she used during softball season. She couldn't imagine her attacker would be bold enough to strike in daylight, but she wasn't taking any chances. Before she sat down, she'd search every corner of the apartment—it wasn't as though checking a one-bedroom apartment would take long. There would be no surprises this afternoon.

She checked the living room first, looking behind the curtains and verifying that the anti-theft bar was still in the track of the sliding door, not that it was really necessary. There was no way to reach her second-floor balcony from outside without a ladder. She even looked behind the couch, though there wasn't room for anyone to hide there unless a Photoshopped super-model from the cover of a magazine was her stalker.

It didn't take long to check the kitchen, her bedroom, the bathroom, and even the linen closet, in case the stalker was hunched on the floor beneath the lower shelf. Nothing. She was alone.

Breathing more easily, Emily returned to her bedroom and took a short-sleeved shirt from her closet. The tension from her talk with Lund followed by the stress of searching the apartment had left her soaked in sweat, and her turtleneck sweater was about as comfortable as a parka in the Sahara.

In the kitchen, she sat at the table with the softball bat on the floor next to her. She opened her laptop and clicked on a new file where she could start fresh in recording her ideas and impressions of everything that had happened this past week. This time, she created four columns and headed each with a name, hating herself with each keystroke but knowing she couldn't close her eyes to any possibilities.

Zach

Brent

Nicole

Justin

She paused and stared at the names. That wasn't all. She needed two more columns:

Rochelle

Bethany

After a painful moment of hesitation, she added another column.

Me

She hadn't killed Monica. But it *was* possible she'd been the one tormenting herself.

The act of listing herself brought an unexpected sense of relief. At last, she was truly facing *all* the possibilities, no matter how much they terrified her. She wouldn't hide from the evidence; she wouldn't fight it. She'd lay it out and analyze it, listing every fragment of information she had about everyone on her list—any reason they might have for either killing Monica or hurting Emily. The clues were there if she could just organize her thoughts well enough to find them.

Steeling herself, Emily added one final name to her list.

Ryan

It was a possibility she could no longer ignore, no matter how far-fetched it seemed.

Typing rapidly, she began entering everything she could think of that might either link someone on her list to any of the crimes or exonerate them. Rochelle thought Justin had been in love with Monica and she had rejected him. Brent had an alibi for the night of the murder; he'd been in Sunnyvale rock-climbing with Logan—although come to think of it, she had only Brent's word for that. She'd better check with Logan.

Absorbed in her work, Emily was so startled by the clunk of footsteps on the outside stairs that she jumped halfway out of her chair. Who was it?

Zach. She couldn't talk to him right now. If she looked into that face she loved, his name would slide right off her list, and she wouldn't be able to evaluate him with any degree of objectivity. He wouldn't know whether she was home or not—she'd left her car in the lot last night, so it wouldn't provide Zach any clues to her whereabouts. If she remained silent and still, Zach would give up and leave, assuming she hadn't come to her apartment.

The doorbell rang. Emily kept her hands motionless, afraid to create even the slight noise of tapping keys. *Later, Zach. I'll talk to you later. I'm sorry.*

A heavy knock followed, though Zach must have been able to hear that the doorbell was working. *Please go away,* Emily thought. *I can't talk to you right now. I'm so sorry.*

A key clicked in the lock.

She hadn't given anyone a key to the new lock. The only person who would have one was the attacker, who might have stolen one, copied it, and used it to enter last night.

Without time to think, Emily slapped the laptop shut, grabbed the bat, and darted toward the first hiding place she saw—the pantry. Her elbow knocked a bag of macaroni to the floor as she worked to flatten herself against the shelves so she could pull the door shut. It was still open a crack when she heard the front door swing open.

Her lungs strained as she held her breath, fearing to make even the smallest noise. Through the crack in the door, she could see part of the kitchen but couldn't see the front door.

Footsteps sounded, distinct on the tile surrounding the door, then more muffled on the carpeting of the living room.

Emily's terror mingled with fury, and she gripped the bat harder. She wasn't insane. *This* was the person who'd been tormenting her—Monica's killer. The attacker didn't think she was here. That's why he'd rung the bell, to make sure Emily wasn't home. Wildly, Emily thought of the way Tricia had liked to ring the bell when they arrived home to an empty house. Emily had always said the same thing—*"Who do you expect to answer?" "I'm just giving the burglars a heads-up,"* was Tricia's stock response.

The footsteps drew closer, but Emily could see nothing of the intruder; the crack through which she viewed the kitchen revealed only the back part of the room, not the dining area that the intruder would enter first.

She heard a familiar click. The invader had opened her laptop. He'd see what she'd written. The columns with names. Her speculation on possible motives. And he'd see today's date that she'd written automatically at the top of her work and the way she'd stopped in mid-sentence. He'd feel the warmth of the computer and know she'd been working on it a few minutes earlier.

Who was it? In her mind's eye, she pictured Zach leaning over the computer, Zach pushing his fingers through his hair the way he did when he was thinking. *Don't be an idiot. It's not him. It can't be.*

Emily shifted her weight, and her foot nudged the fallen bag of macaroni. The crackle of cellophane wasn't a loud noise, but in the silent apartment, it was distinct.

She froze. From outside the pantry, she could hear nothing. The intruder must be as motionless as she.

A voice spoke, calm, familiar. "Hello, Emily. Come on out and be civil."

It was Brent.

CHAPTER 23

"Have a seat, Mr. Sullivan."

Zach sat at the table. Trying to organize his whirling thoughts was like trying to count grains of sand while the wind blasted them into his face. What did he hope to achieve by talking to Detective Lund? *Whatever is best for Emily.* At this point, he had no idea what that was.

"Thank you for—" The ringing of his cell phone cut off his words. Embarrassed, he fumbled in his pocket to grab his phone and silence it but ended up dropping it on the floor.

"Sorry." He snatched it up, but before he hit the button to switch it off, he saw the number on the screen. *Timing.* Did the call he'd been waiting for have to come now?

"If you need to take the call, go ahead," Lund invited.

"No, that's—"

"It's all right." Lund gestured for him to proceed. Simultaneously glad and embarrassed, Zach answered the phone.

"Hello, this is Zachary Sullivan."

"Tyler Markham here. I've got some preliminary information for you." At the satisfaction evident in the voice of the private investigator, Zach yanked a pen out of his pocket, ready to take notes. Realizing he had nothing to write on, he looked at Lund.

"Can I have a sheet of paper?" He figured Lund was sizing him up as a total idiot, but her expression remained impassive as she tore a sheet off her notebook and handed it to him.

"All right, I'm ready," Zach said into the phone.

"No police record," Markham said. "But here's the part that might interest you. Brent Amherst was involved in a nasty divorce six years ago when he was living in Boise. He—"

"Divorce! He's divorced?"

"What century are you living in, Sullivan? It's not that shocking."

Lund's gaze made Zach feel like a guilty student in the principal's office. "He makes a big deal of this death-before-marriage attitude. We all thought he was a perpetual bachelor."

"I'm sure his ex wishes he'd stayed a bachelor. According to her, every-thing was rosy for the first couple of years, and he treated her like a queen. Then he started acting jealous and accused her of cheating on him. She denied it. The marriage fell apart. She claimed he was stalking her after the breakup—leaving her threatening notes, breaking her stuff, stealing her cell phone, running up huge bills for international calls and then slipping the phone back in her purse before she noticed it was gone. She could never nail him for anything. When she started up with a new boyfriend, that guy reported harassment as well, but again, they couldn't prove anything against Amherst. Four years ago, he moved to Los Coros, to the ex's great relief. None of this is official—like I said, no proof and no police record, but the ex-wife swears he's a creep who loves torturing people with mind games."

"Thanks." It wasn't definitive—Zach knew too well how he-said-she-said stories could vary—but it was enough to give to the police. If Brent *was* a creep, and if he'd become obsessed with Emily, might he have decided to torment her with memories of Ryan? And what about Monica? Had Brent secretly been in love with her? If she'd rejected him flat-out, what might he have done to her?

"Want me to keep digging, or is this enough for now?" Markham asked.

"It's enough. Thanks."

"No problem." Markham hung up.

Lund gave him a slight smile as he slid his phone in his pocket. "Interesting news?" she asked.

* * *

Emily's throat was so dry that she couldn't swallow. What a fool she'd been to think she could get away with pretending she wasn't home. In addition to the laptop on the table, her purse was sitting on the counter. The jacket she'd worn last night—Brent had seen her put it on—was draped over the back of her armchair. She should have grabbed the phone, locked herself in the bathroom, and dialed 911.

Brent. Her mind struggled to connect the dots. The bloodied scarf—how could someone take her blood without her knowledge? They couldn't, unless she was insensible at the time. Drugged. Monday night after Justin left, Brent had brought that bottle of sparkling grape juice. He'd poured her a glass with his back to her so she couldn't see what he was doing. She'd been so sleepy that night; she'd gone to bed early and slept without waking. Brent could have come into her apartment and made a small cut somewhere on her body where she wouldn't notice it—her back, maybe? Or had he used a needle to draw blood? And that was the night Bethany had received the 2:00 AM phone call from Emily's phone while Emily lay drugged and oblivious. And last night's attack? Nicole was wrong; she must have arrived the instant after Brent darted into his apartment. That's why she hadn't seen him.

"I can't believe you think hiding will do you any good." Brent's voice was still coming from the direction of the table. "It's not that big of a place, kiddo."

Emily forced herself to breathe slowly and silently. Maybe he hadn't heard the crackle of the macaroni bag. Maybe it was just the sight of her purse, jacket, and laptop that told him she was here, and he didn't yet have any idea where to look for her. If he headed toward the back of the apartment, she could race out the front door.

"Are you practicing for when you'll be hiding from the police? They'll be looking for you soon. They'd like to close the file on the Ryan Tanner case. Find his murderer."

The edge of a pantry shelf was digging into her spine. Any moment now, Brent would notice that the pantry door was ajar.

"They'll find solid evidence this time. You were just playing with them before, but this time it's serious business. You won't like prison, Emily. If I were you, I'd go for an insanity defense. Could work. After all, everyone already thinks you're nuts."

Solid evidence. How could Brent have any kind of real evidence to plant, unless—

Unless he'd killed Ryan himself.

Monica and *Ryan too? Why?*

His footsteps came toward her. Every muscle taut, Emily gripped the bat and waited, acutely aware of the pain in her bruised neck. *Why, Brent?*

The door to the pantry flew open. Emily swung the bat as hard as she could and struck empty air. The momentum from the swing spun her around, and the bat crashed against the wall, shattering the glass face of the clock.

A shove from behind sent her hurtling toward a kitchen chair. The top of the chair caught her hard in the gut, knocking the wind out of her. Brent grabbed her arm, and a wrenching pain in her wrist made her release the softball bat.

"Nice try, Em." He stepped back.

Fighting for breath, Emily staggered sideways, putting distance between them. Brent was wearing his friendly, country-boy expression, but this time the expression chilled her.

Brent rested the tip of the bat on the floor. "So how'd you get clear of your zookeepers? I thought they were taking you to a shrink today."

Brent remained standing several feet away from her. Emily took her chance and lunged toward the front door. Her fingers hadn't even touched the knob when Brent caught her arm.

If Emily could have drawn any air into her lungs, she would have screamed. Brent brought the side of the bat under her chin and yanked her backward with the force of the bat against her throat.

Suffocating under the pressure, Emily grabbed the bat, struggling to push it away, but Brent was too strong.

"Stop fighting, and I'll let go of you." His voice was a snake's hiss in her ear. "Stop fighting before I smash your larynx."

It was either cooperate or suffocate. Emily let herself go limp against Brent, her arms falling to her sides.

Brent lowered the bat. Holding her by one arm, he dragged her to the couch.

Clutching her throat, Emily stared up at him. "How did you get a key to my apartment?" she croaked.

He grinned. "Is that the best question you can think up?"

He looked so normal, so *Brent*. "How did you get it?"

"The first or the second time?"

"Both."

"First time—people who don't want keys stolen and copied ought to be more careful about locking their apartment doors when they step out for a few minutes. Second time—you *were* more careful after you thought someone had broken in, but locking your keys in your desk at school doesn't do a whole lot of good when the thief already has copies of all your school keys."

Emily drew a deep breath and tried to make her voice stronger. "Why are you doing this to me?"

Brent drew something out of his pocket. He was wearing latex gloves. "I came to drop this off. Have a look." He tossed the object into her lap. It was a brown leather wallet. She flipped it open.

Ryan's face smiled up from his driver's license. "You killed him," Emily rasped. "Why?"

"Is this supposed to be a confession session? The villain blabs all? I didn't kill Ryan. You did."

Emily opened her mouth to protest, realized how stupid it was to argue with Brent, and remained silent.

"You sure do fool people, Emily. The sweet schoolteacher. Bashing her fiancé's head in and hiding his body. Then weeping into her lace-edged handkerchief and collecting condolences."

Horror mingled inexplicably with relief. At least she knew—at last—what had happened to Ryan. But *why*?

"As long as you're here, we might as well let you have some fun." Brent swung the bat up so it rested against his shoulder. "Come into the kitchen and have a seat at the table."

"I'm not cooperating with you."

He chuckled and bounced the bat against his shoulder. "I *really* think you'd rather cooperate."

Emily imagined the damage a few swings of the bat could do to her. Disgust and fury at the way she'd provided him with a weapon made her stomach clench. Why hadn't she taken a split second to see where he was standing before she swung blindly?

"Hurry up, Em."

She moved slowly into the kitchen with Brent following her. At his gesture, she sat in the same chair she'd been occupying when he rang the doorbell.

If only she'd *answered* the door, Brent probably would have smiled and said he was checking to see if she was home, and how was she doing? He would have left her safe and ignorant and would have come back later to plant the wallet.

Brent opened the kitchen drawer where she kept pens and phone books. "Okay . . . let's see . . . ah, yes." He took out a pair of scissors.

"Brent, we've always been friends. You helped me so much—you've been here for me through everything—"

His eyes went flinty, and his boyish face was suddenly stone. "That's when I thought you deserved it."

Emily tried to swallow, but it was like forcing sand down her throat. "What do you mean?"

"I thought I'd finally found a woman who was different. Who was faithful."

Faithful? Emily's mind raced back to what Logan had said, hinting that Brent was in love with her. Had Brent imagined a relationship between them where none existed? Had he done the same to Monica?

"I thought Ryan was lucky to have you. And when he disappeared, you were still devoted to him. Waiting for him, loving him. Sure, you'd date now and then to stop Nicole from pestering you, but I could tell your heart wasn't in it. You belonged to Ryan and you were keeping yourself for him, keeping the promise you made when he put a ring on your finger. And then out of the blue, you're engaged to Sullivan. You wait until I'm out of town, and you get engaged! You're just like your sister—a cheating, filthy little—"

"Tricia wasn't—"

"Tricia couldn't keep herself focused on one man for a month, let alone a lifetime. She let me fall for her, then kicked me in the face. Gave me the silly speech about how she didn't want to get serious, we were just friends."

"Brent, if you loved her, I'm sure she didn't know. She—"

"Doesn't matter now, anyway. Tricia got what she deserved." He smacked the scissors against one palm. "Roadkill."

"Were you the one who—?"

"Did I run her down? Come on, Emily! That was divine justice. Lot's wife got turned into a pillar of salt. Sapphira got struck dead on the spot. Jezebel got tossed from a window and eaten by dogs. Tricia Ramsey got splattered over the bumper of an SUV. As for Emily, I guess she's getting off easy. All she's losing is her mind." Brent walked to the covered window next to the table and cut the cord dangling from the top of the drapes.

Brent couldn't have killed Tricia. He'd arrived at the party after the accident, and his car wasn't damaged. Emily's mind spun in confusion, but one thought was clear. Brent had killed Ryan, and he was going to kill her. If she was going to die, she wasn't going to die sitting here and meekly submitting.

Emily sprang to her feet, swooped the wooden chair up, and hurled it at Brent with all her might. It slammed into him, knocking him against the window. Seizing that instant while he was off balance, Emily sprinted for the front door. She twisted the deadbolt, grabbed the handle, and wrenched the door open a split second before pain exploded in her skull and everything went black.

* * *

Lund punched the button to shut off the recorder and rose to her feet. "Next time, Mr. Sullivan, I'd advise you to come to us first instead of trying to investigate or diagnose issues yourself. Delaying a report of last night's attack on Emily Ramsey was extraordinarily foolish, whether or not you suspected that Miss Ramsey had staged it. And if you had suspicions about a friend of hers, a simple phone call to me would have negated the need to hire a private investigator."

"I know. I just didn't want to smear Brent's reputation when I had nothing to go on but a gut feeling."

"I understand how your experiences at your former school sensitized you to the danger of false accusations, but I assure you we can investigate someone without smearing their reputation."

Zach nodded. If he'd felt any more sheepish, he would have sprouted wool. But at least things were moving in the right direction. The police would investigate Brent Amherst. The thought of Brent behind bars and Emily safe and at peace brought Zach feelings of both intense relief and intense guilt. He'd questioned Emily's mental stability, and she knew it. Would she ever be able to forgive him for that?

But she didn't even trust herself. Would she expect more of me?

"I need to speak with Miss Ramsey again," Lund said as she led the way out of the interview room.

Zach wondered how Emily would react to the things he'd told Lund. She was fond of Brent—would she instantly dismiss the unsettling findings in the PI's report as the fabrications of a vindictive ex-wife and Zach's suspicions of Brent as jealousy? If Brent was what his ex-wife claimed, he was eel-slippery; he'd managed to go a long time without getting charged with any crimes. What if the police couldn't find any evidence this time around either? Zach's hands clenched into fists. If it was Brent who had attacked Emily last night, Zach would hound him to the grave before he'd let him get away with that.

Zach stepped into the lobby and stopped in his tracks, looking around the room.

It was empty.

"Wasn't she waiting for you?" Lund asked.

"Yes, I thought—maybe she's in the restroom." Zach glanced questioningly at the woman behind the glassed-in counter.

"Mr. Sullivan? Miss Ramsey left a message for you." The woman pushed a piece of paper through the opening in the window.

Dismay dragged Zach's heart down like it was too heavy for his chest. "Thank you." He unfolded the paper.

"Problems?" Lund asked as Zach refolded the note.

Zach tried not to sound as worried as he felt. "She said she wants to be alone for a while. She's heading back to her parents' house at four. That's when she has the appointment with the psychiatrist."

"She didn't say where she's going now?"

"No. Let me call her." Zach opened his phone and tried Emily's cell phone number. She didn't pick up. He tried her home number. No answer there either.

Lund's frown gouged creases on either side of her mouth. "Does she often ignore her phone?"

"She doesn't hear her cell phone half the time when it's in her purse, but I don't think that's the problem now. She knows I'll be trying to call her. I don't think she wants to talk to me."

Lund held out her hand, and Zach passed her Emily's note. She read it and handed it back. "The things I discussed with Emily rattled her badly. This is not a good time for her to be on her own."

Zach was already punching buttons to call Nicole. "Let me try Nicole Gardiner. If Emily's stressed out, she might call Nicole—" Abruptly, he lowered the phone.

"You don't think Emily would go to Nicole Gardiner after Mrs. Gardiner's role in the incident last night?"

"I guess not."

"Unless, perhaps, she thought she could glean some information from Mrs. Gardiner to reconcile their differing versions of events?"

"Could be." He pressed the button to complete the call.

"Hey, Zach." Nicole sounded anxious. "How's Emily?"

"I was hoping you could tell me. We're here in Los Coros; we were planning to go back to her parents' house this afternoon so she could talk to Dr. Kincaid. But we've had a rough morning, and she ran out on me. I was hoping maybe she'd contacted you."

"A rough morning? What *now*? How hard can it be for you to keep an eye on her?"

Zach squelched the urge to lash back at Nicole. "If you hear from her, call me immediately."

"I doubt she trusts me enough to call me right now."

"She might try to talk to you about last night. To figure things out. She's not answering my calls, but maybe she'll answer yours."

"I'll try her right now. Have you gone to her apartment?"

"Not yet. I'm at the police department. Emily wanted to talk to Detective Lund."

"You *idiot*. Why did you let—oh, never mind. I'll call her, and if she doesn't answer, I'll head to her apartment to see if she's there. I'll call you back in a few minutes."

"Nicole—" Zach glanced at Lund, not sure if he was supposed to say this, but unable to let Nicole go without a warning. "Be careful of Brent Amherst. I've learned some potentially unsettling things about him. If you meet up with him, act normal, but . . . be cautious."

"Okay . . . that sounds like a story, but I'll get it later. Let me call Emily." Nicole hung up.

CHAPTER 23

HER CHEEK RESTED AGAINST SOMETHING hard and cold. Her head throbbed with a sickening ache that augmented the mounting nausea in her stomach. Emily forced her eyelids to stay open, but it didn't do much good. Everything was blurry.

"Are you okay?" A friendly voice spoke in her ear. "You fell and hit your head. Do you remember?"

Hit her head . . . Monica Fife . . . the floor of Monica's workroom . . .

Something was digging into her shoulders. The edge of a table. She was sitting at her kitchen table, her head resting on the tabletop.

Hands grasped her shoulders and eased her to a sitting position. Pain blasted her skull, and the room spun around her. She tried to grab the edge of the table to steady herself and realized her hands were tied behind her.

"You slipped on a wet patch on the kitchen floor and hit your head on the counter. Do you remember that?"

"I . . . that's not what . . ." *Brent. Brent killed Ryan.*

Brent's hands closed around her neck, his cool fingers pressing lightly against her bruised flesh. "You fell, Emily. *Do you remember?*"

Realizing Brent wanted agreement, Emily nodded woozily.

"Good girl. You're not hurt too badly. There's no need to call an ambulance."

He's crazy. He's insane, completely insane. The softball bat and Ryan's wallet both lay on the table next to her laptop. Emily drooped forward, wanting to rest her aching head against the table. Brent's hands shifted to her shoulders, pinning her against the back of the chair.

"You're going to make a couple of phone calls. People have been calling. They're worried about you. You're going to explain what's happening."

"What do you want from me?" she whispered.

"I'm just a friend, here to help." Brent pushed a piece of paper in front of her. "This is what you're going to say. Can you read this?"

Emily blinked, trying to focus on the paper. Zach's name was written at the top of the paper and then, in her own handwriting, the words Brent wanted her to speak. He could forge her handwriting. He'd written the note on the sack taped to Zach's mailbox.

Blearily, she scanned the lines. "I won't say this . . . it's not true . . ."

"Your choice." Brent's hands moved in front of her eyes. Stretched between his hands was a narrow white cord. The cord from the drapes.

He drew the cord back and circled it around her throat, tightening it enough so it pressed into her skin but didn't interfere with her breathing.

"You thought you were strong, didn't you?" Corrosive hatred seeped up through the amusement in his voice. "Flaunting yourself, attracting men and then betraying them like you did Ryan. Like my mother did to my father. Like my ex did to me. But you didn't have as much power as you thought, did you? One silly picture on your door, and you're a wreck. Same with Monica. I knew she'd blame you for that little calling card. All I had to do was sit back and let you tear each other apart. Great entertainment. That's the only reason I bothered with her, you know. She wasn't worth my notice on her own. But I knew she'd make things harder for you."

He leaned close to her ear. "All I had to do was lift a finger, and you'd lose another piece of your sanity. Who's the one with power, Emily?"

"I never claimed to . . . I didn't want . . ."

"You're going to make some phone calls now. It takes, what—four minutes for a brain to die without oxygen? If you think you can say nothing—or say something other than what I wrote for you—and help can get here in less than four minutes, go ahead and take your chances."

"I don't see what difference it makes. You're going to kill me anyway."

"Don't be silly." Brent traced his index finger along her cheekbone in a caress that made her shiver. "If I wanted to kill you, I would have done it already."

"You killed Ryan."

"Not true."

"You killed Monica."

"Also not true. I wasn't sorry to see her go, mind you. She deserved worse than she got."

"You won't let me walk away, not when I can tell the police—"

"Emily." Brent rested his chin on top of her head. "You don't have any proof. You can tell the police anything you want and they won't believe you. They all think you're a wacko. Even your parents think you're nuts. Considering what you did to Ryan, it's not surprising that you finally snapped. You thought you could cope with the guilt, but getting engaged to

Zach brought it all back. And finding Monica like you did—that made those blood-soaked nightmares a little bigger than you could handle."

"No one will ever believe I killed Ryan."

"They'll believe it when they find the evidence. The wallet is just the tip of the iceberg. I'm clean as a whistle, Em. It'll be your word against mine—and everyone knows you're a raving psychotic. So if you want to stay alive, make yourself sound good and crazy. I'll write to you in the psych hospital. We'll be pen pals."

It wasn't possible that Brent would let her go . . . was it? If he was convinced the police thought she was crazy and no one would believe her . . . I *did* doubt her sanity, and so did everyone else . . . but Brent was a killer. Why would he take any kind of risk to keep her alive?

"I like you, Em." Brent spoke with his lips against her hair. "Even with your wicked little Jezebel ways, I still like you. Why would I want to kill you? You just need to talk to Sullivan and Gardiner and make sure they don't think you're here in your apartment. I don't want anyone to bother you. You need rest."

If she played along, it would buy time. If she didn't—

"All right," she said. "Dial the number."

Brent's latex-encased finger rapidly punched at her cell phone keys, locating and dialing Zach's number. "Remember, Emily." The cord dug a little more deeply into her flesh. "Just say what's on the paper. And put some heart into it."

Brent pushed the button to put the call on speakerphone. The phone started ringing.

Emily drew rapid, shallow breaths, hyperconscious of the cord held in Brent's strong hands.

"*Emily.*" Zach answered the phone. "Where are you? Are you all right?"

"Zach, I'm sorry," Emily read from the paper. Brent ought to be pleased with how much her voice was shaking. "I can't talk to you right now. You and the police all think I'm crazy—"

"Emily, *no.* No, we don't. Listen to me. You've got to come back to the police department. Detective Lund needs to talk to you about last night. I told her what happened. She needs to talk to you. She needs to search your apartment for evidence."

Still holding the drape cord in one hand, Brent snatched the pen and scrawled something on the paper. Emily read the new line. "She's already got plenty of evidence against me."

"She doesn't assume you imagined the attack."

Brent crossed out a line and pointed to the next one. "I'm so sorry. I never meant to hurt anyone."

"Emily . . . what are you talking about?"

"I'm sorry, Zach. You should forget about me. I'm not worthy of you. There's too much blood on my hands." *Help me. Can't you tell these aren't my words?*

"Where are you? Tell me where you are. Are you at your apartment?"

Brent had anticipated well. The next line already read: "No. I can't go home. The police might find me there." Behind her back, Emily's fingers curled into fists, her nails sinking into her palms. "I never meant for it to happen. But Ryan had—" At the sight of the next words on the page, Emily couldn't go on. She looked at Brent, silently beseeching him.

He pulled the cord taut, momentarily cutting off her air, then relaxed the cord and mouthed, *"Go on."*

Tears trickled down Emily's face. "He'd gotten involved with Tricia while I was away at school. I accused him and we argued."

"Emily. *Where are you?* Let me come get you. I'll take you wherever you want to go. We don't have to go back to your parents' house. You don't have to talk to Detective Lund. You don't have to talk to Dr. Kincaid. Let me come get you. We'll go for a drive—we'll just drive until you want to stop. We can go anywhere. We can drive across the country if you want."

Brent was right—Zach certainly thought she was insane. But would it be enough to make Brent feel safe? Or was she reciting her own suicide note?

"Darling, listen to me." Zach's voice was half soothing and half desperate. "We'll deal with this together. I need to know where you are. Tell me where you are, and I'll come get you."

I'm at my apartment. Help me. He's going to kill me. Emily couldn't have spoken the words even if she'd decided to take the risk; Brent had pulled the cord too tight to allow for speech. "End the conversation," he whispered in her ear. "Read the last lines." He loosened the cord enough so she could speak.

"I'm sorry, Zach." Emily choked the words out. "I never meant—"

"Emily, listen to me. I might know who's been stalking you. I did some checking. Brent Amherst has been accused of this kind of behavior in the past, and with him living so close to you, it would have been easy for him to get into your apartment. The police are investigating him. Emily, we can sort this out—we can stop the things that are happening to you—"

Terror as sharp as a steel blade sliced through Emily's heart. Bent over the table, his head next to hers, Brent stood frozen, his hand halfway to the pen. If he'd ever thought he could stay safe even with Emily accusing him, he couldn't think so anymore. He was going to kill her. Now.

With all the strength she could gather, Emily slammed her head sideways, crashing her skull into the side of Brent's face. There was a savage yank on the cord around her throat, which was quickly released as Brent reared back, clutching his face. He fell to his knees.

"Zach, help me!" Emily shrieked. "I'm at my apartment!" Pushing her feet hard against the floor, she shoved her chair back from the table and jumped to her feet. Dizziness swished through her, and she stumbled. "Brent's going to kill me—*Brent's going to kill me*—"

She had to get to the door. She lurched, the floor seeming to rise and sink beneath her feet . . . *the door, unlock the door* . . . She twisted her body, frantically stretching her bound hands toward the deadbolt. Brent was rising to his feet—

Something struck her shoulder, and she stumbled backward. A bone-rattling jolt shook her body as she hit the floor.

Blackness.

* * *

"Emily!" A frantic female voice spoke her name. Nicole was leaning over her.

"Brent—" Emily gasped.

"Out cold," Nicole said, and Emily realized Nicole was holding the soft-ball bat. "I was about to ring your doorbell when I heard you screaming something about Brent. I tried the door; it was locked, but then I heard the bolt open. I came crashing in. I think I knocked you down. I'm sorry. Brent jumped at me so I grabbed the bat—"

"Help me up," Emily said, though she felt so sick she knew she'd be better off remaining on the floor. "And call the police."

"I will." With a firm grip on Emily's arm, Nicole pulled her to her feet. Emily caught an unfocused glimpse of Brent sprawled on the kitchen floor.

"What *happened*?" Nicole asked. "Brent's the one who's been stalking you?"

"Yes. And he killed Ryan. He wanted to frame me for it—he's got Ryan's wallet, look—" With her hands tied, Emily had to use her elbow to gesture at the table. "Get me to the couch before I fall over. My head—"

But Nicole didn't seem to hear her. She released Emily's arm, snatched the wallet, and flipped it open.

"Nicole, could you please—"

"How did he get this? *How did he get this?*"

"I don't know—he didn't say—"

"Was there anything else of Ryan's?"

"I don't know." Emily's stomach convulsed with nausea, and she swayed on her feet. She managed two shuffling steps forward and collapsed into a kitchen chair. Leaning against the back of the chair in an effort to brace herself, she watched in confusion as Nicole shoved the wallet into her purse.

"What are you—what—" Emily couldn't finish the question. It took all her concentration to stay upright on the chair. On the floor, Brent twitched slightly.

Nicole leaned over Brent. "Was there anything else besides the wallet?"

"No . . . he didn't . . . what are you doing?"

Nicole had the drape cord in her hands. She wound it twice around Brent's neck and yanked it tight.

"*Stop!* What are you doing? You'll kill him! Let the police—the police will take care of him—"

Nicole knotted the drape cord and sprang to her feet.

"Nicole! You're killing him—he can't breathe!" Emily slid off the chair so she was on her knees next to Brent.

Nicole raced into the kitchen and yanked open a cupboard while Emily twisted, reaching for the cord that was strangling Brent. "You can't do this. The police—"

Nicole caught Emily under the arm and yanked her to her feet. Something poked Emily in the ribs, and she looked down to see the blade of one of the razor-sharp knives her mother had given her for Christmas.

"You're coming with me. If you say one word to anyone, I'll sink this straight into your heart." Nicole removed the wool cape she was wearing and threw it around Emily's shoulders, concealing her bound hands. The cape draped around the knife and Nicole's hand, camouflaging them.

"You're hurt, and I'm taking you to the hospital," Nicole said. "That's the story. Don't say anything to anyone."

Nicole hurried her toward the door, moving so fast that Emily couldn't contend with anything except the dizziness sweeping through her. Dimly she heard the sound of their feet banging on the stairs, felt the hardness of the sidewalk beneath her shoes, the point of the knife against her ribs. Nicole's rigid arm curved around her, supporting her.

Nicole unlocked her BMW and pushed Emily into the passenger seat. She drew the seat belt across Emily, snapped it shut, and raced around to the driver's side.

Sirens, Emily realized. Sirens, growing louder, then cutting to silence.

"Get down." Nicole grabbed Emily by the hair and forced her below the level of the dashboard.

Not until she'd driven for several minutes did Nicole relax her grip on Emily's hair. Stiffly, Emily sat up. They were speeding along the on-ramp to the freeway.

"Where are we going?"

Nicole's face was as white and hard as a marble statue. The knife rested on her lap.

* * *

Crying had left Rochelle Elton's eyelids so raw that it hurt to blink. Seth kept shooting anxious looks at her, and she kept thrusting more cookies at him and hoping his favorite movie would keep him occupied long enough so she could figure out what to do.

Every time she pictured the expression on Emily Ramsey's face, her tears started anew. Emily had looked so stunned—so frightened. And Zach—he clearly didn't know *what* to believe, but he must think Emily had lost her mind. The anonymous note had assured Rochelle that her voice mail message had been erased, so there was no record of what she'd said to Emily. No one would have any reason to believe her.

"Keep whatever you think you know to yourself, or little Seth is going to vanish into thin air. Say you only talked to Emily to tell her to leave you alone. Deny telling her you had any information. Everyone will think she's insane." The words of the note she'd found pushed through her mail slot made Rochelle shudder every time they echoed in her thoughts. She'd obeyed the instructions in the note, too terrified to do anything else.

And her information had seemed so paltry, something she hadn't even remembered until she'd made a meticulous list of the events on the night of Monica's murder in light of what Emily had told her about the picture of Ryan Tanner and the red nail polish. When Rochelle had gone into Monica's shop just after closing time, a bottle of red nail polish and a manila envelope had been sitting near the cash register. It was odd to see nail polish there—Monica wasn't the type to sit at her register and repair a chipped nail—but Rochelle hadn't thought much about it; she'd been promptly distracted by the call from her mother about Seth's cut finger.

Red nail polish and an envelope that might have held a picture. Those items had been on the counter when Rochelle had called out to Monica and Monica hadn't answered—when she might have already been dead on her workroom floor. But when the police had escorted Rochelle back to the shop to see if she could identify anything out of place, the nail polish and envelope had been gone. Had someone—the murderer?—come back to retrieve them?

Emily had told Rochelle that she'd given the nail polish and picture of Ryan Tanner to Nicole Gardiner. The thought of Nicole Gardiner had jarred another memory, one domino tipping into the next. When she'd been driving away to meet her mother and Seth at urgent care, a silver BMW had whipped around the corner, crowding into Rochelle's lane. Rochelle remembered the flash of annoyance she'd felt—again, a memory quickly forgotten, pushed out by bigger concerns. She hadn't even realized Nicole drove a silver BMW until she'd seen her car on Monday when Nicole and Brent Amherst had shown up to haul Emily out of Rochelle's shop.

Was it possible that Nicole Gardiner had been there the night of the murder and she'd taken the nail polish and picture to confront Monica with them? Emily had mentioned that both she and Nicole thought Monica was responsible for the picture of Ryan, and Rochelle knew through Monica that Nicole was very protective of Emily—almost strangely protective—and that she'd been the one to bring Zach and Emily together. If she thought Monica was threatening that relationship, would she have confronted Monica?

It had all seemed incredibly far-fetched—it was ludicrous to imagine that Nicole Gardiner could have had anything to do with the murder—but Rochelle had wanted to mention it to Emily anyway and get her opinion. No way did she dare take such wild conjectures to the police without talking to Emily first. Nicole Gardiner's husband was some high-powered business executive, and Rochelle could picture herself losing her store, her house, and everything else she owned when Mitchell Gardiner sued her into oblivion for damaging his wife's reputation. Besides, she was almost sure that her theory was nonsense.

Then the note had arrived.

Rochelle rose to her feet and started to head for the kitchen for a drink of water, but in the doorway, she stopped and turned, unwilling to let Seth out of her sight.

If her information was worthless, why had someone—Nicole?—threatened her?

She needed to call the police. She needed to tell them what had happened. But Seth—how could she risk him? Rochelle wanted to snatch him up and run away, fly across the world, go to Australia or China and hide there.

Rochelle picked up the playful blue-and-yellow polka-dot candle that sat on a lamp table. Was she such a coward that she'd shield the demon who had taken Monica's life? What if the murderer killed again? What if Emily Ramsey was the next victim?

Rochelle would protect Seth, no matter what. But she wouldn't collude with a murderer.

She didn't dare just call the police. What if the murderer had tapped her phone somehow? She'd go straight to the police department.

Her decision made, Rochelle strode across the room and switched off the TV. "Seth, come on. We need to go for a drive."

CHAPTER 24

"NICOLE, TALK TO ME." Emily squirmed in her seat, but even if they hadn't been speeding along the freeway at seventy miles per hour, she didn't have a chance at escape. With her hands tied and the seat belt pinning her, she was trapped, and the enveloping cape eliminated even the possibility of contorting her body at an angle that might allow her to release the seat belt or open her door. "What's going on?"

"I'm sorry." Tears welled in Nicole's eyes. "I'm really, really sorry. I never wanted to hurt you. You're such a good person—you've suffered enough—"

"Why did you do that to Brent?"

"Because he *knows*. There's no other way he could have gotten the wallet."

"Ryan's wallet?" Emily's head ached so badly that plain words didn't seem to make sense. "What do you mean?"

Nicole lowered one hand from the steering wheel to touch the handle of the knife, as though wanting to make sure it was still there.

"Brent killed Ryan." Emily tried to sound calm. "He must have kept the wallet. He wanted to frame me."

Nicole stared out the windshield.

Facts tangled and twirled in an incomprehensible formation. Nicole had murdered Brent. She'd taken Emily hostage. She'd taken the wallet.

"He knows. There's no other way he could have gotten the wallet."

Nicole had been afraid to let anyone find the wallet. Afraid of what Brent could tell the police.

Afraid of what Emily could tell the police.

The night Ryan had disappeared—Nicole's trembling voice on the Tanners' phone, right after Emily arrived, while she was still looking around the house for Tricia. *"I tried Tricia's cell phone, but she's not answering. Can you tell her I won't be able to make your party? I'm sick—throwing up—food poisoning, I think—"*

Emily had never seen Nicole that night.

The question seemed absurd, but Emily had to ask it. "Did *you* kill Ryan?"

"I didn't *want* to. I never wanted to. I just didn't know what else to do."

"Why didn't you know what to do?"

"I'm sorry." Tears dripped down Nicole's face. "I'm so sorry. It was an accident. Just an accident. But he was going to call the police. And it wouldn't have done any good. It was *useless*. I knew she was dead. She had to be dead—I was going so fast, and I was driving that big SUV—"

For an instant, Emily's heart stalled. "An accident—Nicole—"

"I'm sorry. It was an accident. But I'd been drinking just a little. I'd been on the phone with my dad. It was an ugly conversation—he didn't want me to invite my brother to my wedding . . . said if I did, he wouldn't pay for it. I was upset and needed something to unwind me. I wasn't *drunk,* but I did have a few . . . I knew the police would check for—Emily, it would have wrecked my life. I could have gone to prison. And what good would it have done to call the police? Tricia was already gone. She wouldn't have wanted me to go to prison. Would she?"

"No—of course she wouldn't," Emily choked out.

"But Ryan—he wasn't thinking, he was just reacting, freaking out. He was with me in the car. I'd met him when I stopped at Safeway to pick up the napkins for the party. Tricia had forgotten the napkins. He was stranded, so I offered him a ride. He didn't know that I'd been . . . and it was raining so hard that night, it was almost impossible to see. I didn't even see Tricia until the instant before I hit—I'm so sorry. And Emily, I honestly didn't mean to hurt Ryan. I didn't even think about what I was doing. But he yelled at me until I stopped the car. He had his cell phone in his hand, and he was going to call—I panicked. All I could think of was my picture on the front page of the paper. Mitch would have dumped me. He'd never have married me after something like that. My parents would have disowned me. I would have lost my family, lost everything—"

Cold sweat drenched Emily's skin. "What did you do to Ryan?"

"I hit him in the head. I had a flashlight in the glove compartment, one of those metal ones, the heavy kind. I *had* to stop him from calling the police. I'm *sorry*. Your sister and your fiancé, in one night. I wanted to die, I felt so awful."

Emily strained against the cord binding her wrists and felt scorching pain as the cord dug deeper into raw skin. Her head hurt so much that she could hardly focus her eyes, but she wished the pain were worse—sufficient to block out Nicole's confession.

Nicole's words were coming faster now, a well of pain gushing out. "I couldn't do anything for Tricia or Ryan, but I *could* help you. Did you notice, Emily? Did you notice how I helped you? I was a good friend, wasn't I?"

"Yes."

"You and Tricia were so close. She used to talk about you all the time. I knew her death would leave a horrible gap in your life. I did everything I could to fill that gap. I helped you, didn't I? Didn't I make things easier?"

Emily closed her eyes. Looking at Nicole's familiar, beloved face hurt too much. How many times had she been grateful for that very thing—that Nicole had done so much to fill the void left by Tricia's death?

"But Ryan—I couldn't take his place, could I?" Nicole swung her BMW around a slow-moving Volkswagen. "I knew I had to find someone for you. You didn't make it easy, you know, being so picky about the guy sharing your religion." She laughed and accelerated. "But the minute I met Zach Sullivan, I knew he was perfect for you. I did well there, didn't I? I was right—Zach *is* perfect for you, and I made it happen. And then *Monica.* That sneaky, nasty little—oops. Soap, right?" She laughed again. "She would have messed things up for you. I knew it. And I wasn't going to let you lose Zach. You'd lost too much."

"You killed Monica," Emily whispered.

"I didn't plan on it. I thought she'd sent you that picture of Ryan. I was going to confront her with it, threaten her that if she didn't lay off, I'd see her arrested. Mitch is friends with the chief of police. I figured I'd throw his name in her face."

"You took the red nail polish to her." *Red nail polish. Rochelle had wanted to tell me something about red nail polish.* "You didn't really throw it out like you said."

"Yes. But she just laughed. She thought this was *your* game—trying to scare her then telling everyone *she* was the one planting horrible pictures. She said if you thought you could make her look bad with some freaky tactic like that, she'd be happy to give you the number of a good psychiatrist. She was so cocky. She said she'd send you a wedding announcement when Zach and she got engaged. I just lost it, Emily. I didn't mean to hurt her, but I couldn't let her do that to you. Not after what you'd been through. You'd lost so much because of me. I wouldn't let you lose Zach too, not when I could keep it from happening. I honestly didn't plan to hurt her. It just happened. But she would have ruined things. What was I supposed to do? Let her take Zach?"

You should have trusted that Zach wasn't stupid enough to fall for her again. Emily didn't dare say the words.

"I killed Monica for *you*. You can forgive me for that, can't you?"

"You threatened Rochelle Elton into denying what she told me, didn't you?"

"I had to. I didn't really think she knew anything important, but I couldn't take the chance."

"What did you do with Ryan's body?"

"I took him up to the yoga cabin. I . . . left him there, in the garage. I couldn't stand to do anything else. What was I supposed to do? Scratch out a hole with my fingernails and bury him in the woods?"

Emily fought back an image of Ryan's body abandoned on the floor of Nicole's garage. "What about your car? There must have been damage—"

"There were some dents—nothing too bad—it was that old SUV, the one my parents gave me because they thought I'd be safer in a big car. I drove three or four hours away and took it to some sleazy repair shop. I cleaned Ryan's blood up first, of course. I paid a pile of cash to get the dents fixed, and they didn't ask questions. I sold it as soon as I could. But Brent . . . Brent must have . . . I don't know how he figured it out. Maybe because I denied seeing anyone last night when you were attacked. It must have been *him*. Was *he* the one who gave you those awful pictures?" The fury that contorted Nicole's face made Emily shrink back. "If I'd known, believe me—"

"If you were trying to help me, why did you lie and say there was no attacker? Why were you trying to make me look like I was having a break-down?"

"I didn't want to hurt you, but you were scaring me, the way you were starting to play Nancy Drew. I was afraid of what you might figure out. It would be better if people thought you were losing your mind. That way they'd ignore anything you said. I'm sorry. I know it was hard for you, but it would have all blown past. Maybe you would have spent a little while in a hospital, some medication, something like that. And truly, Emily, I thought maybe you *were* losing it. That creepy note . . . But your parents would have helped you, they wouldn't have minded that you were damaged. And Zach was so sweet, he just wanted to take care of you."

Nicole brushed tear-dampened hair off her cheeks. "But I made a mistake there. I must have made Brent suspicious, because he knew I'd seen someon run out of your apartment, and then I denied it. The yoga cabin— maybe he went up there to hunt around for any dirt on me. Tricia must have told him where it was. When he found Ryan, he must have decided it would be more fun to torment both of us with what he'd learned than to call the police. He's a freak." Nicole pulled her foot off the accelerator. "I'd better slow down. I don't want a speeding ticket."

"Where are we going?"

Nicole's expression closed. "I just need to get a little farther away, and I'll let you out, okay?"

She was lying, and so badly that Emily marveled she'd ever been able to conceal her crimes with such finesse. "You're taking me to the yoga cabin, aren't you?"

"I never wanted to hurt you."

But you will. You're going to kill me and leave my body with Ryan's. "Nicole, please don't do this. You can't cover this up any longer. Even if Brent's dead—and I'm dead—there will be people who saw you arrive at my apartment, people who saw us walking away—"

"You'd be amazed at what people don't notice."

"But you can't assume no one—" Emily closed her mouth. *Zach.* Zach had been listening on the phone when Nicole walked in. He might have heard her voice.

More than that. Zach must have told Nicole she was missing, or Nicole wouldn't have assumed Emily was home. Zach must know that Nicole had gone to Emily's apartment. He'd tell the police. And Nicole's fingerprints—no, they wouldn't be on the bat. Nicole was wearing suede gloves that matched her hat.

Wincing at the pain evoked by turning her neck, Emily glanced over her shoulder, hoping for a glimpse of a highway patrol car. She saw nothing but the usual line of traffic.

"Please listen to me." It would have been easier to sew a quilt out of rocks than to make her voice calm, but Emily did her best to sound soothing. "You don't have to go on with this. You don't want to hurt me. Nicole, listen. You can get help. I'm sure Mitch knows top-notch lawyers—"

"Do you really think future president of the United States Mitch will do anything for me? He hates scandal. He'll divorce me in ten seconds flat. Besides, no lawyer can get me out of a triple—I mean quadruple—murder charge, unless he can also cancel the law of gravity and make the sun rotate around the earth."

"Lesser charges—none of these deaths were premeditated. Your parents could help you find a lawyer who—" Emily stopped. Nicole was laughing through her tears.

"You have no idea, do you? You think my parents are like yours. They might get mad at you, but they'll love you in the end no matter what. It doesn't work that way in my family. You know about my brother. They haven't spoken to him for eight years because he married a girl they hated. They didn't want her low-class genes in our precious gene pool. If they find out what I've done—but they won't find out. They can't find out."

Up ahead, brake lights flared. Nicole cursed and touched the brake to keep from rear-ending the car in front of her. "What's up with this traffic? We're going the wrong way for rush hour to—"

"Killing me won't help you," Emily said. "The police will find out you were at my apartment. They'll know—"

"So what if they know I was there? I'll say I got there and you were hysterical. You'd strangled Brent. I tried to save him, but you forced me out of the house at knifepoint and ordered me into my car. I'll hide the car at the cabin and tell the police you let me out and drove off in it. Why wouldn't they believe me?"

The pain in Emily's head was so excruciating that passing out would have been a relief. Could Nicole possibly be right? Would Zach and the police fall for that? No one had ever questioned Nicole's sanity.

Had anyone seen Nicole and her exiting the apartment, with Nicole plainly in control? Emily didn't remember seeing anyone.

Nicole's cell phone rang. Nicole reached for the purse she had tossed near Emily's feet. She pulled the phone out and glanced at it.

"Who is it?" Emily asked.

Nicole rolled her window down partway and dropped the phone out of the car. Emily pictured her telling the police about that incident. *My phone rang. Emily ordered me to throw it out the window, so I did. I didn't know what else to do—she had a knife—*

Traffic in front of them slowed to a crawl again, and Nicole stomped the brake harder than necessary, causing the car to lurch. Emily looked out her window, trying desperately to make eye contact with another driver or passenger, even though she knew it wouldn't do any good. What was she hoping for? A lip-reader who could decipher, *Help me, she's going to kill me?*

"Nicole." Emily tried again, not knowing what to say but desperate to fracture Nicole's determination. "You don't want to do this. You can't live with this. Please, let's stop and—"

"I'm sorry." Nicole's voice had hardened, and no more tears flowed. "I'm really, really sorry, Emily . . . This *traffic!* There must be an accident up ahead."

Nicole signaled and pulled off at the next exit. Emily wondered if this indicated a brief reprieve. The longer it took Nicole to drive to the cabin, the longer Emily would remain alive. Unless Nicole decided she didn't want to wait. Her hand kept dropping from the steering wheel, fingering the knife, then returning to the wheel. How would it feel—razor-sharp steel, plunging into her chest, penetrating her heart—

If she was to have any chance at escape, it would have to be now, while they were in the stoplight-ridden suburbs. Once Nicole was back on the freeway, there would be no hope. Trying to move slowly enough that she wouldn't attract Nicole's attention, Emily shifted her body, working to make the cape fall away.

Nicole glanced in the rearview mirror and drew a sharp breath. Emily looked over her shoulder. A police car was tailing them.

"If you do anything to attract attention, Emily—anything at all—you'll be dead before that cop can turn on his siren."

Emily turned back and looked straight ahead. Nicole drove carefully, maintaining the speed limit, glancing repeatedly into the rearview mirror. Emily didn't have to check behind them to know the police car was still there—she could tell by the look on Nicole's face.

Emily repressed the urge to beg Nicole to surrender before she made things worse. Nicole's eyes were wild, darting to Emily, to the mirror, to the knife.

A right turn. A left turn. Was Nicole heading somewhere in particular, or was she driving randomly, hoping the police car would turn in another direction? Nicole's breathing accelerated to a ragged pant, and Emily knew the officer was still behind them.

Emily braced herself. "He's following us. You can kill me now if you want, but it won't help you."

Nicole licked her lips. "He's not following us. If he wanted to pull me over, he'd turn on his lights. It's just coincidence." She swung onto a road that formed a loop in the center of a business park. Cars filled the surrounding parking lots, but the road itself was deserted.

Emily risked another glance over her shoulder. The road curved, allowing her to see that not one but *two* police cars were now following them.

Hope sent Emily's heartbeat on a frantic sprint. Zach had called the police and sent them on the hunt for Nicole's car. They might not know whether Nicole or Emily was the criminal, but they were moving in.

"Stop looking behind us!" Nicole snapped.

Emily turned back. Nicole had taken one hand off the steering wheel and was gripping the handle of the knife.

"There are two police cars," Emily said.

Nicole said nothing.

The brief whoop of a siren made Emily jump. Despite Nicole's warning, she glanced behind her. The light bars on the police car were flashing.

"Pull over," Emily said. "You have to pull over."

Nicole kept driving, staring straight ahead. Dizziness rippled through Emily. Was Nicole going to turn this into a car chase? She couldn't possibly be stupid enough to think she could speed away from this. And she *wasn't* accelerating—just driving steadily, one hand on the wheel, one hand on the knife.

Another blast from the siren jolted Emily's eardrums. They were nearly to the end of the U-shaped loop. They'd be emerging soon, heading back toward the traffic of the main road. Did Nicole think she'd be better off in traffic—that if she tried to elude the police, they'd let her go rather than risk other drivers in a high-speed chase?

"Driver, pull over." An electronically magnified voice boomed from the car behind them. Nicole's face went gray as she gave an abrupt twist of the wheel, steering the car to the curb. She jerked the gearshift into park.

Relief filled Emily—relief that lasted only as long as it took Nicole to turn toward her, raising the knife.

"Stay still and I won't hurt you." Nicole wore a desperate, almost feral look that Emily never could have imagined on her face. She leaned toward Emily, one hand reaching for the back of Emily's neck, the other hand bringing the knife toward her throat. Instantly, Emily understood. Nicole planned to use her life as a bargaining chip, the only one she had left.

A standoff—a hostage negotiation—Nicole growing ever more panicked—

Instinctively, Emily yanked her knees up to her chest, twisted toward Nicole, and kicked out as hard as she could. One foot caught Nicole in the chest; the other caught the arm holding the knife. Nicole lurched backward, gasping, slashing savagely at Emily's legs. Ignoring the pain, Emily kicked out again, her feet hammering Nicole.

Nicole yanked the door handle and tumbled out of the car, the knife still in her hand.

"Drop the knife," an officer shouted. *"Drop the knife."*

Nicole froze partway to her feet, her legs bent, her body arched forward. Through the open doorway, Emily could see Nicole's stricken face, her eyes staring at nothing. The wind caught her hair, wafting golden strands across her smooth cheekbones, and Emily knew this was all wrong, all a dream. Nicole Gardiner could never hurt anyone—

Nicole straightened and charged toward the officer, knife held high.

"Nicole, *no!*" Emily screamed. *"No!"*

Gunfire shattered the air, and Emily crumpled against her seat as reality crashed around her in countless broken pieces.

CHAPTER 25

"IN MY HEART, I THINK I knew all along." Bethany Tanner whispered the words in Emily's ear, gave her a final squeeze, and broke the embrace. "But I couldn't stop worrying he was out there somewhere, needing me. To say he was dead felt like abandoning him."

"I understand." Emily's gaze rested on the flower-covered casket that stood ready to be lowered into the ground.

Bethany kissed Emily's cheek. "Come over for dinner soon, all right? You and Zach." She stretched out her hand to Zach, who stood a little behind Emily.

Emily stepped back from Bethany and turned to Logan Tanner, who was waiting a few feet away, his dark hair ruffled by the mild afternoon breeze.

Logan hugged her. "It sounds callous to say that I'm relieved, but it's good to know Ryan isn't suffering," he said.

"I feel the same way." The emotion filling Emily at the moment was one of closure and relief, not grief. Her grief for Ryan had stretched over the past three years, sorrow rendered more bitter by uncertainty. Now she could finally let it go.

Logan's smile was melancholy. "An apology sounds so inadequate, but I'm sorry for not catching on to what Brent Amherst was."

"Don't apologize. I knew Brent as well as you did—probably better—and I didn't catch on."

"That doesn't make me feel any less rotten. Looking back, thinking of the things he said to me—the way he talked about women and the way he totally idolized you but always hinted he didn't want to make a move because of loyalty to Ryan—I don't think Ryan had anything to do with it. He didn't make a move because if you became real to him—a real woman in a real relationship—he couldn't love you."

"What do you mean?"

"I think he could only love an imaginary, idealized woman. And as long as you belonged to Ryan, you didn't belong to anyone, so Brent could worship you to his heart's content. When you got engaged to Zach Sullivan—ouch. Nosedive off the pedestal."

"I don't think it had anything to do with love," Emily said, chilled by the same coldness that always accompanied her memory of the things Brent had said to her. "Obsession, maybe. Power, definitely."

Logan shuddered. "I'm just grateful you're all right. You've been through a living nightmare, with Brent and Nicole Gardiner . . . Well, if you ever need anything, call me. You'll always be part of the family."

"Thank you."

Emily and Zach joined Emily's parents as they walked away from the graveside. Zach reached tentatively toward Emily's arm as though to steady her then dropped his hand. She read the discomfort in his posture; he didn't know if his touch was welcome at the moment or an intrusion on her mourning for Ryan.

"How are you holding up?" Carolyn asked.

"I'm good."

"Are you tired, honey?"

"A little. I'm okay, Mom." Emily offered a crooked smile. "*Really* okay, not fake leave-me-alone okay."

Carolyn chuckled. "All right. We'll see you at home. I've got beef stew in the Crock-Pot. Apple-pear tart for dessert. No hurry—we can serve it anytime." They had reached her parents' car. Lloyd opened the door for Carolyn, but she hesitated, anxiety deepening the creases around her eyes as she looked at Emily. "You'll be careful, won't you, sweetie?"

Emily knew her mother was referring less to the simple act of driving to Morgan Hill than to everything Emily would do for the rest of her life. Emily stepped forward and wrapped her arms around her mother.

"I love you." Emily rested her cheek on Carolyn's shoulder.

"I'm being overprotective again, aren't I?"

"After the past couple of weeks, you're entitled."

"Get in the car, dear." Lloyd patted Carolyn's hand. "Don't worry. Zach will take care of her."

"He'd better." Carolyn spoke with a half-teasing, half-serious note in her voice.

Zach and Emily started toward Zach's car. Emily glanced back toward the cemetery plot where members of the Tanner family were still gathered. Her gaze caught on a man standing underneath a tree several yards away, facing the funeral gathering but keeping himself separate.

"That's Mitch Gardiner," Emily said in surprise.

Zach followed her gaze. "Was he at the funeral?"

"I don't think so. I didn't see him." Emily hesitated, watching Mitch. Dressed in a long, dark coat, he stood unmoving, his hands in his pockets.

"I'm going to go talk to him," she said. "Do you mind waiting here for a minute?"

"Take whatever time you need," Zach said, and Emily appreciated his understanding why she wanted to approach Mitch alone.

As she neared him, Mitch turned toward her. His handsome features were sharper, as though the sculptor had returned and chiseled out the curves, leaving only bone and hollows. "Emily," he said simply.

"How are you, Mitch?"

Not replying, he turned his gaze back to where Bethany and Ted Tanner stood. Emily stood next to him and waited.

"I'm sorry I didn't take your calls," he said after a moment.

"Don't worry about it. I just wanted you to know that I cared."

"Thank you." Mitch slid one hand out of his pocket and gestured toward Ryan's casket. "I can't get my mind around this. Any of it."

"I know what you mean."

"Her parents didn't want a funeral." He slid his hand back into his pocket. His shoulders hunched as though against the cold, though it was a beautiful, sunny afternoon. "I didn't think I wanted one either. I thought the only reason people would come was to gawk, and I worried about the media, so I just quietly . . ." His voice trailed off. For a silent moment, he watched as Ted Tanner embraced a gray-haired man Emily recognized as Ryan's uncle Paul.

"I regret it now," Mitch said. "I think there are people who genuinely cared about her. People who would have come remembering the good things."

"I remember the good things." Emily's tears welled and spilled over.

"She loved you." Mitch's voice cracked. "That may sound strange after what she tried to do to you, but I think she cared more for you—and your sister—than for anyone else in the world."

"Except you," Emily said.

Tears drew shiny lines down his haggard face. "It haunts me. Am I what she thought? She thought I cared more for my career, my future, than I did for her. That I would have rejected her because of a moment of poor judgment, because of a tragic accident. That she had to . . . that the only way to hide her mistake was to—"

Emily slid her arm through Mitch's. They stood silent for a moment.

"If you'd like to hold a service for her, I'd be happy to help in any way," Emily said.

"Thank you." He pressed her hand. "I need to go talk to the Tanners. Take care, Emily." Shoulders straight, he made his way toward Ted and Bethany.

Emily walked back to where Zach waited, walking heavily on her toes to keep the heels of her shoes from sinking into the grass. The partially healed cuts on her legs throbbed as she moved. Her tears flowed steadily, and she let them come. It felt far better to cry for Nicole than to hold the pain inside.

Zach wrapped his arm around her shoulders. "You okay?"

Emily nodded, pulling a tissue out of her purse. "I'm ready to go."

Zach was quiet as he drove out of the cemetery. Emily glanced at him. He looked pensive. Remote.

"That was a beautiful service," he said at last.

"Yes." Emily wanted to say more but couldn't choose something from the thousand thoughts crammed into her head.

"Do you mind if we don't head to your parents' house right away?" Zach asked. "Your mother said there was no hurry, and I'd like a little time to talk with you in private."

Emily's heart jerked, and she looked at the diamond ring on her hand. Zach and she hadn't talked on more than a superficial level since the day of Nicole's death. He'd visited Emily in the hospital, brought her flowers, visited her at her parents' house where she was staying, but they hadn't even tried to talk about their relationship.

"That's fine," she said, her mouth sticky-dry with apprehension. She sensed Zach looking toward her, and she tried to smile, but she knew what was coming. Zach would say he needed time to sort things out after everything that had happened. He'd ask for his ring back. It was over.

Zach pulled into the empty parking lot of a nearby preschool and switched off the engine.

"Why are we here?" Emily asked in surprise.

"To talk." Zach reached toward her, took her face in his hands, and kissed her, a kiss that sent torrents of warmth through her body. When he finally drew back, tears shone in his eyes. "I love you. I can't even imagine how bad things have been for you, and I'll understand if you don't want me around for a while. But I want you to know I love you." He smiled wryly. "I wish I could explain how much I love you, but I'm a math teacher, not a poet. Just know that I'd do anything for your happiness."

Tears flowed down Emily's face. "I love you, too. I was afraid that you wouldn't want—that after everything . . ."

Zach gripped her hand. "I can't even begin to tell you how sorry I am that I let you down. I didn't believe in you when you needed me."

The sleeve of her sweater had ridden up a little, exposing the remnants of the abrasions left by the drape cord. Emily pulled her sleeve down to cover them. "Zach, I didn't even fully believe in myself. Brent did such a good job of making me look crazy that sometimes I thought I *was* losing my mind. But you were always there for me, always trying to protect me—even if that meant protecting me from myself. I love you for that. And if we're trading confessions . . ." Emily's throat suddenly felt like it was filled with gravel. She didn't want to go on, but she knew she had to. "By the end, I was scared of everyone. Including myself. Including you. Most of me trusted you, but there were moments—Brent did everything he could to stir up my suspicions of you . . ."

"I know. I'm not surprised. The more he could isolate you, the happier he was. That picture of Monica and me—" Zach grimaced. The report had come from Detective Lund: Zach's watch had been digitally added to the picture, a fact that became apparent once the picture was enlarged. It chilled Emily to imagine Brent sitting at his computer, cheerfully doctoring the photo to give Emily reason to doubt Zach's fidelity.

"And I'm sorry I never told you the whole story of why I left Sacramento," Zach said. "Rochelle told me that she told you about it. You shouldn't have had to hear it from her, and I'm sure hearing it that way didn't help you trust me."

"I'm sorry for doubting you," Emily said. "If you don't want *me* around, I'll understand. I'm kind of a mess right now. Have been for a while, actually, but I didn't want to admit it."

"If you want to get rid of me, you're going to have to do the dumping. Trying to trick me into dumping *you* isn't going to work."

"That's the last thing I want."

"Emily, I love you. When I heard you screaming over the phone and realized Brent was . . . that you . . . that the police might not get there in time—I'm going to have nightmares about that for the rest of my life. If I hadn't been such a fool that you felt you had to run off from the police department . . ."

"*Zach.* That wasn't your fault at all. I was so scared and so confused by that point that I wasn't acting rationally. Promise me you won't blame yourself."

"I can't help it."

Emily extricated her hand from Zach's. She opened her purse and removed a pen and an apple-shaped notepad.

"What are you doing?" Zach asked.

"Making a note for myself." Emily pretended to write. "'At next appointment, ask Dr. Kincaid how to get Zach to stop blaming himself for things that aren't his fault.'"

Zach laughed. "Fine, okay, put the pen away. So are you finding Dr. Kincaid helpful?"

"Very, and my mother now has full legal rights to say 'I told you so.' It's a tremendous relief to be able to talk about things I didn't think I wanted to talk about. Also, I'm thinking I owe him a couple new boxes of Kleenex."

"I'm sure he buys them in bulk."

"He'll have to, to keep up with me. Especially to get me through Brent's trial. I'm sure Brent will do everything he can to convince a jury that I'm a lunatic and he was the victim."

"If the creep has any brains at all, he won't even try. His best bet would be to plea bargain and try to avoid a conviction for attempted murder."

Emily reached for Zach's hand again and held it tightly. She'd experienced a relief that surprised her when she'd learned the police had arrived at her apartment barely in time to save Brent's life.

One less murder on Nicole's hands.

The picture was burned into her mind—Nicole rushing toward the police officers, the knife clenched in her hand. She wasn't trying to attack them. She was committing suicide.

"I just wish . . ." Emily let her voice fade. There were too many things to list. "I can't believe Nicole killed Monica for me."

"Nicole killed Monica because she'd already scarred her conscience to the point that she thought murder was a legitimate way to deal with a problem. But what a hideous waste. There *was* no problem. I never would have gone back to Monica."

"Justin Driscoll is moving," Emily said. "Did I tell you that?"

"No."

"He talked with me at Monica's funeral. He's going to San Diego—he's got a job offer in the works. He said he can't endure staying in Los Coros any longer. Everything hurts here. He apologized to me, by the way."

Zach's jaw tightened. "I hope so."

"I can't be angry with him. He was so desperate to see Monica's murderer punished that he was determined to cast *someone* in that role, and I was the most likely suspect—at least initially."

"He should have put his brain in gear before he started throwing accusations around and attacking your reputation."

"He knows that. He apologized."

They lapsed into silence, but it was a comfortable silence.

"My students sent me the cutest batch of get-well cards you've ever seen," Emily said.

"You're not going to rush back to work, are you? You need time to heal."

"I know. I'm taking it easy. Truth is, my head still hurts when I move it the wrong way. Like forward, backward, sideways, up, down . . . take your pick. Don't worry, I'll wait until my neurologist gives the thumbs-up before I go back to work."

"You're assuming your mother will let you go."

"Well, with all the knocks on the head I've taken lately, she *is* a little worried that my brains resemble scrambled eggs."

"Scrambled eggs? From your mother, it's more likely she thinks they resemble a frittata with prosciutto, grilled portobello mushrooms, and yak cheese."

"Yak cheese?" Emily laughed. "Either way, I'm counting on Dad to hold Mom back so I can sneak out the door."

Zach touched her cheek, his fingers gentle. "If there's anything I can do to carry any of your troubles for you, I will."

"Be careful what you offer. I've got a stack of about fourteen hundred papers to grade."

"Deal. And if I help you with your work, will you marry me?"

"I thought I already answered that question." Emily displayed her left hand.

"I want to make sure you haven't changed your mind."

"Never," she said.